D0913936

THE LONGMIRE DEFENSE

THE LONGMIRE DEFENSE

CRAIG JOHNSON

THORNDIKE PRESS
A part of Gale, a Cengage Company

GALE
A Cengage Company

GALE
A Cengage Company

**LIBRARY OF CONGRESS CIP DATA ON FILE.
CATALOGUING IN PUBLICATION FOR THIS BOOK
IS AVAILABLE FROM THE LIBRARY OF CONGRESS.**

ISBN-13: 979-8-88579-690-3 (hardcover alk. paper)

Published in 2024 by arrangement with Viking, an imprint of Penguin Publishing Group, a division of Penguin Random House LLC.

Print Number: 1   Print Year: 2024
Printed in Mexico

For Dan Quick,
who never drove angry

Chess is ruthless: you've got to be
prepared to kill people.

— Nigel Short

ACKNOWLEDGMENTS

There are writers who most outdoorsmen read, and for westerners one of them is Elmer Keith, world-renowned Montana cowboy, big-game hunter, and firearm enthusiast. I first encountered Keith in my father's copious library of hunting, fishing, and general outdoor topics, and I went on to read just about everything the man ever wrote.

I enjoyed his easy writing style and the fact that he didn't always stay on topic, sometimes drifting into areas that might not seem to connect to the subject at hand but eventually do — and there was one such story that has stayed stuck between the pages of my mind for most of my life.

The book is *"Hell, I Was There!,"* Keith's life story. Within it is a hair-raising tale from his youth when a state official is killed under questionable circumstances immediately after WWI. Keith doesn't pull any punches

9

in the story, telling it as it most likely happened, and just short of naming names he relays to us what took place at that elk camp in Montana all those years ago — stating plainly that the men who committed murder got away with it.

It's too bad Walt Longmire wasn't there.

Well, in my version he is — perhaps after the fact as his father tells him the story years later, but when the rifle that did the deed appears and turns out to belong to Walt's grandfather Lloyd, it sets the good sheriff on an investigation very different in tone than any before.

During my travels I was talking to an old sheriff who used the term *proud flesh* in conjunction with a case he'd worked on, and I asked him about it. I knew the term in an equestrian sense, where a horse can have granulated, highly vascularized material fill in a wound too quickly and need to be carved out so that proper nerve-related tissues can occupy the space. He explained that the old-timers used the term when describing how a detective can sometimes rush to conclusions that eventually have to be excised from investigation because they're simply not correct.

Anyone familiar with my novels knows that Walt's relationship with his grandfather

10

can be referred to as rocky, to say the least. I like to think of Walt as the most ecumenical and fair-minded detective in the game, but when the prime suspect becomes Lloyd Longmire, then a very different game is afoot.

The Longmire Defense was a joy to write, finally giving me the chance to delve into the relationship between Walt and his grandfather, which has been referred to for years. There were some specialists I consulted before telling this story; people whose disciplines I'm familiar but certainly not an expert in, and I'm pleased to have the opportunity to list those folks here.

First off I'd like to thank Adam Weatherby and the fine folks at Weatherby Inc., a little north of Sheridan, Wyoming, for all the time they allowed me in their museum/library, and especially his wife, Brenda. My buddy Reeves over at the Sports Lure, who really doesn't look like the Swedish Chef on *The Muppet Show.*

Second, my good buddy Chet Carlson, who knows more about finance than Walt and me. I can't balance my checkbook either.

Gail *The White Rook* Hochman, who can move in any direction both vertically and horizontally without jumping and has many

11

times on my behalf. Marianne *The Black Rook* Merola, who assists Gail in castling in the kingdom of Hochman.

Brian *The Black King* Tart, who moves in all adjoining squares and never leaves me in check. Jenn *The Black Knight* Houghton, who moves in diagonals and keeps us all on our toes.

Ben *The White Knight* Petrone, who always moves in right angles and keeps me out of corners. Johnathan *The White Bishop* Lay, who's always willing to sacrifice himself for my good. Michael *The Black Pawn* Brown, en passant, who defends me horizontally. Christine *The White Pawn* Choi, who is always shooting for the back rank and a quick development into any piece on the board.

And the checkmate of my heart, Judy *The White Queen* Johnson, who can go any-where, anytime.

1

"Where have you been?"

I looked out amid the grove of aspens that led to the beaver pond where Hero trimmed the smaller saplings and dragged them into the water, ever building, ever improving his tiny world near my family cabin in the Bighorn National Forest.

Herodutus was the beaver's entire name, the title a gift from my father, and knowing that the average beaver lifespan is only ten to twelve years, I had a sneaking suspicion I was witnessing the labors of his great-, great-, great-, great-grandson.

I wished I had his energy.

I lowered my book on the back of my sleeping granddaughter and glanced at Cady, feeling guilty for lying in a hammock and reading while she cross-examined me. I noticed she was holding a framed photo and a wet, soiled paper towel as she examined the picture. "Great-grandpa Lloyd was a handsome guy." My daughter came closer and lowered the picture frame she was cleaning and then studied the man in the black-and-white photo, my grandfather. "You two didn't get along, did you?"

I closed the book, *The Histories,* as chance would have it, and gave it some thought. "We were . . . a lot alike."

She continued examining the framed photo in her hands, part of the great spring-cleaning effort she'd decided to give the vintage cabin, a project I had, until now, studiously avoided. "Why is he wearing a suit?"

Placing the book alongside my grand-daughter, I stretched out a hand. "I'm not sure which one that is." Taking the tarnished metal frame, I turned it and looked at the image of seven men standing on the side-walk in downtown Durant, Wyoming.

They were all wearing suits and those old Tom Mix–style cowboy hats, and my eye was drawn to the tallest of the bunch who was standing at the end to the left. A little over six feet, which was considered tall at the time, I could still feel the piercing of those nickel-plated, gray owllike eyes, the ones that searched out any flaw. The others were smiling, but not him — grim as the reaper, it was as if he knew I'd be looking back at him someday.

I handed it to her. "Bank of Durant, I think that's the board of directors that bought up the collateral after the crash, probably sometime in the dirty thirties."

She turned and continued to study it. "They bought the bank?"

"It had failed and was going to go into receivership, so this consortium of the biggest ranchers in Absaroka County got together and bought it at a bargain-basement price — pennies on the dollar." I nodded, readjusting Lola on my chest. "Your great-grandfather being one of them."

"We owned the Bank of Durant?"

"Part of it, until sometime in the midfifties when the consortium broke up and they sold it back to some proper and more experienced bankers."

"How come I never knew any of this?"

I shrugged. "Lloyd had his fingers in a lot of pies."

She gazed back at the photo. "Who are the other six?"

"I don't know the two on the end, board members, I guess. I mean, I suppose I could figure it out, but I've never been interested."

Her own cool, gray eyes came up to mine, hers not looking that much different from her great-grandfather's. "What happened?"

"What do you mean?"

"Between you two, what was it?"

"What, am I under investigation here?"

"Just curious." She pushed the hammock in illustration of her dissatisfaction with my answers, handing me the framed photo again, and then leaned down to take her child. "You never talk about him."

I watched her turn away, climb the steps of the tiny cabin, and pull open the screen door. I felt the door slapping shut behind her as Dog, my hundred-and-fifty-pound backup, nosed it open and came out onto the porch.

I was about to follow Cady inside when I noticed on the four-wheel-drive, two-track road an Absaroka County Sheriff Department vehicle approaching: a sleek, swift-looking piece of modern law-enforcement equipment with a sleek, swift-looking driver at the wheel.

My undersheriff, Victoria Moretti, pulled to a stop, opening the door and stepping onto the running board, looking at me over the top of her unit. "Nice place you've got here."

I lay there, tucking the frame under my arm. "It has its benefits."

"Like no cell service?"

"In case you've never noticed, I never have

cell service."

She glanced around. "And being way the hell out in the middle of fucking nowhere?"

"Obviously not far enough."

She laid her naked forearms on the sheet metal, resting her chin on them, and continued to look at me. "You've been convalescing for three weeks now, so I thought you might like to go out and do a little sheriffing for a change?"

Dog moved down beside me as I swung my legs from the hammock and ruffled his ears. "I'm having quality time with my family."

She raised her head and nodded. "What's that, under your arm?"

"Ancient history."

She smiled, and it was dazzling. "Well, in current affairs it might interest you to know that a woman from Minnesota took the advice of her phone navigation and attempted to go over the mountains on Forest Service Road 31."

"31 doesn't go over the mountain."

"No, but unknown to Google you can get far enough so that when you bury your two-wheel-drive piece-of-shit Honda in a snow-drift you can hike to Sheep Mountain Lookout and get cell service long enough to call out, telling the world how totally lost you are."

"Is that where she is now, the Lookout?"

"No. Evidently she decided to strike out on her own, abandoning walls, a roof, and emergency supplies for better reception." My deputy stepped off the running board and walked around her truck, then leaned against the grille guard. "Search and Rescue caught a ghosting signal on 911 and are under the impression that she continued walking on 28 into the Cloud Peak Wilderness area. Your thoughts?"

I mapped out the trails in my head. "It's possible, but if she took 28 in the other direction, they'd find her on the way up. Unless she took a wrong turn on 636, 447, or 449."

"Or?"

I sighed. "Or she returned to her car and then doubled back, figuring she'd at least get to a paved road."

Vic pointed a manicured finger at me. "Exactly." She walked over to the edge of the porch and reached out to grab at one of Dog's paws that he had lowered in a reasonable position of play. "I'm going to do the 31 loop and thought you might need a break from quality family time." She looked over at me. "C'mon, it'll be an hour or so of sheriffing, just enough to get your feet wet."

18

I was having a hard time figuring out a way to not do it.

Reaching out and pulling at Dog's other paw and then expertly avoiding his play bite, she placed the same hand to the side of her mouth and shouted into the cabin. "Hey Cady, can I borrow your dad for an hour to do sheriffy stuff?"

After a moment my daughter's voice came back through the closed screen door. "Take him, he's not doing me any good."

I sat there for a moment and then raised a finger to hold off Vic, and then stood up and climbed the steps, opened the screen door, and found Cady pulling more artwork and photos from the wall. "I don't really feel like going."

She propped the stack of frames on her hip, Lola on the other, still asleep. "I don't really feel like driving back to Cheyenne this afternoon, but it's my job — and you always do your job."

"Who told you that?"

"This guy I know who used to do sheriffy things."

"Ouch." I crossed the room and leaned on the rock mantelpiece and tipped my hat back. "So, what you're telling me is that it's time to get back on the horse?"

"That or put it out to pasture." I nodded,

19

saying nothing as she crossed toward me in order to place the frames on the mantel-piece. "But I think you should ride one more time before you make any hasty decisions."

Glancing up on the mantelpiece to escape her eyes, I found another pair of eyes in another one of the collected frames. "You sound like this woman I used to know."

"Used to, huh?"

"Yep." I plucked it down, studying the photo of my deceased wife, Martha. "I've been having a lot of dreams about your mother, lately."

"Oh, yeah?"

"It's in a library, and she's dancing."

Cady swiveled her hips, swaying with Lola in her arms. "She was a good dancer, as I recall."

"Yep, she was."

She waited a moment before asking. "Are you ever going to tell anybody about what happened up there in Montana?"

A silence settled between us. "No need to, it's over."

She stepped in closer, cradling her child and looking up at me. "You're sure about that?"

I nodded. "Yep."

"Leave me the keys to your truck in case

you get stuck somewhere and I need to get back to the ranch and get my Jeep." She glanced over my shoulder. "Your second-in-command can drop you off at home."

"I'm not going to be gone that long."

"Uh-huh." She stuck out her hand, and I dropped my keys into her palm, the cool, gray eyes staying focused on me. "Go for a ride, it'll do you some good." Then she took the photo from my other hand and stacked it with the others for cleaning.

There wasn't too much snow at the beginning of the route, but that was because the land was still open, and the sun could get to it. Once you got into the tree line, the shade would protect the snow, and it would begin to mount up, not too deep at first but that would change.

Granted, I had a thing about cell phones, but this was not the first time their navigation had led unwary travelers astray. There was a glitch in the program that led motorists off the highway and toward the dump and a dead-end road that eventually led nowhere. The number of travelers got so bad that the dump manager finally put up a billboard that read: THIS ROAD DOESN'T LEAD ANYWHERE BUT THE DAMN DUMP NO MATTER WHAT GOOGLE SAYS!

Expertly traversing the rutted-out road and growing drifts in the Banshee II, as I referred to it, Vic followed the passenger car tire tracks, shaking her head. "What is wrong with people, anyway? Do they ever think of stopping and asking somebody?"

"So, Search and Rescue isn't checking 31?"

"No, I told them we would."

"They didn't think she would go back to her car?"

"They figured she wouldn't know where it was."

"What's her name?"

She glanced at me. "Does it matter?"

"I'd rather not roam the mountain calling Lady from Minnesota to the tune of 'The Girl from Ipanema.' "

She snatched a sheet from her metal clipboard and handed it to me. "Trisha Knox."

I nodded and read. "This is the transcript from the 911 call from last night?"

"Yeah."

"She sounds pretty worried."

"At no point was she more than a mile from the paved road."

"People get turned around, forget which way they came, things look different . . ." I shrugged and then threw out a hand. "Stop."

She locked up the brakes, sliding to a halt. "What?"

"Prints, on the side of the road." Cracking open the door, I stepped down and then held it for Dog, who got out and promptly sat, looking up at me as Vic killed the high-performance engine.

Down the road I saw that the prints came along in the snow and then suddenly turned to the left and disappeared into the woods. "This is the point where 31 goes from being Pole Creek Road to being Lost Cabin Road."

Tromping in the melting snow, Vic came around the truck. "And why is that?"

"Because the road crosses Pole Creek, and if I were making a guess, I'd say that's where she went."

"The creek?"

"People generally don't get lost uphill . . ." I glanced around. "Water goes downhill, and so maybe she had enough sense to know that's the direction she needed to go — not bad logic." I peered down the wash and into the trees where the set of prints followed. "As long as she doesn't fall into the creek, she should be fine."

"Do you ever think that what we're doing

23

here is against the laws of nature?"

"Meaning?"

"That the Darwinian maxim of survival of the fittest should extend to search and/or rescue?"

"We'd be out of a job."

"What do you want to do?"

"Turn around and head back to the paved road and drive down to the Pole Creek cross-country skiing site and work your way up 457 as far as you can go. If I find her, I'll flush her out and we'll meet you there — and if not, it'll just be me and Dog."

"Why there?"

"Because it's downhill."

"Why you and Dog?"

"Because I already have my Sorel boots and mountain gear on, and I could use the exercise." Reaching down, I ruffled Dog's ears. "And so could you."

Sighing, she opened the driver's-side door of the truck, and pulled out a coyote-brown assault pack and a two-way from behind her seat. "At least take the bug-out bag, in case you fall in the creek, get hungry or thirsty, or cut off your head?"

I saluted my second-in-command, clipped the radio to my jacket, and took the pack, throwing it up over the shoulder of my Carhartt parka and reading the words printed

24

on the flap in Magic Marker: SHIT YOU MAY NEED. "Does it have dog treats?"

"Always." She started around the front and climbed in the truck. "If she's cold and stiff when you find her, don't haul her out and just wait for me?"

"Will do."

Dog and I watched as she threw the latest of her frightening vehicles into reverse, rooster-tailing snow at us as she whipped around between the trees and vroomed into the far curve of the Forest Service logging road.

"Can you believe the county commissioners bought her another one like that?" Reaching down and pulling his ear one last time, we headed out into an absolutely pristine May Day.

Most people would be surprised to know that the Bighorn Mountains get the majority of their glacial snowpack in March and April, but here I was, wading through the stuff about knee-deep. Dog seemed to be having a better time of it as we moseyed along, following the prints. "I would say that is a Scarpa Terra GTX hiking boot in size seven."

He paid no attention as he hopped his hundred-and-fifty-pound body from spot to spot, paying more heed to the angry squirrels that barked down at us for disturbing their solitude. "My grandfather sometimes made us eat squirrel stew when I was a kid — always tasted like rat to me." Stopping to take a breather, I glanced around. "Maybe that's why I didn't like him."

There was another treeless area heading northeast that ran into the drainage, and I tried to think when the last time I'd been in this particular portion of Elk Area 35, as the Game and Fish Department romantically referred to it.

There had been some elk hunters that had gotten caught in an early fall storm who holed up at the Pole Creek Cabin until we could get them out. There had been a young man from Casper who had committed suicide, and a motorcyclist who had ridden his street bike up the trail far enough until he flipped it, breaking his leg before crawling the better part of two miles to get back to the main road. There were a couple of snowmobilers who had gotten lost and buried their machines in the creek itself. But the most recent incident had been a year ago, when two kids had the presence of mind to climb up on a ridge and call us and then sit with their father, who had been thrown from his horse and accrued a broken leg, jaw, and other assorted injuries.

We'd gotten here in forty minutes and in seventy-five the man had been airlifted via chopper to the hospital in Billings. When we'd found his wife back at their campsite, her only prosaic response had been, "Hell, he never could ride."

Swinging the pack off my shoulder, I unzipped the top, pulled out the canteen, and then unscrewed the top to take a swig. Dog bounded over toward the trees to the north and then turned back to look at me as if I were supposed to climb the tree or shoot a squirrel for him.

"I'm not that desperate yet." I stuffed the canteen back into the pack, zipped it up, slung it on my shoulder, and started off again.

Rounding some rock ridges, I could see farther down the draw where it connected to some others and a few parks without much snow on them, the warm sunshine doing its work.

The snow dropped down to about six inches and I couldn't help but feel good chugging along with the rays of the sun warming my back and doing one of the things I really enjoyed: putting a little effort out to help someone. I sometimes wondered how I'd ended up being a sheriff — if it had simply been the path of least resistance from being a marine investigator in Vietnam, becoming a deputy when I'd gotten back stateside, and then eventually running for the office. I like to think it was more than that, and the thing I usually settled on was being of assistance when people needed it the most.

I know it sounded corny in the modern era, but it was what I was good at, something I did well.

Loosening the collar of my parka as the temperature rose, I glanced back at the sun, calculating how much daylight we had left — figuring a good two hours, more than enough unless she'd sidetracked.

Everything just felt good after all these weeks, and I really didn't have any worries that we wouldn't find Trisha Knox — it just might take some time.

In the next stretch, I became aware of a rock outcropping to my left, overlooking another park due north, and had a sudden recollection of my father bringing me here elk hunting a long, long time ago.

Watching and waiting for the migrating elk to shift out from the trees, we sat there above the timber line, my father's big Remington rifle lying across his knees as his hands nimbly worked, the only part of him

28

that really did.

Other than that small movement, you would've thought he was a sphinx, his pinch-front cowboy hat seated on the back of his head.

"There were times in these mountains when a man carried what law there was with him, but I would like to think that those times have passed."

His hand lifted, and he licked the side of the smoke, tucking it in the corner of his mouth to light it with a brass Zippo decorated with a bucking bronc, the glow of the ember lighting his face on one side as the sun set and everything became dramatic in what the old guys called the golden time.

"The first man I ever saw die was right around here."

I looked out at the peaceful park, trying to imagine. "Really?"

He nodded. "You don't remember Bill Sutherland do you, I believe he was before your time — '48 or '49."

"I'm fifteen, now."

Ignoring me, he continued. "Big Bill Sutherland, he was from out on the Powder River Country, but worked down in Cheyenne . . ." His eyes narrowed as he thought about it, his hands closing the lighter and tucking it back in his double-lined pants.

"It was a hunting accident, or so they say."

"What happened?"

He nodded to himself in contemplation. "Are you sure you want to hear about it?"

"Yep."

He plucked the cigarette from his lips, flicked the ash, and turned back to look at me. "Don't tell your grandfather I told this story to you."

"He was there?"

"Yep."

"Why would he care?"

"It was here, at his elk camp." My father's eyes went back to the park, still watching and still aware through the telling. "Bill had been away during the war but had wanted to get back up here in the mountains and take an elk home to his wife, Jean. So he called up your grandfather who has a way with such things and got him a tag." He took a drag on the cigarette and then slowly let it out, the trail of smoke in the late afternoon looking like a ghost escaping his body. "Well, like everything else in Cheyenne, it couldn't remain simple, and a couple of Bill's friends from down there decided that they wanted to come and try their luck too."

"Sir?"

"I see 'em." A heavy cow elk had pointed

her nose out from behind a Fraser fir but had stopped. "Fella by the name of Harold Grafton and another, Bob Carr." Tucking the cigarette in the corner of his mouth, his hands silently fell to the wooden stock in his lap. "How far?"

I judged the distance. "A thousand yards."

He slid the bolt-action silently and adjusted his scope. "I'd say just shy of twelve hundred — dropping about twenty-four inches per five hundred." Dialed in, he lifted the weapon to his eye. "I wasn't much older than you, but I got to go because I could handle the horses and could pack out the meat while the older men kept hunting." He glanced at me with the eye. "And drinking and playing cards." The cool eye returned to the scope. "This was back before the Pole Creek Cabin was ever built, and we made do with a couple of wall tents with stoves that I was responsible for setting up and keeping fed with logs. Dad had talked Clarence Standing Bear, who is the best damned elk stalker in two states, to come help in that he figured the fellows from Cheyenne would turn out to be relatively useless, and he was right, they were."

"Clarence, Henry's dad."

"Yep."

The heavy elk took another tentative step

31

but then stopped again.

"We'd broken up into three groups, hunting the valley with Dad and this Bob Carr from down in Cheyenne taking the north fork, Big Bill and me taking the middle, and Clarence and the other fellow from Cheyenne, Harold Grafton, on the south."

The elk didn't move, and neither did my father.

"As we were getting ready to leave camp that morning, I remember Dad throwing his rifle sling up on his shoulder and adjusting the .45 revolver he kept on him all the time in this cross-chest holster and saying that if there was any trouble to just fire three shots in the air and we'd all come running. Well, I'd never heard him say anything like that before but just figured that it must've been for the benefit of those two from down in Cheyenne."

He stayed steady and so did the elk.

"Big Bill and I decided to head out a little ways before taking on some serious hunting, and at one point he sat on a log and looked around and said he had a funny feeling about this trip and that he wasn't sure he was going to make it through the day. I found that puzzling and told him so, and he said that he'd had that same feeling one time in the Ardennes when a German sniper had put a bullet through his helmet, permanently parting his hair. He took his cap off and reached out and took my hand, running my fingers across a groove in his scalp."

The elk retreated back into the tree line, and my father waited a moment and then lowered the Remington.

"We both laughed about that, and then he told me he was going to cover the basin so I could take the hillside since my legs were young and spry. He went off, and I worked my way up the hill — only making it about halfway when I heard voices behind me. I was pretty sure it was Bill arguing with somebody, both of them getting hot. I thought about going back down, but all these men were acquainted with each other in a business way as far as I knew, so I decided to just stay out of it."

His eyes shifted to where the elk had been but then turned back to me. "Do you have any of those sandwiches your mother packed?"

Sighing, I hauled the rucksack up from the rocks, sitting it between us and unrolling the top, handing him the thermos with the hot coffee that she'd also prepared, and a sandwich wrapped in wax paper. I watched as he unwrapped the sandwich and took a bite, chewing. I knew better than to ask and just waited; it is what Longmire men do.

Still looking at the meadow below, he twisted the cap off the thermos and then spun off the stopper before pouring himself a steaming cup.

Finally, as usual, I had to break the family edict and ask, "What happened?"

"I shot an elk."

"I meant about the man, Big Bill?"

"I'm getting to that."

He sipped his coffee and took another bite out of his sandwich.

"I got back to the camp later than everybody else, trying to get done what I could in dressing out that old buck, bringing the liver and tenderloin back to camp. We ate well that night, and the next morning Bill said he'd team up with me and help me quarter and skin that elk before heading out and getting a shot for himself. I thought that was quite grand of the fellow and agreed." He took another bite of sandwich and looked down at the park again. "It was getting late by the time we'd finished, and it had started to snow, and I told Bill we'd better get moving if we were going to get him an elk."

His face froze for a moment, and he didn't move what seemed like a long time.

"Dad?"

"We'd just started off when I felt something go by me, like a hummingbird — just a quick zip and then nothing." The gray eyes unfroze first, and he looked at me. "I'd never been shot at that close, but I knew what it was . . . Bill gasped and then reached a hand out to me before falling over. I scrambled behind a rock outcropping and just sat there in case whoever it was was looking to fire another wayward round. I yelled and yelled, hoping that whoever was out there would hear me, but nobody yelled back. Remembering what your grandfather had said, I pulled out the .38 I had and fired it in the air three times — still nothing."

My father folded up the rest of his sandwich and handed it back to me, his appetite suddenly disappearing.

"By that time, I was getting a little put off and reloaded that .38 and circled back around those rocks and worked my way over to where I thought the shot had come from. There was a depression where someone had been lying but nothing else. I stood there listening, but there wasn't any sound and I thought I'd better get back and check on Bill."

He brought the silver cup up to his mouth but didn't drink.

"He was lying on his side when I got to

him and pulled him over with part of a lung sticking out of a hole in his chest. He kept telling me that he was okay and that I just needed to help him up, but you could see different — his breath was short, and his eyes were just starting to roll back."

"What'd you do?"

"There wasn't much I could do. I had a clean bandanna and poked that part of his lung back in the hole and tried to stop the bleeding, for all the good it would do. Trussing him up, I told him I'd go back to camp and get help, but he didn't want me to leave him. I knew he'd just die if I stayed, so I propped his head up with my jacket so that he wouldn't drown in his own blood and took off like a scalded dog."

He sipped his coffee and glanced back at the meadow.

"It was snowing heavy by then, really coming down, and I had to struggle to find my way back, crossing the creek with the ice breaking. All the way down the valley, I'd raise that .38 and fire it three times in succession but never heard anything until I finally could see the tents up ahead and men roiling out."

Lowering the cup, he studied the steam rising from it.

"Your grandfather was the first to get to

36

me, and I remember him reaching out and taking the .38 and then grabbing me by the shoulder and asking what was wrong. I told them that Bill Sutherland had been shot, and I remember Bob Carr was the next face I saw, and he wanted to know if I'd shot Bill. I told him no, but that Sutherland had been arguing with somebody the day before and what exactly had happened after the shot had been fired that hit Bill and that I'd yelled, fired warning shots, and even snuck around and found the spot where the shooter had been. Harold Grafton laughed and said I was being overly dramatic, and where was Bill? Well, by that time I was good and mad and told them that he was back there on the trail where I'd left him until I could get back and get help and if they weren't going to do anything then give me a blanket, medical supplies, and a quart of Who-Hit-John and leave me to it."

He smiled into the cup.

"Dad put his hand on my shoulder and looked at all of them and said a few words, really low. After that, they all joined me, and we slogged our way back to where Bill was still lying on the ground, now covered in snow. I remember going up to him and kneeling and knowing he was dead. Your grandfather Clarence Standing Bear and I lifted him up and moved down to a flat spot where I started a fire, figuring we were there for the night. Dad pulled out a handkerchief and began collecting all Bill's personal items, his glasses, watch, wallet, and jewelry, tucking it all in there before tying it off and stuffing it in his pocket."

His mouth curved in the sad smile again.

"Bob Carr started making noises about heading back to camp in that Bill was now in the hands of the Almighty, and I remember your grandfather stepping around the fire to intercept them and saying that Bill was our friend and that the least we could do was sit up with his body and keep it safe that night. There was more arguing, but I remember it ended when Clarence Standing Bear pulled out a stag-handled knife and said he'd kill any man who tried to leave."

The sun had started to set, and the golden glow was fading from the mountains, replaced with a shuffling breeze that promised dark and cold.

"That next morning, we had to break him loose and hang him over a horse and let me tell you young man that's the hardest piece of work there is — breaking loose the frozen body of a friend." His eyes redirected to me. "I hope you never have to attend to a business like that, son." My father smiled at me, the saddest smile I'd ever seen. "That was the longest night of my life, I can tell you that — I'll never forget those sounds."

"Who shot him?"

He shook his head while emptying out the cup and replaced it on the top of the thermos. "They never found out." Swinging his rifle sling onto his shoulder, he stood, and I watched him walk down off the rock outcropping, looking after the disappearing sun and the invisible elk. "I came back up the next day with the sheriff, Lucian Connally — I believe you two have met recently?"

I lowered my head. "Yes, sir."

"We found a shell from a .300 H&H Magnum near where the shot had been fired, but none of the men in the hunting party had been carrying that caliber. At the autopsy, they recovered the slug and determined that it had been that caliber weapon that had done the deed."

"So, somebody just shot him and then ran off?"

After a moment, he turned to look at me. "It happens. A man makes a mistake he can't live with and ends up running away from it for the rest of his life. In a way, it becomes his life."

■ ■ ■ ■

"Excuse me?"

I lowered my face from the robin's-egg blue sky so bright the color seemed to fade along with my musings and found a somewhat hard-looking, twenty-something-year-old woman wrapped in what appeared to be about five coats and a car blanket. "Trisha Knox, I presume?"

From under the froth of dirty-blondish curls leaking out from under her knit cap, she smiled as Dog stood at her side, paying an inordinate amount of attention to her. "Are you *looking* for me?"

"I am." Shrugging the pack off my shoulder, I opened the top and gave her a bottle of water, which she readily drank as I pulled my two-way from the clip on my shoulder and turned up the gain, hitting the toggle. "Unit two, this is unit one — Hey, Vic, I found Ms. Knox." I hit the toggle again. "Unit two." Lowering the radio, I listened and looked down at the green LED display but heard and saw nothing. Lifting it to my mouth again, I hit the toggle. "Vic, you out there?"

"Excuse me, but are *you* a policeman?"

I pointed to the embroidered star on my

40

parka. "Sheriff of Absaroka County."

"*The* sheriff?"

"Yes, ma'am."

She studied the stitching. "Is that *where* we are, Absaroka County?"

"Yes, ma'am." Raising the radio again, I hit the toggle. "Vic, are you there?" I clicked the thing. "Oh, just any carbon-based life-form on the planet, come in?"

Nothing.

She studied Dog. "Is this *your* wolf?"

"Yes, ma'am."

"Are we *lost*?"

Reaching into the pack, I mused on the fact that she appeared to emphasize one word in every sentence she spoke and handed her a PAYDAY. "No, ma'am . . . Well, at least I'm not. I'm just trying to raise my deputy to let her know I've found you."

She chewed on the candy bar. "Actually, I think I found *you.*"

I searched for higher ground in hope of increasing my reception. "Yes, ma'am."

"What were you *doing*?"

"Thinking."

She looked concerned. "Before, I thought you might be having some sort of *fit.*"

"Yes, ma'am, the two bear a striking resemblance." Finally seeing a ridge with a gentle slope, I figured that was my best bet.

"Would you like to take a little walk with Dog and me up to the top of that ridge where we might get better reception on my radio?"

She smiled again. "I'd be happy to."

Crossing from the snow in the basin to the sunshine-coated hillside, the ground became drier as we hiked. There was a thin strip of uncovered rock at the top of the ridge with an overhang of about six feet. We stopped and looked back through the high country of the Bighorn Mountains, the Powder River breaks unfolding far down below.

"Do you come to this *spot* often?"

"No, ma'am." I hit the toggle again. "Unit two, this is unit one, come in?"

She held out a plastic turquoise case encrusted with rhinestones. "Do you want to use *my* phone?"

"Sure." Dialing the number, the response was predictable.

"Where the fuck are you?"

"I'm just north of the Pole Creek Cabin with Ms. Knox." Speaking quickly before Vic could say anything else, I formulated a plan. "Hey, she seems fine, so if you're down on the cross-country ski access area we'll just continue that way and meet you?" I looked back to the west. "Looks like we've got another couple of hours of daylight left."

"I'm here, for fuck's sake."

Handing Ms. Knox back her decorated phone, I smiled at her, taking a little time to notice that she was rougher looking than I'd at first thought. "My undersheriff, she can be an acquired taste." I pulled my pack off, then sat and unzipped it and grabbed another bottle of water, unscrewing the top and drinking. "Were you on your way somewhere, Ms. Knox?"

She nodded, sitting in the grass a little ways away. "Looking for a *new* life, I guess is what you'd call it."

I watched as Dog paid attention to us for a moment and then circled around and began sniffing at the crags in the rocks, probably looking for marmots. "Decide to take a little detour?"

She nodded. "I did, it just seemed like there was so much to *see* that wasn't on the roads . . ."

"I know May is a lovely month back in Minnesota, Ms. Knox, but here in Wyoming at this altitude, it can get awfully wintry."

"Is there *somebody* who can retrieve my car?"

I listened as Dog scratched at the rocks under where I was sitting. "I'm sure we can attend to that when we get back down to

43

the main road."

She broke a peanut off the remainder of her PAYDAY and ate it. "And how *far* is that?"

"About a mile." Dog continued scratching underneath the rocks. "Dog, knock it off."

"Is he after *something*?"

"He thinks he is, until whatever it is bites his nose." Securing my water, I popped it back in the pack and stood. Circling around the rocks, I bumped Dog's rear quarter with my leg. "C'mon, knock it off."

I kneeled and pushed Dog aside enough to see he had his teeth wrapped around a leather strap that had broken off as he backed up and sat, presenting it to me. "What've you got here?" It was dry and brittle but looked like a piece of tack.

"What's *that*?"

I turned to find that she'd gotten up and come over behind us for a better look. "I'm not sure, but I'm hoping it's not the rest of a horse or a sleeping marmot or a fox that is not going to appreciate me reaching into their den." Slipping on a glove, I nudged Dog out of the way and reached in the crack of the rock as far as my arm would allow, feeling something there. It was another part of the strap, but when I pulled it broke again, so I reached to the side and felt something stronger, a small metal piece that afforded a little more leverage.

I could tell it was something smooth, so I pushed it with my fingertips, pulling at the thing until I started making some headway, finally reaching a change in the contour.

Realizing what it was, I pulled the elongated item from the crack in the rock and held it up. The surface was rusted and appeared flat and aged in the sun.

I turned it in my hand, placing the butt in the palm of the other and studied the medallion embedded in the stock, my mind racing. "Unless I miss my guess, Ms. Knox, that is a memorial coin of the fiftieth anniversary of the great state of Wyoming, and this . . ." I sighed with a deep resignation. "This is some kind of custom .300 H&H Magnum, circa late 1940s."

2

I stared at Reeve the Swede across the counter at the sporting goods store, fully expecting him to break into the nonsense speech of the Swedish Chef on episodes of *The Muppet Show* that I had watched with Cady when she was a child. The Swede adjusted his round glasses and blew through his mouth, causing the mostly salt and not much pepper mustache to poof out.

"Dropped?"

"Perhaps, with emphasis."

"Somebody threw it down?"

"Maybe, but if you dropped it from a height, it would do the same thing." He rolled it over on the rubber pad. "The stock is broken in two places, but there are no marks where it would've hit rocks — it's almost as if someone broke it apart with their bare hands."

"What about the medallion?"

He snorted a laugh. "You tell me, Sheriff."

"Old, but not like a challenge coin exactly."

"No, not particularly."

"Any idea what year?"

He shrugged. "Might be on the other side, they used to do these commemorative coins, fifty-year anniversary and such." He ran a hand across the weapon. "I can roughly tell you the date of manufacture."

"Late forties?"

"Maybe 1947 to be exact. I would say this is one of the original prototypes that came out in 1948."

"Prototype of what?"

"A Weatherby, one of the originals from when they were out there in Los Angeles making custom guns for big-game hunters and movie stars like John Wayne, Gary Cooper, and Roy Rogers." He examined the action. "It doesn't have a serial number, so I don't see how it could've been sold on the retail market or anything like that. A gift from the manufacturer, I suppose . . . Heck if I know."

"No way to check the registration?"

"No, no way at all. It doesn't have any numbers, Walt. I could take it apart and see if I can find some under the furniture, but I wouldn't hold out much hope, if I was you." He stood there studying me as I contemplated the rifle. "You want me to take it apart?"

"Not just yet — I may send it down to Cheyenne."

"Why don't you just take it over to Sheridan? I mean that's where Weatherby is located. They moved from California just last year, north of town toward Ranchester. They've got their own museum and research library over there." He held the rifle out and studied it, his eyes widening a bit behind the steel gray frames of his round glasses. "Some cold case, huh?"

"Do you remember a man by the name of Bill Sutherland?"

He thought about it and then shook his head. "Can't say that I do, but maybe that was before my time. What'd he do?"

"Died." I gestured toward the weapon. "Wrap it up for me, would you?"

He began wrapping it in brown wax paper before handing it to me. "You guys aren't making that a crime, are you?"

I tucked the rifle under my arm. "According to the circumstance."

Turning, I walked past the glass cases full of handguns and ammunition and the racks of long guns, chained up like a gang attempting to nod off and catch a few z's.

Pushing open the glass door, I stepped

48

out onto the sidewalk and looked around at my town. It was mid-spring and the tourists hadn't arrived, but the grass was green and the flower boxes were tended to by the American Legion, so all was right with the world. Then I felt the weight of the rifle under my arm — well, mostly right with the world.

Taking a left, I started up the street when I saw Trisha Knox. She looked a little more rested than the last time I'd seen her and was wearing only one coat. "Howdy, Ms. Knox."

She clapped her hands together. "Sheriff, how are *you*?"

"I'm fine."

"Still carrying that *rifle,* I see."

"Yes, ma'am. How was your night at The Virginian?"

"Great. Did you *know* they have a blue-grass jam on Monday nights in the saloon?"

"Yep, I'm aware." I watched as she glanced around. "What's the story on your car?"

"They're *supposed* to have it towed out by tomorrow."

"It's been nice seeing you again, Ms. Knox. I hope you enjoy your time here." With that, I stepped around her and continued up the sidewalk in hopes that that was the end of that.

■ ■ ■ ■

I rested the rifle on my dispatcher's desk but picked it up when she slid a plastic binder underneath. "What's this?"

"Checks for the troops. I've taken the liberty of arranging them in a binder to make it easier on your next dispatcher."

"I wish you'd stop saying that." Propping the rifle beside the counter, I held out a hand in which she deposited a pen. "So, what happens if I don't sign these?"

"Revolution."

"I'd better sign, then." I began signing. "Did Woody Woodson call me back?"

"No."

I finished signing my name and slid the binder back to her. "He must be busy."

"It is fishing season."

"Hmm." With that, I continued to my office and sat at my desk. I stared at the rifle still wrapped in the brown wax paper that lay on my desk like a giant cold cut. "A .300 H&H Magnum, late forties . . . Has to be."

"Has to be what?"

I looked up to see Santiago Saizarbitoria, one of my deputies as well as a representative of the Basque contingency, at my doorway. "Did you look up that name I gave you?"

He stepped inside and tossed a thin sheet onto my desk. "There wasn't much, considering Bill Sutherland was the state accountant for five years — two before the Second World War and then three after." He sat in my guest chair as I picked up the sheet of paper. "This state of yours wasn't much into the record-keeping thing back in the day, huh?"

"An obituary, that's it?"

"One small notice from the local paper saying his death was the result of a hunting accident, intimating he might've even shot himself."

I read the short article below the obit. "As reported by Bob Carr?"

"Him there's a bunch on — he was the state treasurer."

"And Harold Grafton?"

"Chief clerk of the Wyoming State Treasurer's Office."

"So, they all worked together down in Cheyenne at the time?"

He nodded. "Sutherland was the local connection. I guess he had a family ranch out on the Powder River, near Absalom." He gestured toward the cut piece of paper in my hands. "He had a wife, Jean, but there

51

isn't anything more on her."

"Know where the ranch is?"

"Like I said, out near Absalom, but that's about as detailed as it gets. You want me to head over to the Courant office and see if they've got anything going back that far in their newspaper archives?"

"Yep, maybe check the library too." I attempted to hand him the paper.

"No, you keep it, I've got a copy."

"Are you sure you don't mind doing this stuff?"

He stood. "Nope. I actually enjoy it."

"Good for you."

"Two questions?"

"Sure."

"They mention a Clarence Standing Bear — any relation to Henry?"

"His father."

"They also mention a Lloyd Longmire. Is he your father?"

"Grandfather."

"I've never heard you mention him."

My eyes went back to the obituary. "Nope, you haven't."

He disappeared, and I lowered the sheet of paper. Why hadn't my father included this information when he'd told me the story? Possibly because I was a fifteen-year-old kid and it hadn't seemed pertinent, or maybe because he himself hadn't known, although I doubted that. What could have been my grandfather's connection to these individuals? As the head of the board of directors of the local bank, I was sure he'd known all of them.

The first question would be whether this actually was the rifle that had killed Bill Sutherland.

And so the first step of the coldest of ice-cold cases would be to find the slug and then the location of the body of Bill Sutherland — the cemetery in Absalom seeming a good place to start.

"Watch out for that rattlesnake near that stone on the end — as mousers go, he's a good'n."

This was not the first time I'd followed the small man around, searching for an unmarked grave or misplaced cemetery occupant and dodging rattlesnakes in the process.

Jules Beldon lifted a flask and took a sip. "Sutherland, huh?"

It was also not the first time I suspected he was drunk, but he did a remarkable job in keeping the old cemeteries clean and well kept. So much so that his services were in demand across two counties in the little townships across the Powder River Country.

"Bill Sutherland." Pocketing the flask, he nodded and fished a round container from his pocket and dipped out a pinch, carefully placing it between lip and gum. "They had a homestead south of town, *just* south of town, and that was back in the day when folks just dug a hole and planted 'em." He glanced around, calculating. "How'd he die?"

"Shot."

He glanced at me and rubbed a hand over the seven o'clock shadow on his grubby chin as he spit a brownish stream to the side. "Seems like that's always the way with the ones you're looking for, isn't it?"

"It seems that way, doesn't it?" I walked through the next row. "I'm not seeing any Sutherlands."

"No, Bill would be the only one, I believe his wife run off back to Idaho, where she was from — I seem to recall her being in a nursing home in Ketchum."

"That'd be easy enough to check on, but until I find Bill's body and have the Division of Criminal Investigation exhume it, there's no reason to go any further."

"Well, you're in luck."

Following his voice, I switched over to the next row of plots and came to where he stood, before a low stone marker that simply read B. SUTHERLAND. "Gotta be him."

"Yep, gotta be." He started off toward his Jeepster, Wilma, with its missing floorboards through which he'd lost the ashes of an uncle, I believe. "I'll get my shovel and pickax —"

"Jules, we have to get a court order —"

"Not out here we don't."

I called after him. "Yes, Jules, we do." About three feet down, I was saying the same thing, striking the hard dirt with the pickax and then climbing out so Jules could throw the dirt clods from the hole. "What we're doing here is against the law. I should know, in that I am the law."

"Not against anything unless we find something." He climbed in, digging and shoveling from the hole.

"The technical term is *grave-robbing.*"

He shrugged. "I like to think of the law as more of a guidance than a hard line, you know what I mean?"

I adjusted my hat and leaned on the pickax's handle and looked back at Dog, who was resting in the shade underneath a juniper bush. "I know it's not something you've considered as the gravest importance in your life, the law."

"Yeah, I just think you can get carried

55

away with any kind of ethical construct, you know?" He looked down at the yawning grave. "Not to change the subject but have you ever heard of taphephobia?"

"Can't say that I have."

"The fear of being buried alive." He wiped the sweat from his face. "You know that term, saved by the bell?"

"Yep."

"In the late 1800s they had so many cases of folks being buried alive that they came up with this bell system when they buried people where they'd attach strings to the head, hands, and feet. If the cemetery watchman heard the bell, they'd shove a tube down into the casket and pump air into it till they could dig 'em out. 'Course if the body swelled, which they do as they decay, that'd set off the bells and you'd just be digging up a rotting corpse."

"That's pleasant."

"You remember Emily Edgecombe from over in Campbell County?"

"Jules, is this a story I'm going to want to hear?"

He thought about it. "Sure, it is . . . Maybe a little before your time, but she was married to Darwin Edgecombe and died. Well, they took her to the funeral parlor over on South Warren Avenue by the railroad

56

tracks and laid her out. There was this kid that worked there, and he had his eye on a ring that Emily was wearing so he volunteered to stick around and prepare the body, sending everybody else home. Late that night he started pulling on that ring, trying to get it off her finger and don't you know she rose up and looked him right in the eye and said, "Stop that."

"You're kidding."

"Nope, the kid had a heart attack and died right then and there, and then she got off the slab and walked four blocks home in her nightgown, not that things like that are uncommon in Gillette even these days." He pointed vaguely in an easterly direction. "That road by the railroad tracks — the old-timers used to call that Emily Walk."

I kneeled by the hole and looked at the old sodbuster. "Hey, Jules?"

He paused in the digging, looking over at me. "Yep?"

"Where are my parents buried?"

He smiled a sly grin and then spit. "Durant Memorial Cemetery, section C, row 36, B and C."

"My grandparents?"

"Which side?"

"Paternal."

"Buried on the family plot on the ridge

57

above your grandfather's place on Buffalo Creek."

"My wife?"

"Durant Memorial Cemetery, section C, row 36, D."

"I guess that means I'll be section C, row 36, E?"

"Yes, it does."

I smiled myself. "Do you mind if I ask you a personal question?"

"I don't see how anything you ask can be more personal than where you'll spend eternity."

"Seeing as how you're an expert in the field, what are your feelings on the afterlife?"

"In what spirit is this question asked, if you don't mind my asking?"

I thought about how I wanted to phrase it. "Do you think they're up there, out there somewhere keeping an eye on us, Jules?"

He studied the hole. "I think we have responsibilities, but I think that's as far as it goes. Whenever I'm arguing with someone about that I always ask 'em, 'Do you remember anything before you got here?' And generally if they're honest they'll say no. Then I ask 'em what makes 'em think they'll remember anything when they're gone?"

"Seems logical."

He began digging again and the tip of his

shovel struck something, something hard but that sounded hollow, then stopped. "Yeah, but that doesn't necessarily mean it's true." He began digging again. "They say that as long as one good man remembered him and raised a toast to his name every year, he figured he'd be immortal." He pulled the flask from his pocket and unscrewed the cap, handing it to me. "To Big Bill Sutherland."

I took a swig, and it was the worst thing I'd ever tasted in my life. "Embalming fluid?"

He took it back, had a slug, and then twisted the cap on, returning it to his pocket before tapping the shovel tip on what sounded to be wood. "I think we found Mr. Sutherland."

"It's not unusual, you know."

We stood there, staring at the empty box. "As in?"

"Some folks want the deceased buried in one spot and some want 'em buried in another. Then there's the cremations; sometimes the deceased would request a cremation, but some members of the family might object so they'd go through the motions of a burial."

"So, you don't think there was ever a body

in this box?"

"No, I don't believe so." He gripped his shovel and looked at me. "Even by '40s prices that was a pauper's coffin, and as near as I can tell, this fellow Sutherland was a man of means. Nobody would've ever buried him in a simple pine box like this." He gestured with the shovel. "You mind if I fill it in?"

"No, and if you've got another shovel, I'll be glad to help."

"That's all right, I believe I can handle it." He shoveled a bit of dirt in. "If you want me to, I can take a look around on that ranch of theirs tomorrow and see what I can find?"

"Nobody lives down there?"

"Nope, it's pretty much deserted down that way. I know a few people in that direction, and I'll let them know what I'm looking for, and they might be able to help."

"Well, if you don't mind . . ."

"Gimme something to do, but if I was you, I'd also check the registration at the cemetery in Durant, just to be sure."

"I thought you were sure."

"You never can be sure enough." The sunburned ball of bailing wire smiled again with a few missing teeth, watching the cloud bank building in the northwest. "You and that dog of yours ought to load up and get out of here before the rain starts."

Still holding the pickax, I gestured with it. "Want me to throw this in your Jeep?"

"No, I'll just gather my things up when I get done."

"Thanks, Jules."

He waved me off. "I'll call you if I find anything."

"Call me even if you don't."

He didn't answer but continued throwing dirt in the hole, racing the clouds.

Dog fell in beside me as I got back to my truck where I could hear someone talking over the two-way. Reaching in, I grabbed the mic and keyed it. "Unit one."

Static. "Where the hell have you been?"

"Robbing graves. You?"

Static. "Everything you're supposed to be doing, like trying to get an emotional wreck of a twenty-year-old out of a motel room that she hasn't paid for . . ."

"Ministerial aid?"

Static. "It's that Knox woman you rescued. I tried, but she doesn't want to talk to anybody, she just wants to stay in the room for free."

"How does the motel feel about that?"

Static. "Not real charitable, as you might imagine."

61

"You want me to talk to her?"

Static. "That'd be nice, in that my patience is starting to fray."

"I'll be back in town in a half hour and take care of it. You mind doing something else?"

Static. "Like what?"

"Like going over to Durant Memorial Cemetery and checking their registration to make sure Bill Sutherland isn't buried there?"

Static. "This would be under the subheading 'old guy nobody cares about anyway'?"

"Um, yep."

Static. "Yeah, well I'm still waiting to find out why you care."

"I'll tell you sometime."

Static. "How about tonight over a pizza and a bottle of wine — I haven't seen you in more than a week."

"It's chess night at the Durant Home for Assisted Living."

Static. "Let me get this straight, you'd rather go play chess with Lucian Connally than have pizza, wine, and sex with me?"

"This would also be under the subheading 'old guy nobody cares about anyway.' "

Static. "What time?"

"The usual."

Static. "See you there."

■ ■ ■ ■

The lodging in question was a Best Western franchise among a number of motels near the intersection of both major interstate highways that had the benefit of being right at the base of the off-ramp.

It was pouring rain when I arrived under the canopy. I had left Dog in the truck and then thought better of it; in my experience with upset people, they're a little intimidated by the beast at first, but after discovering his true nature, they want to adopt him.

"I understand you have an intractable lodger by the name of Trisha Knox?"

The young woman looked up at me. "Hi, Sheriff. Do you remember me?"

"You're the one getting a law-enforcement degree over at Sheridan College."

"Yes, I am." She glanced down the hall. "She came in very late last night, so I let her have the corner room on the right facing the highway. It's noisy, which is why I can discount it, but when housekeeping tried to get in the room at eleven, she wouldn't open the door."

"Okay, I'll take my backup here and go talk to her."

Wandering down the hallway, I got to the room in question and knocked. I could hear a TV on inside and there was some rustling but no answer. "Sheriff's Department, can I speak to you, please?"

More rustling and then the same female voice with the strong upper-midwestern accent and the emphasis on a single word per sentence answered. "What do *you* want?"

I leaned against the doorjamb. "Well, just to talk to you first, Miss Knox."

The voice came closer to the door. "I haven't *done* anything."

"No, but we have this rule here in Wyoming where you have to pay for rooms at motels."

"I paid."

"You paid for last night, Miss Knox, but not today or what is rapidly becoming tonight."

Her voice was right on the other side of the door. "I made a *deal* with the woman at the desk . . ."

"I'm afraid that was for one night — last night."

There was a long pause. "Can't you just go *away*, please?"

"I'm afraid not. Hey, look, how about you open the door and talk to me, because I'm feeling kind of stupid standing out here talking to the door. I promise, whatever the problem is, I'll work with you on getting it straight, okay?"

"Like that *deputy* who was here earlier?"

I sighed. "She can be difficult."

"You can say that again." There was another pause. "I think I've had enough *rough* lately."

"If you open the door, I promise I won't be rough — besides, my dog needs some water."

"Wait, you've got that same *dog* with you?"

"Yep."

There was another pause and then the unfastening of a chain as she turned the handle and opened the door about six inches, looking up at me a second before there was a bright flash. "Hi, Sheriff."

Turning my head, I scrubbed a thumb and forefinger in my eye sockets in an attempt to regain sight. "Do you mind telling me why it is you just took my picture with that very bright flash?"

She lowered her phone, and I watched it disappear. "I take a picture of everyone when I first meet them under certain circumstances."

She looked different; her hair was matted, and it looked like she'd been crying. There

65

was some bruising under one eye and possibly a little swelling at the jaw. "His *name* really is Dog?"

The pupils weren't dilated or constricted. "Yep, I wasn't feeling particularly creative when I adopted him."

She reached a few fingers out, and he licked them. "Okay." A moment passed and then the door closed for a few moments more. She opened it again, allowing Dog and me to enter.

The room looked as if a bomb had gone off in a dry cleaner with clothes strung up and hanging off everything. The television was playing some soap opera, and I was surprised that such things still existed. "Do you mind turning the TV off?"

With a sulk, she slumped on one of the queen beds and picked up the remote as I'd requested.

She was wearing a pair of gym shorts and a Grain Belt beer T-shirt. Her leg was skinned and, for lack of anything else, she'd attached toilet paper to it to stop the bleeding.

"You're hurt?"

"It's nothing." She motioned around the disheveled room. "It's kind of a mess."

"It's all right, I have a daughter."

For the first time, she smiled, and even

66

laughed. "I was *washing* my clothes and hung them all out to dry."

"Where did you wash them?"

"In the sink."

I glanced around, figuring there were about enough clothes for a large backpack. "Any luck with your car?"

"They said tomorrow." She shrugged, finally looking toward the partially covered window where the rain pelted the glass. "You ever feel like you're at the *end* of your rope, Sheriff?"

I waited a moment before answering. "Many times."

She turned her brown eyes back to me as Dog went to her and she began petting him. "Look, you seem like a *nice* guy . . . Maybe you and me can make a *deal*?"

I sat on the other bed so as not to tower over her. "I'll save you the trouble, here's my deal — I'll cover your one more night here at the motel, but tomorrow come eleven o'clock you're out and gone, sound good?"

She nodded her head not looking at me. "You don't want to hear *my* deal?"

"Nope." I watched as she played with the toilet paper attached to her leg. "You hungry?"

Of all the things I was prepared for, an

outburst of tears was perhaps the last, but it was what I got as she cried out and then converted it into a sob of laughter. "I'm *dying* . . ."

Sitting in the far corner of the newly remodeled Dash Inn, we ruminated over Super Dashburgers, of which she had already eaten two. "So, they don't have food back in the Twin Cities?"

She glanced up between chews.

"It was an educated guess, between the accent and the Grain Belt T-shirt."

"Bemidji."

"Never heard of it."

"North."

I sat there watching her eat like she hadn't had anything in a week — so young but so many hard miles. "So, what brings you to Wyoming?"

"A car." When I didn't say anything, she continued, fumbling with the words but still finding one to emphasize in each sentence. "I . . . I was in Denver, *working.*"

I nodded, reaching over and taking a fry from the communal pile in the hope that she wouldn't eat my hand. "What kind of work?"

"Does it matter?" I didn't say anything again, just studying her until she felt compelled to add. "Dancer."

"Denver Ballet?"

"Hardly." She snorted, eating a few more fries. "I left there and was in a place down in . . . south of here, what is it, the friendly ghost town?"

"Casper."

"That's it, yeah." She continued eating, devouring my fries along with hers. "There was a guy there, not bad looking and he had a *bitchin'* car. So, I met him again at a bar over here by the highway."

I sipped my iced tea. "How did you skin up your leg and bruise your eye?"

She leaned back in the booth, averting me. "That's my *business.*"

"Okay, but if somebody hurt you, I can look into it."

"Why?"

"Because people shouldn't do the things I think have been done to you."

"And what do you think's been *done* to me?"

"I think you've been manhandled."

"Did you just say *manhandled*?" She laughed the guttural snort again and then rolled her eyes back to me. "I bet you've done some manhandling in your day."

"Not like that."

"Other kinds of manhandling?" She studied me. "Where'd you get that *scar* over your eye, and why's part of your ear *missing*?" A very unpleasant smile slithered across her lips like something poisonous. "Yeah, I bet you've done some *manhandling* in your time — I bet you've done a lot." The smile faded. "How 'bout you gimme that big gun you got on your hip, and I'll just take care of myself?" I stared at her, saying nothing until she stood, wiping her hands on a paper napkin and tossing it back on the tray. Pulling on her nylon jacket, she pushed her hair back from her face. "We done here?"

"I suppose so."

I started to get up when she stuck a hand out to stop me. "I can walk from here."

"Sure about that?"

She ignored me and started for the side door. "Thanks for dinner."

"Hey, can I ask you a question?"

She stopped and turned. "Sure."

"If you take somebody's picture at your door as a security measure, why wouldn't they just take your phone once they got in?"

She pulled the device from the back pocket and held it up where I could see the turquoise cover encrusted with rhinestones. "Waterproof case . . . After I take the picture, I just drop it in the toilet tank —

nobody ever looks for a phone in there."

"Smart." I watched her go, looking out the window at the receding thunderheads and the shine they had left on everything. Scooping up the remainder of our fries, I redeposited them into the container and dumped the tray and carried them out to the parking lot where the air smelled clean and laden like fresh laundry.

My trusty backup sat in the back of the truck with his enormous head hanging out the partially lowered rear window.

Slowly feeding him fries, we both watched as she made the sidewalk, turned left, and strutted off, almost getting run over by a motorist who had taken the off-ramp. A few words and gestures were exchanged before she continued into the underpass toward the motel.

Taking a fry for myself, I sighed. "How much trouble do you think this world could divest itself of if we all didn't think we were so tough?"

3

Watching as she filled my glass, I had to admit that the pizza warming in the oven of room thirty-two of the Durant Home for Assisted Living smelled pretty good. I also couldn't help but wonder if we all couldn't use a little assistance in living.

Vic handed the wine to me and then crossed her arms. "So, you put her up for another night?"

"I did. I also bought both of us Super Dashburgers and she ate both mine and hers, except for a few fries, which I shared with the Grendel over there." The monster opened his eyes to slits from his resting place on the tufted leather sofa in order to see if the pizza — or, more important, the crusts — had come out of the oven. Disappointed, he closed his eyes again.

Lucian leaned over the chessboard to study the situation. "Had a fellow that used to do that to us every spring, he'd just move around and hit up the sheriff's departments of each county. Got away with it for a pretty long time, as I recall."

I watched as Vic filled the retired sheriff's glass, and he reared back to study her and her killer smile. "What'd you do?"

"Put him on a county work detail, back when we had such things. He lasted about a day and then disappeared, and we never heard from him again — hell, for all I know he got run over by a train." It seemed that whenever Lucian Connally lost track of anybody, the specter of train dismemberment always reared its head.

He smiled up at her. "I'm trying to figure out if you're getting better looking every time I see you."

She finished pouring herself a drink and turned to retreat into the kitchenette. "It's because I bring you a jug of wine and a loaf of bread. It's an illusion that Roman women have been using for centuries — that and knifing you in your sleep."

He watched her go and then looked back at me, his finger still on the rook. "Man oh man, she is one butter-and-egg fly."

I didn't bother trying to figure out what that meant exactly. "Big Bill Sutherland."

He turned back to stare at me. "Who?"

"Big Bill Sutherland, the fellow I asked

you about."

He continued to study me, and I couldn't help but think it was a few seconds too long. "I'm not coming up with anything."

"The state accountant that got killed in the hunting accident back in '48 I was telling you about?"

He thought some more and then his eyes moved to the rook. "What is it you want to know?"

I leaned forward, getting a sense of what he was attempting to do in the game, among other things. "Your case?"

"Wasn't much of a case, as I recall."

"They never figured out who shot him."

He puffed a little air out with his lips in dismissal. "By *they,* you mean *me*?"

I sighed. "No, that's not what I mean."

His dark eyes stayed on the board. "You mind if I ask what's brought all this up?"

"I found a .300 H&H Magnum up in the mountains, an odd piece without manufacture numbers and a State of Wyoming fiftieth anniversary medallion embedded in the stock. I was talking to Reeve over at the Sports Lure, and he said it was one of the early Weatherby models and that I should take it over to Sheridan and have them look at it."

He grunted and put his finger on a knight.

74

"From what I'm to understand, Sutherland was killed with that caliber rifle, but I
can't find any reports or filings on the
incident. Was the autopsy done here or
down in Cheyenne?"

"Hell if I know — that was a long time
ago. Who knows if there even was an autopsy?"

"Do you know where he was buried?"

He moved the knight. "No."

I lowered my face to catch his gaze.
"You're not being a lot of help here."

The mahogany eyes flickered across my
face. "Ancient history. Some fellow gets
himself shot in an elk camp, and we can't
find the weapon, and suddenly you stumble
onto it more than half a century later? Well,
congratulations — let me know how that
plays out."

"It was my grandfather's elk camp."

"Oh." He relaxed in the leather wingback
chair and continued to study me, slightly
shaking his head. "So that's what this is all
about."

"What's that supposed to mean?"

"Well, I think we can, without much
contradiction, refer to the relationship
between you and that grandfather of yours
as a rocky road."

"Meaning?"

75

"Is that what's got a bug up your ass? That this might concern Lloyd Longmire?"

"And my father."

"Wait." He shook his head as if to clear it. "How is he involved?"

"He's the one who told me the story of how Sutherland was killed — and he also said you and he went back up there the next day."

"And when did that conversation take place?"

"Quite a while ago, when I was a teenager."

"What'd he know about it?"

"He was there when it happened."

He studied me for a long while. "I don't remember that."

"He and Sutherland were out hunting near Pole Creek when the man was shot —"

"I know where it happened, damn it." He thought, massaging the stump where his leg used to be. "To the best of my recollection there was some other fellow involved from down in Cheyenne —"

"Bob Carr, the state treasurer."

"And what was this Sutherland fellow?"

"State accountant, who'd just come back from the war."

He sipped his wine as Vic came in from the kitchen and leaned in the doorway with

76

her own glass and listened. "That was a lot of us that made that particular trip."

"And there was another one from Cheyenne, Harold Grafton, chief clerk of the Wyoming State Treasurer's Office — now, doesn't that strike you as odd?"

"What, that a bunch of assholes from Cheyenne came up here and couldn't shoot straight?"

"Lucian . . ."

"If there'd been any funny business, we would've done something, but you say there was an autopsy?"

"That's what my father said. He also said Clarence Standing Bear was there too."

He thought about it, gripping his chin like a knuckleball. "And they determined that this fellow Sutherland was killed with a .300 H&H? The same gun you say you found leaning against a tree up here?"

"Stuffed in some rocks, actually."

"Well, the Division of Criminal Investigation isn't going to have records going back that far, not on some random hunting accident."

"Where would the DCI records be if it had been done here — and more important, where would the slug be?"

He thought about it. "When did Isaac Bloomfield start working at the hospital?"

"You would know better than me, but I'd imagine sometime after the war."

"I'd start with him and see if they've got anything over there, but I wouldn't get my hopes up." He looked out the window and into the darkness past the sliding glass doors. "Now, what's this about the body?"

"We can't find it."

"Well, I'd start with Jules Beldon."

"I was grave-robbing with him earlier today out in Absalom and all we found was an empty coffin." I sipped my wine. "He says Sutherland had a family place south of town and might be buried there."

"Well, go look for him."

"You don't remember him?"

"Who?"

"Bill Sutherland." He said nothing. "The accountant for the State of Wyoming was from around here and you don't remember him?"

"Well, I can't be expected to remember every case in the last century, but if there had been anything to it, I'm telling you we would've followed it up." The old Doolittle Raider sipped his wine and then glanced around. "Hey, are we ever going to get anything to eat in here?"

"He's lying."

"Yep." I opened the door of my truck and let Dog jump in as I stood there, and I hung an arm through the window. "But about what, and more importantly, for whom?"

Vic leaned against the fender of her race truck, Banshee II, crossed her arms, and looked up at me. "How well did Lucian know your grandfather?"

"I have no idea."

"How well did you know your grandfather?"

"That's a good question." I sighed, looking out toward Fort Street and the hazy streetlights there. "He came up in the conversation yesterday morning at the cabin. Cady was cleaning a photo of him that she'd never seen, one of him and the other bank directors standing on the sidewalk."

"Bank directors?"

"I suppose that's who they were, seven of them." My eyes came back to her. "There was a time when my illustrious grandfather was the chairman of the board of directors of the Bank of Durant, I guess keeping it from going under."

"So, let me get this straight — the state treasurer, the chief clerk of the state treasury office, and your grandfather, the de facto bank president, all go hunting and the state

79

accountant turns up dead?"

"Seems a little funny, doesn't it?"

"This place is starting to sound like North Philly." She unfolded her arms and stuffed her hands in her jean pockets. "And your father was there?"

"Yep, he told me the story when I was a teenager. He said it was the first man he'd ever seen killed, but as I remember there were other disturbing factors."

"Like what?"

"After Sutherland was killed, the men wanted to just leave his body out there overnight."

She made a face. "I don't know much about hunting etiquette, but that seems fucked up."

I nodded. "Highly."

"Anything else?"

I laughed, thinking about what my father had said all those years ago. "Henry's father offered to carve up any of them if they left."

"The Bear's father was there too?"

"Yep."

She pushed off her truck and stepped toward me. "And what happened after-ward?"

"That's what I'm trying to piece together."

She brought both hands up, flattening the lapels of my jacket. "And you really think

80

your grandfather might've been involved in all of this?"

"Let's just say I'm not excluding the possibility."

"Wow, just . . ." Grabbing the lapels, she shook me. "Wow."

"I know."

"Look, maybe your grandfather wasn't involved, maybe it was just these guys from Cheyenne."

"It was my grandfather's elk camp."

"So?"

"So, in a way he was responsible, along with his financial ties."

"You think this Sutherland guy found something out that he wasn't supposed to?"

"His tenure as the state accountant was interrupted by his military service, whereas the others didn't serve and worked here throughout the war."

She let go of my lapels and leaned on the door beside me. "So, you think he got back and discovered that these guys had been up to something?"

"It seems like a logical supposition."

"And you really think your grandfather was involved?"

"Why would Lucian lie to protect Carr and Grafton, two men he hardly remembers?"

81

She stared at me for a moment. "I'm going to ask a question, and mind you, it's just a question."

"Okay."

"You think Lucian could've been involved?"

"Well, I don't want to take anybody off the list, but my father only mentioned him after the fact."

"After Sutherland had been shot."

"Yep."

"Doesn't mean that he couldn't have been involved." She glanced back toward the brick building. "That ol' coot has killed more people than typhus, Walt."

"I don't think you can count strategic bombings."

"I'm not."

She stepped toward her truck, then turned to me. "So, do you want to go back to my place and have sex or do you want to go to your place and have sex?"

"My daughter and granddaughter are at my place."

She started back around to her truck toward the driver's seat. "My place it is."

"I think I'm going to have to take a rain check. I'm kind of worn out from grave-robbing."

She stopped on the other side, laying her

arms on the hood and glowering at me. "It's been over a month."

"I am aware of that."

"Is there something I need to know?"

"No, nothing like that."

"Then." She rested her chin on a forearm. "What?"

"Nothing, it's nothing." I pushed off and walked over to the opposite side of the Banshee II hood. "Just a lot going on right now, and then I find out my grandfather may have been involved in a murder . . ."

"Seems to me like you're rooting for it."

I stared at her.

"I mean it's no great secret that you two didn't get along. I don't know jack shit about your family, but I know that."

"I don't think that's the case."

"Okay."

I thought about it. "It seems like that?"

"Yeah, well, yeah." She raised her head from her arms and moved toward the door of her truck.

Something strange happened in that moment, words I wasn't even sure if I remembered or how to say them. "Marry me."

She leaned to the side, her tarnished gold eyes just visible past the front pillar by the windshield. "What'd you just say?"

I swallowed and then worked up the nerve

to repeat myself. "Marry me."

I don't think I'd ever seen her so surprised in my life. "What?"

I said it again, simply because it seemed like the only words I could come up with at the moment. "Marry me."

"No."

I wasn't quite sure what to expect but don't think this was it. "No, you won't marry me?"

"No, don't you ask me like that in the fucking parking lot of the Durant Home for Assisted Living."

I glanced around. "I know it's not —"

"No, it's not." She charged back around the truck and planted herself in front of me and pointed a finger in my face like a deadly weapon. "This is the definition of not." She glanced around at our surroundings. "Now?" She spun around. "Here, in the parking lot is where you decide to ask me the most important question of our lives?" The finger withdrew and joined its brethren as she placed both fists on her hips. "For years I've been waiting for you to ask and now, now is the time you get it into your head to pop the question?"

"I know it doesn't seem like —"

"Why not the fucking IGA while we're cadging jurors?"

84

"Look, I know —"

"Why not at the Kum and Go, you know, while we're filling the fucking truck up with gas?"

"Vic, I . . ."

She turned and walked away from me, standing there, and looking out at the dusty parking lot, finally raising her arms. "Boy, here it is, world — the most romantic spot that Walt Longmire could come up with."

"C'mon —"

"No."

I stood there for a moment, wondering if I'd heard her right. "No, what?"

"No. No is the answer if you need an answer right now."

I took a couple of steps toward her, staring at the back of her head. "I don't . . ."

"I need time to think about it, okay?"

"Sure, sure."

She stood there for a moment more and then walked around her vehicle, snatching open the door and jumping in and then grinding the seven-hundred-horsepower truck to life and throwing it into reverse, barking the tires, and then burning out onto the main street, where she drifted sideways and then laid another strip of rubber before disappearing into the night with a roar of supercharged heat.

I stood there silent for a moment and then glanced back at Dog. "You know, I don't think that went the way I thought it would." He said nothing, and I climbed in my own truck, backing out and heading home at a reasonable speed.

"I thought it went without saying."

"In my experiences with women, it is better to adopt a posture where nothing goes without saying."

I watched as Henry Standing Bear continued closing out the register of the Red Pony Bar & Grill. He probably hoped I'd go home. I had gone home first but had seen the red Jeep parked in front of my cabin, which alerted me to the fact that my daughter and granddaughter had indeed elected to stay the night rather than face the nearly five-hour drive back down to Cheyenne.

In the face of current dialogues, I felt the need for a little conversation and didn't want to burden Cady. Instead, I was watching an old black-and-white episode of *Have Gun — Will Travel* on the Sony Trinitron in the corner, where a very young James Olson locked Richard Boone behind bars. I raised my empty can of Rainier and rattled it. "So, do you think no means no?"

He sighed, turned from the cash register,

and looked at me. "In what way?"

"As in, 'No I'm not going to marry you.'"

"I do not know, in that I was not there."

"But I've described it to you."

He picked up his tonic water with the lime twist, what he always drank while working his bar, and glanced up at the TV screen as Paladin, the main character of the show, explained to a young sheriff that using the municipal code from a large city, Philadelphia, wasn't going to work in the frontier town. "Yes, you have, a number of times."

"Well, what do you think it means?"

"I think it means no, that she needs time to think about it."

"Well, I know that's what she said, but what do you think it means in the larger scope of things?"

He glanced at the watch on his wrist. "In the larger scope of things, I think it means no and that she wants to think about it."

I rested an elbow on the bar and looked at him. "Can I have another beer?"

"No, and in the larger scope of things what that means is that I am closing and that you need to go home."

I looked down at Dog, who had raised his head at the word *home.* "I don't feel like going home."

The Bear sighed again and then reached

in the cooler to pull out another can of Rainier, then taking the empty and replacing it as Dog's head returned to the floor. I took a sip, feeling moderately better.

The phone rang, and he picked up the receiver. "It is another beautiful day at the Red Pony Bar & Grill and continual soiree, but unfortunately we are closed and no longer taking reservations."

As he hung up the phone, I glanced around at the threadbare indoor-but-mostly-outdoor carpeting, the ancient jukebox, the pool table with its torn felt, and the patches in the wall where we had once searched in vain for the original fuse box. "You have to have reservations to get in this place now?"

"Not really, but it keeps out the riffraff." Reaching over, he began polishing glasses he'd already polished and watched as the civic argument on the TV began winding down. "If you do not mind me asking, why did you choose to propose to her now?"

"I don't know, it just kind of happened — a spur of the moment kind of thing."

Returning the glasses to rest lip down on the bar towel, he nodded a grim nod. "Not good planning then?"

"I suppose not."

"Then you are simply going to have to wait."

We both watched as the gunfighter, dressed in black, smoked a cigar slipped from his boot and attempted to get the young sheriff to release him so that he might assist him in holding off some bad guys who were coming to town. "Waiting is hard."

"Yes."

I took another sip of my beer as Boone threw open a door, drawing the fire of the bad guys as a few hit the dirt. "What if I — ?"

He turned, pulling the liner from the trash can and resting it on the floor, then tying the plastic ties. "No."

"You didn't even hear what I was going to say."

"I do not have to."

"But —"

"No." He straightened, staring down at me. "I am going to go battle the gang of raccoons and throw the trash in the dumpster now, but when I get back the answer will still be no."

Watching him as he exited through the side door and into the lot at the back of the bar, I sipped my beer, my eyes drifting to the screen where Paladin fired a shotgun into a saloon.

No.

Of all the answers I'd expected, that wasn't one of them. Maybe Henry was right, but it seemed like I'd put a couple of years of thought into it. She'd never said she wanted to get married, but then she hadn't said specifically that she didn't want to be married. I remembered a conversation where she'd said she wasn't looking for hearth and home.

Maybe I'd overstepped my boundaries.

Maybe it was the job.

Maybe it was somebody else.

Henry came back in and began putting a new liner in the trash can. He slid it back in place and looked up at the screen.

"Maybe there's somebody else."

His eyes came back to me as he sighed again. "Who?"

"She was back in Philadelphia three weeks ago, maybe she met somebody."

"You know, you can truly be an idiot sometimes." He leaned his arms on the bar. "Walt, how long have you two been together?"

"In the biblical sense?"

"Yes."

"I don't know, maybe four years?"

"You do not think that if there was someone else, we would know about it by now

— especially, seeing as how you are in the investigative business?"

I nodded at the TV in an attempt to change the subject. "I always liked that show."

"Yes, my father and I used to watch it when I was young."

I watched as Paladin explained the basic unwritten law of jurisprudence, and how you can't enforce a law that goes against the wishes of the majority and how there's a name for people who do, *tyrant.* "Pretty weighty issues for a fifties television series."

"He is the one who had the card."

I nodded. "Lived in a hotel in San Francisco."

"His other totem was a chess piece, a knight as I recall." Leaning against the bar, his eyes came back to me. "So, what is the story of this rifle you have found up on the mountain at an elk camp that included my father?"

"It's out in the truck, would you like me to get it?"

I watched the conflicted look on his face as he finally said, "Certainly."

Dog started to get up as I stood, but I settled him with a gesture and went out the front, then walked over to my truck, opened the door, and pulled the custom rifle from

91

the back seat. I'd just started to close the door when I saw a set of headlights coming from the distance, traveling way too fast.

It looked like a modern SUV and could've been a highway patrolman, so I stepped forward and watched as it approached at well over a hundred miles an hour, figuring they'd see a fully dressed and armed Wyoming sheriff and possibly slow down.

It was a dark-colored SUV and flashed by in an instant.

Looking for the plates, I could see from the running lights that they were Wyoming registration, but the plate light was out and the thing was going so fast that from the angle I couldn't make out the numbers or county designation.

I thought about jumping in my truck and giving chase, but in all honesty I wasn't sure I could catch the SUV by the time I got my truck started and took off after it. I figured I'd just radio ahead to the two state routes it could take, which I did.

Hanging the mic back up and closing the door again, I carried the rifle inside and laid it on the bar.

Henry looked over my shoulder. "Something going on out there?"

"Just some SUV going by like the proverbial bat out of hell. I radioed both counties

to the west so that if Richard Petty contin-
ues, they'll get a welcoming committee."

Pulling the rifle out of the wax paper, he
looked down at it for far too long.

I took a sip of my beer. "Something?"

"I know this coin."

"You're kidding."

"No." He reached out and touched the
piece of metal embedded in the stock. "I
recognize this."

"What do you — ?"

"Let me think for a moment." He continued studying the rifle and then turned and
hit NO SALE on the vintage brass cash
register behind him. Carefully lifting the
cash tray, I watched as he rooted around for
a moment and then grabbed a coin from
the bottom and turned to show it to me
between thumb and forefinger. "Unless I
am mistaken, this is the exact same coin."

It was.

I took it, turning it over and examining
the other side that proudly pronounced the
fiftieth anniversary of the state. "Where did
you get this?"

"My mother gave it to me. I recall that I
was very impressed by the coin, and I
remember asking my mother about it."

I looked down at the coin. "What was it
she said?"

"That the draped figure in the center holds a staff and flowing banner that reads *Equal Rights;* she explained that the words symbolized the passage of the territorial suffrage amendment from 1869 giving women the right to vote, the first state to do so." He shook his head. "Of course, my people did not receive that right until 1924."

I studied the coin as he picked the rifle up and held it in the light. "It is a beautiful gun."

"Except for where the stock is cracked."

"In two places."

"Possibly weaknesses in the stock that over time?"

"Possibly."

"How do you think your grandfather was involved with the death of this man Sutherland?"

"I didn't until Lucian started lying to me about it."

"Lying?"

"Well, maybe that's too strong of a word, maybe 'not forthcoming' would be a better phrase."

"And you think he is attempting to protect your grandfather?"

"Who else?"

"Himself?"

"Another possibility."

"And there are no records of this incident?"

"None that I or any of my trusty staff can find." I watched as he turned the rifle in his hands, sighting his eyes along the scope but not flipping up the covers, almost as if they might reveal too much. "What about your father?"

"What about him?"

"Did Clarence ever mention this incident?"

He smiled the paper-cut grin. "No, he would have filed this under the heading WMP."

I waited.

"White Man Problems." He lowered the rifle and stared at me. "You honestly believe your grandfather might have been involved?"

"I'm not discounting it as a possibility."

"But you don't suspect your father?"

"No."

"Or mine?"

"No."

"Very complex, these White Man Problems."

"Our fathers weren't in the financial sector."

He lowered the rifle, carefully laying it back on the wax paper. "And you have to

95

be, to have done this?"

"It seems a reasonable suspicion."

"Rather than simply an accident?" He picked up the remote and turned off the TV, leaving Richard Boone to his own devices. "Odds would say that this was likely an accident."

I handed the coin back to him. "In case you haven't noticed, I'm not in the accident business."

He flipped it in the air, caught it, and then slapped it onto the back of his other hand. "Yes, I sense that." Removing his hand, he looked at the coin and then returned it to its resting place under the cash drawer in the register.

"Heads or tails?"

"Yes." He turned to study the rifle and then me.

For the lack of anything else, I stated the obvious. "I just want to know what happened, Henry."

"And that is all you want?"

"Yep." I glanced at the weapon. "The chances of me uncovering anything after all this time are pretty slim, but I'd like to know the truth if Sutherland was killed."

He smiled at me. "It goes without saying?"

"In both women and murder investigations . . ."

I was about to pursue more on this thought when a thunderous crash shook the building.

Dog stood and barked as both Henry and I braced ourselves against the bar so we could look around. "What the heck was that?"

"Possibly an asteroid . . ." He started moving around the bar and toward the front door. "But from previous experience, I would say that someone has run their car into the building."

Getting up, I followed him. "That happen a lot?"

He nodded, pushing open the screen door. "Yes, when people have been at other establishments and possibly been overserved."

When we got outside, he darted to the left and I followed as he turned the corner and disappeared around the building. Before I could get the screen door closed, Dog shot out and followed Henry, leaving me to bring up the rear.

As I turned the corner, I was more than shocked to see it was Jules Beldon's rusted-out turquoise Jeepster, Wilma, crunched into the wall of the converted Texaco station that had become the Red Pony Bar & Grill.

Shaking my head, I walked over to where Henry had reached in the open window of the sputtering and dying contraption, pulling the aged gravedigger back up and looking at him. Placing a hand against his neck, he glanced back at me. "He is breathing."

"Well, that's good. Is he drunk?"

"There is a strong smell of liquor, among other things."

"I bet." I had a little trouble opening the door where the fender had pushed into it but finally leveraged the thing open with a crunch of sheet metal. "I was doing a little excavation work with him out in Absalom earlier today, and he'd already started drinking."

He was not wearing a seat belt. It appeared the vehicle didn't have any. Henry scooped him up and carried him toward the front of the building as I hurried past to open the screen door. I pushed everything on the bar to the side as the Bear lifted the small man up and onto the surface before leaning forward and listening to his breathing. "He is hurt."

"I'd imagine." I studied the older man, even going so far as to peel an eyelid back to reveal a constricted pupil and then doing the same to the other. I stabilized his head and pulled my penlight from my shirt pocket. "It looks like there's some blood at the back of his head."

"We will need to get him into the hospital in Durant."

I nodded. "He's concussed."

As I started to lift Jules, Henry stopped me and pulled back the man's jacket where you could see that the entire side of his body was saturated with blood. "I am afraid it is more than that." His face came up, the dark eyes all but glowing. "He has been shot."

4

"Three rounds."

I stared at the old doctor whom I'd entrusted with my life numerous times. "Three?"

Isaac Bloomfield leaned against the wall with the clipboard in his knotty, veined hands, his large hazel eyes peering at me through the upper lenses of his thick bifocals. "Two in his side and one that glanced off the back of his head."

I stuffed my hands in my jeans and looked at him and then his partner in medicine, David Nickerson. "This is where I make the joke about Jules's hard head."

"We're hoping the cerebral swelling will subside, but he's incommunicative at this time." David shook his head. "You say he was driving and ran into Henry's bar with his automobile?"

"Yep."

"I'm surprised. There is damage near his

spine from one of the slugs — I wouldn't have thought he would've been capable."

"He's tough."

The young man looked sad. "In all honesty, I don't think he'll walk again, Walt."

The early morning hallway at Durant Memorial was empty. "What was the caliber?"

"We don't know." Drawing a ziplock bag from behind the clipboard, Isaac extended it to me. "A rifle, I'm assuming."

I took it from him and studied the two pieces of malformed metal. "Hmm, possibly a .223 Remington, or . . ."

The older man adjusted his glasses. "What?"

"Oh, one of those NATO rounds, but I don't see anybody running around the Powder River Country with a combat rifle — not that they're not out there, but who would shoot Jules with one?"

"A hunting accident?"

"Not in May." I thumbed the slugs, rolling them in my fingers. "Too much of a coincidence." I looked back at Isaac. "I was just out near Absalom with Jules yesterday. We were attempting to find a long-dead body buried in the cemetery out there. We didn't find the deceased in question, but he said he knew that the fellow's family had a place south of town and he'd go look around there."

"You think someone shot him for trespassing?"

"Not three times." I continued studying the slugs. "No, this was somebody trying to kill him, for whatever reason, and I sent him out there."

"You can't blame yourself for something crazy like this." He pushed off the wall, and the three of us began walking toward the nurses' station. "If you don't mind my asking, what are you doing exhuming bodies out on the Powder River Country?"

"It's funny you should ask, Doc." I pulled up and stopped, glancing over at Janine Reynolds and figuring she knew how to keep her mouth shut, being the granddaughter of my dispatcher, or maybe she was her niece. "I don't suppose you remember a hunting accident involving a man by the name of Bill Sutherland from back in 1948?"

He stared at me.

"I know it's a long time . . ."

He sighed. "You've seen my office."

Few things in life have sent a shudder down my spine, but the mere mention of Isaac Bloomfield's cubbyhole of an office with its filing cabinets and reams of files and folders stacked in precarious piles to the ceiling did just that.

He threw a hand onto his associate's shoulder. "The good news is that I'm retiring at the end of this month and David here is taking over, which means that my lair is going to have to be cleared out, with a snow shovel, if necessary."

"Does the incident ring any bells?"

"What was his name again?"

"Sutherland, Bill Sutherland. He was the head accountant for the state and was shot elk hunting in '48 with two buddies of his from down in Cheyenne — the Wyoming State Treasurer Bob Carr and his chief clerk, Harold Grafton. My father, Henry's father, and my grandfather were all there as well."

"That does seem familiar. Was he a big man?"

"I'm assuming. His nickname was *Big* Bill Sutherland."

"This is one of Lucian's cases?"

"Yep."

"As I recall he was somewhat fast and loose with his reporting when he started out as sheriff."

"He never was one for the paperwork."

He placed the clipboard on the counter edge of the nurses' station. "I'll have to start

103

going through the files, and that's going to take some time."

"Are you really going to throw them out?"

"No, they'll be transferred over to computer files." He glanced at David. "But that won't be my job."

Nickerson turned to Janine. "Or mine."

The head nurse sighed, mostly I'd imagine, because there was no one else to turn to.

"Not quite a mile wide but certainly no more than an inch deep. Let 'er buck. The three of us stood on a ridge and looked at the banks of the Powder River just south of Absalom. "Seven percent . . ."

The Bear crossed behind Dog and me. "Seven percent?"

"Seven percent of the population of Wyoming joined up during World War I, where the phrase came from. Some say it was cowboys on cattle drives, but it gained worldwide recognition with the 361st Regiment of the 91st Infantry Division. When they went over the top they'd yell 'Powder River, let 'er buck.' "

"Among my people it was referred to as the Powder River because it was believed that it held gunpowder because of the lightning that would touch off the natural gas bubbles in the water."

"I've never heard that."

"My father used to refer to it as the River of Flatulence." With that, he turned, walked past my truck, opened the door, and unlocked the shotgun from the hump in order to take it out. "It is amazing the things you hear when you have been here thousands of years before anyone else."

I gestured toward my Wingmaster shotgun in his right hand. "What's that for?"

He lip-pointed toward the skyline. "Someone is shooting people out here, so I thought it wise to have a weapon."

"Kind of close range."

"My preference." He walked toward the old shack and a terminally leaning barn in a wash about a hundred yards away. There was a ditch and a spot where a cattle guard had been, but it was gone, holding motorized vehicles in abeyance, although the two of us and Dog hopped across rather easily.

"We are sure this is the Sutherland place?"

Trailing along behind him as I patted my leg to get Dog's attention away from a Western cottontail, I called out. "I'm not, but from the tire tracks I'd say Jules was."

"There were no bullet holes in the car." He gestured toward the ground. "And there is no blood."

"No, but if I know Jules, he drove up here and got the lay of the land and then turned around and found a way to get in closer — he doesn't strike me as a walker." Looking across the miles of sagebrush, it was easy to see why Sutherland's ancestors would've taken the risk of being in the tertiary basin to be closer to the water. The shelf where the little homestead stood was high enough to avoid any except the worst every-hundred-year flooding.

As Dog and I veered toward the house, Henry continued toward the barn with the 12-gauge on his shoulder, the two of us having separate ideas as to where a private cemetery would be.

The front door hung open on one leather shoe-sole hinge, creaking in the ever-present wind. I always thought about the high-plains dreams that had constructed such places out in the middle of nowhere, ones that had bloomed, grown, withered, and died. The foundation was slip-formed with crude cement and indigenous rock, but it had withstood the rigors of time better than the clapboard planks that has been nailed crooked along the exterior walls, gray and indifferent. All the windows were broken, and a few sheets of the corroded tin lifted with a resigned salutation to every wind gust that passed.

Stepping onto the rough-cut planks of the porch, I watched as a pack rat scurried below, disappearing into a crack in the foundation, much to Dog's interest. "Not much to pack away around here, my friend."

I couldn't help but take a look inside where newspapers had been glued to the walls in lieu of wallpaper. Knowing that with my weakness for the printed word I could stand inside there all day reading the articles on the walls, I tested the floor on the other side of the entryway and walked forward with Dog in tow toward the back door that swung open at the other end of the short hallway.

It was warm in the little house as I got to the back and stood there in the opening, looking out at the sun-drenched landscape, thinking about my grandfather.

Knowing that I would be leaving for USC's summer football camp, he had moved up the branding at our ranch on Buffalo Creek, which was fine with me, because it meant I wouldn't be wrestling the four-hundred-pounders he usually had us working with in the late fall.

When I had gone beyond six feet and two hundred pounds, he had decided I no longer needed to be on a horse. As the riders would separate the calves from the heifers, they would then usher them into a corral where we would tackle them and hold them down as they were vaccinated and neutered. As the day wore on, other hands got hurt or were simply worn down by the pace the old man had set, until finally I was the only one left standing in the corral.

Backlit in that hard sun, he looked down at me with the contempt that only those on horseback have for those afoot. "How much longer do you think you can go?"

I panted, attempting to catch my breath. "As long as you want."

He nodded, looking away. "I figure we've got another dozen or so."

I wiped the sweat from my face with the side of my hand.

"I guess you figure this is the last time you'll ever be doing this, huh?"

I stood there, silent.

"You know what I think? I think you'll be back here in no time with your tail between your legs, and I'll then decide if I wanna hire you all over again."

"You've never hired me in the first place."

He studied me for a long moment.

"At least you've never paid me."

He nodded, looking down at the rope in

his hands, and then turned his horse and trotted away, calling back. " 'Bout what you're worth."

"Find anything?"

Startled back to reality, I turned to see Henry standing at the corner of the old house. "Nothing but ghosts."

He joined me, walking out where I'd been staring with the 12-gauge in his hands as Dog joined him. "There is nothing near the barn and nothing around the house here. I suppose we should take a look on the ridge up near that hillock?"

I nodded and followed as Dog led the way along an old, overgrown path. "You think people put cemeteries on hills so they're closer to God?"

"It would explain why my people build platforms."

This path was less traveled, probably because the mule deer and wayward cows saw no need to visit a grave site, if there were any up there.

We'd just gotten to the flat area when Henry stopped, pointing with the shotgun. "Blood." Snatching Dog's collar before he could trot in, I saw the dark stains brushed on the brittle leaves of the sage. "He must've fallen here."

Following the Bear as he circled to the left, I could see the trail where the gravedigger had come from and could now see a number of weathered headstones. There were only a few left standing, although one had tools leaning against it, and on closer inspection you could see the pile of dirt that had been removed and shoveled next to the grave.

And the blood.

The Bear's head angled to one side. "He was shot while digging in the grave."

We moved forward as a buzzing sound swarmed near my head and I swiped at what I assumed was a mosquito or hummingbird.

Henry set up camp to the left of the grave, staying a few yards out so as to not tamper with the site. "Then Jules must have scrambled up and that way toward the road." The Bear stood on tiptoes, looking into the sagebrush. "He was hit again there, about halfway to the pullout, which is where he must have parked his vehicle."

"And the third shot?"

"I would say that was made as he tried to get in the vehicle, but it would only be a guess."

The whirring went by my head again, and I was starting to think it was some kind of bird attempting to guard its nest. "Where would you shoot from?"

He glanced around, finally pointing the shotgun across the road and to the hills to the west. "Somewhere over there."

"But if he'd been hit, why would Jules run toward where the shots were coming from?"

"Confusion? He had been hit once and then twice, and he was knowledgeable enough to know that if he didn't get to his vehicle, he would most certainly die out here alone, or be finished off."

"By whom?"

"That is always the question, is it not?" And with that he turned directly toward me, the shotgun rising deftly in his hands, leveling off and firing.

Automatically ducking, I caught myself with a hand on the rough ground and straightened, stretching my jaw, and trying to get my hearing back as Dog stood to the side barking. I stared at the Cheyenne Nation, my voice echoing in my head as the words came out. "You mind telling me what that was all about?"

Calmly walking past me, he handed me the shotgun and continued a good twenty yards out into the sagebrush before stopping to look around and then stooping and lifting something from the ground. Walking that way with Dog, we got there just as the

Bear held the black, metal contraption up, one of its four propellers hanging limp like a broken wing.

He smiled at me. "Pull."

"A drone, and a very expensive one."

"What does it do?"

Santiago Saizarbitoria glanced at me as if I'd just asked where you wound it up. "It takes pictures, video, graph locations . . ."

"Where?"

"Where what?"

"Where does it take pictures?"

He lowered his face down to the level of the thing on the table in the basement of our offices, using a pencil to point at a lens mounted on the abdomen of what appeared to me like some sort of giant insect. "Right here."

"But where does it store them?"

"Not on the device, it transmits the signal to a controller."

"Is it recording now?"

"No, I took the battery out of it — one of those mAh LiPo batteries."

Henry folded his arms. "What would the range on something like this be?"

"I'm guessing, without knowing what kind it is, but I'd say anywhere from three to seven and a half miles. Why?"

112

The Bear lowered his face to look at the thing. "We saw no one in the surrounding area, and we looked."

"This thing is really well built, not like the stuff on the commercial market. See how the pieces are all custom made? With all these big motors, I bet this thing could lift a hundred pounds if it had to."

"Where would you buy something like this?"

The Basquo shook his head. "I have no idea, but the battery would be close to a thousand dollars."

"How much?"

He grunted a laugh. "I'm just guessing, but for the whole drone I'm betting fifty, a hundred thousand dollars."

"Military?"

He shrugged. "Possibly, but why would the military be out there flying around the Powder River country?"

I leaned over the thing, still not completely sure that it was dead. "Any way to trace it?"

"Not without taking it apart."

"Take it apart."

He made a face. "What if I can't put it back together?"

"I don't care."

He looked at the carcass. "Boy, somebody's gonna be pissed."

"Good." I pointed at the gadget. "Whoever was flying that thing might be the ones responsible for shooting Jules Beldon, and I'm dying to meet them." I turned and started toward the stairs as Henry followed me. "When you get through with that, I volunteered you for another job."

Saizarbitoria picked the drone up, turning it over and examining it. "What's that?"

"Going over to Durant Memorial and going through Isaac Bloomfield's files to see if you can find anything on that incident back in '48."

"Cool."

As we continued up the steps, the Bear glanced at me. "Has he ever seen Isaac Bloomfield's office?"

"No."

He shook his head, and I followed him the rest of the way up to the main floor where my dispatcher was doing paperwork. "That's two empty graves in twenty-four hours."

He leaned on the counter with me. "You are, officially, oh-for-two."

Glancing over, I could see Dog at Ruby's feet. "Where's Vic?"

"Took the day off."

I stared at her. "She never takes a day off."

"Well, she did today; called it in this morning."

"Is she sick?"

"No, she just took a personal day." She glanced up at me. "Did you say something to upset her?"

I glanced at Henry and then we both turned back to look at her. "No."

"Good." Her head dropped as she went back to her paperwork. "She said she checked the grave registration at Durant Memorial Cemetery, but they had no record of any Bill Sutherland. You have Post-its on your door facing."

"Right." With another look at Henry, I started toward my office and began pulling off the square pieces of paper as if I were plucking a chicken. I read the first one and turned back to her as Henry passed me and sat in my office guest chair. "Who is Carole Wiltse?"

"That would be the state treasurer."

"Of what state?"

"Ours."

"What does she want?"

"Walter, why don't you call her and find out?"

I stared at the stack of papers in my hand. "Are we in some kind of trouble?"

"Not that I'm aware of."

115

"How 'bout I don't call her back, then we're sure to not be in trouble."

She got up and walked over to me with her arms folded. "That's not how it works with Cheyenne, Walter. If you don't call them back, they just keep calling; they have unlimited funds as far as telephoning is concerned, that and metered mail."

"Have I ever met her?"

"Probably not, unless she's been involved with some kind of criminal activity, which I doubt." Ruby leaned against the doorway and surveyed me. "Your deputies have been calling down there about this hunting accident concerning the state accountant back in 1948, so I would imagine it has something to do with that."

"Right."

She reached out and tapped the small square of paper with a fingernail. "Just call her, Walter."

"Right."

She pushed me toward my office and returned to her desk. I walked there, sat in my chair, and looked across my desk at my best friend in the world. "Vic never takes a personal day."

"Perhaps she is thinking."

I tossed the Post-its on the surface of my leather blotter. "That's a lot of thinking."

"It is a big step." He stretched his long legs out and studied me. "Have you thought about this?"

"What's that supposed to mean?"

"The changes you are going to have to make in your life?"

"What changes?"

He laced his fingers together over his abdomen and smiled. "You are going to have to finish your house."

"You think?"

"Women like completed bathrooms and kitchens."

I thought about it. "She's never complained before."

"You were not married to her before."

I gave it some prescribed thought. "It's probably about time."

"Overdue, actually."

The phone outside rang, and after a moment Ruby called out as the little red light on our cojoined phones glowed. "Carole Wiltse, *Wyoming* state treasurer, line one."

I stared at my arch nemesis, the red light on my phone, as it began blinking like a tapping foot or someone jangling their car keys. I punched the red blinking button along with the speaker phone. "Absaroka County Sheriff, Walt Longmire speaking."

"What the heck is going on up there?"

"Excuse me, but who is this?"

"This is the state treasurer, Carole Wiltse, and I'd like to know what's going on up there?"

"Well, Ms. Wiltse, it's a beautiful May day here in Absaroka County, with the temperature hovering at about seventy degrees with a southeasterly wind of about three miles an hour —"

"You know why I'm calling, Sheriff."

"No, I'm afraid I don't."

"This Bill Sutherland situation."

"You mean his death?"

"I do."

"Well, we happen to have stumbled on some things that might shed some light on his demise back in '48."

"Such as?"

"A murder weapon." The line from Cheyenne was quiet. "From the best of my information, it would appear that Mr. Sutherland was killed with a .300 H&H Magnum, a weapon that no one in the hunting party appears to have been carrying."

"And?"

"I think we might've found that weapon."

"I see."

I glanced over at Henry, who raised an eyebrow in response. "You don't sound particularly pleased with the idea of closing a long-standing cold case, Ms. Wiltse."

"I'd just like to make sure that we're not just dredging up a lot of vintage mud in the media for nothing."

"Well, I don't think finding a man's murderer could be referred to as nothing."

"This is the incident involving Robert Carr and Harold Grafton?"

"Yes, ma'am."

"You're aware that this doesn't reflect well on the Wyoming State Treasurer's Office?"

"If it has anything to do with the department, it was three-quarters of a century ago."

"Perhaps, but we have a hard enough time conveying a respectable appearance to the outside financial world and not looking like a bunch of cowboys."

I had to smile at that one. "Well, you might not have anything to worry about in that we're having a great deal of trouble finding the body."

"Of whom?"

"Big Bill Sutherland."

There was another long pause. "That's because there is no body."

"Excuse me?"

"Bill Sutherland was cremated."

The Bear and I stared at each other as I sat forward, speaking carefully into the mic

119

on the phone. "And do you mind telling me why it is that you would be privy to that kind of information, Ms. Wiltse?"

"Sheriff, Big Bill was my great-uncle."

"So, why did you not tell her that you think it was your grandfather who may have killed him?"

"I thought it might be a little premature in a murder investigation for that kind of revelation." I paused as Dorothy Kisling, the owner and operator of the Busy Bee Café, sidled up to the table, pen and pad in hand. "Howdy. Whose murder?"

I sat my menu back on the table and looked out the window at the ducks treading water in Clear Creek. "An old one."

"What, you're running out of current ones?"

"Thank goodness."

"Well, if you're not going to confide in me, then what do you want for lunch?"

I glanced at Henry, who appeared to be engaged in his own battle with the menu and then back at her. "What's the special?"

"There isn't one today."

I stared at her, incredulous. "There's always a special."

She stuck the pen behind her ear and tucked the pad under her arm and studied me. "Your deputy was just in here and got the last one to go."

"Saizarbitoria?"

"The Terror."

I glanced at Henry, who was now looking at me, and then back at Dorothy. "Vic was just here?"

"About twenty minutes ago."

I handed her the menu. "I'll have the usual."

She glanced at the Bear, who shrugged. "When in Rome . . ."

We watched as she turned and disappeared through the swinging door at the end of the counter. "She's out and about."

"It would appear." He sat back in his chair. "Sometimes it takes food to think."

"Is it me or is this getting weird?"

"When you asked Martha to marry you, did she say yes, immediately?"

"She actually said no."

"So, you are oh-for-two."

I stared at him, which had no effect whatsoever.

"But in the end, she did marry you. Maybe this is a pattern."

"I hope so."

Dorothy returned with two glasses of water and then departed as the Bear began sipping his and then joined me in watching the ducks outside before hearing the tinkling of the front door in time to see the assistant attorney general of the State of Wyoming enter with my granddaughter on her hip.

Plopping down in the seat between us, she handed Henry the heir apparent and looked at me. "Did you order?"

I glanced back toward the kitchen. "I think we did, but you can never be sure."

Henry scooted his chair out and stood with Lola cradled in his arm as she played with his hair. "What would you like and please do not say the usual."

"Chicken tenders with ranch, please." She poked her daughter in the belly. "I can share them with the monster."

The monster giggled as Henry carted her away to add to our order.

"Good morning."

Cady turned to me. "It's the afternoon, and just for the record, where have you been?"

"There was a shooting."

She took a sip of my water. "Anybody I know?"

"Jules Beldon."

"Oh, no . . . Is he all right?"

"No. He got hit three times with a high-powered rifle, but he's still hanging in there."

She made a face, folding her arms. "That's ridiculous; somebody not happy with the way their relative was buried?"

"It might have to do with something I had him looking into."

"The last time I saw you, you were doing a search and rescue up the mountain."

"I found that woman, but I also found a rifle that might've been involved in a murder back in 1948."

"You're kidding."

"And possibly your great-grandfather."

"You have got to be kidding."

"I'm afraid not." I sat back in my chair. "Hey, living down in Cheyenne, that nest of iniquity, what do you know about Carole Wiltse?"

"The state treasurer?"

"Yep."

She thought about it. "I hear she's tough, fair but tough."

"Ever meet her?"

"Briefly, at one of the governor's shindigs. She's a tall woman, silver hair, and very, very blue eyes. I hear she's amazingly competent. I mean the PWMTF is at a market value that's hard to argue with." I stared at her, blankly. "The PWMTF is the Permanent Wyoming Mineral Trust Fund. It's an investment trust and the state's biggest sovereign wealth fund." I continued to look at her blankly. "It's worth over eight billion."

"Dollars?"

"Yes." She shook her head. "So, how is Carole Wiltse involved in all of this?"

"Her great-uncle was the one killed at your great-grandfather's elk camp, a story your grandfather, my father, told me about back when I was a kid."

"Oh, my . . ."

"And I think I might've just found the rifle that did the deed."

Henry returned with Lola as they sat, and my granddaughter turned to look at me with the exact same eyes as her great-grandfather. "Not to change the subject, but what are the chances that the drone is connected to the shooting of Jules Beldon?"

Cady looked up at him and then back to me. "A drone?"

I sighed. "It's crossed my mind, but does it take two hands to operate one of those things?"

Cady nodded. "A drone, yes."

"It could've been the same individual, first shooting and then spying on us with the drone. It seems odd that the two wouldn't be connected."

The Bear grunted. "Especially considering the cost of the drone."

Lola reached for her mother.

"Saizarbitoria says the thing is worth well over fifty thousand dollars."

Cady sat Lola on her lap, but then my granddaughter reached for me. "Do you think Jules is involved with something?"

The Bear laughed. "You mean besides digging up graves for your father?"

She glanced at him and then at me as I settled Lola on my lap, who began playing with the star that was pinned to my chest. "I doubt it, but it could also be a case of some trigger-happy individual trying out their new rifle and drone."

Dorothy arrived with the food, pulled pork sandwiches for Henry and me and what I assumed was chicken parts and dipping sauce for my family. "This is the usual?"

"It is today." She turned and walked away.

Cady plucked out a battered chicken part and blew on it before breaking off a piece, dipping it in the ranch dressing, and feeding it to Lola. "This all sounds a little doomsday prepperish, doesn't it?"

"Yes, it does, but the thing that gets me —"

The Bear picked up his sandwich. "Why shoot him three times?"

"Exactly." I looked at my food, not particularly hungry. "I guess I'm going to have to go and knock on some doors out on the Powder River and see if anybody knows anything."

Cady dipped and then took a bite for herself. "You could always send a deputy."

"I appear to be fresh out."

She chewed and glanced between Henry and me, pulling a wayward strand of red hair from her too-smart-for-her-own-good face. "Wait, is there something I'm not getting here?"

5

"How 'bout I buy you a real car?"

"Real car!" She continued fastening Lola, my repeating granddaughter, into the child seat as I held open the door.

"I like my Jeep."

"It's five hours down to Cheyenne, don't you think you and your kidneys would be more comfortable in something with an actual suspension?"

"Sure, and then I couldn't get around in the snow or be able to get to the cabin when you're hiding out up there."

"I don't hide out there."

"Hide out!"

She glanced at her daughter, finished rolling up the window, and then took the door from me to close it. "Uh-huh."

I followed her around the Wrangler and stood there at the door as she climbed in and sat in the driver's seat, handing my granddaughter her stuffed buffalo, Boomba, to occupy her. "I just think you and Lola would be more comfortable not bouncing down the highway —"

"You asked her to marry you?"

I stood there looking at her and then hung an arm through the window, leaning on the vehicle I was trying to replace. "I, um . . . I was going to talk to you about that."

She turned to look at me with the cool, gray eyes. "Why? You're a grown man."

"I just thought that it was something we should discuss. I mean, it's going to have an effect on all our lives."

She nodded, looking at her daughter and then moved the buffalo around to keep her attention. "You talk like it's a foregone conclusion."

I laughed. "Oh, it's far from that. I haven't spoken with her since I asked."

"And when was that?"

I had to think, the lack of sleep and discomfort getting to me. "Early last night."

"When you didn't come home."

"Yep, I felt like I needed a little conversation, and I didn't want to burden you."

"Burden me?"

"Well, yeah . . ."

"Dad, do you think I don't know that you and Vic have been in this quasi relationship for a few years now?"

I stared at her.

"Mom's been gone for a long time, and you know the one thing I want out of all of this? For you to be happy. It just seems like it's been such a long time since I saw you happy." With this, she climbed out of the Jeep and wrapped her arms around me, standing there on Main Street with her head pressed against my chest. "I think we've earned a little happiness . . . you know?"

"I know."

She pulled her head back and wiped away a tear. "So, she didn't say yes?"

"That is correct, she didn't say yes."

"But she didn't say no."

"She said she needed to think about it."

She finally climbed back in the Jeep as I gently closed the door behind her.

Firing the thing up, I watched as she connected her seat belt and then turned back to me in the open window, handing me the framed photo of my grandfather from the cabin. "Here. Since he's suspect number one, I thought you might want the photograph of him."

I took it, looking again at the seven men and their Tom Mix hats.

"You really think he had something to do with all this?"

"I don't know, but I intend to find out." I

129

glanced back at her. "Just because you're a Longmire, doesn't mean you get a free pass."

"Tell me about it." She studied me for a long while, smiled, and then turned to Lola. "Say goodbye to Poppy."

The little one dropped the stuffed toy and then lunged at the center console with her arms outstretched. "Poppy!"

I reached across my daughter and gripped the tiny hands. "Bye, Peanut."

"Bye, Peanut!"

I stepped back as Cady handed her daughter the dropped toy. Smiling at her, she put the Wrangler in gear and was about to pull away when she pushed the red hair from her face and slipped on her sunglasses, looking at me sideways. "Just for the record, she'd be crazy to not want you, Pop."

"Pop!" Peanut chimed in as they pulled away.

I stood there on the street watching the little red Jeep drive off, towing my heart to Cheyenne.

Tucking the framed photo under my arm, I walked up the steps to the courthouse, then walked around it, past my office, and across the street.

"Of course, we have records — that's what

we do in a bank is keep records."

"And money."

"And money." Wes Haskins, the president of the Bank of Durant, looked down at the framed photo lying flat on his desk. "I can see a resemblance."

"Please don't say that."

"These five on this side are all from the original board, but I don't know these two. You and Lloyd didn't get along?"

"No."

"Well, this bank wouldn't be here if it weren't for him." Wes looked at me, sitting like a giant problem in his guest chair. "Any idea what it is we're looking for?"

"Nope."

"Well, that's helpful."

"Any irregularities in that period I mentioned, just before, during, and after the war."

He took off his glasses and stared at me. "Irregularities."

"Yep."

"Like what?"

"Hell, I don't know, Wes, you're the banker — banking irregularities."

"Right." He glanced back at the photo. "I never met him, but I knew a few old-timers who did. The previous bank president, Dave Conrad, said he was at one board of directors meeting when Lloyd pulled off his boot and began banging it on the table to get everybody's attention."

"Subtle, he was not."

"And I guess there was another time when two guys tried to rob the bank back in 1933 and your grandfather happened to be here and shot them both dead right out there in the lobby."

"Effective, he was."

"And they say there was the time he won the Mendizabal ranch in a poker game, all ten thousand acres of it, and brought in a straight flush as collateral when old man Mendizabal claimed the game was under ace-to-five-low rules . . . Lloyd had four signed affidavits from the other players saying that it wasn't, and the five cards of his hand stapled together." He glanced around, smiling. "Believe it or not, I think those cards are still in his safe-deposit box down in the basement."

I stood, having heard the stories numerous times. "My grandfather has a safe-deposit box?"

"He did. I'm not sure if it's still down there. It was mostly bank papers and stuff — you know, records?"

"If you would, pull it? I'd like to go through anything he left."

Wes cocked his head, looking more than doubtful. "Can I ask you something?"

I stood there in the doorway. "Sure."

"What was it between you and him?"

I thought about it. "It's a long story."

"That much I know. Any idea why he got off the board back in the fifties?"

"From what I know from my father, he got tired of it." I started to go and then added. "He got tired of a lot of things."

After walking back across the street, I retrieved Dog from Ruby and then climbed into my truck and thought about driving over to Vic's house and knocking on the door but then decided against it. Driving north out of town, I figured it was time to be the Powder River Avon lady.

As I drove, I thought of that long story and tried to remember a single moment when my grandfather and I had gotten along. I failed miserably. It seemed as long back as I could remember we'd been at odds.

The relationship with my father and him was no less rocky, but by the time I'd come along they'd reached something of a détente and just avoided each other.

My mother never spoke of him.

He'd died while I was in Vietnam, and

even though I'd obtained a hardship leave, I hadn't bothered coming home. I figured we'd stopped talking long ago and that there was nothing to say now.

On the drive out to Absalom, I slowed and took the left at Buffalo Creek toward a rutted-out dirt road that led to a back gate to what appeared to be a very old and prosperous ranch. Driving past the gate with the handmade ironwork, I nosed up to the knoll that overlooked the surrounding area and pulled to the side and parked.

I climbed out and let Dog accompany me as I stood there, letting the sun warm my face. I closed my eyes and could still see every trace, ripple, and crease of the land where I now stood. It probably would've been faster to go through the front gate, but I hadn't wanted to disturb Tom Groneberg and his family, if they were still there. A month ago, Tom had told me that he'd been offered a job managing a cattle ranch up in Montana and I'd amicably ended the lease.

As far as I knew, the old homestead was sitting down there, empty.

I'd been meaning to make my way here and just check things out, possibly with Cady and Lola, but just hadn't gotten around to it, or maybe I just hadn't wanted to. I walked to the edge of the ridge where

Dog stood and looked down at my grand-father's place. From a distance it appeared as if Tom had kept the ranch in order and had, in fact, improved it in a number of places.

Personally, I hadn't darkened its doors in almost thirty years.

Crossing back to my truck, I looked to the left where a small, fenced area sat with two headstones, just as Jules had said. I never met Olive, my grandmother, who had died in a car accident while I was still very small, but my father and mother had told me she was an extraordinary woman, dedicated to her family and the community as a whole.

They also said that her death changed my grandfather, that he became more isolated and callous. When I was young, there were times when my mother and father would go on short trips and leave me with him, but mostly I remembered his housekeeper, Ella One Heart, who had doted on me as I'd played with her daughter, Ruth.

Lloyd, however, had taught me how to play chess.

"Which one are you?"

"Excuse me?"

My grandfather sat there in his ornate

leather straight-backed chair, his gnarled hands matching the lion claws that clutched at the globes on the ends of the armrests. "Which one of these pieces is you?"

I sat there with my legs dangling from my own chair, my arms folded on the table with my chin resting on them, looking at the chess set from a worm's-eye view. "I don't know."

"What do you mean you don't know?"

I stared at the board and the myriad pieces there. "I'm not any of them, I'm me."

He reached over in order to take a tumbler of an amber-looking liquid. "That's why you're going to lose."

"I thought it was because you are better than me."

He leaned forward, his craggy face highlighted by the vertical light of the Tiffany lamp. "I am, but there's a reason. In a bacon-and-egg breakfast, do you know the difference between the chicken and the pig?"

"No, sir."

"The chicken is involved, but the pig . . ." He raised a bushy eyebrow, which made him look even more like a wizened old owl. "Now that pig, he's committed." He sat the glass down and studied me with those gray eyes, gray like a coming storm. "Have you

136

ever heard the term *skin in the game*?"

"No, sir."

"It means you have something to lose."

I slumped back in my oversize chair. "It's just a game."

"Listen up . . . But what if it weren't?" He placed the leather elbow pads of his hunting shirt on the edge of the table, cradling his chin in his interlaced fingers. "You start disregarding the challenges in your life and you end up disregarding your life as a whole — it becomes a habit. You get my drift?"

"So, I have to start treating everything I do as important?"

"No, you can go through life as a trifling man. Do you know what that means, *trifling*?"

"Not important?"

"Close, but more like insignificant, inconsequential, frivolous, or small. Do you want to live a small life, Walter?"

"I don't think so, sir."

"You don't think about something like that, you need to know."

Ella One Heart entered from the main hall, bringing me a root beer on a silver serving tray, carefully placing a linen napkin down before putting the frosted bottle on the leather surface of the partner's desk. She glanced sideways at my grandfather.

"Are you torturing the boy?"

He sat back, looking at her. "I'm teaching him."

"Hard to tell the difference, the way you do it."

I liked Ella. Heck, I loved Ella. She always called me *the boy*, but it wasn't demeaning the way she said it — more like a title, like royalty.

She draped one of her thick arms over the back of my chair. "It's after the boy's bedtime."

"Staying up a little late won't hurt him any."

"His mother might think so."

"His mother be damned."

She stared at him in a way that nobody else did, and I never knew why she got away with it, but she did. "I'm fixing to go home, Mr. Longmire."

"So?"

"Somebody will need to put the boy to bed."

"He can't find his bed on his own?"

Her hand came down and ruffled my hair. "Given the chance, he'll stay up all night, just like my granddaughter."

"Well, let him."

"Mr. Longmire."

"All right, all right . . . Will you allow us

138

ten minutes to finish our game?"

"We just got started, sir."

"I'll be done with you in ten minutes, young lad."

He sometimes called me *young lad,* but it was different than *the boy* that Ella used.

Ella sighed and started off toward the kitchen. "Ten minutes."

He shook his head at her and then tapped a fingertip on the tiny horse near the corner of the board. "Do you know what that is?"

"It's a knight."

"Very good. Chess is based on chaturanga, an Indian game that had a piece that is the oldest defined and most unique." He tapped the horse again. "That is you."

"A knight?"

He nodded. "It might not be who you are forever, but it's who you are now — the most versatile piece on the board. It can move in eight different directions over any obstacles, always unexpected."

I studied the board in front of me. "And the king?"

"That is me."

Confused, I studied the piece in front of him. "But it's not the most powerful piece."

"No."

"Then why aren't you the queen?"

He chuckled, glancing toward the kitchen

139

where Ella was singing a song in Crow. "You have to have something to aspire to in life."

I moved my bishop. "Is that a small life or a big life?"

"You tell me."

I studied the piece he'd pointed out at the corner and pondered what he was saying. "Why a knight?"

"Your job so far is to threaten and protect the monarch." He slid his queen along the side of the board.

"I thought that was the king?"

"That comes later — what's a king without a throne?"

"A knight?"

"And a knight without a horse?"

I moved my knight, taking a pawn. "A pawn?"

"Very good, Walter." He picked up his glass and took another sip. "Don't ever aspire to be a pawn."

I thought about it. "Why am I the one to protect?"

He stood, pushing his chair back in order to walk past me to pluck an iron from the rack and poke at the logs that were crackling in the fire. "Building a home is one of the greatest things you'll ever do in a lifetime." He glanced at the portrait of the lovely woman above the fireplace. "Do you remember your grandmother?"

"No, sir."

He nodded. "You were only about two when she passed." He turned, studying the dark-paneled walls, the oriental carpets, the moss-rock fireplace where the logs flamed, banked against the fire. "Why do you think I built this place?"

"Because you could?"

"No, something more than that." He looked back at the painting of my grandmother. "You know, I thought I did it for her, but that wasn't the case." He didn't move for a moment. "A man has to stand for something in this world, he has to make a mark, and there are as many ways to do that as there are men, but I chose to build something, something that I hope will last."

I glanced around with him. "It's a pretty fancy place."

"Fancy?"

"Yes, sir."

"I think *steadfast* is the word you're looking for but, nevertheless, wood warps and decays, rock falls away — these things don't last forever, at least not without care. Who do you think I built this place for?"

"Yourself."

"Well, partially . . ." He laughed. "You know I'm not going to be around forever, right? That I'm going to die someday?"

"I guess."

"You guess?"

"It's hard for me to imagine, sir."

"Well, good. I'd rather you not summon up the image too clearly or too soon." He moved past me, looking at the bookshelves. "How old are you, Walter?"

"Six, sir."

"Do you ever suppose that you'll amount to much?"

I swallowed, trying to be honest. "I don't know, sir."

"You don't know." He sighed and returned to the board, then sat and extended that same finger in order to make a decisive move with his queen. "Check."

I loaded Dog in the truck and then jumped in and backed out, turned around, and headed down the hill for the ranch gate.

Getting there, I noticed the heavy logging chain that held the metal gate closed with a massive brass padlock. Reaching into the center console of my truck, I pulled out a large ring of assorted keys, some of them going all the way back to being skeleton ones.

Climbing out, I walked over to the lock, looked at the number stamped in the brass,

142

and then found the matching key with the same number and unlocked it, pulling the chain free and watching the gate swing open.

I got back in and drove down the rest of the way into an open area where a sandstone fountain sat dry in front of the main house, all the structures built of stone eighteen inches thick. After sitting there for a long while, I suddenly heard Dog grumble a growl, then I opened the door and got out, allowing him to jump down after me.

Overwhelmed by the waves of memories that washed through my mind, I surveyed the surrounding area with the ranch pushed up against the cliffs and the river out ahead and thought about how the place was built like a fort. There had been a bridge and the pylons remained, stone sentinels standing there with water and time flowing by with little or no effect.

There were no vehicles around, so I assumed that Tom and his family had headed north.

The barn, cow barn, bunkhouse, laundry/icehouse/coal room, chicken coop, and outbuildings all looked as if the stone had been quarried across the river only months ago.

Patting my leg, I began walking toward

the main house, large even by today's standards. Five bedrooms, a parlor, dining room, a study, main hall, and a kitchen. I didn't have to go in. I had it all memorized.

I walked up the recently swept, heavy stone steps and noticed the tongue-and-groove ceiling of the porch, recently oiled. I flipped on a switch attached to one of the sandstone supports and watched as absolutely none of the yellowish bug lights flickered to life all along the fixtured eaves of the wraparound porch.

My grandfather hadn't electrified the place until 1960, and evidently the Rural Electric Association and the Powder River Energy Corporation had taken the same position since the bills hadn't been paid. I knew there was a generator back in the icehouse with a breaker in the tunnel below, but I had no idea what condition it was in.

The sun was starting to set, and the water reflected the twilight sky, making the river look like slow-flowing mercury.

Dog went to the door and sniffed at the old wooden-framed screen door as I started to remove the ring of keys from my pocket but instead reached up and removed a small piece of stone above the doorway. Sticking my fingers in the cavity, I pulled out an old key.

144

I swung the screen door back along with the attached rubber ball meant to keep it from slapping against the frame and then slipped the key in the lock, turning it and watching the thick door swing wide open.

Dog entered, but I stood there.

It was as if I were looking at a museum of my mind, and except for the sheets hung over the artwork and furniture like ghosts in repose — nothing had changed.

Scuffing my boots on the front mat from habit, I returned the key and the stone and then stepped in onto the geometric designs weaved into an old Navajo rug and studied the dark gleam of the wide-plank fir floors. The banister to the left circled the entryway to the balcony on the second floor, where more sun-faded rugs hung, all of them at least a hundred years old.

Pushing the brass button at the switch as a second try, I watched the elk antler chandelier remain dark. Luckily the vanishing sunshine from the open doorway cast a golden light on the one uncovered piece of furniture, the entryway table, where a lone envelope lay.

Stepping the rest of the way in, I reached down with a finger and turned the envelope toward me and read my name.

WALT

Picking it up, I ran my finger under the flap and tore it open to find a marvelous, month-old letter from Tom and his family, thanking me for the privilege of living in and taking care of the place for the last almost seven years. They'd gone to a great deal of trouble in trying to clean the place as well as they could and hoped I'd be pleased. Tom ended the letter with all their contact information near Great Falls if I should need to get in touch with them.

I lowered the letter to the table and glanced around at the place that had been cleaned and polished to within an inch of its architectural life, but the dust had begun to settle and there were more than a few cobwebs drifting in the breeze from the open door.

Moving to the left, I gazed through the dining room and toward a swinging door with the porthole that led to the kitchen in the back. Entering that room, I trailed a hand over the sheet that covered the table, thinking about the arguments that had started, ensued, and ended here, and then kept going.

I stood at the kitchen door and remembered the woman who had cooked for my grandfather all those years — Ella, whose biscuits I could still taste, and her daughter, Ruth.

Pushing the door open, I looked at the gleaming porcelain of the aged appliances and the black-and-white tiles that covered not only the floors but the walls. The old propane refrigerator still stood there, probably because it weighed more than Ella and nobody wanted to wrestle with it.

The glass in the cabinets gleamed, revealing dishes and glasses I hadn't eaten on or drunk from in more than a quarter of a century. I turned and walked back through the swinging door and through the dining room into the entryway. Looking across the room and into the archway to the right, I found myself drawn in that direction.

The study had always been my favorite room in the house, the place I could go to and hide, immersing myself in the leather-bound books and worlds and words of distraction.

The old grizzly-skin rug still lay on the floor, looking a little worse for wear, and there were other mounts, including a moose, two buffalo, a few mule deer, and an antelope, all of them staring down at me in an accusatory fashion.

There was a moss-stone fireplace with a piece of art covered with another sheet and the vast, mission-style partner's desk with an old bronze lamp with red panels depicting the *End of the Trail.*

I stared at the heavy, metal chess set that sat there paused in mid-game and, strangely, the miniature Kewpie doll that had taken the place of the missing knight that had mysteriously disappeared in my youth.

Over by the built-in shelves there were books stacked in cardboard boxes, a few having been absorbed into my own collection or maybe auctioned, and it was as if the house now had no soul. I picked a book out of one of the boxes and read the binding: *The Count of Monte Cristo.*

I stood there leafing through the pages, thinking about how much I'd loved the book when I was young, how I had seen myself as Edmond Dantès, adventuring my way through a world of intrigue and vengeance.

"They didn't sell."

I turned to find a tall Native woman filling out an old flight jacket, standing in the archway with Dog sitting beside her, having an ear scratched.

"You know . . ." I studied her, having a strange feeling that I knew her from somewhere before. "That dog usually alerts me to situations such as this."

148

She smiled with all the muscles in her bronze face, her teeth, dazzling as she flipped back her long raven hair with a halo of silver around her features and revealing surprisingly steely eyes. "I have a way with dogs, especially male ones."

I nodded and looked back at the boxes of books. "Didn't sell?"

"They were going to have an auction, but the auction house decided to dispose of them as an estate set, and nobody bought them."

I studied the marbled paper of the inside covers. "Nobody wants to take the time to read anymore."

"You must make time for reading or surrender yourself to self-chosen ignorance."

I carefully placed the book back in the box and stepped toward her, extending a hand. "Confucius."

"Funny, you don't look Chinese."

I smiled, my hand still hanging there between us. "Walt Longmire."

She ignored my gesture and circled around me toward the bay window that looked out and onto the front where my truck sat parked. "I know who you are."

"Well, then you have me at a disadvantage."

She turned away, toward the window, her

leather jacket hitched up to where I could now see a 9mm in one of those hard plastic holsters at her hip. "I always have."

"I'm sorry, but . . ."

"I've got some family pastureland that I bale to the east of this place, and I sometimes check in when Tom and his family are away, especially if I see strange vehicles parked out front."

"I'm not strange." I glanced past her and at the stars and bars on my three-quarter ton. "I'm the sheriff of Absaroka County."

"I know that too." She nodded, tugging on Dog's ear the same way I did. "Did you know that there's a tunnel from the kitchen all the way to the laundry, the icehouse, and the coal room, and that there's a railed handcart that you push back and forth between the buildings?" She took another few steps around the desk, first looking at the chess set and then at the empty fireplace. "They built it for when the snow got too deep in the winters."

I studied her a bit harder.

"And did you know that you can ride in those handcarts if you've got some big dumb white boy to push them?"

I snorted a laugh and then shook my head. "Are you who I think you are, Ruthless One Heart?" She spread her arms, walking back toward me as I pinched the bridge of my nose between thumb and forefinger in an attempt to dissuade the embarrassment. "Ella's daughter."

"You know, you're the only one I ever let call me that."

I stuck my hand out again, but this time she took it. "I always wondered what happened to you."

"I moved around a lot, finally settled in, but I came back." She patted her sidearm. "Special agent with the ATF's Rapid Response Teams after a stint with Air Force Intelligence."

"Justice."

"Yeah."

"Impressive."

She released my hand. "I tried to keep in touch, but after your grandfather died Ella stopped working here and I lost track."

"I'm assuming Ella's gone?"

"A long time ago."

"I'm sorry."

"She had a good life, and she always spoke well of you — and him."

I looked down at the floor. "Him."

She went over to the boxes of books, pulling the one from my hand back out. "Looks like Tom and his family took care of the place."

"They're good people."

She flipped a few pages and then looked at me, her hair hiding half her face. "Your reading tastes haven't changed. I was surprised when no one in your family was living here anymore — I figured there had to be some Longmires out there somewhere who would come back."

"Oh, it was always my grandfather's place."

She continued studying me. "You gonna sell it?"

I sighed, looking around at the furniture and the sheets. "I don't know."

She replaced the book in the box. "You want a drink?"

I breathed a laugh. "And where would we get that?"

She smiled. "This old house has a lot of mysteries, some of which she's shared with me over the years." Walking to the mantelpiece, I watched as Ruth reached up to the woodwork and pulled open a secret door, revealing a bottle with a small tin cup covering the cork.

She handed me the bottle and I took it, studying the peeling and yellowed label. "What the hell is Gilbey's Spey Royal?" I stared at her. "You know, we're likely to go blind drinking this stuff." She snatched the tin cup off the top and held it out so that I was obliged to pull the crumbling cork and pour her one. "There appear to be things floating in here."

She raised the tiny cup. "To the Laird of Longmire."

Raising the bottle, I made my own toast. "To the line of Daasáwatash, One Heart."

I'd made a fire, and she had joined me in putting the books back on the shelves, neither of us able to leave them in the boxes. We'd made pretty good progress, except for the points when we took to reading each other excerpts from our favorites. Dog lay on the uncovered tufted red leather sofa and snored.

"You were married, weren't you?"

I nodded, arranging the O. Henry alongside Mark Twain. "I was . . . She passed away."

She poured herself another cheap scotch. "Kids?"

"The Wyoming assistant attorney general."

"Oh, my."

"And a granddaughter who bosses around the assistant attorney general." Ruth attempted to hand me the tin cup, but I waved her off. "How 'bout you?"

She downed it and placed the cup on the

mantelpiece next to the bottle. "Two failed marriages — thanks for asking."

"Kids?"

"None, thank God." She picked up a few more books but appeared to have lost interest, finally lowering them back into the box. "I sound bitter, don't I?"

"A little."

"That's probably because I am."

I glanced around at the dimly lit room, the lamp on the desk and the fire providing the only light. "Ranching can do that."

Tucking her hands into her jeans, she walked toward Dog, sat on the sofa beside him, and stroked his broad head. "Maybe I'm spending too much time out here alone."

I gestured toward her sidearm. "Is that what the Sig is for?"

She leaned back in the sofa, folding her arms behind her head. "I don't know, you get used to carrying them, right?" She nodded toward mine. "That why you carry the blunderbuss?"

I reached to the small of my back and felt my 1911 with the stag grips. "What I got used to." I flipped my jacket back to reveal my star, a redundancy in that she'd already seen my truck. "Anyway, still working."

She peered out the window into the darkness. "This place isn't what it used to be."

"What's that supposed to mean?"

She stretched her legs out, crossing them at her boots. "I don't know, it just isn't the same as when we were kids."

"What is?"

"Touché." She cocked her head and continued to knead her fingers in Dog's thick hair. "So, what are you finally doing out here, Walt Longmire?"

I pulled a few more books and assembled them like a wall against illiteracy. "Oh, checking on a man who was shot out near Absalom yesterday."

"Shot?"

"Three times."

She pushed out a mouthful of air as if she'd been punched. "Well, there's my point. Do you ever remember that kind of thing happening when we were kids?"

"No, but I know those kinds of things used to happen because this shooting might have something to do with another one I'm investigating from back in 1948."

"Another what?"

"Shooting."

"Wow . . ." She sat up and pointed toward the bottle on the mantelpiece. "Pour me another and sit down and tell me the story."

Retrieving the bottle, I gave her the *Read-*

er's Digest version of the case, leaving out some of the more personal and salacious details as we sat there in the chairs by the fire.

She listened without interrupting until I'd finished talking, finally standing in order to adjust the logs in the fireplace. I turned back to her as she sat there mesmerized by the flames. "Cui bono, huh?"

"They were people he worked with at the state Treasury."

"How are you going to track it?"

"The gun."

She sipped from the cup. "But the body was cremated, so it's not like you can get an autopsy."

"There was one done; I just need to find the slugs."

"Yeah, but the chances of them going back and finding it . . . ."

Throwing caution to the wind, I took the bottle from the mantel and had a small swig, gritting my teeth. "I've got another resource."

"For the autopsy?"

"The report, yep."

"So, say you get the report, and it confirms that the weapon that did the deed is this infamous .300 H&H Magnum, then what?"

"I find out who owned the gun."

"And that means they're the killer?"

"Not exactly, but it's a start."

"So, who pulled the trigger, the treasurer or the chief clerk?"

"One, the other, both, or neither . . ."

She stood and walked over, just a little unsteady, and placed an elbow on the mantel. "And your dad told you the story?"

"Yep."

"I can't imagine him being involved in something sordid like that — your scary old grandfather, yes, but not your dad." She removed the sheet from the painting hanging above the fireplace where a portrait of my grandfather glowered down at us. "How 'bout it, old man? You shoot him?" Toasting him, she tipped the remainder of the contents back and drank what was left in the cup.

I said nothing, and she studied me for just a little too long.

"You're kidding."

"Excuse me?"

"That look on your face." Her eyes narrowed. "You really think your grandfather did it?"

"I'm not discounting anyone who was at that elk camp at this point."

She thought about it. "So, how does this case connect with the guy near Absalom that got tagged three times?"

"He was looking for the body of Bill Sutherland for me."

"And you think somebody shot him for doing it?"

"I'm looking at it as a possibility."

"Seems kind of far-fetched. You're sure this guy . . . what's his name?"

"Jules Beldon."

"Ol' Jules didn't just have some old enemies out there somewhere?"

"That could be the case, but the timing seems odd, and how do you explain the drone?"

"Oh, that could be the same person. I just think connecting it to this homicide from the middle of the last century is a bit of a reach."

"Agreed."

"You know, if you need help on that drone, I could probably help you out. I had some interactions with those things back in the day."

"I've got someone on it now." I pulled out a pen and then tore off a piece of cardboard from one of the boxes and gave them to her. "But if I run into a dead end, I'll give you a call?" She scribbled her number down and handed the pen and cardboard back to me, and I noted the number. "202, DC?"

She patted a pocket in her jacket. "Cell phone. I never got around to changing it." She yawned and then stretched. "Anyway, I'm glad it's your problem and not mine, Walt Longmire." She glanced at the painting one last time and then started for the entryway and the front door. "I'm going home, unless you want to head down in the tunnel and race the handcart from the laundry?"

I smiled at the thought of how much time we'd spent as children down in that tunnel, avoiding the world above. "I think I'm a little too far gone for that. What about you?"

She paused at the opening and turned, leaning against the jamb. "What about me?"

"Are you okay to drive?"

"Is that an offer?"

I took a breath. "More of a concern."

She pursed her lips. "Get back to me when it's more of an offer, will you?" She then turned, and I listened as she went out the front door. "You've got my number."

I walked over to the window, and Dog got off the couch to join me. We watched her start up a one-ton with a large bale lifter and navigate around the dry fountain and circle back, the taillights following the river and then disappearing west.

I glanced back at the fire, now having died

down to some smoldering embers, and then put the cork back in the scotch and placed the tin cup over it, hiding the entire thing back in the cubby of the woodwork.

Starting for the door, I allowed Dog to jump ahead and lead the way. Closing it behind me, I crossed the porch and then stepped down in the weeds and on dry ground, walking out to the old fountain.

I'd always loved the thing, an Indian maiden kneeling at a body of water, a pot in her hands, tipped forward as she held it. I remember when there had been water piped to it from the Powder River and the water had flowed in an unending cascade from that clay pot in her hands.

In my mind's ear, I could still hear the water splashing into the main pool of the fountain, constructed of the same sandstone as the house.

The pot was broken now, along with the maiden's right arm and a portion of her nose, both of which appeared to be missing until I glanced in the fountain and could see the arm lying there. Reaching in, I picked up the limb and held it to where it should've been, but broken as it was, I couldn't get it to stay. "Milady, you must remain unarmed."

Suddenly feeling a little woozy, I turned

and sat at the edge of the fountain, where I still held the arm and looked back at the house.

You had to give credit where credit was due — the old bastard had placed his mark on the land, an imprint of his hand that had lasted to this day. Sure, the weeds, dust, field mice, and spiders were having their way, but that was mostly my fault.

Spite. That's what my mother would've called it — a case of unmitigated spite.

I raised the arm. "I know you thought you brought me up better than that, but there you are."

I suddenly felt very tired and thought about sleeping in my truck till morning.

Looking back at the house, I had to consider it very hard — sleeping under my roof or his?

I finally struggled to my feet and stood there holding the arm. "He's dead."

Carefully laying the arm at the edge of the fountain, I trudged toward the house. Dog stood at the truck, unsure of what to do.

At the steps I called back to him. "C'mon."

He stared at me, even going so far as to whine.

"I know, I know . . . C'mon." Getting to the front door, I opened the screen and was

161

confronted with the lock. Taking a moment to remember, I reached up and skillfully knocked the rock off and into my eye. "Damn it . . ."

Kicking the rock, I felt for the key, finally recovering it and pulling it down to slip into the lock.

Dog had given up hope of going home and had now joined me as the door creaked open like an effect in a bad horror movie. Stumbling through, I headed immediately for the study, stopping in the archway, and staring at the portrait over the fireplace where the moonlight framed the ancient and unforgiving head of the family.

I addressed the house in its entirety. "Did you hang it there so that it could be il-luminated all night, like the flag?"

Predictably, he stared down at me, silent.

I sighed and shuffled over to the red leather sofa and sat, shucking off my boots. I stared at him as Dog joined me, taking a little more than half of the available space. "What were you involved with, old man?"

There was still no response.

"If I were to head up on that hill and unearth you, would I get some answers about more than just this case?"

Still nothing.

I leaned back on the sofa and pulled my

hat down over my face. "Just so you know, I'm going to play this string out to the end."

6

I knocked on the door, not particularly expecting anybody to answer, which was just as well because I was ready to sell my soul for a cup of coffee from whoever did.

Standing there, I tried to get a read on how far we were from the old Sutherland place and family plot where Jules had been shot. As near as I could tell we were about a mile away, but not by line of sight. There were hills over toward the river where the breaks completely hid the place.

"There a problem?"

I turned to look at the crusty individual behind the screen door who was adjusting the wad of tobacco between his gum and lip. "Walt Longmire, Absaroka County Sheriff."

"Yeah, I seen your truck."

"And you are?"

"Niall, Mike Niall."

"I think we've met, haven't we, Mr. Niall?"

He studied me with the algae-green eyes. "Don't think so."

"Can I ask you a few questions, sir?"

He scrubbed a hand over his chin, the sound like sandpaper on rough-cut wood. " 'Bout what?"

"Have you seen anything strange out this way lately?"

"Strange, how?"

"Vehicles, people . . . ?"

"Son, there's always some asshole drivin' up and down the Upper Powder River Road. They get off the highway, thinkin' they gotta see the Powder River because they saw Van Heflin in some damn movie." He pushed open the door, and I stepped back, letting him go out to the railing on his porch and look toward the dirt road. "Had a fella come up through here in March, one of the snowiest months we got, and had his wife and four kids in a minivan." He spit off the porch and then turned to look at me. "Three feet of snow, and this asshole decides to go look for the Bozeman Trail in a two-wheel-drive minivan."

I joined him at the edge of the porch and leaned against a post. "I was thinking of more recently?"

He nodded, still looking at the road and pointing past an old '55 GMC that sat to the side of his house. "There was a black SUV setting down there at the pullout the other day."

I thought of the car that had blown by as I'd stood outside the Red Pony Bar & Grill. "A black SUV?"

"Yeah. Set down there for a good forty minutes, so I walked over to see what the problem was, and they took off when I got near."

"Plates?"

"Wyoming, but I don't know what. Hell, they were Wyoming plates, as many varieties as they got, I could still tell that."

"Anything else you can tell me about the car, make, year?"

"Oh, hell no."

"Get a look at the driver?"

"Not really."

"Have you heard any shots lately?"

"What kind of shots?"

"Rifle."

He thought about it. "No, but when I ain't got my hearing aids in I don't hear a thing, which is most of the time."

"Live alone, sir?"

"Yeah, for about twenty years now."

"Who are your neighbors?"

He peered to the south. "Dave Thompson's place is about three miles that way, and then there's some kid about a mile north that lives in a camper that his relatives bought him. I think just to get him out of the house since he come back."

"Back from where?"

"Afghanistan or some damn place."

"Does he have a name?"

"Most likely, but I have no idea what it could be, but I think his uncle works at a welding shop over in Gillette."

I stepped off the porch and started for my truck. "Well, thanks, Mr. Niall."

"You look different."

I stopped and turned to him. "How's that?"

"That scar over your eye, it wasn't there the last time I saw you."

"No, it wasn't."

He spit again. "You did a fine job savin' that woman and her horse a few years back."

"Thank you."

I started to turn, but his voice stopped me. "You never said who got shot."

"No, sir, I didn't."

He stared at me for a moment more and then went back in his house, the screen door slapping like the period on a sentence.

The trailer was about a mile north, just as he'd said, but the opening to the road looked like a little used cattle guard. Where the thing was parked on the southwest side of the hill, it was possible to miss it when traveling south toward the highway.

Driving across the cattle guard, I circled up the road and then pulled onto a dirt patch beside a relatively new camper. More of a hunting-camp size, it didn't look like the type of thing you could live in year-round. There were no vehicles or much of anything else other than a lone camp chair, just the trailer sitting there on a spot that looked like it might have been scraped off with a backhoe only days ago.

Making Dog stay inside the truck, I climbed out and looked around. The mid-morning wind was picking up, and I took advantage of the solitude by walking to my left and looking down a draw that led directly to the Sutherland place, which you could see from here.

Going up to the small camper, I knocked on the door and waited but could hear nothing, at which point I stepped up onto the aluminum stairs and peered between the curtains on the door at the inside of the trailer.

Everything seemed very much in order. Neat as a pin. As if it were still on the showroom floor. There didn't seem to be a single personal item in sight — no pictures, clothes, nothing.

Taking a breath, I stepped back down and looked around again for anything that might identify the owner, but there was no mailbox or anything to indicate who that might be. There was a flapping of something, so I kneeled to look under the trailer where a piece of paper was stapled to some wires. Reaching under, I pulled a sheet from the undercarriage and stared at it — a schematic of the camper's wiring.

Carefully folding it, I kneeled again and stuffed it back behind a metal brace.

I stood and turned to look about a hundred yards away, where there was a much-used backhoe setting beside the road and thought maybe it was the one that might've cleared the area for the trailer. Deciding to head that way, I'd just started to circle around the front of my truck when something caught my eye.

A flash of metal in the sagebrush.

Walking over, I kneeled and plucked the pen from my pocket, lowering it to the ground to poke the point into the front of a cartridge so that I could tip it up to look at the brass case for any markings that might be stamped there, but there was nothing. It was a rimless, tapered bottleneck, not particularly remarkable, but it was fresh.

After walking back to my truck, I snatched a plastic evidence bag from the door and placed the cartridge in it. I was about to climb in when I noticed a five-yard dump truck coming up the road with a heavy-duty trailer, slowing as it passed the backhoe and then pulling over and stopping.

I climbed in my truck, petted Dog, and then drove back down to the road in order to pull in behind the backhoe when a middle-aged man got out of the dumper and walked back toward me with a resigned look. "So, what is it, my mud flaps are a quarter of an inch too narrow?"

"Actually, they look okay to me."

"I've got log dogs with rust on them?" He stopped a few paces off. "What is it?"

"You wouldn't happen to have been the fellow that flattened out that spot where that camper is setting up there, would you?"

He studied me. "You got some dirt work you need done?"

"Not exactly." I gestured toward the camper. "You know the owner?"

"I do." He shifted a greasy ballcap back, revealing a very white forehead. "Why?"

"You know, most people answer my questions rather than asking them back."

He moved past me, pulled on some gloves,

began disconnecting the chains that held the ramps, and then flipped one down onto the road with a loud clank. "I'm not like most people."

I watched him. "I'm getting that."

He flipped the other one down and then turned to look at me, his hands on hips as the dust settled. "What do you want to know about him?"

"A name, for a start."

"Heller, his name is Jordan Heller.

"Does he live here?"

He glanced around at the desolate landscape. "I guess he's gonna."

"Where does he live now?"

He walked around the ramps and past me. "Over in Gillette."

"Got an address?"

He stopped and turned. "Look, what is this about?"

"I'd just like to ask him some questions, if you don't mind and actually even if you do."

"The kid's a veteran, okay?" He took a few steps toward me. "He did two tours over in that shithole Afghanistan and then come back. He's having a hard time of it, and you come around here askin' questions about him and then get all pissy because I won't answer?"

"I wasn't aware I was being pissy."

171

"Well, you are." He stared at me.

"Well, I'm about to go back here and check the registration on this trailer and if I discover your name is also Heller, then things are going to get a lot pissier." I started to walk away.

"He's my nephew."

I stopped and turned back.

"I'm a little protective of him these days."

"Understandable."

He walked back, sitting on the fender of the trailer, and taking off the gloves. "He was an army sniper, and now he's over in Gillette changing tires for a living."

I sat on the fender beside him. "A man was shot out here yesterday, and I was wondering if he might've heard anything."

"Shot."

"Yep."

"You think Jordan shot somebody?"

"Not just yet, but I'd like to ask him if he heard anything. Do you have any idea if your nephew was even out here yesterday?"

"He might've been — it was his day off." He gestured toward the lawn chair in front of the camper. "He comes out here and just sits there, staring at nothing."

I wasn't sure what to say until the words fell out of my mouth. "I've heard there are parts of Wyoming that look an awful lot like

Afghanistan."

"God, I hope not." He rolled his gloves up and stuffed them in his back pocket, then fished a pack of cigarettes from his shirt and bumped one up, offering it to me as I turned it down. Biting it from the pack, he pulled out a Zippo and lit it, taking a deep drag and then blowing it out in a steady stream. "You serve?"

"I did."

He studied the side of my face. "Viet-nam?"

"Yep."

"Well . . ." He took another drag on the cigarette. "They didn't give you guys a royal welcome back either."

"Not so much, no."

"My sister — his mother — didn't want him out here, but he wanted to be away from everybody."

"Long way to drive to a job in Gillette."

"Oh, he won't stick with that for long. Somebody'll say something wrong to him and he'll threaten to stick his boot so far up their ass their breath'll smell like KIWI shoe polish."

"Anger issues?"

"Oh, hell no — no issues with anger, he's got plenty." He puffed his cigarette. "Who was it that got shot?"

173

"A fellow by the name of Jules Beldon."

"The gravedigger?"

"Yep."

He thought about it, making a face. "Who'd want to shoot him?"

"I'm trying to find that out."

"He dead?"

"Nope, not yet."

"Well, then, Jordan didn't shoot him, because if he had, he'd most certainly be dead."

"I'd still like to talk to him."

"He'll be back out here tonight." He glanced up at the abbreviated homestead, taking a last draw on the butt and then flicking it out onto the gravel road. "He'll be up there, sittin' in that chair, smokin' cigarettes and seein' nothing."

"Where have you been?"

I always knew that there was a disaster whenever Ruby met me on the steps of the office, and I always attempted to meet it with the utmost of grace. "Something up?"

She held the door open with one hand and produced a clipboard, festooned with Post-its. "The entire state government would like a word with you."

"The entire state government?" I took the clipboard and began reading the luminaries requiring my attention, and her remark didn't seem that far off. "I already spoke with this Carole Wiltse . . ."

She followed me as we tromped up the steps. "Well, she wants to talk to you some more."

I continued reading the names of potential political landmines. "Joe Meyer, the attorney general, my daughter's boss, something about the PWMTF . . ."

Meeting me at the landing, she looked up. "If you don't mind my asking, what in the earthly world is the PWMTF?"

Recalling the conversation I'd had with Cady at the Busy Bee, I recited the words in a very offhand manner. "The PWMTF is the Permanent Wyoming Mineral Trust Fund and is an investment trust and the state's biggest sovereign wealth fund — worth over eight billion." I turned to look at her. "That's dollars."

In the many years I'd known Ruby, this was the most dumbfounded I'd ever seen her. "You can't balance your checkbook; what do you know about all of this?"

I went back to the Post-its. "Linda Roripaugh?"

"CEO of the PWMTF."

I read another. "Tom Rondelle?"

"He's the head of trustees for your pre-

175

cious PWMTF."

"Mike Regis?"

"Somehow connected to Tom Rondelle."

"*Wyoming Tribune Eagle, Casper Star-Tribune, High Country News, Forbes, The Wall Street Journal, The Washington Post, The New York Times . . .*"

"What did you do?"

I took a deep breath and let it out slowly. "I'm not sure, and that's what's so worrisome."

Before she could remark, her desk phone began ringing. She moved in that direction and then glanced back at me as I started for my office. "I'm sure it's for you, would you like to answer it?"

"Under no circumstance."

I made it into my office, stepping over Dog, who sometimes sought sanctuary there when things got busy out front as Ruby called. "It's Joe Meyer!"

"Under all circumstances." Reaching over the rifle that I'd found in the mountains, still wrapped in wax paper, I sat in my chair and punched the little red light that blinked at me like a nuclear fail-safe. I put the receiver to my ear. "Joe, before you say anything, don't ask me, because I have no idea what's going on."

"What the hell is going on?"

"I told you not to ask me that."

"I've just had the governor sitting here in my office . . ."

I leaned back in my chair, listening to it groan. "Tell him I said howdy."

"Walt . . ."

"Joe, I found a rifle at my grandfather's elk camp, and I think it's the one that was used to kill Bill Sutherland in a supposed hunting accident back in 1948."

"And who, pray tell, is Bill Sutherland?"

"The state accountant at that time but also present were Robert Carr, the state treasurer, and Harold Grafton, the chief clerk of the state Treasury, who had held office while Sutherland was away in the war."

"Oh, shit . . ."

"It looks bad, doesn't it?" Saizarbitoria was leaning against the doorjamb with some papers in one of his hands. "To make matters worse, Bill Sutherland is the great-uncle of the current state treasurer, Carole Wiltse."

"Oh, shit . . ."

Fishing the shell in the evidence bag out of my shirt pocket, I tossed it onto the desk and shoved it toward the Basquo, who picked it up with one hand and examined it through the plastic.

"You mentioned something about your grandfather?"

"It was his elk camp where Sutherland was killed, and at that time, he was the chief of the board of directors at the Bank of Durant."

"Oh, double shit . . ."

"We're trying to find the autopsy on Sutherland and attempting to trace the ownership of the rifle, but we haven't come up with anything yet."

Sancho raised the papers and rustled them at me.

"But we might be getting somewhere . . ." I gestured for my deputy to have a seat, which he did, tossing the papers on my desk. "Joe, why is the entirety of the fourth estate and everybody associated with the Wyoming State Treasurer's Office and the PWMTF trying to get ahold of me?"

"Oh, the horse's ass trustees of the PWMTF just fired the CEO, Linda Roripaugh, who is a good friend of Carole Wiltse's."

"Why?"

"Well, the fund was up 15.2 percent, outperforming every other statewide sovereign wealth fund in the country this year — so, why not fire her? It was for political reasons, I'm pretty sure. She was opposed to this paying out of much bigger dividends to state residents instead of protecting the trust, which pays about a third of the state budget."

"Why would the trustees want to do that?"

"Because they are horses' asses who want to buy votes before the next election."

"Okay, but what does this have to do with me and my little investigation up here in the hinterlands?"

"I'm sure what they're trying to do is tie in the inherent lawlessness of the Wyoming financial institutions — political maneuverings are one thing, but a nice tasty murder to top things off will sell a heck of a lot more newspapers."

"Boy howdy." I sighed, sitting forward and cradling my chin with a fist. "Second question: How did all these reporters find out about my investigation?"

"Oh, Walt, this ship of state has more leaks than the *Andrea Doria.* Did any of your people call down here and ask some questions?"

I glanced at Saizarbitoria. "Possibly."

"Then somebody calls somebody or texts somebody else or they meet at the water fountain . . . You get the picture?"

"Okay, so what is it you want me to do, great general of all the attorneys?"

"Stay out of it. This is a great big Cheyenne shit sandwich, and my advice to you is to not take a bite."

"Sounds like good advice."

There was a pause. "So . . . You really think these two fellows from the state treasurer's office offed the state accountant back in '48?"

"Talk to you later, Joe." I hung up the phone and looked at my deputy.

He shoved the papers toward me with one hand, still studying the shell in the evidence bag. "Before you start telling me how tough your life is, I want to remind you that I just spent eight hours in Isaac Bloomfield's office digging up an autopsy report from the middle of the last century."

I picked up the papers. "I see you made it out alive."

"We had only three avalanches, but we bivouacked and made it up the north face and around the high ridge." He held up the bag. "And from careful ballistic deduction I can tell you that this is not the bullet that killed Big Bill Sutherland."

"No, but unfortunately it might be one of the ones that shot Jules Beldon."

"Why unfortunately?"

"Oh, some kid who did two tours over in Afghanistan, and now the only thing he can do is sit in a lawn chair out on the Powder River."

"This a 5.56x45mm NATO?" Sancho continued to hold the baggy with the shell. "It's the right cartridge."

"I figured."

"Where'd you find it?"

"Out by the kid's trailer. His uncle says he was an army sniper over there."

"You think he was out doing a little target practice?"

I stared at the brass cartridge. "Jordan Heller, from over in Campbell County — run him."

"Got it." Sancho stood, reaching into his jacket and tossing another plastic bag onto my desk with a malformed piece of lead inside. "I'll trade you."

Picking the thing up, I stared at it. "What's this?"

"The slug they dug out of Big Bill Sutherland back in '48"

"You're kidding . . ."

"You wouldn't believe the stuff Isaac has in that Ripley's-Believe-It-or-Not! office." He stood to leave, reaching out and tapping the rifle. "Just for the record, I believe what you have here is a murder weapon."

I looked down at the .300 H&H Magnum. After reading the report and notes, I stepped over Dog and wandered into the main office to give Ruby another shot at me, which she took. "That woman that you tried to get out of the motel the other day?"

"Trisha Knox?" It seemed like eons ago, but I did remember. "What about her?"

Ruby lowered the glasses on her nose and raised her eyes. "She didn't."

"Didn't what?"

"Get out of the Best Western."

"She's still there?"

Ruby attempted to hand me another Post-it. "Evidently. They just called."

I stared at the tiny square of paper. "Do you have stock in the Post-it company?"

She stuck it to my arm. "Better than the PWMTF."

"You have no idea . . ." I pulled the paper off and looked at it. "Can't somebody else do this? I've got a lot of things I'm dealing with here."

"Double Tough is covering down at Powder Junction and Vic is still off, so unless you want to promote Barrett to road deputy?"

I thought about my full-time Cheyenne, part-time dispatcher. "No, I'm not quite that desperate yet."

She waved a hand at me. "Off you go then."

"Vic is still out?"

"Yes."

182

I thought about that, then turned, slapped my leg, and moved to the top of the steps. "Dog, let's go."

There was no response.

"Dog?" Ruby stared at me as I leaned to one side where I could see the beast's legs and that they hadn't moved. "Did you wear out my dog?"

"Maybe you did. Just out of curiosity, where were you last night?"

I sighed and started down the steps alone. "Sleeping in a haunted house."

It was a nice day, so I tried to concentrate on that as I drove over to the Best Western and parked in the shade under the canopy.

When I climbed out, the same young woman met me at the door. "She won't let us in the room, and I'm sorry but I didn't know who else to call."

"No, you did the right thing." Moving past her, I walked down the hall to the same room and knocked. "Absaroka County Sheriff's Department."

There was no answer.

I knocked again. "Absaroka County Sheriff, hello?"

The voice was soft and seemed to be coming from just on the other side of the door. "Go *away.*"

I placed a shoulder on the door facing and leaned there. "Open up, Trisha, or I'll go and get a key from the front desk." There was a heavy sigh as the door opened about six inches, the security chain still attached, and I could see a deeply swollen eye peering up at me. "Howdy."

"Go *away.*"

"That's not how it works, even back in Minnesota." I pushed off the facing and watched as she flinched. "Are you hurt?"

"No."

"You look hurt."

"A little."

"Open up and let me get a look at you."

A few seconds passed and then the door closed, only to open back up again and swing wide in her hand. The eye was swollen, along with the majority of one side of her face. She was wearing a tattered bathrobe and limped back toward one of the rumpled queen beds and sat on the corner, barefoot.

I entered, leaving the door open and sitting on the edge of the counter that held the TV. "Something happen?"

She clutched herself, looking out the opaque curtains covering the window. "Yeah."

"What?"

"Look, I'm not *feeling* very well, can't you just *leave* me alone?"

"No, I'm afraid I can't." I surveyed the relative disaster of the room with shoes, clothes, and cosmetics scattered everywhere. "Do you have somebody you can call?"

She guffawed a hollow laugh, placing a hand on the mattress to lean an arm there but missing. She caught her balance and turned her head to look at me as I studied the bruises on her wrists. "Yeah, that worked out *really* well."

"I'm afraid I don't understand."

"I called *somebody,* okay?"

"Is that the person who hurt you?"

"I needed *money,* and it was the only number I had, okay?"

"Who was it?"

"It doesn't matter, *okay*?"

"It matters to me." I stood. "C'mon, let's get going."

She moved back, almost collapsing into the bed. "I don't have *anywhere* to go."

I stood over her. "I'm taking you to the hospital."

"I . . . I have to go to the bathroom first."

I stepped back and out of the way. "Certainly."

She tried to get up but was unsteady, so I reached out a hand, taking her elbow. "I just need to go to the bathroom."

"Okay." I led her in that direction, noticing that as she walked, she kept her legs together in an awkward fashion. Getting her to the door, I stopped as she entered, closing the door behind her. I waited a moment but then thought it best to give her privacy, so I moved back toward the open door and leaned against the wall. "Do you want me to get some clothes together for you or something?"

I hoped she would say no, because I had no idea what it was I should actually get.

Looking down at the bed, amid the flotsam and jetsam, I saw a black moleskin notebook with receipts and a few other pieces of paper sticking out of it, held fast with a large paper clip.

Lifting my head, I called out again. "You okay in there?"

There was no response.

"Hello?" Still hearing nothing, I pushed off the wall and approached the door. "Hello?"

I rapped a few knuckles on it and watched as it opened just a bit, revealing the young woman lying on the floor with a blood-saturated T-shirt wadded up between her legs.

Pushing the door the rest of the way open,

I kneeled down and scooped her up, wrapping the robe back around her as her head lolled against my chest.

As I carried her out, I spoke to the young woman at the desk. "Would you mind opening the passenger-side door of my truck?"

"Is she bleeding?"

"Yep." She followed me and opened the door as I placed Trisha, then buckled her seat belt and closed the door. I went around with the young woman from the front desk trailing behind. "Has she been in that room the whole time?"

"I don't know. I just came on this morning."

I climbed in and fired up the V10. "Find out for me, and in the meantime lock that door and don't let anyone disturb anything in there, got me?"

"Got it." She gave me a thumbs-up and a towel as I pulled away, flipped on the lights and siren, wheeled out onto the main drag toward Durant Memorial like an internally combusted missile.

Standing there by the empty nurses' station and thinking about the conversation I'd had with the AG, Joe Meyer, I couldn't help but think that now would've been a good time to go on a vacation or possibly a honey-moon.

Two personal days she'd taken off.

Maybe the thing to do was go by and knock on her door, exactly what Henry had warned me not to do.

I was getting the feeling that patience was not a personal virtue of mine.

"She could've bled to death." Isaac approached, looking through Trisha Knox's paperwork on a clipboard. "We're lucky you brought her in when you did."

"She's beaten up pretty badly."

"You could say that." He flipped through the papers. "Detached retina, contusions, lacerations, a concussion caused by blunt force trauma, and the pelvic swelling and internal damage to the vaginal lining, which wasn't helped by the urinary tract infection."

I waited a respectful moment before asking. "But she'll be all right?"

"With time, I would assume so."

I nodded, thinking I should change the subject. "I checked in on Jules. Is he doing any better?"

"His readings are strong, but he's acquired quite a bit of damage for a man his age."

"You'll keep me notified if there's any change?"

"Of course."

I noticed the doc was looking a little sad so I changed the subject again. "I understand you and Saizarbitoria had quite the paper chase in your office?"

He smiled. "He is a very nice young man and very thorough."

"Well, I appreciate you finding that autopsy for me, and I can't believe you still had the slug."

"Did it connect the gun to the killing?"

"Probably. Now if we can just find out who owned the rifle, we'll be on our way to finding out who did the deed." I watched as his eyes dropped. "Something wrong, Doc?"

"Oh, I've been giving careful consideration to my life and career."

I waited a moment, and then when it appeared that he wasn't going to continue without prompting, I asked. "Are you really going to retire?"

"I am. I can't help but think it's time." Looking down at the clipboard, he started walking toward the double swinging doors that led to the waiting room. "I've come to the conclusion, as a lot of elderly people do, that the times are growing worse in this godless, indifferent, chaotic universe, where social structures that disguise the true horrors of existence are rapidly falling away and that things are indeed getting worse."

I stared at him as we arrived at the doors. "All that written on that clipboard, Doc?"

He smiled at me. "But then I'm reminded of the horrors I endured from an earlier time and am strangely placated." He studied the star on my chest. "What are your thoughts, Walter?"

"I think you should go out and take a walk, maybe get some air."

"Perhaps you're right." I started to push open the door when his wrinkled and veined hand came up and rested on my arm, his great hazel eyes looking at me, the thick bifocal glasses making him look like an aged tortoise. "Did you notice the marks on the young woman's wrists?"

"I did."

"Handcuffs. Was she arrested?"

"No, and those marks weren't there when I first met her."

"I thought not." He lowered the clipboard and then held it there against his chest in both hands. "She was handcuffed and raped."

I took a breath. "I had assumed as much."

"But not with a member . . ." He paused for a moment. "From the lacerations, I would say with a handgun."

7

"Who?"

The disaster had worsened to the point that Ruby was now meeting me in the parking lot with Dog. "Mike Regis — he's somehow connected to that mess in Cheyenne."

"Then I don't want to talk to him."

"He says he's here to help." She scrubbed the beast's head.

"People from the government like to say those kinds of things, but they don't really mean it." I looked at Dog's collar and the leash clipped to it, the first time I'd ever seen him with one. "What are you and Dog doing out here?"

"This Mike Regis is sitting in a chair waiting for you, and I thought I'd intercept you before you came in, in case you wanted to run for it."

I glanced at the old Carnegie Library we call home as I put my arm around her shoulder. "Oh, I'm too busy to escape."

"He seems like a very nice young man, very professional. I guess Tom Rondelle, the head of the trustees for this LMNOPDQ or whatever it is, sent him up here to help you out with this investigation."

I stood a little straighter as we walked toward the building. "Help me out."

"That's what Mr. Rondelle said."

"What, is this Sherlock Holmes coming in here to help us break the big case?"

"Something like that."

I looked up in time to see a medium-size individual with a short haircut, a dark, stylish suit, and a flaming-red tie approaching from the steps with his hand stuck out. "Mike Regis."

I stared at the hand.

He pulled the hand back and smiled, raising both in supplication. "Tom sent me to see if I could be of any help, but if you don't want me, I'll just get back on my horse and ride."

"Who, exactly, are you, Mr. Regis?"

"A problem solver, Sheriff. I work for Tom Rondelle at the moment, but I have lots of other clients here in the state."

"And you're here to help me solve my problems?"

Ruby, sensing how far and fast the conversation could go south when people tried to tell me how to do my job, took Dog's leash and waved a quick goodbye before backtracking toward the office with the beast in tow, even though he wanted to stay.

Regis watched them go and then turned back to me. "I have been held at bay with the best, but she's good."

"Mr. Regis, why would your Tom Rondelle give the remotest tinker's damn about my vintage murder investigation?"

"Actually, he doesn't. Tom's under a lot of pressure right now in a situation that I really can't help him with —"

"Firing Linda Roripaugh, the CEO of the PWMTF?"

He was surprised. "You heard about that?"

"From what I understand she was doing a pretty phenomenal job."

"She was, she was . . . The problem, from what I'm to understand, is that she was starting to treat the fund as her personal fiefdom, and the trustees were getting tired of being told what to do by an appointee — but that's neither here nor there."

"Sheriff, can we go get a cup of coffee or something where we can talk in private?"

"I don't think we're going to be talking that long, Mr. Regis."

He breathed a laugh and then stepped

back, once again raising his hands. "C'mon, Sheriff, give a guy a break. I'm on Tom's payroll, and there's nothing I can do to help out with this cluster in Cheyenne, so I told him I'd drive up and try to assist you. I'm actually pretty good at this stuff."

"What stuff, Mr. Regis?"

He laughed, again. "Is it the suit and tie, Sheriff? Is that what it is? If I'd shown up in boots and jeans, would you cut me some slack? For the record, I was born in Idaho, CAG Tier 1 SMU — SEAL Team 6, government contractor, and a lobbyist." He studied me. "You were military, right?"

"Just a marine."

He smiled. "Well, I just wanted you to know I had jobs before I started working with Tom."

"As a solver of problems?"

The smile faded. "For lack of a better term. Wherever the fires are, I go and try to put them out."

"And I'm a fire that needs to be put out?"

He raised his hands again. "Okay, look, I give up. I thought this would be fun and that I could get out of that political hot seat down in Cheyenne for a few days and maybe even get in a little fishing, but I can see that I'm not welcome here." He handed me a business card and walked toward a sparkling green Land Rover that I hadn't noticed before. He slipped on his sunglasses. "It was a pleasure meeting you, Sheriff. If the situation changes and you think you might need me for anything, just let me know."

Watching him go, I could see Saizarbitoria coming down the steps with the busted drone in his hands. "Hey Boss, there's some kind of barcode I found on this thing, but I've tried and can't find anything on the internet about the manufacturer or model numbers."

We met at the base of the steps, and I glanced at it and then turned to find Mike Regis standing beside the door of his SUV with his hands in his pockets. He was staring at the ground and smiling, and for the first time I noticed he wasn't wearing socks. "Hey, you know anything about these things?"

His head raised and the smile grew. "Everything."

"It's a Talon XPV, but it's a new model I've never seen."

I sat on a metal stool outside the jail cells in the basement of our building and sipped coffee while watching the two men laboring over the mechanical insect. "Military?"

195

Regis nodded, tapping on a tiny laptop computer he had found a way to plug into the drone. "Exclusively."

Sancho sipped his coffee. "How did you know how to open that thing — I tried everything."

With his jacket off, his sleeves rolled up, and his tie tucked in his shirt, Regis tapped in more information before flipping the thing over and showing us the open bottom. "You have to know the trick to get the thing open, but worse yet, all the manufacturer info is only visible in infrared. So, you could look forever, but if you don't have an IR flashlight, you'd never find it."

"What can you tell us, other than it's military grade?"

He picked up his coffee from the table and took a sip, making a face. "Not much, but I know a guy who can."

"You don't like our coffee?"

"It's not that it sucks, it's just that it sucks." He pulled an expensive-looking cell phone from the jacket hanging off his own stool and began punching in numbers. Holding the thing to his ear, he sat. "Hey, Bethany, it's Mike, is Giles in?" He adjusted the phone. "Right. Well, when he gets in will you have him give me a call at this number? I've got a downed bird of his and I need to run the numbers." He waited a moment and then added. "Sure, that'd be fine."

He hung up as I continued sipping my coffee. "Who is Giles?"

He started to sip his own again but then caught himself, setting it on the table beside the drone with a sense of finality. "Giles Hasselblad, the president of Talon Aerodynamics."

Saizarbitoria and I looked at each other. "And you're on a first-name basis with this guy?"

He smiled the dazzling smile once again. "With his secretary I am, yeah."

He glanced at the high-tech drone and made a face.

"Something?"

He shook his head. "Who in the world would be out here using this kind of technology, and to shoot a . . . What did you say this Jules Beldon was?"

"A gravedigger."

"You weren't kidding." He studied me. "You mean he literally digs graves?"

"Yep."

"That makes no sense whatsoever."

I shrugged. "You wanted to help." Lumbering up, I stood and downed the rest of what was deemed as wretched coffee. "Do you want to see the rifle upstairs?"

"Is the coffee better there?"

"Not really, but there are windows."

Regis and I started up the stairs as Saizar-bitoria paused and looked at his phone, then called after us. "I've got to go over to Sheridan, Boss."

I stopped at the landing as the man from Cheyenne rolled his sleeves back down. "What's up?"

"I contacted Weatherby and had them search for the rifle and see if they could find anything."

"And they did?"

He pocketed his phone and smiled as he passed us on the landing and continued up the stairs. "I'm going over there now to find out."

"You know, I'll take that one."

He looked disappointed. "Okay."

"But you can head over to the newspaper and see if they can find anything."

He saluted and headed out. I called after the Basquo as he took a left at the entryway and exited the building. "Keep me informed."

We stopped at the next landing and Regis watched Sancho cut across the lawn of the courthouse and down the steps toward Main Street. "Good man."

"The best, and possibly the next sheriff of

this county."

He slipped on his jacket. "Really?"

"There's a strong Basque contingency here along the Bighorns."

"Basque?"

I started up the stairs again. "When the federal government opened the National Forest to pasture leasing, there were areas that weren't particularly suited for cattle, so a lot of ranches diversified and brought in Basque shepherds."

"I thought cattlemen and sheep ranchers didn't get along?"

"Aren't you from Idaho?"

"Boise." He raised a fist. "Go Broncos — I was the best third-string quarterback they ever had. I don't know anything about this cowboy stuff." He studied me. "You play?"

"Offensive tackle."

"Where?"

"USC."

"No joke?" He caught up with me at the top of the stairs. "Were they any good when you played?"

"Not bad." I leaned over the counter to get Ruby's attention. "Anything?"

She spoke without looking up. "All quiet on the newspaper front."

My dispatcher went back to typing as we continued toward my office where Dog once again lay on the floor. Stepping over the snoring animal, I gestured toward my guest chair. "Have a seat."

Regis did, looking at his phone. "I'm guessing at your age, but from your nonchalance I'm assuming you beat Wisconsin in a Rose Bowl?"

"I had some help."

"Why didn't you go pro?"

"I'm guessing from your age you might not have heard of it but there was this thing called Vietnam . . ." I pointed to the shell in the plastic bag, still lying on my desk where Sancho had left it. "What do you make of that?"

He picked it up. "5.56x45mm NATO."

"Not a .223 Remington?"

"No."

"You're sure of it?"

"Yes. Same family, but I've seen a million of these things. The difference isn't in the shape or thickness of the brass cartridges but in pressure ratings and chamber lead length." He tossed the bag back on the desk. "It's a 5.56x45mm NATO, I'm certain of it. Assault carbine for close-quarters combat, Sheriff. That's a military weapon you're looking for."

"M16?"

"No, something newer. Newer than 1980

at least."

"I'm assuming your experiences as a SEAL are what made you knowledgeable about those things?"

"Yeah, I could tell you about it, but then I'd have to *bill* you."

"I'm assuming your experiences as a lobbyist are what made you knowledgeable about those things?"

He nodded. "Most people would rather be killed than billed." He glanced at the other plastic bag on my desk that held the older slug and sat forward. "What's this?"

"The lead they dug out of Big Bill Sutherland back in '48."

He looked down at the rifle on my desk. "May I?"

"Sure."

He carefully unwrapped the hunting rifle and raised it to the light. Expertly handling it, he turned it over and noted the splits in the stock. "She's had some rough treatment, but even with the age she looks relatively new."

"Only fired once."

"No manufacturer marks, nothing."

"My expert tells me it's probably a prototype Weatherby model that got auctioned off or donated."

"Boy, you wouldn't be able to do that

nowadays."

"No."

He examined the medallion embedded in the stock. "What's with the coin?"

"We think it's the fiftieth anniversary of the State of Wyoming."

"And what year was that?"

"Nineteen forty, so it could've been any year after that."

He studied the rifle. "What could these two guys from the treasurer's office have done to make them want to silence the state accountant for good?"

"You tell me."

"Something they shouldn't have." He lay the rifle back on the paper on my desk and stared at it. "The triangle of fraud . . ."

"What's that?"

He started, as if I'd woken him. "Oh — incentive, opportunity, and rationalization." He stuck out three fingers and began counting them off. "The first leg, incentive, is pressure to commit the crime. A person is looking for a way to solve their financial issues due to an inability to pay their bills, drug and/or alcohol addiction, or simply status, wanting to have a bigger house or drive a fancier car." He counted off another finger. "The second leg is perceived opportunity, where the individual identifies ways to commit fraud with the lowest amount of risk, like lying about the number of hours worked, inflated sales or productivity to garner higher pay, creating false invoices for products never purchased and pocketing the money, or selling proprietary company information to competitors." He counted off the last finger. "The third leg of the triangle, and this is an important one, is where individuals persuade themselves into believing that they're doing the right thing. They convince themselves that they're just borrowing the money or feel entitled to it through perceived low pay, uncompensated hours, lack of respect, or trying to provide for their family."

"Okay, but what pushes two men whom we assume are relatively upright individuals into going so far as to kill someone?"

"A lot of money."

I laughed.

"I'm serious. If these guys were siphoning funds out of the state treasury to the tune of, say, millions during wartime? First, there's no way they could ever pay the money back and second, they could be tried as traitors for profiteering, or worse. As I recall, they used to hang people for that kind of thing." He stood and moved toward the door. "So, can I buy you dinner?"

I glanced down at the brass in the plastic bag. "I think I have to run by Weatherby and then go out on the Powder River and talk to a Jordan Heller."

"Jordan Heller?"

"A young man out there, Afghanistan vet with some issues. I found that brass out at his place."

"Would you like me to go with you? I've got a lot of experience talking guys down from PTSD issues."

"No, you've done enough." I stood and extended my hand. "I think I owe you an apology."

"No need — I would've probably reacted the same way." He shook my hand. "So, where does a guy go to get a steak and a bed around these parts, Sheriff?"

I stood in the reception area of the newly relocated Weatherby Inc., just a little north of Sheridan, with the paper-wrapped rifle under my arm and took in the impressive taxidermy mounts that surrounded the stone-and-timber walls.

I knew and respected the brand and the man who had started it all, Roy Weatherby, a poor tenant farmer from White City, Kansas, who started modifying hunting rifles after selling the farm and moving to

Southern California. Weatherby began developing his own cartridges; by the mid-forties he had opened his storefront in Long Beach, and over time became a favorite of big-game hunters and the Hollywood elite, sports figures, and others leading all the way to the White House.

Moving toward the back of the room, I entered an area with racks of different rifles held in glass cases with photographs of many of Weatherby's more notable customers, the likes of Roy Rogers, Gary Cooper, Elmer Keith, and Jack O'Connor.

There was also a photo of Weatherby himself, standing with John Wayne, sharing a laugh.

Angling to the left, I stared at the early models Roy had modified and could see there were similarities to the one under my arm. The average Weatherby ran about a hundred and fifty dollars at the time and, though it didn't sound like it, was a big-ticket item. Who could've afforded such a thing, and how could they have gotten access to such an exotic weapon, if it was the one that killed Bill Sutherland?

"My father used to say my grandfather could sell a rifle to a Quaker." I turned to see a young man in a ballcap and black fleece with a golden "W" on the chest extending a hand and had to admit that he bore more than a passing resemblance to the founding grandfather. "Adam Weatherby."

"Walt Longmire." We shook as I surveyed the room. "I think his work spoke for itself."

He noticed the elongated package under my arm. "I understand you think you might have one of ours?"

I patted the rifle. "I may."

"C'mon, we'll take a look at it in the boardroom."

I followed him toward the front where we took a left at the reception area into a room with a massive table where a striking blond woman labored over some vintage newspaper clippings that matched the framed advertisements on the walls. She pulled her hair back and then readjusted the clippings on a mat board. "Adam, these aren't going to fit together . . ."

"This is my wife, Brenda."

"Howdy."

She looked a little embarrassed. "Sorry, I didn't know you had somebody with you."

"He's the sheriff from over in Absaroka County."

She began gathering her things. "I'll get out of the way . . ."

He settled her in her chair with a gentle

hand on her shoulder. "No, we might want your input in this." He glanced at me. "Brenda does all the archival work, and I'd swear she knows more about the older stuff than I do." He gestured toward the walls. "She did all of these."

Brenda stood, shaking my hand. "Because no one else wanted to do them."

Adam pointed at the bundle. "Can we take a look?"

I sat the package down and watched as he opened the paper and then carefully turned it toward his wife. "Wow . . ."

"Is it one of yours?"

She answered for the two of them. "Yes."

"It's one of the earliest sporterized Mauser 98's . . ." Her hand moved over the still-gleaming stock. "California Claro Walnut with one of those ultra-high Monte Carlo cheekpieces."

"Rosewood for end tips." He pointed at the small, white spacers at the pistol-grip cap. "That's our hallmark, but this is a really early design." She flipped it over. "Something of a missing link — postwar, but very early . . ." She ran her fingers over the coin. "Fiftieth anniversary?"

I provided what little information I was sure of. "The State of Wyoming."

Adam leaned forward, studying the action

mechanism. "This is before Granddad and Fred Jennie encased the head in a counter-bored bolt face that had three vents on the right to carry gases away from the shooter if they encountered a blown primer or casing. They upped the locking lugs to nine, which gave it a 54-degree lift on the bolt, which meant you didn't have to bend the handle to have room for a telescopic sight."

Brenda's hand rose to her chin as she stared at the rifle like a binary computer. "I've seen this gun before."

We both stared at her, Adam the first to speak. "You're sure of it?"

She nodded. "In the archives, I'm almost positive."

"Where, do you think?"

She shook her head and slowly turned her gaze to me. "I don't know, but I swear I've seen this rifle or one very like it somewhere."

He glanced at me. "She's scary that way."

The sun was angling toward the Bighorn Mountains when I took the cutoff toward Absalom, driving across the new bridge and easing through the small town. I was tempted to grab a six-pack from the bar for the conversation but decided that might not be the proper thing to do.

Maybe I just wanted a beer.

When I got to the turnoff to the little trailer, I could see an old green International Scout in the gloom with the outline of an individual sitting in the camp chair in the yard and smoking a cigarette.

Turning the truck, I drove the rest of the way and parked, climbing out to look at the tall, very lean individual as he held the cigarette away from his face. "You're blocking my view."

"Sorry." As I walked up, he flicked the ashes into a Maxwell House coffee can. "You keep a good camp; I wasn't sure if anybody actually lived here."

"I'm not so sure I actually live anywhere."

I took another step toward him and stuck out a hand. "Walt Longmire."

"The sheriff. Yeah, my uncle said you'd be by." We shook and I noticed his hands were filthy and bandaged, blood tracing from under the adhesive as he noticed my interest. "It's the steel-belted tires, when they wear out the belts fray and the wires stick out of the tires and go in your hands like butter."

"It must hurt."

"Most things do." He took another drag from the cigarette. "There's another camp chair inside the door if you want to sit and watch the water go by — I've counted at least three gallons in the last hour." Realizing an opportunity when I heard one, I started for the trailer as he called after me. "There's also a sixer of Coors in the fridge, if you'd like to join me in one."

Opening the trailer door, I lifted the lawn chair out and leaned it against the aluminum side and was still able to reach to my right and open the refrigerator door without going in.

The six-pack and a jar of pickles were the only things in there.

I pulled two of the cans off the plastic ring and I carried them and the lawn chair back to where he waited. I handed him a beer, opened the chair, and sat, whereupon we both cracked the tabs on the beers and toasted. "Always carry whiskey in case of snakebite . . ."

We touched cans and his face looked like it was made of stone. "And always carry a small snake, man." He took a drink. "Uncle said you were a big fucker; what'd you do over there in the jungle?"

"Just a marine." I took a sip of the beer. "He says you were a sniper?"

"He never gets it right, or else he just wants me to be a sniper." He shook his head. "MOS 0306, CW02 weapons specialist — I guess that's where he gets mixed up."

"Gunny."

"Yeah."

Knowing full well that a gunner generally carried twenty to thirty extra pounds on patrol, I made an observation. "You've lost weight."

"Yeah."

"How was the food in Afghanistan?"

"The American food sucked, but if you could get the kabuli pulao, the ashak dumplings, or the chopan kabob, it was really great."

"I enjoyed the Vietnamese food when I was over there."

He took another drag on the cigarette. "You do patrols?"

"Only when I had to."

He chuckled. "Well, it hasn't changed much. Did you guys use the roads on sweep-clearance missions?"

"Yep, I'm afraid we did."

"Stupid."

"Yep."

"Crossing linear danger areas is a lost art, especially when you've got squad leaders that'll walk a quarter mile along an irrigation ditch to find a foot bridge that goes across. I think all but three of our casualties happened that way with IEDs . . ."

"We didn't have those so much in Vietnam."

"Eye contact too. I was always telling the new meat to look at the guys around them and know what the heck was going on, proper dispersion and mixing up the timing on your zones. We had this one guy who always did these four-hour patrols like clockwork. We'd come in one side of a village and then go out the other and the Taliban knew it'd be another four hours before we came back through. I started setting up covering an AO in twelve-hour patrols and everybody was complaining, but my guys started pacing themselves, noticing more and talking to the locals. That's how they got their rest, but they also knew that they weren't going to be back at base watching *Buncha Cars on the Prairie* with Wanda Lottaknockers via satellite until the job got done." He glanced at me. "I'm boring the shit out of you with this stuff?"

"No, not really."

"I think that's one of the problems . . . is that I don't have anybody to talk to about the shit that happened over there."

"What about the VA?"

"No offense, but those guys are older than petrified dirt."

I smiled. "The VFW?"

"Same."

"Maybe you'll meet a nice girl."

"Yeah, they're falling out of the trees." His turn to smile as he surveyed the barren landscape, continuing to smoke. "Seen any trees lately?" We sat there in the cool of the evening and listened to some coyotes vocalizing in the distance. "So, who is this guy I've supposedly tagged?"

"A fellow by the name of Jules Beldon was shot, and I'm just trying to figure out who might've done it. Have you heard anything?"

"Shots fired, you mean?"

"Anything — strange people, vehicles?"

"You know, I work about ten hours a day and then I come out here and sit in this chair until I fall asleep, and then I drag my ass in that trailer and lie there staring at the ceiling until I get up in the morning and start it all over again." He stubbed the cigarette out on the inside lip of the can and then dropped it inside. "So, no I don't see anybody out here all day because I'm in Gillette, changing tires. I get out here around six if I'm lucky — and I can tell you that I haven't seen or heard anything like that."

I nodded, sipping my beer. "Do you have any firearms?"

He turned to look at me. "What do you think?"

"Would you like to tell me what you've got?"

"Would you like to tell me what you think I've got?"

I turned to look at him. "I'm hoping you haven't got anything that fires a 5.56x45mm NATO."

He stared at me. "Why the hell would I have something like that? It's not like I hauled anything back with me."

"Any idea why I would've found the shell of one right out there in the sagebrush?"

He seemed genuinely surprised. "Here?"

"Yep."

He thought about it. "I don't know, maybe it fell out of my clothes, equipment, or the trailer — another souvenir from the Near East."

"Do you have any weapons on the premises?"

I stood and walked over to the battered old Scout and leaned against it, watching as he glanced around and then resigned himself to stand and turn back toward the trailer. Walking that way, he opened the same door as I had before reaching in and pulling out a small rifle. He then returned and handed it to me — a single-shot, bolt-action .22 Long. "I had a little trouble with a porcupine."

"Had?"

"He has retired to that great pincushion in the sky, and you know what? I miss the little fucker." Looking at the sluggish river, he walked past me. "He was the only regular visitor that I had."

On the drive into town, I was tempted to go north and back to the homestead but then decided against it because I was getting tired and figured the best place for me was home and bed, especially since I hadn't been there in days.

The lights were off at the Red Pony Bar & Grill, so I wasn't tempted to look for Henry as I drove by, and I continued to my little cabin. Pulling up out front, I looked at the small structure in a different light — why would a woman want to live here, and more important, with me?

I remembered back when Martha and I had built the place, how proud we were that we were striking out on our own and not relying on either of our parents. We were going to add to the place, but in all these years, the only thing I'd done was build a front porch and that was mostly because Henry had forced me.

Lugging myself up the steps, I missed Dog and figured he'd gone home with Ruby as he usually did when I left him behind.

I couldn't take care of a dog, let alone a wife.

Opening the door, the first thing I saw was a vase sitting on the piano with some wildflowers in it, a gift from my daughter. There was a sheet of paper that had been ripped from a spiral-ring notebook and folded in half.

I picked it up and read the note:

I know you're down, and I know it has something to do with Mom, and I just want to tell you that she'd want you to be happy, more than anything else in the world. I want you to be happy, Lola wants you to be happy, even Dog wants you to be happy — so if marrying Vic makes you happy, then we're all for it. Okay?

— The Greatest Legal Mind of Our Time

I stood there holding the note until I became aware of the teardrops that were striking the paper. I folded it and stuffed it in my shirt pocket over my heart. I wiped my eyes and had just started to turn to go into the bedroom when I saw the blinking light on the answering machine.

A smart man would've ignored it, but I've never considered myself to be all that smart

216

and punched the button.

Ruby's voice rose from the tinny speaker. "Walt, I'm visiting my sister tonight and as you know, she's allergic to anything with fur, so I'm going to have to leave Dog here at the office. I wanted to make sure you knew to come in and get him. Call me if you can't and I'll try to make other arrangements. See you in a few days."

After staring at the machine, I pulled out my pocket watch and figured there was no way I'd have caught her, so I grabbed my truck keys from my pocket. I climbed back in the Bullet, closing the door behind me, fired her up, backed around in a sweeping turn headed down the dirt road, and then turned right to get back into town.

I could leave the poor guy there at the office but felt bad about it and drove steadily on.

The traffic lights were blinking when I got into town but it was still a weekday so there wasn't much traffic on Main Street as I drove past the office. Regis's Land Rover was parked in front of The Virginian and the red neon glowed in the slight haze of the saloon and I thought about stopping in and talking some more shop. I hadn't been very nice to the guy, and I was thinking that he might've had a point in saying that part

217

of my mistrust was from his suit.

Maybe I was some kind of class warrior.

I continued south and then took a right and a left, pulling up in front of the small craftsman house with the red door, where I knew I was going the whole time.

There were no lights on in Vic's place, but her truck was there, and I started thinking about scenarios for going up and knocking on the door, anyway.

I lost my dog; can you help me come look for him?

Selling tickets to the Sheriff's Ball?

Avon calling?

Or you could just be a big boy and knock on the door.

Pulling the truck into gear, I drove around the block and circled back around to the office and parked in front of the main door, figuring I wasn't going to be long.

He was waiting for me, his head cocked in admonition.

Turning the key, I opened the door only enough to slip through, knowing full well that he'd blow past and try to get in the truck without me. He watched me climb the steps but stayed there by the door, not likely to be left behind again.

At the top of the stairs, I could see a few Post-its on my door and decided to check them out while I was here. Pulling them off, I saw that they were both progress reports from Durant Memorial and a note about a shoebox that sat on my desk.

There had been no change in Jules Beldon's condition, but his vital signs were growing stronger. I hoped that trend would continue, and I could find out what the heck had happened out there on the Powder River.

Jules had, as near as Isaac could tell, been shot during the day, so it would be easy enough to find out if Jordan Heller had been working at the tire store at that time.

The second pertained to Trisha Knox. She too was in stable condition but was now secured to her bed so as to not do damage to herself.

The third was about the contents of my grandfather's safe-deposit box, indicating that all his official papers were still at the bank and that these papers were copies, along with some odd items that Wes thought I might like to see.

Crossing the room, I sat, opened the box, and began sorting through his finances, stocks, bonds, and even the deed for the ranch, along with a hand of cards stapled together. The last item I came to was a duplicate diploma from Wellesley College for Ruth One Heart, and I had to smile at that one. So, the old guy had paid for Ruth's education — more than he'd done for me.

I was just getting ready to close the box when I noticed a few more things rolling and sliding around in the corner. Reaching in, I pulled out a collection of World War I medals and a chess piece.

A knight.

I sat there looking at the metal horse in my hands.

Outside, in the greater office, I could hear something clattering away, a machine of some type. Stuffing the knight in my shirt pocket, I walked out and attempted to find which machine had sprung to life. Approaching Ruby's desk, I saw a machine there I wasn't sure I'd even known existed. I don't know how long the fax machine had been under there, let alone that the thing was still plugged in or still had paper in it.

Calmly waiting, I pulled the sheet out.

The address was from Weatherby, Brenda Weatherby to be exact. She apologized for taking so long to get back to me, but other than a phone number, she said the only contact had been a fax number and it had taken awhile for them to figure out how to send the photograph below through.

The vintage photograph was from November 2, 1948.

It was the same seven men in the photo from the cabin, even wearing the same clothes and large Tom Mix cowboy hats that had been so popular at the time, and I couldn't help but think that the two photos must've been taken on the same day.

They all stood in a semicircle with my grandfather in the middle, smiling like I'd never seen.

His arms were raised and in his two hands was the custom Weatherby .300 H&H Magnum with the medallion embedded in the stock, the murder weapon that lay on the back seat of my truck in the parking lot.

Boy howdy.

221

8

"It does not mean he killed Sutherland."

"It doesn't mean he didn't or at least didn't have something to do with it."

Henry shook his head as he sipped his coffee. "Is that how you intend to proceed with this wholly unbiased investigation?"

I studied the printed photo on the corner table of the Busy Bee Café and ignored him. "It was a raffle at the VFW, and I guess he won the thing."

"I did not know your grandfather was a veteran."

"And neither did I. World War I, I guess he was seventeen when he ran off and joined — never talked about it."

Dorothy interrupted the conversation by coming over and taking away my plate as she perused the photo. "That grandfather of yours was a good-looking man."

"So they tell me."

"Your grandmother was better looking,

though."

I glanced at the owner and proprietor. "Olive. You knew her?"

"From afar. She was quite the grande dame around these parts. I don't think there was a cause or civic betterment that she wasn't involved with, including that building you call an office."

"She helped with the Carnegie Library?"

"Along with just about everything else in this town."

"She died when I was young." I folded the paper, resting it on my leg. "And surprisingly, there aren't that many photos of her."

"I think your grandfather might've had something to do with that."

I glanced at Henry and then back to her. "In what way?"

"He didn't like her to be photographed. I'm not sure why, but I remember hearing that at one point."

"I guess he didn't have any problem having his own picture taken." I looked down where my family history grinned back at me like a Cheshire cat. "Including the portrait in the study out at the big house."

The Bear finished his coffee. "You went out there?"

"Yep, I was checking on the area where Jules got shot."

223

He and Dorothy shared a look. "Those two places are not remotely close to each other."

"No, but I wanted to check on the ranch since Tom Groneberg and his family moved up to Montana."

"There is no one living there?"

"No, and I'm afraid the place is going to fall to ruin."

Dorothy pointed her chin toward our empty mugs. "You guys want a refill?"

"No, ma'am, but I'll take a bill." She nodded and headed back toward the swinging doors that led to the kitchen as I turned back to Henry. "Hey, do you remember Ruth One Heart?"

He shook his head. "Ruthless, yes, and I remember the Awaasúuachiikaxiia bar and her mother Ella yanking a woman off her husband's lap and dragging her out in the parking lot and whipping on her until that same husband came out to save the woman and Ella whipping him too." He smiled to himself. "I still remember that ass-whipping."

"Awaasúuachiikaxiia?"

"Crow for 'the house that leans.' I am not sure if that was because it did, or that it appeared to after enough drink."

"I used to play with Ruth when I was a

kid — one of the few pleasant memories of my childhood at my grandfather's place."

"She lives out there?"

"Nearby, I guess. She did a stint with the military in intelligence and then ATF with their Rapid Response."

"Sounds like she took after her grandmother."

"Maybe she yanked people off bar stools in DC . . . . She's retired, I guess, but she still looks fit. Her parents passed, and she took up the mantle of the family ranch."

He stood, stretching like a great cat, and followed me as I walked to the cash register, pulled out my wallet, and handed Dorothy a few bills. "You have never been tempted to live out there?"

"My grandfather's place? Too far to drive into work."

He watched as Dorothy made change, handing it back to me as I dropped the coins in the can for donations to the animal shelter and stuffing my wallet back in my pants. "What about when you retire?"

I glanced at him again as we started toward the door.

"Everybody retires sometime."

"I'll cross that burning bridge when I get to it." I pushed the door, the bells tinkled, and we walked out into a perfectly gorgeous high-plains spring morning. "I guess I thought I was keeping it for the future generations, but I don't think Cady is ever going to want to go live out on the Powder River."

"Have you asked her?"

I paused about halfway across the bridge that spanned Clear Creek and dropped a quarter into the fish-food vending machine. Turning the handle, I caught the tiny pellets and tossed them to the hungry brown trout that lurked below. "No, but . . . it's out in the middle of nowhere, Henry — and I think she's kind of a city girl."

"What about Lola?"

We turned and walked back north toward the office. "She's only two years old — it's a little early to be thinking about that, isn't it?"

"You are going to have to find someone to inhabit it if you are not willing." He shrugged. "What is the acreage?"

I stopped at the stairs that led up to the county courthouse and my office. "Twenty-five."

He turned to look at me. "Thousand?"

"Yep. Some people collect stamps — the old man collected ranches."

"That is not a hobbyist-size ranch."

"No."

We continued up the concrete steps as he shook his head. "More of a going concern . . . . Tom was running cattle on the place?"

"Yep."

He stopped, leaning against the iron railing. "You will need a regular outfit and hands to keep it operating."

"That, or I just let it crumble to the ground."

"That would be a shame." I started to turn, but he held out a hand. "That place, it still haunts you, does it not?"

"Even more so, now that I think he was a killer."

"He was always a killer."

"Not like this, this is . . . dirty."

"All killing is dirty."

I nodded, looking at my boots. "I want to know what his part in all this was, and I'm not stopping until I find out."

"You have heard the phrase allowing sleeping dogs to lie?"

I laughed. "So, you think he did it?"

"It is possible that he did it, but what is the need of knowing?"

"To know, that's why."

"In the words of Virgil White Buffalo, your protector and guide, sometimes it is better to sleep."

"Can you honestly tell me that if confronted with this same situation within your family that you wouldn't want to know?"

Studying me, something caught his eye farther up the steps. "Perhaps not."

My eyes followed his — Ruth One Heart stood at the top dressed in the well-worn flight jacket and jeans and was smiling down at us. "Sho'daache, Standing Bear. I thought you would've been long dead by now."

We started up the steps but held a step down where she stood as tall as Henry, who grinned at her. "Not for a lack of trying."

She reached out and thumped his chest with a fist. "You still deflowering virgins on two reservations?"

"Good work, if you can get it." He continued to smile at her.

She turned to me. "And this one, he tried to poison me the other night."

"I believe you're the one who found the secret bottle. Anyway, what are you doing in town?"

"Out for a quick flight and thought I'd pop in and give you the lowdown from the old neighborhood." She glanced at Henry, who immediately got the drift and stepped past her.

"I have to get going, but I would love to catch up with you, Ruthless."

She glanced at me and then shrugged. "That's only the second time I've heard that nickname in years." We both watched him head off toward the office behind the court-house as she laughed. "Damn, he just doesn't age, does he?"

"Doesn't seem like it." I turned back to her. "Did you say a quick flight?"

"I've got a Husky taildragger that I bought after trading my dad's old Piper Super Cub a few years ago — he had a short strip and an old Quonset hut that he used for a hangar." Her voice took on a little irony. "I thought I was going to have to call you from Durant International . . . Did you know that you only have one taxi in this town?"

"We have a taxi?"

"Sort of . . . Anyway, can I get a ride back to what you folks euphemistically refer to as an airport?"

As the truck climbed the hill, she reached in the back and petted Dog. "There was an SUV out at your grandfather's place with some guy in it."

"Black?"

"No, it was a white guy."

"I meant the car."

"No, it was silver or a light gray."

"Wyoming plates?"

"No, Colorado, actually." She turned in the seat to look at me. "You looking for somebody?"

I navigated the winding road at the base of the mountains. "Out where Jules Beldon was shot, there was a black SUV and that night that same vehicle blew by Henry's bar before Jules crashed his Jeepster into the side of that same bar."

"Beldon is the guy you said may have been shot concerning this case from back in 1948?"

"Seems like a reach, but yep."

"No, this was a Realtor out of Jackson, you know, one of those groups that specialize in high-end ranches for the rich and famous."

"How did this guy hear about my grandfather's place?"

"Heck if I know; word gets around. You might want to close the gates on that place and keep them chained to keep the riffraff out."

"I guess so."

"I can do it if you don't want to drive all the way out there."

"No, no, I can do it."

"Maybe put up some signs."

"Yep." I parked at the small terminal and got out and walked through the open chain-link gate that led to the unguarded flight line where a frighteningly fast-looking yellow-and-black beast sat like a gigantic wasp. "It looks like the bush pilot stuff I used to see in Alaska."

She placed a hand on one of the oversize tires and reached up to open the side window and door. "They make 'em over in Afton, a genuine Wyoming product."

"Who knew?"

Her hand stroked the shiny surface of the fuselage. "Fast, and they can take off and land on a Mercury dime."

"I bet."

"Want a ride?"

"Not on your life."

She laughed. "What, you don't trust lady pilots?"

"I don't trust anything that flies, unless it's a case of life or death."

She lithely climbed in, pushed the elevator trim forward, and wrapped the headset around her neck. "You're missing out in life."

"I'm just trying to hang on to it for a little while longer."

"You mind pulling those chocks from the wheels and handing them to me?"

I did as she asked and gave them to her through the window as she hit the ignition, and the noise from the engine roared with me yelling to be heard. "Hey, thanks for coming all the way down here to let me know about what's going on out there!"

"I'll keep an eye on the place!" She turned her head, slipping on her aviator sunglasses. "Are you going to sell it?!"

I backed away, getting clear of the tail structure. "I'm not sure!"

"Gimme first rights of refusal?!" she yelled.

"You've got that kind of money?!"

"No, but I might want to help pick my neighbors!" She smiled. "Clear!"

I watched as she dropped the window closed and throttled up, the capable-looking aircraft leaping forward.

I stepped farther back as she taxied down the runway before pivoting the thing like a ballet dancer. True to her word, I'd never seen an airplane take flight that quickly in my life. One moment it was ripping down the tarmac and the next the massive, balloon-like tires were flying over top of me.

Watching her bank with the wingtip point straight at the ground, I was happy for my stomach that I hadn't accepted the offer of a ride. The engine roared, carrying her north as she straightened out and paralleled the mountains in the golden light of the midmorning sun.

Walking back to my truck, I saw Julie Lu-ehrman, the part-time airport controller, in one of the windows, waving down at me and thought about another flight I'd made years ago.

I took advantage of the opportunity and open ground with grass to let Dog out and relieve himself, sniffing along the parking lot as I plucked the mic from my dash and keyed it. "Base, this is unit one — are you there, Ruby?"

Static. "Base to unit one, what do you want?"

"Is Vic around?"

Static. "No, she took another personal day."

I stood there, holding the mic.

Static. "Do you read?"

"Yep, I heard. Is she sick?"

Static. "Sounded fine to me."

I stood there some more.

Static. "In further news, Isaac Bloomfield called — the young woman you took to the hospital is awake. He thought we might want to send somebody over there to take a statement."

I keyed the mic. "Got it."

Static. "That nice young man from Chey-enne is in the basement with Saizarbitoria,

233

and I have no idea what they're doing down there . . ."

"I think they're trying to figure out who owns that drone Henry shot out of the sky."

Static. "Woody Woodson called, but I told him you didn't need DCI's assistance with the rifle anymore."

"Actually, I think I do."

Static. "I thought there was a ballistic match with the slug that killed Sutherland?"

"There is for the caliber, but I'd just as soon get an actual match on the lands and grooves."

Static. "I'll call him back. Are we shipping the rifle to Cheyenne?"

"I'm not sure, I might just drive it down."

Static. "Suit yourself, I hear southeastern Wyoming is beautiful this time of year."

I stared at the radio and then keyed the mic again. "I'm headed over to the hospital."

Static. "Roger that. See if they can check you for a sense of humor?"

"Any change in Jules?"

"Steady." He straightened the stethoscope on his chest as if it were a tie. "But with his age and physical condition, we'll have to think about how long we want to leave him like this. I don't suppose he has any next of kin?"

"Not that I'm aware of, but I can check. How's Trisha Knox doing?"

"Much better, but she's still extremely weak from blood loss." Isaac sat in his all but empty office and was looking at me as I stood there in the doorway. "I get the feeling she's been living on the streets or at least hasn't been taking the best care of herself."

"Did you run a rape kit?"

"Yes, but that's about all she would let us do."

"Can I speak to her?"

"I was hoping you would." He stood, straightening his back. "I tried to talk with her, but she didn't seem to want to tell me anything. She did brighten up when I mentioned your name."

"That's not what usually happens in my line of work."

"She's been through a lot, and I think she looks upon you as something of a protector."

"Some job I did, huh?" I started to back out of the way and then gestured toward the small desk, the chair, and pile of folders on the floor only about a foot high, the office looking very different from all the time that I'd known it. "Are you going to sublet the place after you're gone?"

He chuckled. "No one appears to desire it."

"What, they want amenities, like a window?"

"I suppose so." He glanced around the tiny room. "I think it was a closet when I arrived, and I think that's what it's going to revert to."

"You did an awful lot of good from this little cubby, Doc. You saved a lot of lives over the years, including mine a bunch of times."

He peered at me through the thick-lensed glasses. "Do you think so, Walter?"

I placed a hand on his slender shoulder, careful not to put too much weight there. "I know so."

As we walked down the hallway, he turned the tables on me. "What about you, Walter? I hear that young deputy of yours has been approached by the Basque community to stand for sheriff."

"Did he talk about that while you guys cleaned out your office?"

"No, it's just the rumor around town."

I nodded, sage-like. "Yep, he told me about it."

"And?"

"I told him I hadn't made up my mind as to whether I was going to run or not."

236

"I think he would make a good sheriff, don't you?"

"Yep, I do."

We stopped outside one of the doors. "It's always an easier decision to make when you can hand your life's work off to someone you trust."

"Like you're doing with David?"

"Like that, yes."

I studied him as I placed my hand on the door handle to Trisha Knox's room. "I'm going to miss you, Doc."

"We all have to go sometime."

"Truer words having never been spoken." I pushed the door open and stepped into the room to find the young woman propped up and staring out the windows with one unpatched eye on the big cottonwoods that occupied the hospital grounds, the breeze moving the leaves that looked almost chartreuse in the glimmering light.

"Some of those trees are a hundred years old."

She ignored me and continued to gaze out the window.

"They planted them when they built the hospital." I crossed over to the bed and pulled out the guest chair. "When they expanded the place about twelve years ago, the architect refused to rip any of the trees out, so they built around them."

She still didn't move.

"How do you feel?"

"Crappy, how 'bout *you*?"

"Oh, I've had better weeks."

"I seem to be a reoccurring problem for you."

Shrugging, I leaned back in the chair and listened to it squeal. "I've had worse."

She waited a moment, then turned to me and began bargaining. "Tell me about one?"

I figured telling her about a case stemming from the middle of the last century wouldn't do much harm. "I think my grandfather may have been involved in the murder of a man back in 1948."

"Wow."

"Yep, wow."

She went back to looking out the window. "What was he like?"

"My grandfather? A disciplinarian who hated my guts."

"Why?"

"I can't honestly say I know, other than I didn't follow the path he'd laid out for me."

"And that was?"

"Being under his control."

She nodded. "I never met my father, let alone my grandfather."

"Back in Minnesota?"

"Yeah."

I waited a moment and then asked, "Do you want to tell me what happened?"

"What are the laws in Wyoming concerning prostitution?"

I thought about it and then quoted the law. "A person who knowingly or intentionally performs or permits, or offers or agrees to perform or permit an act of sexual intrusion, as defined by Wyoming Statute 6-2-301, for money or other property commits prostitution, which is a misdemeanor punishable by imprisonment for not more than six months, and a fine of no more than seven hundred and fifty dollars, or both."

"Sexual intrusion, huh?"

"Sounds a little odd, doesn't it? Would you like to hear the statutes for rape, assault with a deadly weapon, reckless endangerment, and sexual assault in the first degree?"

She turned to look at me again. "What is it you're trying to say?"

"That I'm more concerned with who did this to you than I am about what led to it."

She stared at me. "In my experience, there are always side effects when you team up with the law."

"Like putting whoever did this to you behind bars?"

"Not this guy."

239

"There's no sliding scale of justice in my county."

"Yeah, I've heard that one before."

I scooted my chair in. "Look, whoever did this is a danger to others."

"Yeah, that's usually the next thing they say."

"Well, this is a personal decision that only you can make, but even if you're not pressing charges there are things you need to do beyond medical attention. For now, you're in a safe environment and no matter who he is, he can't get at you here. When you are discharged in a few days, that'll be a different story. Do you have any family, anybody you can call?"

"No."

"Okay, we'll have to see what we can do about that. In the meantime, did Isaac or one of the nurses explain the rape kit to you?"

"Sorta."

"Well, it's an evidence-gathering kit that can be crucial in prosecuting whoever did this. If you do decide to press charges, then I'll take possession of the kit and a chain of custody will be established, but until you do, it'll stay here at the hospital."

"Okay."

"Can you do me a favor?"

"What?"

I pulled a notebook from the inside pocket of my jacket along with a rollerball pen and handed them to her. "Can you write down what happened?"

She stared at the notepad and pen.

"Just for yourself, whether you decide to go through with this or not, you need to get it down on paper, focusing on the details of the assault and the perpetrator before those things start becoming vague."

"I don't think I'll ever forget a single thing about it."

I motioned with the notepad and pen again. "You'd be surprised."

"So, what's the prognosis on your sense of humor?"

I stopped at the top of the steps as Dog continued on, curling up around the bottom of her stool as I looked at the empty office. "I'm thinking it might be terminal."

"How so?"

I tossed the photo onto the counter in front of her, my grinning grandfather front and center.

She turned it to look at it. "So, this is the murder weapon?"

"It sure looks to be. Did you get ahold of Woody?"

"He said to just send it down and they'd put it through the paces."

I glanced at the door to my office and could see no Post-its on the frame. "I'm assuming the media storm has passed?"

She still studied the paper. "It would appear, but if they find out about this . . ."

"I wasn't intending on making it public just now." I picked up the photo and tucked it under my arm. "Still no Vic?"

"No Vic. You two have an argument?"

"Something like that."

"Like what, if you don't mind my asking?"

"I asked her to marry me."

She stared at me as we both stood there listening to the clock ticking on the wall. "Excuse me?"

"Married — people still do it, or so I hear."

She sat back in her stool and shook her head. "And when did all this happen?"

"Just before this disappearing act of hers."

"My goodness . . ."

I leaned a hip against the counter. "That seems to be the general response."

"Does Cady know about all this?"

"Yep."

I tipped my hat back and stared down the short hall at Vic's office door, which was hanging open. "And she's in favor, so long as it makes me happy."

"And will it?"

"I think so."

"You think so?"

"Why do I get the feeling I'm walking around in a minefield here?"

She leaned forward, adjusting the cat-eye glasses with the string of pearls retainer. "It raises some unique ethical questions."

"Such as?"

"Oh, Walter . . . A sheriff married to his undersheriff?"

"I'm sure it's not the first time it's happened."

"It will be here, and you know how people love to talk."

"What's the harm?"

"Are you going to support her as the next sheriff, because if she runs against Saizarbi-toria and the Basque mafia she will most certainly lose."

"You're so sure?"

"Yes."

"Mind if I ask why?"

She flung out three fingers, counting them down with each point. "One, she's a woman. Two, she's not from here. Three, her mouth."

I laughed. "I'm not so sure I can beat

Saizarbitoria and the Basque Syndicate either."

"Well, if you're going to retire in a year, it really doesn't matter."

I pushed back from the counter, pulling the photo from under my arm and slapping my thigh. "It doesn't matter, anyway. My personal and professional lives are two different things."

"Not if she says yes."

"Ruby, what do you think is going on?"

She sat back in her chair and folded her arms. "She's scared."

"You think?"

"I know." She sat there, studying me. "She was married before, for what? A year or two, and then her husband, after relocating her to Wyoming, decides to take off for Alaska. Have you ever heard her talk about him or mention him in any way?"

"No."

"I think she treasures you as her closest and possibly only friend, and then you drop this bomb on her . . ."

"I thought it was a good thing?"

"Really, did you put much thought into it at all?"

I summoned up the environs of the parking lot at the Durant Home for Assisted Living that night, what seemed like a lifetime ago, and heard the words stumbling from my mouth. "It might've been a blurty kind of thing."

"Blurty?"

"Improvisational?"

"Oh, Walter."

"Did she call in with these personal days?"

"She did, and left a message on the answering machine."

"Each time?"

"Yes."

"How did she sound?"

"Normal."

I took a deep breath and let it out slow, like a Stanley Steemer vacuum cleaner getting up to speed. "Maybe I should go by there and talk with her."

"Why not?"

"Henry says I shouldn't."

She leaned forward, resting her chin on her combined fists and looking at me somewhat amused. "Henry's track record with women somewhat speaks for itself, wouldn't you say?"

I thought about it as I looked around. "Does anybody work here anymore?"

"Well, with Vic MIA and you delving into family history, Santiago has been free to pal around with Mr. Regis — they're at lunch."

"Anything for me to do?"

"The Best Western called and asked what you want to do with that young woman's things."

"I'm not sure just yet."

She studied me.

I put on my best war-movie voice. "It's quiet, Ruby."

She grumbled hers in return. "It's too quiet, Walter — go talk to Vic."

"Okay." Leaning forward, I reached behind her neck and pulled the crown of her head down to where I could kiss it. "Thank you."

Turning, I started back toward the steps and called for Dog.

There appeared to be no stirring from behind the counter.

"Coward." Doomed, I marched down the steps like a man headed for a firing squad, pushing the doors open to find Saizarbitoria and Regis heading up the outside steps. "Hello, men. How goes the good fight?"

"Slow, but I ran a check on that kid out on the PR, Jordan Heller."

"And?"

"He's had a few run-ins . . ."

Regis gave out with a laugh.

Sancho glanced at him and then added. "He pounded some guy in a bar over in Moorcroft, had another altercation with a truck driver at his place of work, as well as a restraining order with an ex-wife." Sancho looked at Regis again and then back to me. "Do you have anything you'd like us to do?"

It was my turn to look at Regis. "Are you heading back down to Cheyenne any time soon?"

"Not really, are you trying to get rid of me?"

"No, it's either you or me who's going to drive that rifle down to DCI."

"I can do it."

"That's okay, I've pretty much decided to do it myself."

He shrugged. "I don't mind . . . I'm not doing much here."

I waved him off. "It'll give me an opportunity to see my daughter and granddaughter."

The Basquo gestured toward the man who had downgraded his ensemble to a sport shirt, windbreaker, and jeans. "We thought we'd drive out on the Powder where Jules got shot and check the area for more cartridges or anything else we can find?"

"Fine by me." I glanced at Regis. "You can buy him a beer at the Red Pony Bar & Grill — give him a real idea of the flavor of the place." Walking between them, I offered one more piece of culinary advice. "Make sure to try the pickled turkey gizzards in the big jar at the end of the bar — they've only been there since 1979."

Sancho laughed as I climbed in my truck and wheeled out of the parking lot, driving the three blocks over to Vic's little craftsman with the red door.

I pulled up across the street and tried to find her vehicle, but it didn't seem to be here. It was possible she'd started using the small garage in the back built for vehicles the size of a Model A, but maybe she'd found a way to get Banshee II in there.

I climbed out, walked across the street, and noticed that the yard needed mowing. Stepping onto the porch, I pulled open the screen door, raised a fist, and knocked on the front door, trying to think of what it was I was going to say. What the heck? Look, when a man and a woman really love each other . . . Okay, let's just forget I asked.

The seconds passed, and I couldn't come up with anything, figuring I'd just go with the spur of the moment — because that'd worked out so well the other night.

I raised my fist again, knocking a little harder this time.

I waited a few seconds before leaning to the side and peeking in the space between the curtains and the window frame, where I could see a portion of the hardwood floor I'd helped sand. There were some crumpled newspapers and a cardboard box.

Leaning a little farther, I couldn't see the corner of the sofa that I'd helped carry into the place, or the end table that usually sat at the arm of the sofa.

Snatching open the screen door again, I knocked one last time before reaching down and turning the knob. It swung open, bumping against the inside wall with a hollow, echoing sound.

Stepping inside, I listened as the floor creaked under my weight. Looking through the small entryway and into the living room, I could see that all the furniture was gone, that there was nothing on the wall, and that there were only a few empty packing boxes along with the crumpled newspaper and some bubble wrap on the floor.

Moving into the kitchen, I could see the drawers hanging open and empty and nothing on the counters.

Leaning to one side, I glanced in the bedroom and saw that it too was vacant.

Backing into the living room, I turned and couldn't help but have the uneasy feeling I'd suddenly been caught in a deluge and was circling down a drain.

9

"What's this?"

"The coffee maker."

I stared at the newfangled black box that sat on the counter and felt as if I were being overwhelmed by progress. "What was wrong with the old one?"

She was in the process of gathering up her things and leaving. "Nothing, but that nice young man from Cheyenne ordered this one and had it delivered."

"How does it work?"

She pulled the strap of her purse onto her shoulder and walked over, with Dog trailing along. "You push that button there." She pointed at a knob on the left. "You can dial down the strength of the coffee by turning it. It makes a really good cup, but we'll have to start using whole beans."

"I've got an entire freezer full of them."

"Cady?"

"Yep." Pulling a mug off the rack, I placed

it on the tray. "Heard anything from Vic?"

Ruby pushed the knob and we listened to the beans grind. "She dropped her truck off over at Michelina's, and Jim called to say it was fixed."

"What was wrong with it?"

"The check-engine light had come on, so I guess she brought the truck in and was going to pick it up on Monday."

I watched the mug fill. "Monday."

"Yes." She studied me. "Why are you drinking coffee this late in the afternoon?"

"I think I'm going to drive down to Cheyenne."

"Well, you've been talking about it."

"I figure I can light a fire under Woody if I hand deliver that rifle. Besides, I want to meet this Wiltse woman and some of the other players in the PWMTF saga. Is Barrett coming in?"

She looked at the old Seth Thomas on the wall that was showing us it was two minutes away from closing time or whatever closing time was in our line of work. "Should be here any minute."

After the coffee finished brewing, I took a sip and had to admit that it wasn't bad. "Do you ever miss being married, Ruby?"

She thought about it. "Well, Roger and I were married for twenty-six years before he

251

passed and I missed him terribly, but then I just got used to being alone."

"I don't think I've ever gotten used to being alone."

"Are you okay?"

I turned to her. "Yep, why?"

"You just seem out of sorts."

"Vic mention going somewhere or anything like that?"

"No, why?"

I thought about keeping it to myself until I knew the entire score but decided to go ahead and tell my trusted dispatcher to see if between the two of us we'd be able to puzzle it out. "I was just over there, and all her stuff is gone."

She stared at me, taking a moment before speaking. "Her house?"

"Yep."

"What do you mean, gone?"

"Furniture, everything . . . The place is empty."

For a moment, Ruby looked like I felt. "You mean, she's gone?"

"Sure looks like it."

She studied me for a moment more and then turned, starting back for her desk. "I'm calling her."

"No."

"I've got her cell number." She picked up

the receiver, running a finger down the list taped to her desk and began punching numbers.

I walked over and calmly pushed the tab and disconnected the call. "No."

Whipping off her glasses, Ruby glared at me. "Walt . . ."

"No." I sighed. "I mean, this isn't the response I expected, but I need to respect her choices and just wait till she's ready to get in touch with me."

"Well, I don't."

She started dialing again, and I disconnected the call again. "I've taken you into my confidence here."

Hanging the phone up with a slam, she shook her head. "What is she thinking?"

"I honestly don't know." Looking for something to do as I thought, I took another sip of the high-test coffee. "Maybe she needs some time away to get her head straight —"

"And take her furniture with her?"

"I guess she wants to keep her options open."

"Where would she go, back to Philadelphia?"

"Ruby, I honestly don't know, but if she's on a plane, then the question has already been answered."

"How can you just stand there?"

"Well, I've been giving it some thought and maybe I don't want to hear the answer."

She folded her arms, still looking at me. "I think that's pretty low, to run out on you like that."

I sipped my coffee. "I'm trying to not make judgments here, until I know what's going on."

"Well, that's very mature of you."

"Thanks."

"So, she ran off and now you're going to run off too?"

"Just down to Cheyenne, and then I'll be back tomorrow or Sunday — according to how long Woody needs the rifle."

She continued to study me. "I assumed you were going to drive."

"I am, why?"

She folded her arms and looked a little contrite.

"What?"

"I might've mentioned to Lucian that you were going to Cheyenne."

I listened, as my own voice dropped two octaves. "You what?"

"He called here, and it just slipped out . . ." Her eyes came back to mine. "You could just pretend like you didn't get the message — just leave." She stood and

254

stepped forward, her arms crossed as she bumped her head into my chest. "I'm sorry."

He was waiting on the curb in an old CPO jacket with his Stetson Open Road hat perched on the back of his head and a flight bag slung over his shoulder. "Well, it took you long enough."

I rolled the window down about six inches and called to him. "What are you doing, Lucian?"

He hobbled over and yanked on the door, finding it locked. "Hitchin' a ride to Cheyenne with you, I reckon."

"No."

He readjusted the strap on his shoulder. "What do you mean, no?"

"I mean I'm not taking you to Cheyenne."

He tried the door handle again, but it was still locked. "Why the hell not?"

"Because you're a big pain in the ass."

He stared at me. "Open this door."

"No." I watched as he waited a moment and then fumbled inside his jacket, slipping out his .38 Special S&W Victory Model and drawing it back as if to break the side window. "Lucian."

He lowered the revolver. "Open this damned door; it'll be like one of those buddy movies."

"You've never even seen a buddy movie."

He pointed the barrel at both Dog and me, breaking every gun-handling rule in the book. "*Sons of the Desert.*"

"What?"

"Laurel and Hardy, 1933."

"That's not a buddy movie."

"The hell it wasn't, it was a movie, and they were buddies."

Sighing, I unlocked the door, and he climbed in as Dog bailed for the back.

The old sheriff threw his bag on the center console and stuffed the .38 back in his shoulder holster. He turned to me and pulling out a flask, which he carefully unscrewed, took a sip and then offered me one for the road, which I declined. Fourteen minutes and thirty-two seconds and many sips later, he was asleep against the passenger door, snoring like a Husqvarna chain saw.

I'd thought about going home and packing some clothes but then decided I couldn't face the empty little cabin. There were stores in Cheyenne, or so they told me, and I figured if I needed anything I could just buy it — including a toothbrush and dog food.

Dog sat in the back passenger seat watching the bucolic scenery of central Wyoming pass by the window as I drove south, thinking about the situation in which I'd found myself.

It didn't take long to redirect my line of thought, and for five hours I contemplated the investigation I was conducting.

When I pulled up in front of the Barrett Building on Central Avenue in Cheyenne, the lights were off, but I wasn't worried.

Driving around to the side, I parked and quietly opened the truck door, letting Dog out to go to the bathroom. With one last glance at Lucian, I turned and studied the rather imposing building that housed the Wyoming State Archives — then did what I normally did when confronted by massive quantities of pomp and bureaucracy and went to the side entrance.

Knocking on the steel utility door, I waited as Dog patrolled the area.

After a few moments there was some noise from inside and then a crash and a tirade of cursing. Eventually the door opened, and a young woman looked up at me from the darkened hallway. "You'd think they could afford to keep the lights on, wouldn't you?"

"Maybe they don't want to attract attention after hours. I'm Walt."

"Nina." She stuck out a hand which I shook. "Come on in before the governor

257

walks by."

Nina Yadav had been a long-distance friend of mine for a number of years; a reference archivist for the state, she'd buried herself in the government organization after graduating from the University of Wyoming just down the road. I'd gotten in the habit over the last few years of contacting her whenever I needed the assistance of the archivist and was to the point where I considered her my personal staff.

She kneeled and petted Dog, swinging her dark hair to the side to reveal her smiling face and looking up at me. "It's nice to finally meet you."

"You too."

She stood and gestured that we should follow. "You usually exclusively phone in for my services."

"I was on my way here when it dawned on me, so I stopped at a pay phone in Chugwater."

She paused at the end of the darkened hallway, before opening the door. "You still don't have a phone?"

"No."

"Or a computer?"

"I did for a while, but they took it away from me."

"You're making this research thing more

difficult." She swung the door open, and we entered a brightly lit room with cabinets all around, along with a large table at the center with an illuminated surface where piles of material already stood.

"You've been busy."

"You don't usually contact me about a murder."

"Potential murder."

She made a warning sound in the back of her throat, like a cat. "Potential murders, plural."

I turned to her. "What?"

She took a seat on one of the stools, then pulled out some official-looking documents and handed them to me. "The late Harold Grafton, chief clerk of the Wyoming State Treasurer's Office."

"No, Bill Sutherland is the guy I'm looking into."

She gestured toward the papers in my hand. "Well, you better broaden your investigation, because as near as I can tell, his boss was killed too."

"Holy smokes."

She picked up another stack and handed it to me. "And this guy Bob Carr, the state treasurer? He disappeared about a year later."

I stared at the death reports, looking at

the dates. "Grafton three weeks afterward and Carr a year after Sutherland was killed."

She sat back on her stool. "Did we leave anybody out?"

"Yep, my grandfather."

She slid a stack toward me. "That would be the aforementioned Lloyd Longmire?"

"Yep."

"Why wasn't this big news?"

"It was." She laughed and gestured toward the collected papers. "The state launched an investigation; it's all there."

"But how do you get away with something like this, even back then?"

"This is my guess, and it's only a guess, mind you . . . Someone was very, very crafty."

Nina had been kind enough to order out, so we sat there in the same room and ate dal bhat from Yadav's Nepalese and Indian Bistro, a restaurant that Nina's family owned, which also explained the gargantuan proportions.

I took a sip of my tea and finally dropped my fork in surrender. "Your parents tried to kill us."

Smiling, she nodded. "It's a wonder I don't weigh four hundred pounds."

"So, what is a nice Nepalese researcher

260

like you doing in Wyoming?"

"I heard there were mountains."

I sipped my tea. "They're bigger where you're from."

She brightened. "Have you ever been?"

"No, but it's been a lifelong desire of mine, to see the tallest mountains in the world."

"You should go."

I sat my cup down by the pile of papers. "Oh, I think I'm getting a little old for that foolishness . . ."

"Travel is foolishness?"

"At a certain age, yes."

"You're not that old and, besides, you're never too old for travel or new experiences."

"Are you working for the Nepalese Travel Bureau?"

She shrugged, still smiling. "I just don't like to think of people not doing what they want most in life. People never end their lives thinking about things they wish they'd bought, but they do think about things they wish they'd done."

Wrapping up the remainder of my food, I returned it to the bag and moved it to the counter by the door, figuring there was less of a chance of me spilling anything on one of the state archives worktables. "Speaking

261

of doing, I guess I'll need copies of all this stuff?"

She stood, packing up her food and placing it with mine as Dog followed her, figuring her as more of a mark. "I can make the copies now, or I can get it together and have it for you tomorrow morning."

I glanced at the digital clock on the wall and thought about how late I wanted to show up at Cady's little carriage house away from home, especially with an unannounced Lucian Connally. "The second option might be best since my daughter has a two-year-old."

"You have a daughter and a granddaughter?"

"Assistant attorney general and then the assistant to the assistant AG, but I'm not so sure the two-year-old is of much assistance."

"They're here in Cheyenne?"

"They are."

She stood there, looking at me. "I'm learning so much about you."

"There isn't that much, truth to be told."

Reaching toward the counter, she took a couple of sheets of paper, folding them and handing them to me. "Well, I found some stuff out about your grandfather that was quite interesting."

"I stared at the papers. "What's this?"

"Your grandfather's war record." She stuck out a hand. "Never tell a researcher that there isn't much to know, it only makes us dig deeper."

Stuffing the papers in my jacket, I smiled and shook her hand. "A pleasure to finally meet you, Nina."

"They'll be open tomorrow at nine, and I'll leave a packet for you at the front desk under your name."

"Thank you." We walked down the darkened hallway, and I pushed open the door, letting Dog through and then following him. "Can I give you a lift?"

"No, I want to get this done and then I'll ride my bike. I've got a little house I'm fixing up near the air base."

"You're sure?"

"Yes, I like the exercise." Her eyes drifted up and she stood there, transfixed. "Oh, look . . ."

I followed her gaze and could see the North Star between two buildings, perfectly framed. "Polaris, it's bright tonight."

"Dhruv Tara."

"Excuse me?"

"Its name in my language is Dhruv Tara."

"Good to know." I nodded, walked toward my truck, and waved at her one last time as Dog climbed in and I followed suit, firing

263

the V10 up and pulling out of the parking lot.

The old sheriff shook himself awake and looked over at me, more than a bit bleary. "Where the hell are we?"

"Cheyenne."

He peeked out the side window as we pulled away. "Yeah, but what building is that?"

"The Wyoming State Archives — you've probably never heard of it."

He grunted then looked out the window as I drove to Cady's place. I thought about what I'd learned and then pulled down the alley and parked under the deck in one of her spots.

Joe Meyer, the real AG, had been kind enough to rent my daughter the carriage house of their place and even cadged his wife, Mary, into Lola-sitting every once in a while.

I glanced over and could see that Lucian had fallen back asleep. Quietly reaching into my jacket, I pulled out the sheets of paper and read them. After I'd gone through them twice, I opened the door, first letting Dog out, then collected the rifle and circled around to retrieve the half-asleep sheriff, picking him up and throwing him over my shoulder.

Dog went ahead as Lucian and I got about halfway up the stairs when we heard the screen door open and a familiar voice call out softly, "I've got a gun."

"Me too."

"Yeah, but I was taught how to shoot by the best in the business."

"Who was that?"

"My mother."

Arriving at the landing with the wrapped rifle in one hand and Lucian draped over my shoulder, I glanced at my daughter in her bathrobe, who looked remarkably like the woman she'd just mentioned. "Am I waking you?"

She opened the door wider as Dog barged his way in. "Nope, Ruby called and said there might be three of you." She took the old sheriff off my shoulders and into her arms, giving him a hug as she escorted him toward the sofa.

"She did, did she?"

As I approached, Cady kissed the scruff on my chin, then guided the old sheriff onto the sofa, where he curled up his legs and went back to sleep. She took off his hat and placed it on the coffee table and then covered him in an old blanket with stars and planets. "C'mon, cowboy — I'll buy you a beer."

We took a hard right into the kitchen. "I only drink one brand."

She opened the refrigerator and pulled out a bottle of Rainier. "Well, you're lucky because that brand is still here from the last time you visited a month ago." Twisting off the top, she handed it to me and looked over at the rifle I had just set down on her table. "So, you're running guns from the northern part of the state?"

I took a sip. "Something like that."

She glanced at the watch on her wrist. "What took you so long? Ruby said you left more than six hours ago."

"I made a stopover at the state archives."

"Okay?"

"I've got a specialist over there, Nina Yadav, whom I consult from time to time." I took another sip. "It turns out that within a year after Big Bill Sutherland was killed, the chief clerk, Harold Grafton, was killed, and the state treasurer, Bob Carr, went missing in Montana."

"Oh, no."

"Oh, yes." I turned the beer in the small ring of condensation on the Formica surface of the table. "Harold Grafton was at a conference in Gillette and was found dead, an apparent suicide, and Bob Carr was supposedly on a fishing vacation on the Bighorn

River near Fort Smith and disappeared . . ."

She sat there staring at me. "Seems a little too convenient, doesn't it?"

"Yep."

"So, you think somebody was cleaning up their mess?"

"It seems possible."

She shook her head, subconsciously pulling her robe and closing it a little tighter as if she might be cold. "Correct me if I'm wrong about this, but it's one thing to accidentally kill someone at an elk camp out in the middle of nowhere, and another thing to track two individuals down and premeditatedly murder them, one on a city street?"

"It is."

"You still think it was great-grandpa Lloyd?"

"I hate to say this, but who else is there? My father was there, but he didn't have any connections to the financial world and neither did Henry's father. The only one left alive a year after the shooting of Big Bill Sutherland was my grandfather, and he had connections to all three men."

"What could've motivated him to do such a thing?"

"Money . . . a lot of it."

"Was Great-granddad really that avaricious?"

"There was a point when he was collecting ranches like baseball cards . . ."

"You're saying . . ."

"The ranch, the trust — all of it."

"Our family's entire wealth?"

"Along with the financial underpinnings of the Bank of Durant."

She sat back in her chair and studied me. "What does Wes Haskins have to say about all this?"

"He says the previous bank president watched Lloyd shoot two men dead in the lobby of the bank in 1933, a story I'd heard but thought up to now was just a legend."

"So, he had killed before."

I reached into my pocket and pulled out the folded sheets of paper that Nina had given me. "Have you ever heard of the Belleau Wood?"

"No."

I laid the pieces of paper on the surface of the table, smoothing them out and sliding them toward her. "It's in France, an old hunting preserve near the Marne River. It was one of the first battles for American troops in World War I, and compared to some of the others, it was a relatively small but sordid affair, fought across dark overgrown fields with poison gas, fixed bayonets, and hand-to-hand combat. It was where the

Corps went from being a small-skirmish force into the mechanized wholesale of slaughter."

"The Corps." She leaned forward, studying the papers. "Wait, Great-grandpa was a marine too?"

Finishing my beer, I stood, walked over to the sink, and rested the empty bottle there. "Can you believe it? Third Battalion, Sixth Marine Regiment, and the sonofabitch never said a word when I was drafted — not a word."

"Unbelievable."

I laughed and shook my head. "The Germans had machine gun nests everywhere, and it was one of the largest number of casualties suffered by any single American brigade of the entire war; over four thousand wounded and a thousand dead, one of the largest single losses in marine history to date."

"And Grandpa was there?"

"Victorious ends require bloody means . . . There was a huge plaque on the wall at boot camp." I turned and leaned on the counter. "Nina found the records and gave them to me; she tracked them down in the marine records at the National Archives." I gestured toward the sheets of paper lying on the kitchen table. "He was a part of the first attack late in the afternoon. They walked across a field into enemy fire and the majority were wiped out." I looked at her, trying to remember if they'd met. "You don't remember him, do you?"

"No, he was dead before I was born."

"The man could fall asleep anywhere, and that might've been what saved him. The survivors hit the ground and stayed there to avoid getting hit by the machine guns and artillery. Well, Lloyd must've fallen asleep and missed the call to retreat. He woke up in the middle of the night and figured the attack was still on and started crawling toward these four German divisions hidden in the woods."

"Alone?"

"Alone." I shook my head at the idea. "Pretty soon he comes on this machine gun nest and finds all of them asleep. Then they wake up and come out of the hole at him, and he shoots all four of them before two more come over and he bayonets them."

"Jeez, Dad, this is Sergeant York–type stuff."

I reached over and shuffled through the papers. "Wait, it gets better. So, it's morning and back in the American lines they hear the shots and start the offensive again, but by this time Lloyd has repositioned the German machine gun and aims it to his left and opens fire, wiping out another nest. Well, the American offensive gains ground and they get into the woods on the right side where they start chasing the Germans wholesale. Your great-grandfather kills two more before they put a bullet through his chest and the rest of his brigade found him crawling after the Germans, bleeding out." I turned the page, reading the last part. "It says he won a Medal of Honor and a Navy Cross and even a French Croix de Guerre but I never saw them. The Germans called the marines Teufel Hunden — Devil Dogs. Legendary, the battle that turned the tide of a World War." I looked at her. "I never even knew."

She leaned forward, taking my hand in hers. "Dad, how could the man you just described have killed those three men?"

It was me speaking, but my voice seemed very far away, as far away as a dark forest deep in France. "The mechanics of killing were not unknown to Lloyd Longmire."

Her hand squeezed mine. "That can be said about a lot of the members of this family."

Later, I couldn't sleep, scenarios of the Battle of Belleau Wood unfolding over and over again in my head, and found myself creeping back into the kitchen. As Lucian snored, I looked at those same pieces of paper when I heard a noise coming from outside on the deck.

Opening the door and screen door, I stepped out and looked around but couldn't see anything; so, like a good hunter, I stood there motionless and listened.

The small noise I'd heard was coming from below, so I eased each door shut behind me, walked to the railing, and looked down into the alley. My truck was parked at my daughter's garage door, so nothing seemed out of the ordinary. At one end of the block I could hear a motorcycle idling but that wasn't anything new in a town the size of Cheyenne either.

I'd just started to turn and head back when a man appeared in the alley from underneath the deck. He was walking away toward the sound of the running bike. "Can I help you?"

It was a guy in his forties, dressed in a leather jacket, the slap of his hard-sole boots echoing off the buildings.

"Hey?"

He stopped and half-turned toward me. "Yes?"

"Can I help you?"

His accent was eastern European. "No, just looking for an address."

"At two in the morning?"

He turned to look up at me. "What, you are neighborhood watch?"

"In this neighborhood, I am." I pointed below the deck. "You see that truck down there with the stars on it? That's mine."

He glanced at my truck and then sighed. "I had buddy call me drunk . . . He gave me wrong address. That okay?"

"What's the address?"

He stared up at me, still not turning his face completely so that the majority was still hidden. "What?"

"The address your buddy gave you, what was it?"

"Don't know, two thousand something."

"East Twentieth, that's four blocks south, and the alleys are half numbers."

He nodded, waving, and then started off. "Thank you."

I watched him go and listened as the unseen motorcycle revved up and roared away to go annoy some other neighborhood. Turning, I quietly pulled open the doors and went back inside, but now heard some noises from the bedroom beside Cady's.

Padding in that direction in my bare feet, I went to the door as Dog slipped off the

273

sofa beside Lucian and joined me. There was more noise, and I turned the knob, cracking the door open to find my granddaughter standing in her crib, looking at me, evidently awoken by the conversation outside her window. "Poppy!"

"Hi, Peanut."

Her arms shot out at me, begging to be picked up and delivered from incarceration.

I held a finger to my lip, whispering as I approached. "You have to be quiet, or we'll be in trouble."

She held a finger to her own mouth. "Trouble!"

"Shhhh . . ."

"Shhhhhhh . . ." I scooped her up and started to turn when she reached behind her. "Boomba!"

"Shhhh . . ." I handed her the stuffed buffalo, and she crammed its nose in her mouth.

Dog followed as I carried Lola into the living room and thought about where I could take her so that she wouldn't get us both in trouble and awaken Cady or Lucian. Reaching over, I took another blanket from the reading chair where I'd been quasi-sleeping and trailed it after us as I went out onto the deck and into a velvety, warm night with just a touch of the continual Wyoming breeze.

Sitting in one of the deck chairs, I placed her in my lap and watched as she played with the toy, Dog lying down near my feet. As Lola galloped Boomba across my chest, I looked at the starry night. With all the ambient light of the city, the view was better out at my place, but this one wasn't bad.

Looking down, I could see Lola following my gaze up and into the sky. "Stars."

"Very good. Which one is your favorite?"

She pointed to the badge on my chest. "Um, that one."

I swallowed, attempting to find some words, any words. "Yep, but up there, which one is your favorite?"

She took a moment to stare into the sky and then picked the one I figured she would. "That one."

"The bright one? That's the North Star, or what the Cheyenne call the Star That Does Not Walk." She nodded as I pointed. "You can always see it on any clear night, you just have to find the Big Dipper."

"Dipper."

"Big Dipper."

"Big, um, Dipper."

I poked at the stars that assembled the pattern. "The two stars at the end of the

Dipper's cup point the way to the North Star, which is the tip of the handle of the Little Dipper."

She regarded me the way she did when she thought I might be trying to get something over on her. "Little Dipper."

"Right, or the tail of the little bear in the constellation Ursa Minor."

She looked back at the stars, trying to find Uncle Henry. "Bear?"

"Two bears — a big one and a little one, just like you and me."

"You and me."

"Polaris is another word for that star." I thought about the brief conversation I'd had with Nina outside the State Archives building. "And Dhruv Tara is another one."

"Dhruv Tara," she repeated, expertly.

"There's nothing here, Sheriff. I'm very sorry."

I stared at the receptionist at the Wyoming State Archives. "Are you sure? Nina Yadav was going to get things together for me."

The young man reached for his phone. "Let me call her."

I waited as he dialed but then watched as he listened for a moment and then spoke the way you do to machines. "Nina, this is Michael at the front desk. We've got a

Sheriff Walt Longmire down here to pick up some materials that you supposedly have for him, so if you would, please give me a call." He waited a moment and then hung up. "She's not at her desk, but to be honest I don't think she works today with it being a Saturday."

"She was going to put these things together for me last night."

"Is this important?"

"It's a murder investigation."

"Oh." He picked up his cell phone and scrolled through it. "I've got her home phone number, and I'll give her a call?"

"That'd be great, thanks." I walked away, far enough to not be hovering but close enough so that he could get my attention if he found her. There was a display called "A Brief History of Bear Hunting in Wyoming" with two armed men in front of the largest bear skin I'd ever seen, almost three times their size.

"She's not there, but I left her a message — are you in town for long?"

"I've got some work to do over at the DCI crime lab."

"Well, give me your cell number and I'll call you when I hear from her."

"I don't have a cell phone." Pulling one of the cards, I bent the corner back to straighten it and handed it to him. "Just call my dispatcher and have her contact me."

He looked rather dubiously at the weathered card that had been riding around in my shirt pocket for months. "Will do."

"Thanks." I turned and walked out into the perfectly gorgeous day and my truck, where Lucian was waiting in the passenger seat with his arm hanging out the window. As I climbed in, he pulled his hat from his face. "Damn, why'd you let me drink all that bourbon?"

"You seemed determined."

Avoiding the interstate, I headed south and then east, circling around the community college and parking in front of the new building that replaced the old supermarket that used to house the operation.

Lucian sat up. "So, this is where all our tax money is going."

The building was in a relatively vacant area, so I opened the door, grabbed the rifle from the back, and let Dog out. Then I came around and opened the door for Lucian. He organized himself before walking past me with his cane, approaching the cantilevered structure with the glass-block entryway.

Arriving at the front door behind him, I found it locked so I pushed the button for the intercom. A moment later, a tinny voice sounded from the speaker.

Static. "Can I help you?"

"Is Steve Woodson around?"

Static. "He doesn't work here anymore."

"What'd he do, join the circus?"

Static. "No, he's trying to get out of law enforcement."

Lucian shouted at the speaker. "Damn it, Woody, you wiseass, we know that's you."

The buzzer sounded, and I pushed the glass door open to let Lucian and Dog in. Woody appeared from a corner behind a reception area wearing an Orvis sweatshirt and a bucket hat with an assortment of dry flies stuck in the liner. "Just so you know, this stuff is interfering with my fishing."

I handed him the rifle. "You fish too much anyway."

He tucked the Weatherby under his arm and reached over to shake hands with my old boss. "How are you, Lucian?"

"Hungover, so don't screw around with me."

He smiled and petted Dog. "This is jiffy service, driving this thing down yourself. Did you go see your daughter, and more importantly your granddaughter?"

"I did, but I also had some things to do over at the archives."

Straightening, he held the wax paper–covered rifle out. "Something to do with this?"

"Yep."

"Well, let's go see what we've got, shall we?"

Following him, we all entered the inner sanctum of the Division of Criminal Investigation and then down a hallway to a lab connected to a shooting range. He sat the rifle on a felt-covered bench and unwrapped it. "Whoa . . . What's this, the case of Walt Longmire and Jurassic Park?"

"Custom Weatherby .300 H&H Magnum."

"Somebody wanted someone dead." He glanced at me. "I'm assuming no print run?"

"All you'd find after all this time would be mine."

"You'd be amazed what we can find." I watched as he drew the bolt-action back and used illuminated magnifying glasses to check the bore and breech. "Amazingly good shape, other than surface rust — like new." He looked at me and then at Lucian. "I'll just do a little maintenance and then we'll fire her into the ballistic jelly to get a slug and then compare the two. You brought the other lead with you?"

Fishing into my pocket, I handed him the

vintage evidence bag. "I did."

Lucian leaned forward, looking at the malformed lead. "Where the hell did you get that?"

"Isaac Bloomfield."

Woody interrupted. "You're telling me you were able to locate a slug from an unsolved hunting accident from 1948?"

Giving Lucian one last look, I glanced back at the DCI director. "We run a tight ship."

He rolled his eyes and began getting the rifle ready to fire. "This might take a little while to get up to speed, have you got something you can go do for twenty minutes?"

Lucian grumbled. "You mean besides standing here and bothering you?"

"That's exactly what I mean."

I took Lucian by the shoulder and steered him along with me. "I've got a water bowl for Dog, so I can take him out for a short walk." I started us for the door. "You'll let me back in before you leave to go fishing, right?"

Preoccupied, he waved me off. "It's going to take another twenty minutes to find a sample round to run through this thing."

"We'll be back." Opening the door, I motioned to Dog who followed me down the hallway and into the entryway.

"Isaac Bloomfield, huh?"

I looked down at the old sheriff as he limped along. "Yep, can you believe he still had the lead from that incident?"

"Nope, I hardly can." He stared at the floor as we walked, pulling his hat down on his head and sheltering his eyes as he stopped at a sofa in the entryway. "I need to sit down."

"Okay." He sat there, batting the cane between his knees as Dog sat beside him. "You ever heard the term *proud flesh*?"

"Sure, my father was a blacksmith — it's the granulated tissue that rapidly fills in the wounds on a horse, but sometimes has to be carved away because it's just fiber and blood vessels without nerves."

"That's one definition. The old-timers used to refer to it when you jump to conclusions in an investigation and rush in with answers before you have any."

"You think that's what I'm doing?"

"I know that's what you're doing, and I thought I trained you to be a better detective than that."

I stared at the tile floor, my hand on the bar of the glass door. "Just because he's my grandfather, Lucian, doesn't mean he gets a free pass."

"Doesn't mean he's guilty either." He pointed one of his truncheon-like fingers at me. "You just keep in mind that every wrong answer you pack into this investigation, you're gonna have to carve back out to get to the truth."

"Proud flesh, huh?" I'd just started to push open the glass door when I saw a black luxury SUV parked behind my truck. I stared at it for a moment and then pushed the door open. I stood there for a few seconds longer as Lucian joined me, and then I started to run over as Dog passed through the door, blindsiding me, tangling my boots, and causing the both of us to fall onto the concrete.

I attempted to scramble back up as the SUV whipped away and out of the parking lot at a high rate of speed. Limping over to my truck, I joined Dog, and we watched as a big Lincoln darted between two other buildings and disappeared.

Resting a hand on the fender of my truck, I could now see that whoever it was had busted out the rear driver's-side window and had left the driver's door hanging open.

Brushing the grit from my jeans, I glanced back to see Lucian standing at the front of the truck with his pistol drawn again. "Damn, this is a rough town."

10

"I blame the political element myself."
Woody turned back to me after studying
the new window that the technician had attached and handed me the bill. "I would
say that this is the classic example of a crash
and grab, my friend."

Handing the tech my credit card, I
watched as he stuck it into the machine,
running me out a receipt that I signed and
gave back to him. "They were driving a
vehicle that cost as much as my house."

"Thrill seekers."

"Woody . . ."

He used a broom and dustpan to sweep
up the evidence and then straightened to
look at me as the glass repairman hopped
in his vehicle and backed away. "Hell, Walt,
I don't know. Did you have anything valuable in here?"

"Other than that rifle you're testing inside?
Nope."

"Why would anyone want to go to that kind of trouble to steal that rifle?"

"I don't know, but there was some strange guy in the alley behind Cady's carriage house last night, nosing around, and that's got me wondering."

He leaned against my abused truck. "About what?"

"It just seems odd that all these things have coincided with my finding that rifle up the mountain — somebody shooting Jules Beldon, somebody breaking into my truck . . . I don't know, but it just seems strange."

"So, you're thinking that all these things are connected somehow?"

"Maybe."

"So . . . How?"

I stared at him. "Well, Woody, if I knew that I wouldn't be standing here discussing it with you while you clean up the parking lot, now would I?"

He walked past me and back toward his office. "Are you always this grumpy during a case?"

"Generally."

He called back over his shoulder as Dog and I trailed along behind. "Then I'm glad I'm only responsible for a portion of the investigation." He pulled open the door, and we followed him in where he dumped the broken glass into a garbage can beside the vacant receptionist desk. "So, do you want the good news first or the bad?"

"There's good news?"

He continued toward the lab. "We have an absolute match on the bullet that killed Bill Sutherland."

I caught the door, and we continued following him to the counter where Lucian sat in a chair, still batting his cane between his knees. "Let me guess, the bad news is that it's my grandfather's rifle?"

"You got it." He picked up the rifle, handed it to me, and then pushed his fishing hat back on his head. "Perfect match, the lands and grooves are exact. That's what your grandfather gets for having a grandson for a sheriff who keeps the longest evidence custody chain ever seen in the history of law enforcement."

I took the rifle in my hands, flipping off the leather lens caps and studying it.

Lucian's voice carried to me. "Now, I don't have to remind you again that just because this is the weapon that killed Big Bill Sutherland, it doesn't mean that your ol' granddad pulled the trigger."

He continued bouncing the cane between his hands. "It also doesn't mean that it wasn't."

Woody stood there for a moment more and then backed away. "I've got some things I need to attend to in my office before I head out, but I'll stop back by here and see you fellows in a few minutes."

We both watched him go, at which point the old sheriff sat back in his chair and laid his dark eyes on me. "So, what are you planning on doing now?"

"Continuing with the investigation."

He nodded, allowing for a little silence between us. "Walt, how long has the man been dead?"

"A half century, at least."

"Do you mind if I ask what the hell is to be gained by going on with all this?"

"The truth."

"You don't think the truth might be better served by moving on?"

"You're not telling me how to do my job, are you Lucian?"

He breathed a laugh. "I just don't see what good is going to come of all this other than some vague objective. I mean, let's go way out on a limb and say your grandfather's guilty. Who's going to benefit from this? You, your daughter, your granddaughter?"

"It's not a question of benefit — it's a

question of truth."

He shook his head. "There you go again with that word. You're never going to know the truth . . . You may find out who did it, but this long afterward you're never going to know why."

"Well, suppose you tell me. You were there."

He said nothing and walked toward the door.

"You don't seem to have much faith in me as an investigator."

He stopped but didn't turn. "Oh, I've got all the faith in the world in you as an investigator, but let me tell you something, I also know the limitations of what an investigation can resolve — and more importantly, the things it can't." He paused for a moment and then added. "I think you're ghost hunting, young son, and I just don't want you to be too disappointed when you don't find what it is you're looking for."

"And what's that?"

"Peace." He finally turned and pointed the cane at me like a cannon. "Peace with a man who's been dead for more than half a century."

"You got me in trouble with my boss."

"How?"

The greatest legal mind of our time sat back in her cushy leather chair, tapping a pen on her blotter and glaring at me. "He wants to meet with you." She glanced at her wrist to the watch that had belonged to her mother. "Here in about seven minutes."

"Okay, let's go meet with him."

"He doesn't want me there."

"Okay."

"No, that's not okay, because I want to be there."

Sitting in one of her guest chairs, I looked out at the incredible view of the state capitol. It was sometimes hard for me to remember that the place actually existed; it and the surrounding grounds usually were something of an abstract up in the northern part of the state. My daughter and grand-daughter's apartment was real enough, but the state government would always be something of a fiction for me.

"It actually sounds like I'm in trouble with you, which worries me a lot more."

She slapped the pen on the blotter and pulled her coppery-red hair behind one ear. "I am the assistant attorney general of the State of Wyoming, and I feel like I've been put in a playpen while the grown-ups are in the other room talking."

"Would you like me to wear a wire?"

"Not funny." The gray eyes came up to mine. "The state senate is convening a budget and audit committee to call Tom Rondelle, the head of trustees of the PWMTF, on the carpet, and I'm betting that he'll be in on this little meeting in Joe Meyer's office."

"Doing what?"

"Circling the wagons, I'm sure."

I pointed at the complex phone on her otherwise clean and clear desk, the clean and clear something I aspired to but seemed doomed to never achieve. "Call him, and I'll ask him if you can sit in."

"That's not the point, I shouldn't have to have my father ask if I can be a part of a meeting."

"It probably has to do with this Bill Sutherland thing and doesn't have anything to do with you."

"It's our family, so it has to do with me."

"How about you go to the meeting, and I'll stay here."

"Do you know how hard I've had to work to escape your shadow in this state? I should've stayed in Pennsylvania where no one has ever heard of you."

"Please don't say that, and please tell me that you're not really mad?"

She turned her chair away from me.

"Slightly miffed."

"I'll take you out to dinner."

The chair shifted back toward me. "Where?"

"Little Bear Inn." I had raised the stakes by mentioning the venerable roadhouse just north of town that had started out as a stage stop on the way to the Black Hills in 1875. Evolving into a saloon, gambling hall, and restaurant, there were many legends surrounding the place, including how many times the floor had collapsed from overly enthusiastic cowboys riding their horses from the bar to the hundred-foot tunnel.

"I want the filet with the gorgonzola cream sauce."

I stood. "Done."

"And the loaded Little Bear potato."

I moved toward the door. "Right."

"And the red-wine salad."

"Got it." I closed the door quickly, before I went broke, and wondered if I'd just gotten played. I glanced at Cady's secretary. "Maureen, if you were the general of all the attorneys in Wyoming, where would you be?"

The thick-set woman with the stylish gray hair pointed with a pencil. "In the war room, to your right — end of the hall."

"Thanks."

Making a quick getaway, I paused at Joe Meyer's door and glanced at two gray monoliths seated in office chairs as one of them looked at the other. "Bob, I think he thought he could come down here, to our town, and then get away scot-free without seeing us."

The other monolith nodded, studying me with a taciturn expression. "I believe you're right, Bob."

The Bobs were a legend in the state. Bob Delude and Robert Hall had started out as regular highway patrolmen, but through years of outstanding service had risen to be the point of . . . well, I wasn't sure, but they were always lingering around when Joe Meyer was on the job. "Haven't you two retired yet?"

Bob Delude stood, stretching, and glancing at his namesake. "Look who's talking."

Bob Hall also stood, I guess figuring it was going to take the two of them to get me to go in Joe's office. "No joke."

I examined their matching suits. "Did you guys call each other this morning?"

"There was a sale at the tall and big men's shop." Bob stuck out a hand. "Besides, he's wearing a blue tie and mine is green."

I shook the hand. "You're color-blind, Bob."

The other Bob nodded as I shook his hand. "He's right, Bob."

Bob lifted his tie, examining it. "Well, what color is it?"

"Blue. It's just a darker shade."

Bob scratched at a small stain on his tie. "Well, that accounts for something, don't you think?"

The other Bob looked over my shoulder. "Hey, we heard Lucian was tagging along with you?"

"He is, but I left him off over at the capitol building so he could go in there and codger around with some of his state legislature buddies."

Bob dropped his tie. "Talk about in need of retirement . . ."

I gestured toward the closed door of Joe Meyer's office. "What am I walking into here, guys?"

Bob leaned in. "Heck if we know, but that jaybird Rondelle is in there."

The other Bob closed a giant hand around the doorknob. "Yell, if you need us."

I saluted. "Will do."

He turned the knob, and I stepped in, listening as he closed it behind me. Joe appeared to be in conference with a movie-star handsome, silver-haired man in a dark suit. Breaking things off, they both turned to look at me. "Walt, I'd like you to meet Tom Rondelle."

The suntanned man remained seated but grinned a practiced smile and extended his hand. "Nice to meet you, Sheriff."

I shook. "Nice to meet you too."

"Hey, is Mike Regis being any help to you up there?"

I smiled and nodded. "Thank you for that, and yes, he's a fine young man, but I'm afraid he's not getting much fishing in."

Rondelle glanced back at Joe. "Well, that depends on what you're fishing for."

Meyer gestured toward the other chair that looked remarkably like the one I'd just vacated in Cady's office. "Have a seat, Walt."

I did and then glanced between the two men and said nothing.

Joe leaned back in his chair. "We were, um . . . just wondering how this investigation into the death of Bill Sutherland is going?"

"Murder."

The attorney general laced his fingers over his chest. "Murder, we're sure of that?"

"We are. I just came from the DCI lab and Woody Woodson, who confirmed that the weapon I found is the one that killed the state accountant back in '48."

The two shared a look as Meyer turned back to me. "And the owner of that weapon?"

"At the moment, it would appear to be my grandfather."

Rondelle looked at me, his eyes wide. "Oh, my."

I cleared my throat and continued. "There were two other men from down here in Cheyenne involved, Harold Grafton, the chief clerk, and Bob Carr, the state treasurer — one of whom was shot and killed up in Gillette and the other disappeared."

"Perhaps, but what kind of time frame are we talking here, Walt? You can't connect these two random incidents with —"

"One three weeks later and the other within a year."

They both grew silent.

Rondelle breathed a sigh and then stood, walking over to the floor-to-ceiling window and looking down at the capitol lawn with his hands in his pockets. "Sheriff, I'm not so sure how aware you are of current goings-on within the office of the state . . ."

"You mean the firing of Linda Roripaugh, the CEO of the Permanent Wyoming Mineral Trust Fund?"

He turned to look at me. "I mean exactly

that. Now, I'm not going to bore you with the details of why it is that Ms. Roripaugh was dismissed —"

"Please, feel free to do so." He stared at me. "From what I'm to understand she's been doing a remarkable job for the last five years."

"Well, we can debate that at another time, but in the meantime, she was an at-will employee, and it was the board's prerogative to fire her."

"Why?"

He coughed a laugh. "I'm not going to go into an in-depth analysis of everything she did right and everything she did wrong —"

"Is that the stance you're going to take with the senate budget and audit committee?"

"And what do you know about that?"

I shrugged, keeping my confidential sources protected. "Seems to be common knowledge down around these parts."

"Sheriff, I'm not sure if you're aware, but we're kind of in a hot seat with this situation and calling more attention to it isn't going to do this state any good."

"The state or the state treasurer's office?"

His face became more somber, and I had to wonder if it was a look he practiced in a mirror. "I'm not telling you what to do here,

Sheriff —"

"That's good, because that's not something I take to very well."

"I'm not saying drop the investigation —"

"I have no intention of it."

"But I can't help but wonder if all parties might be better served if you were to perhaps take this investigation up again in, say, six months?"

"Six months."

He smiled. "Just until after the next election."

"I'm not concerned with elections."

"Really? I thought that's how you got your job, Sheriff."

"Is that a threat, Mr. Rondelle?"

He took a step toward me. "What I'm saying is that it's easy enough to convene a grand jury and indict a sheriff as a cause of removal, especially if said sheriff's grandfather happened to be a murderer. A sheriff such as that could also be removed for being under investigation for a criminal offense, malfeasance, or incompetence in office, such as trying to cloud a murder investigation because of personal interests."

I said nothing.

"You get my meaning?"

I stood and walked past him to the glass wall where it was quiet for a while.

"Am I boring you, Sheriff?"

"Nope, I'm just wondering if I threw you through this glass how far out you'd go before you fell the four stories to the sidewalk down there."

There was a long pause. "I'm sure that would help your situation immensely."

I listened as he walked across the room and through the door, now safely out of danger. Turning, I stared at my friend, the attorney general. "What the hell was that, Joe?"

He shook his head. "I had a foolish thought that you two could talk this out."

"Well, in a way we did."

"I don't think having you throw him through a window was what I had in mind."

"Whose side are you on?"

"Yours, of course. Up until now he hasn't been that big of a horse's ass, but at least now we know what we're dealing with." He came around his desk and sat on the corner. "Although I have to admit that having your grandfather become suspect number one doesn't do our cause a great deal of good."

"And what is our *cause,* here, Joe?"

"Our duty."

"Then I'm doing it."

"Well, things get a little complicated down here in the big city, Walt."

"Tell me about it . . . Somebody was looking around my truck parked behind your carriage house last night and then somebody broke into said truck, as near as I can tell, to get that rifle we've been talking about." I crossed toward the door through which Rondelle had made his dramatic exit to safety. "You can't tell me this is just a case of avoiding bad publicity."

"Oh, it could easily be. That term, *at-will employee,* covers a lot of us part-timers down here in Cheyenne and when you start talking about billions of dollars that fund the workings of the state, then people start getting nervous and possibly start looking for someone else to take the blame."

"Me?"

"It's all a shell game for these people, Walt, and if they can get the media looking under your shell rather than theirs, then the heat is off."

"What do you know about this Mike Regis he sent up to babysit me?"

"Met him at a fundraiser over at the governor's mansion. Seems like an okay guy, but he got his personals in a ringer when he was caught partnering up with some rich asshole in Jackson and another individual, Max Sidorov, who is some kind of Russian spook."

"Is Regis CIA or something?"

"No, he's more on the private protection side of things. You know, if rich people need tech muscle . . ."

"So, a mercenary."

"They don't like that term, but yeah."

"And he's on Rondelle's payroll."

"For now."

"Meaning?"

"If Tom can't pay him, I'm sure he'll just go on to the next-highest bidder."

"So, what did Regis and this Sidorov get themselves involved in?"

"Setting up Black Swan, a spy school to infiltrate political competitors for their clients."

I made a face in an attempt to express my incredulity. "In Wyoming?"

"Starting there but then going nation-wide."

"Charming. So, do you think he's been sent to me to keep an eye on the investigation?"

"Possibly, but it's also possible that he'd just as soon get some distance from Rondelle and his bunch."

"Rats on a sinking ship?"

"You want a friend in politics . . ."

I nodded and then sighed, mostly to myself. "Speaking of which, I need to go walk my dog." I slipped my hat down tight and turned to look at him. "I'm going to head back north tomorrow and kick this Regis guy to the curb."

"You could." I watched as Joe returned to his seat and settled behind his desk. "You know what they say — keep your friends close and your enemies closer."

"Hey, Joe?"

"Yep?"

"You still have that stainless .41 Mag Mountain Gun in your desk?"

His eyes dropped to the top drawer, center. "Sure do, and I've also got the Bobs out there if you need them."

"No, but you'll all keep an eye out for my daughter and granddaughter?"

"With our lives." As I was about to go through the door, he called after me. "Who is it that said that about enemies anyway?"

"Sun Tzu."

He mumbled as I turned the knob. "I knew you'd know."

"So, is there any reason you didn't tell me you were acquainted with the CEO of the Permanent Wyoming Mineral Trust Fund?"

Cady assisted Lola with her Little Bear Inn sippy cup. She was seated in Lucian's lap as the old sheriff sipped bourbon from his own sippy cup, of sorts. "I didn't think it mattered until your case started getting wrapped up in the PWMTF fiasco."

"Yep." I sipped my own beer. "I'm still not sure how the two are tangentially connected. Joe seems to think the trustees of the PWMTF or at least the head, this Tom Rondelle, is attempting to use me as a distraction." Lucian appeared to be ignoring us by playing with my granddaughter. "Especially since it's looking more and more like your great-grandfather killed Bill Sutherland and possibly two other men, Grafton and Carr."

Lucian, now holding the straw for Lola's sippy cup, shifted his eyes to mine. "Excuse me?"

"The DCI lab confirmed that the rifle in question was indeed the one that killed the state accountant back in '48."

Cady sat back in her chair and then glanced at the old sheriff and then me. "There must've been a good reason."

I placed my beer on the table and turned it in the circle of condensation. "And why is that?"

"Because he's your grandfather and my great-grandfather."

"You never met him."

Her eyes pivoted to the old sheriff. "What

was he like, Uncle Lucian?"

"Tough." He sat his glass down out of Lola's reach. "Old-school tough. He was fair, but you didn't cross him — he was the best friend you could ever have, and he could also be your worst enemy."

I sipped my beer. "Sounds like the kind of man who could commit a murder like the ones we're discussing."

Cady picked up her own drink, a huckleberry martini. "I've never seen you so adamant that a suspect was guilty. I mean you usually approach every investigation with the idea that the suspect is innocent until proven guilty, but not this one."

"Everybody's guilty of something, don't you know that, Cady?" A tall woman with dark hair and glasses was now standing by our table. She extended a hand to me. "Sheriff?"

I sidled out of my seat and stood. "Linda Roripaugh, I presume?"

"Nice to meet you."

I gestured toward Lucian, who still held a drowsy Lola but waved. "Lucian Connally, the previous sheriff of Absaroka County, and my granddaughter . . ."

"The future sheriff of Absaroka County."

I pulled out a chair for the woman and reseated myself. "Well, we're hoping for bet-

303

ter than that for her."

Roripaugh sat, glancing around the table. "Sounds like I've missed the best part of this conversation."

"Not necessarily." Cady laughed. "My father wants to dig up his grandfather and hang him."

"Remind me to never come to a Longmire family reunion." She looked at the waiter, who had suddenly appeared, and pointed to Cady's drink. "I'll have one of those." She then turned back to me, and I was surprised by how fresh and happy she looked for a person under siege. "So, you think your grandfather was a killer?"

Lucian coughed a laugh.

I glared at him and then looked at her. "I know he was a killer; I just don't know if he did these particular killings."

"Killings, as in plural?" Roripaugh smiled. "I'm sorry if I'm sticking my nose in where it doesn't belong, but Cady told me a few details, and I can't help but be curious."

I nodded. "Carole Wiltse, the state treasurer, is a friend of yours?"

"Yes, I know Carole very well."

"And did you know that Bill Sutherland was her great-uncle?"

"I did."

"How does she feel about all this?"

304

"Very curious, but she has a lot on her plate right now."

I nodded some more and then reached over, taking Lola from Lucian and stowing her on my lap, slung in my arm where she collapsed against my chest and fell soundly asleep. "I met Tom Rondelle today."

The waiter arrived, and I watched as Roripaugh took a sip in order to give herself time before responding. "He's a piece of work, don't you think?"

"We didn't exactly hit it off."

"I bet not. He's filed a suit against the legislature if they try and go on with the investigation. Do you mind if I ask where you met Rondelle?"

I glanced at Cady and then shrugged. "In Joe Meyer's office."

"The attorney general."

"He's a family friend."

"I would imagine he was feeling out Meyer to see where he stood with all this. If you don't mind me asking, where does he stand with all this?"

"Without a leg to stand on."

"Did Rondelle threaten you?"

"He tried, but then I offered to toss him through the fourth-floor window."

"Threats are his go-to in communicating." Roripaugh studied her drink. "This investigation through the legislature is supposedly going to depose the trustees, but they're going to slap Rondelle with a subpoena."

"Can I apply to serve it?"

"Maybe there'll be a lottery." She took another sip of her drink. "He's pleading his case in the paper tomorrow morning, bemoaning the fact that it's going to cost the taxpayers a hundred thousand for the special investigation."

"Think that'll fly?"

"Depends on who the legislature taps as the special adjudicator."

"Any idea who?"

"Some retired federal judge out of California who has provided service to the state before —"

"Scott Snowden?"

"That's him — you know him?"

I glanced at Lucian, who conceded. "He's a good man."

Her eyes shifted to mine. "Well, don't tell anybody or they'll drop him, thinking there's some tie between the two of you."

I adjusted my granddaughter in my lap as she drooled on my shirt. "So, why did Rondelle go after you?"

"Politics, pure and simple. He wants to buy votes with these thousand-dollar checks he wants to hand out."

"And you said no."

"As the executive director of the Permanent Fund, my job is to make sure the investment earnings outpace withdrawals, and for the first time in its history, they weren't going to."

I picked up my beer and took a sip. "But Rondelle still wanted to hand out the money?"

"Yes. Now, on the surface, the fund would survive the downturn easily, but I'm afraid it sets a precedent where the fund could be used for political purposes, and the danger of that should be pretty obvious to everyone."

"What are you going to do?"

"Walk away."

I studied her. "Really?"

"I'll cooperate with the legislature and the special investigation, but I've had enough politics to last me a lifetime. Do you know what a private firm would give to have a 15.2 percent rate of return in challenging financial times such as these?"

"I've got a feeling you're going to find out."

"You'd be right." Roripaugh smiled again, glancing at all of us in turn and then picking up one of the menus. "Should we order something to eat? I'm famished."

■ ■ ■ ■

"What do you mean, gone?"

"Keep your voice quieter, please. Lucian doesn't know about Vic." I peered down at the old sheriff who was climbing the stairs below us. "I went over to her house just to check on her after she'd called in a few personal days and everything in her house was gone."

Cady followed along as I carried Lola up the steps to her apartment. "Everything?"

"Furniture . . . everything."

"Holy crap."

"Keep your voice down . . . Yep, that's what I thought. I mean she could've just said no."

"You really think she's gone?"

I stopped at the deck and waited for Cady to catch up. "I don't know what to think. She dropped her unit off with the mechanic in town to get something done, but maybe that was just a way of getting rid of it without telling me."

Reaching the top, she held on to both railings and looked at me. She whispered, "Victoria Moretti avoiding a confrontation?"

"Doesn't sound right, does it?"

"No." She came the rest of the way up

and looked out at the city of Cheyenne. She spoke under her breath. "Maybe she just needs time to get herself together; it's a big step."

"I thought that's where we were headed all this time."

"Maybe she just put all her stuff in storage. Did you guys talk about living arrangements?"

"No."

"So long as we still get a guest room."

"We didn't talk about anything. As I recall, the only thing we talked about was her dissatisfaction with how I'd asked her to marry me."

She reached out and took Peanut as I opened the door and held it, enabling her to carry Lola inside. "Oh, boy."

"Yep." I waited for Lucian as he paused at the landing below. "Are you going to make it, old man?"

He swiped off his hat and then dabbed the sweat from his face with the back of a sleeve. "You two can have this night owl horseshit — I'd just as soon head back to a civilized town where they keep regular hours."

"C'mon the rest of the way, and I'll tuck you in."

"How 'bout you kiss my ass instead?"

I left him there, opened the door, and followed Cady through the living room, where the phone machine was blinking, and then into Lola's room where she carefully lay her in the crib, undressing her and pulling the blankets up around her tiny chin. Then Cady leaned over and gave her a kiss.

She led the way back into the kitchen where we always sat and, as I passed, I snagged a couple of Rainiers from the fridge. "Frosty beverage?"

She sat on the other side of the kitchen table and shook her head. "No, thanks."

Breathing heavily, Lucian appeared in the doorway. "You want a beer, High Sheriff?"

"Piss on the both of you, abandoning an old man like that."

"I pity what you meet more than I do you."

"The hell with both of you, I'm going to bed."

I returned one beer to the refrigerator but sat with the other, pulling the tab and taking a drink because I needed it. We listened as Lucian cursed a bit and then settled into the sofa and in no time at all was snoring.

Cady turned to me. "He's getting old."

"Getting?"

She chuckled. "What do you think of Linda?"

"Smart."

"She's that. It's a shame she's bailing — she's very good at her job."

"I sometimes get the feeling that the best and brightest aren't going into politics these days."

"Including me?"

"You're an appointee, punk."

"Maybe more."

I set the beer down. "What's that supposed to mean?"

"Joe called me into his office after you left this afternoon."

"Yep?"

"He says he's going to retire after this upcoming election."

"And?"

"Wally Fisk's replacement, Robert Lang, asked Joe about me, wanting to know if I'd want the job."

I stared at her. "The attorney general of the State of Wyoming?"

She smirked as she shucked off her shoes, letting them fall to the floor as she massaged her feet. "Think you could stand me as a boss?"

"My world is falling apart around me."

"Oh, c'mon — would it be that bad?"

"My daughter as the highest-ranked law-enforcement officer in the state?" I shook

311

my head. "You're moving up fast."

"Scare you? Because it scares the shit out of me."

"Not really." I moved the Rainier to the side and reached for her hands. "You'd be great — I just wish your mother was here to see it."

She took my hand, resting her chin on an arm and studying me. "There's only one catch. Joe says he offered you an appointment as a special investigator for the attorney general's office and if I take the nomination, you'd be dropped from consideration."

I thought about it and then made a face. "Fisk offered me that job more than a year ago, before Governor Hemmings took office — you don't think they've figured out that I don't want the job?"

"Maybe they were hoping you'd end up taking it."

"Well, I'm not." I patted her arms and she sat back up, and I grabbed my beer. "Saizarbitoria seems to have the backing of the Basque mafia in-county, so I may be out of a job completely in six months."

"I can't say I'm disappointed." Her eyes stayed steady on me. "What would you do with your time?"

"You'll laugh."

"Probably."

"I'm thinking of fixing up the ancestral manse."

She leaned back in her chair in disbelief. "Up on Buffalo Creek? Great-grandpa Lloyd's place?"

"Yep."

"You're kidding."

"No, I went out there to check on things since the lease had come due and Tom and his family have moved to Montana."

"Who's there now?"

"No one."

"You've always hated that place."

"It's growing on me." I sipped my beer. "There's no one there, and the place is going to seed. I just feel . . . I feel like I should be taking care of it."

"For us?"

"Sure, if you want it."

"It's out in the middle of nowhere!" I couldn't help but smile, something she noticed. "What?"

"I told Henry that you probably weren't going to want it."

"Dad, I haven't been out there since I was in college. I'm not sure I even remember it all that well." She shook her head. "You're never going to get anyone to work on it."

"Then I'll do it myself."

313

She stood, still shaking her head as she came around and placed her chin on the crown of my head and hugged my shoulders from behind. "Mr. Fixer-upper . . ."

I listened as she exited the kitchen and dared to hit the button on the answering machine, but Lucian continued snoring. I sipped my beer and listened to the voice murmur on the other end, not quite making out who it was or what they were saying. After a moment, Cady reappeared with the phone in her hand and a more than shaken look on her face. "Dad, do you know a woman by the name of Nina Yadav?"

"Yep, she's a state archivist who is down here and helps me out sometimes. I just met with her yesterday."

She held the phone out to me. "You better call the Cheyenne Police Department back — they say there's been an accident."

11

The CPD was only a handful of blocks south and from there I was directed to an address on Randall Avenue near the air force base. I was there in ten minutes and was met by DCI Investigator Louis Price, who held me on the porch. "She's alive, but just barely. Evidently there was a broken valve on the gas inlet of the stove — one of those corrugated flex tubes that was a couple of decades old and just cracked and fell apart enough to start leaking."

"Where is she?"

Price was tall and lean with ears that held close to his close-cropped hair, giving him the appearance of a Doberman pinscher in a gray suit jacket. "Cheyenne Regional Medical Center."

"Who found her?"

"The mailman — at least he's the one who reported it." We watched as the Cheyenne Fire Department, the DCI techs, and a media liaison officer talked to a television crew in the street, their bright lights illuminating the front of the tiny house. "Came up on the porch this morning and smelled gas; probably saved her life."

I looked at Price. "That means she was in there all night."

He shrugged. "I know what you're thinking, but it depends on when the leak started and how concentrated the gas was." He glanced at the little bungalow. "These old military houses weren't built all that tight. I'm just glad the gas didn't get to a pilot light or a switch and take the whole block with it." He gazed to the east. "Her mother and father are with her over at CRMC."

"How did you know to contact me?"

"The legendary Walt Longmire? We saw you on the security cameras at the archive. You kind of stand out, Sheriff. Besides, Woody said you were in town." He studied me. "Mind if I ask what you were doing there?"

"Discussing a seventy-year-old murder."

He pulled out a notebook and plucked a pen from the inside of his jacket. "This is just for my memory." He clicked the pen. "What, exactly, were you discussing?"

"There was a man killed, a Bill Sutherland, in what was supposed to be a hunting

316

accident back in 1948; he was the state accountant, and it appears there were two other men in the party who were either killed or had disappeared within a year of the incident."

He scribbled away. "Hmm . . . Not exactly a recent crime."

"No, but we've had a few incidents where a man was shot up on the Powder River while attempting to do a little investigating for me."

"What kind of investigating?"

"Exhuming a body."

"Whose?"

"The state accountant I mentioned, who is actually the great-uncle of Carole Wiltse, the state treasurer."

"And?"

"He was cremated." I shook my head. "Someone also broke into my truck earlier today, I'm assuming to get the rifle that did the deed."

He nodded. "Woody mentioned that."

"There are all these things, but it's possible they have nothing to do with this investigation, at least I partially believed, until this." I leaned my back against a post and studied the clapboard surface of the tiny house Nina Yadav was fixing up. "You're sure this was an accident?"

"I'm never sure of anything until Woody tells me I am."

I shook my head, walked to the edge of the porch, and leaned on a post there. "Just for the record, there's nothing we discussed that could possibly be important enough for anyone to attempt to kill this young woman, right?"

"Nothing we know of." He clicked the pen and returned it and the pad to his jacket. "Woody's guys are going over it, but that's all we've got right now — I was just curious as to why you were down here and at the archives."

"That's it." I pushed my hat back on my head. "Can I see her?"

"Probably not tonight, she was dizzy, throwing up, and had breathing difficulties . . . They had a heart monitor on her, but I'm going over to the hospital first thing in the morning, if you'd like to meet me there?"

"Sure, but there's something you're not telling me, Detective."

He broke into a wide smile. "They said you were good . . ." He walked toward me and then stepped off the porch and onto the sidewalk before pulling out a pack of cigarettes. He nudged one out. "Okay, she had a bump on the back of her head, but we're thinking she fell." He pulled out a Zippo from the other pocket, lit the cigarette, and nodded toward the television crew on the driveway who were interviewing one of the firemen. "You want to go be a star?"

"Not really."

"Yeah, me neither." He started off but then stopped. "Let's let the girl sleep. What do you say? Nine?"

"I'll be there."

He stood still for a moment more, smoking and shaking his head. "Fireman — the only job where you wake up to go home."

I watched as he walked out to where the TV light shined and his thirty seconds of fame began.

"So, you fell."

Unconsciously raising a hand to the back of her head, she felt the bandages there. "I guess so." She was not a particularly large woman, but lying there in the hospital bed, she seemed almost childlike. "Is there something wrong?"

The DCI man cleared his throat. "The patrolman that found you said you were lying on your stomach. Now, it's possible that you fell backward and hit your head and then rolled over, or it was something else."

She looked confused. "Such as?"

"How about you go through what happened when you got home after working with the sheriff here?"

She thought about it. "I rode my bike home and went in . . ."

"Was the house locked?"

She thought about it. "I don't remember."

"Not uncommon, go ahead?"

"I remember putting the leftovers in the refrigerator and then feeding the cat . . ."

"Yes?"

"I don't remember anything after that."

I interrupted with a glance to Price. "Where was she found?"

"In the kitchen."

My eyes went back to her. "Where do you feed the cat?"

"In the hallway — that way he can get to it from anywhere in the house." She looked even more confused. "Is the cat all right?"

Price nodded. "Yeah, your parents took him last night."

"So?"

I reached out and touched her arm. "It's possible you don't remember going from the hallway to the kitchen, but you were found face down in another room with damage done to the back of your head. So, the question becomes did you go back in the kitchen, fall backward, and roll over, or did someone strike you from behind and then drag you into the kitchen where the gas leak could finish you off."

"The file . . ."

"Excuse me?"

"The file I prepared for you, was it on the kitchen counter?"

I glanced at the investigator as he stood, moved toward the door, pulled a cell phone from his blazer, and began dialing. I sat forward and patted her arm. "How are you feeling?"

"Horrible." She shook her head, immediately regretting the action. "Do you really think that somebody might've done this to me?"

"We're just not discounting anything at this point."

Price returned. "There was no file on the counter or anywhere in the house."

"There's no way you could've left it at the archives or somewhere else?"

She stared at her lap, her hands folded there. "No, I wanted to make sure I had it when you came by the next morning, and since it's a communal work area, I didn't want to leave it lying around."

We watched as Price turned and disappeared out the door with his phone again.

"What's going on?"

"I'd imagine they're going to treat your house like a crime scene."

"This is so stupid . . . I mean, I can easily look everything up again and give it to you."

"Evidently they wanted the information now." I studied the closed door where the investigator had gone out into the hall. "Is there anything I need to know?"

She took a breath and then her eyes settled on me. "A few things, but I'd just as soon you see what I found. I'm sure they'll let me out of here later today, and then I can go over to work and reprint those things. It's so silly, because I can just reprint everything."

I stood, looking down at her. "Not if you were dead."

After speaking with the physician in charge, who assured us that if Nina's condition continued to improve they would likely discharge her in the afternoon, Price and I walked out and into the parking lot where two gray effigies stood beside a black Yukon with the door hanging open, Lucian Connally sitting in the back.

"You know these guys?"

"I'm afraid I do."

I raised a hand. "Bob." I waved at the other one. "Bob."

The one large man gave a side look to the other large man as they both glanced in at Lucian and then back at us. "Bob, I think our snitch has helped us find our man."

"I think you're right, Bob."

Investigator Price, not wanting to be any part of the vaudeville act, waved at the two of them and ambled off toward his own unit, leaving me to face the Bobs. "What do you two want now?"

"You've got a lunch date."

"I do?" I pulled up between them. "With whom?"

"State treasurer, Carole Wiltse."

"I guess I'll let her pick up the tab then." I nodded and climbed in beside Lucian. "Where's my dog, old man?"

"Taking a walk with your daughter and eating the better part of a hot dog that he got from your granddaughter, the last time I saw him before these two ruffians picked me up off the street like a common felon."

Bob settled himself in behind the steering wheel as Bob, in the passenger seat, turned to look at us as he buckled his seat belt. "I believe you offered to accompany us, Sheriff."

Ignoring him, Lucian glanced out the side window. "Abduction, that's what it was."

Watching as we jetted through the back-

323

streets of the state capital, I settled in. "Did you guys get coffee in him, because if you didn't, he gets like this."

He turned to look at me. "Get like what, damn it?"

Only a few blocks from the state plaza, we pulled up in front of a massive brick Victorian with turrets and glowing windows and intricate, although dead, flower beds stacked against the wraparound porch. The painted surfaces had seen better days, but you could see where the windows were masked and that there were painting supplies and drop cloths scattered across the worn surface of the porch and steps.

I climbed out and circled around as Lucian opened his door and the Bobs got out. "This an episode of *Better Homes and Gardens*?"

Bob sidled along beside me and admired the place. "Three months ago it looked like the house from *The Munsters* — she's done a lot of work on it."

As if the mention of her name were a conjuring, a tall woman with silver hair pulled back in a ponytail appeared on the porch in an oversize flannel shirt and paint-covered jeans and a pair of work boots. "I'm charging a dollar a minute to watch the work."

The other Bob joined his compatriot on the sidewalk with us. "What work? It doesn't look to me as if there's anything going on."

She tossed a thumb over her shoulder. "The painting crew is having lunch on the picnic table in the backyard, Bob Delude." She counted us. "I was only counting on one of you — how many are staying for lunch?"

We all looked at one another.

She made a sweeping gesture, inviting us all in before pulling out a phone and texting on it. "C'mon, I'll feed all of you."

Knowing a good thing when I heard one, I was the first to go up, holding the wrought-iron gate for Lucian as he followed, the Bobs bringing up the rear.

Avoiding the painting supplies, I followed her into the entryway where I could see the mahogany trim was being stripped and refinished. "This is a lot of work you're doing here."

She nodded toward the walls where the paper had been partially pulled off. "My husband thinks I'm crazy."

"And where is he?"

"At our ranch in Fremont County." She approached a swinging door with a porthole in it and turned to look at me. "Bill Wiltse."

I stopped in my tracks. "The sheriff?"

"Yes, Walt Longmire, the sheriff."

I scrubbed a hand across my face in an attempt to hide the embarrassment there. "Have we met?"

She smiled. "Only once, but we weren't properly introduced." She held out a hand. "Carole Wiltse."

We both turned as Lucian joined us. "Howdy, Carole."

As they shook hands, I looked at him. "You knew who she was?"

"Hell, yes."

"And it didn't occur to you to tell me?"

Walking between us, he pushed open the door and went into what I assumed was the kitchen. "If I took the time to tell you everything I know and you don't, we wouldn't get much of anything else done, now would we?"

I glanced back as the two megaliths joined us. "And you know the Bobs?"

"Everybody knows the Bobs." She patted one of them on the arm like he was a wayward child and then followed Lucian into the kitchen, or what had been a kitchen before someone had torn everything out of the place you could cook or store food in. "You and Bill moving to Cheyenne?"

She looked around, and I had to admit that the abounding energy was a little daunting. "Only part time. I came over to this side of town for a meeting of the Wyoming CattleWomen and saw the FOR SALE sign on this place . . ."

"Bill didn't try to stop you?"

She raised a Dutch eyebrow. "He knows better . . ."

"Quite an endeavor."

She waved a hand. "The kids are gone, the ranch is fine, and he's just happy I'm not pestering the shit out of him." She laughed. "C'mon, the hutch over here is still serviceable."

We all crowded into the corner and watched as she went through another door and then reappeared with bags of sandwiches and Arnold Palmers for the troops. "I hope you don't mind — as you can see, the kitchen is out of action, but the sandwiches are from the deli on the corner." She set the bags on the table and began pulling out sandwiches. "I've got Reubens, pastrami and cheese, and an Italian cold cut. Leftovers from feeding the painters."

I slipped out and moved over to a small portion of the counter that still stood and listened as Lucian and the Bobs entered into a conversation about the relative merits of assorted golfers as they ate their sandwiches and drank their Arnold Palmers.

"Not hungry?"

Carole placed a Reuben between us and handed me a drink in a plastic cup, complete with straw. "Oh, a little, I guess."

She unwrapped the sandwich and took half for herself, pushing the other toward me. "Something killing your appetite?"

"Maybe."

"How goes the investigation?"

"It's taken some twists and turns."

She took a bite and chewed, studying me. "Such as?"

"It's looking more and more like your great-uncle might've been killed by my grandfather."

She studied me for a while longer, finally pulling a short stepladder over and sitting on it. "Well, this is awkward."

"Yep."

"No, I mean I was thinking of hiring you to look into this situation."

"You don't have to hire me, Mrs. Wiltse, it's my job."

"Taking on a seventy-year-old hunting accident? I think that might be above and beyond the call of duty."

"Murder."

She took another bite of her sandwich and chewed. "Murder?"

"Yes, ma'am."

328

"And you think your grandfather was involved?"

"It would appear that the weapon that killed Bill Sutherland was Lloyd Longmire's."

She nodded and looked out a window above where I assume the sink must've resided and then turned to me with glacial eyes as she took a sip of her drink. "And why would your grandfather have been involved with the killing?"

"He was the head of the board of directors for the Bank of Durant at that time."

She kept the eyes on me. "That's it?"

"No, the chief clerk of the treasurer's office, Harold Grafton, was at a conference in Gillette and was found dead, shot in his car, and State Treasurer Bob Carr was supposedly on a fishing vacation on the Bighorn River near Fort Smith when he simply disappeared."

"And you think your grandfather also had something to do with what happened to these two men?"

I picked up my drink, directing the straw into my mouth and taking a sip. "Mrs. Wiltse . . ."

"Carole, please."

"Carole, I can stand here and answer your questions, or you can tell me what you know, and we can combine our efforts and really get something done on this. Now, I'm not looking to cover up my grandfather's actions, so you can not only rely on me but stand assured that I'm going to get to the bottom of your great-uncle's death."

She smiled. "My husband said I should just call you . . ."

I sat my cup down. "You did."

"Yes, but not that I should tell you everything I know."

"That might be helpful."

She remained silent for a moment. "Did you know that Bill Sutherland was the father of the Fund?"

I took a deep breath and then let it out slow. "No, I did not know that."

"It was something he worked up in the late thirties, before the war. The state was having trouble keeping the coffers full and Great-uncle Bill didn't think it was fair that these companies were coming in and raking up the profits without paying their fair share to the state. So, he modeled the program after similar ones in Texas, Arizona, and Nevada."

"The PWMTF."

"Actually, the SWF, or Sovereign Wealth Fund. The Permanent Wyoming Mineral Trust Fund was established in 1975."

I gave her my best questioning look. "It was that late?"

"I have been doing some reading."

I took another sip. "Oh, now why do I not like the sound of that?"

"The governor of the state back in '68 . . ."

"Stan Hathaway, who was later the secretary of the Interior."

She nodded. "He is the one that actually introduced a bill in the state legislature to institute a severance tax on minerals — and do you know why he did that? Because the balance on the state bank account in 1968 was eighty dollars."

"Eighty, as in eight-oh?"

"And no cents. The bill passed in 1969 with a one percent severance tax, which saved Wyoming."

"Well, that's good news."

"It is until you look a bit closer and discover that a similar bill, the Sovereign Wealth Fund, was introduced by Bill Sutherland."

I thought about it. "So, what happened, it didn't pass?"

"With the distractions of the Second World War, it was never brought to the floor for a vote."

"So, that was the end of that?"

"Not specifically." She reached behind

her, pulled a sheaf of papers from the counter, and placed them in front of me. "Now, it looks to me as if this Sovereign Wealth Fund was on the fast track after the war and then suddenly disappeared."

"That wouldn't have coincided with the death of Bill Sutherland in 1948?"

"It would have." She thumbed through the pages. "As near as I can tell there were studies on the implementation of this SWF bill, but without Great-uncle Bill's support it didn't get to the state legislature."

"Why would Carr and Grafton — and my grandfather, for that matter — want to get rid of it? And your great-uncle?"

She rested her sandwich on the wrapper. "One can't help but wonder, did they implement it in the confusion of wartime, and is it possible that this Sovereign Wealth Fund has quietly been accumulating since the forties?"

"Do you think it's a parasitic fund hidden in the PWMTF?"

"It makes sense, doesn't it? I wouldn't suspect that this SWF ghost account is as much as the state mineral fund, but it has had a head start of almost twenty-five years — if it exists." She stared at me. "There was a lot of resistance. The problem being that when Uncle Bill got back from the war, the plan he'd proposed wasn't exactly what he had arranged."

"Meaning?"

"It had been broken into a number of funds, only one of them unaccounted for, and that's when he confronted Grafton and Carr."

"After the war."

"Yes, and from what I'm to understand he met with resistance again, but when he threatened to go to the newspapers with the information, the state treasurer's office got on board."

"Okay, but if that's the case, then why kill him — or more possibly have Lloyd Longmire kill him?"

She took a sip of her drink and then sat it down next to mine. "There was not a great deal of transparency in the state treasury back in the thirties and not a lot of careful adjudication in its actions."

"So, not much of a paper trail to follow?"

"Next to none."

"So, what you're saying is that not all of these ancillary funds, including this SWF, might've been liquidated?"

"Exactly."

"And if they got rid of the one government official who was crying foul . . ."

"And with all the attention that Head of

Trustees Tom Rondelle is drawing to the PWMTF right now . . ."

I stood there for a moment, assimilating what she'd just said. "Are you saying that these ghost funds might still exist?"

She stared at me, saying nothing, finally picking up her sandwich and taking a bite.

"How much money are we talking about back in '48?"

She chewed, wiping a bit of Thousand Island dressing from the corner of her mouth with an index finger. "Enough to be worth killing a man."

"And now?"

"A lot more."

I picked up my half a sandwich but then rested it back, maybe even less hungry than I was before. "And you've been able to track this all down?"

"No, which is why I need your help."

"What can I do?"

"Find out who killed Bill Sutherland. If we can track that to who might be controlling these funds now, then we might have a chance of shedding light on this situation."

"And bankrupting the state."

"No, the state PWMTF is fine, but somebody out there has been making a lot of money for a very long time with a little sidecar industry of the SWF, and I think

334

that gravy train needs to stop." She continued studying me, reading the concern on my face. "Something else?"

I thought about what I wanted to say, and how I wanted to say it without sounding like some sort of conspiracy theorist, finally deciding I needed to take someone into my confidence. "I've had some incidences happen recently that lead me to believe that we're not the only ones concerned with this case. When we were looking for your great-uncle's grave, a man was shot, then a friend of mine was possibly targeted in a gas asphyxiation here in Cheyenne, and then somebody broke a window out of my truck, I'm assuming in an attempt to get the rifle that killed Bill Sutherland."

"Your grandfather's rifle."

"Yep."

"Is that all that leads you to believe that this Lloyd Longmire killed Uncle Bill?"

I thought about it and then just answered as honestly as I could. "Let me put it this way, Carole . . . If I were looking for someone to kill somebody at that time, Lloyd Longmire would've been the man I'd be looking for."

"This all sounds a little personal."

"Perhaps, but it doesn't mean it isn't true." I turned, leaning against the counter and folding my arms. "So, if somebody is attempting to protect this ghost fund — who would you suspect? This Tom Rondelle?"

"No, he hasn't got the brains God gave gophers."

"Then who? Because if I'm continuing this investigation, I'd like to know who I'm up against and what direction they might be coming from."

"I wish I could tell you."

"Have you thought about contacting the AG's office or the FBI or the US Department of the Treasury back in DC?"

"And what happens if I get hold of somebody involved and tip them off as to what's going on? They could just disappear or worse . . ."

"Well, I trust Joe Meyer."

"We're talking a lot of money here, Walt, and I don't trust anybody."

"In that case, what makes you think you can trust me?"

"You have everything to lose and nothing to gain from this investigation, but here you are." She took another bite of her sandwich and chewed. "Now, at this point you might be asking yourself why it is you should trust me."

"I hadn't been thinking that, but I'd be

interested to hear what you have to say."

"I am the treasurer for this state, and anything that reflects badly on it reflects badly on me, and if there is something going on with our finances, I want to know what it is." She sat the rest of her sandwich down. "And . . ."

"And what?"

The arctic eyes rose to mine like a shearing glacier. "I want to know who killed my great-uncle, Big Bill Sutherland, period."

"Well, did you learn anything you didn't already know?"

Driving north, I glanced over at him and the rapidly passing landscape of the southern part of our county, slipping past Powder Junction and the end run home. "Yep."

He'd slept most of the way, but after an hour of silence had become conversational. "Such as?"

I remained silent as I waited for an eighteen-wheeler to slowly pass another, or as we referred to it in Wyoming, an elephant race.

"So, that's it, huh? If I don't tell you everything I know, then you don't tell me what you found out?"

"Lucian, you haven't told me anything."

"I've told you everything I remember."

"What about Carr and Grafton?"

"What about 'em?"

I reached down and picked up the photograph that Cady had given me from the cabin. "First off, why didn't you tell me they were the two men in this photograph with my grandfather?"

He studied the image after I handed it to him. "Who told you that?"

"Carole Wiltse."

"Well, that was a wide-ranging conversation you two had."

"You're not answering my question."

He continued studying the photo. "Maybe because I didn't know who the hell they were?"

"You met both of them."

"Over fifty years ago." He tossed the frame onto the back seat, which disturbed Dog's nap enough for him to raise his head. "You know, I hope to God when you're my age that you can draw on all the random crap everybody throws at you."

"Pretty convenient, that memory of yours."

He stared out the windshield. "Stop this truck."

"What?"

"Stop this truck right now, or I'm going to open this door and just step out."

Spotting a turnaround, I slowed and then pulled into the median, finally coming to a stop as he threw the handle and got out, slamming the door behind him.

With a quick look at an expectant Dog, I shook my head no and then climbed out on my side. By the time I got around the front of my truck he was standing there in the newly mowed grass and was looking north. "Lucian?"

"Did you know your grandfather was my biggest backer when I ran for sheriff after the war?"

"No."

"Well, he was." He poked at a tuft of dry sage with his cane. "He came to my rescue a number of times before he died."

I walked toward him. "What's your point?"

"He was a good man." He turned to me. "I'm not saying he was easy to get along with, but brother, if you had your back against the wall and you needed a little assistance — he was your man."

I stepped past and then turned to look at him. "How did he get involved in all this?"

"All of what?"

"The murder of Bill Sutherland."

"It ever cross your mind that he wasn't, that he didn't?"

"Then why all the secrecy?"

"Because I can't say the same about your friends Harold Grafton and Bob Carr."

I stood there with a weight in the trunk of my body as the same two semis passed us, heading up the road due north. I'd had my suspicions, but having them confirmed was like taking a shot to the chest. "He killed both of them?"

He took the pipe from his pocket and clinched the stem between his teeth, then pawed out his beaded tobacco bag and stuffed the bowl. "You are asking me to break a blood oath in answering that question."

"Yep, I am."

He finished loading his pipe and then put the tobacco bag back in the pocket of his jacket. "It was a different time and you —"

"Did he kill those men?"

He studied me for a moment and then lit the pipe and took a puff as more traffic passed us by. "Yes, I believe he did."

"Why?"

"Because they deserved killing." Taking the stem from his mouth, he pointed it at me. "They murdered his friend."

"Bill Sutherland."

He walked toward me, his eyes glistening. "He came into my office after we'd hauled Sutherland's body off the mountain and sat

340

in my office chair and said flat-out that he knew those two men had killed Bill and wanted to know what I was going to do about it. I told him that he knew as well as I did that those men were well-thought-of in the state, and without any way to connect them to the crime with the murder weapon, it was gonna be difficult to charge 'em."

He walked farther out in the grass, and we both heard an unmistakable buzzing sound. "Careful . . ."

"I see him." He pointed with his cane where a prairie rattlesnake coiled in upon itself about eight feet from his right boot in order to take advantage of the early warmth to come out of hibernation. "Isaac had already done the preliminary parts of the autopsy, and we knew it had been a .300 H&H Magnum that had done the deed, a weapon that no one in the party had been carrying but that everyone in the community knew your grandfather owned."

The snake continued to rattle at Lucian, but he ignored it.

"I asked him where the weapon was, but he said he didn't know — that it had disappeared in camp, and he had no idea where it had gone."

"Then what?"

"He stood there in my office and said he had business to attend to. I asked him to not do what it was he was considering doing, that there were just too many ways that a thing like that could go wrong." He lifted the pipe back up and took another puff.

"Did you help him?"

"No, I did not. As a matter of fact, I followed him out of my office and halfway down the steps before I told him that if he set out to do such a foolish thing I'd likely be coming for him."

"And what did he say to that?"

"Come ahead but be ready when you do." The old sheriff took another puff on his pipe, the smoke blowing away between us like a lost trust. "A week later Harold Grafton was sitting in his Nash Ambassador along the railroad tracks in Gillette at approximately 11:00 p.m. and pressed the muzzle of a 9mm Luger to the side of his head and blew his own brains out."

"You and I both know that's not what happened."

"Maybe so, but there wasn't any proof otherwise."

"And Carr?"

He poked his cane out at the rattler, which responded by taking a strike at it before retreating into an s-shaped coil. "He was fishing . . ."

"Alone?"

"Drove all the way up to the Bighorn River . . . There are witnesses who saw him park his truck at a pullout on 313 and a game warden even stopped and checked his license."

"And then what?"

"He disappeared; him, his truck, and everything . . . One minute he was there, and the next he was gone." His jaw set in grim determination, holding his pipe as he poked at the snake again.

"He killed those men, Lucian. You know he did."

The prairie rattler obliged him by striking out at the cane once more, and then, quick as forked lightning, the old sheriff snatched the .38 from his shoulder holster and shot the head off the snake. He turned and walked past me toward the truck as he muttered over his shoulder and from the side of his mouth. "I don't know any such thing."

12

After dropping Lucian off, I drove over to Durant Memorial to check on the two patients, only to find one. David Nickerson was in his office, a proper one, unlike the broom closet that had been Isaac Bloomfield's.

"Trisha Knox?"

He stood, joining me in the hallway with a file under his arm. "Checked herself out — and in answer to your question before you ask it, she did not pull a Longmire but actually discharged herself out through registration."

"Is there a secret meaning in there for me?"

"Yes, the times they are, indeed, a changin' . . . And by the next time you're in here, I'm arranging to have locks put on the doors." He smiled, adjusting his glasses. "I'm assuming the county will be picking up the bill for Ms. Knox?"

"I'd imagine so." I followed him as we walked toward Jules Beldon's room. "Any idea where she went?"

"Nope, just threw her bag over her shoulder and walked across the parking lot and disappeared." He shook his head. "I know you see a lot more of this than I do, but how do people like that survive?"

"A lot of times they don't." I nodded toward the door beside us. "I checked earlier, but he's still unconscious?"

"It's the best shot he's got at surviving, a man that age shot three times . . . I don't know how he's still alive."

"He's tough as a pine knot." I crossed my arms and leaned against the wall. "So, no remarkable improvement?"

"No, but he keeps chugging along." He took the file from under his arm and opened it. "Pulse rate, body temperature, respiration, and blood pressure are all within the reasonable variables . . . That's the amazing thing about what I do, to see how the human body finds a way to survive, and in his case it's above and beyond the norm. Are pine knots particularly tough?"

"Yep. So, speaking of pine knots, is Isaac completely moved out?"

"I think so."

"Another era ends." I thought about it.

"What's he going to do with his time? I mean, as long as I've known him, I've never known him to have any hobbies or anything."

"Did you know he plays the violin?"

"Actually, I did."

"Well, we found the damn thing in its case buried under his papers, and you know he pulled the thing out, tuned it, and played Barber's 'Adagio for Strings.' " He laughed. "I don't think you have to worry about him, he's going on the lecture circuit."

"The what?"

"I guess there's this speaker's bureau in New York that invited him to join, talking about his experiences in the concentration camp, coming to the US, and being a doctor here in Wyoming for the last million years. Hell, he can accompany himself on violin." He smiled. "Do you know how old he is?"

"Old."

He leaned in, almost as if he didn't want the building to hear him. "He's ninety-nine years old, a hundred in three months. We found his citizenship papers from when he came over after the war — he's almost a hundred years old."

"There should be some sort of celebration or something."

"I tried, but he won't go for it."

"You can't get Isaac to do things, you just have to spring them on him."

"Will you help me do something?"

"I'll do better than that, I'll get Ruby on it — she'll come up with something wonderful, I'm sure."

He walked me toward the front door and the reception area where, of all people, Ruby's niece sat. "Hey, Janine, do you think we can talk Ruby into putting together a party for Isaac Bloomfield's hundredth birthday in three months?"

She didn't even look up from her computer screen. "She's already on it."

David and I looked at each other.

"I should have known." I started out the door before I could be even more embarrassed. "It goes without saying that if there's any change in Jules's condition, you'll call me?"

David waved as I went through the double-glass and automatic doors. "Will do."

Barrett Long looked up from the book he was reading at Ruby's desk. "It's Sunday."

I made the top of the steps and looked around at the otherwise empty office as Dog continued over to say hello. "I know it's

Sunday."

He reached down and ruffled the scruff at the back of the beast's neck. "I'm supposed to tell you what day of the week it is when you show up."

"Well, I now know it's Sunday, but it's also after six p.m. — what are you still doing here?"

"We have a lodger."

"We do?" I turned the sheriff prisoner's record, which happened to be lying on the counter, and read the name. "Jordan Heller?"

Barrett nodded, closing *Basic Laboratory Exercises for Forensic Science,* 9th Edition. "Saizarbitoria and the Regis guy found the gun that shot Jules Beldon out at his place this afternoon."

"You're kidding."

"Heckler and Koch HK416, stuffed up under his camper."

"Did they check it?"

"I think they were waiting to see when you were getting back from Cheyenne. I guess they figured if you were down there that you might want to be in charge of checking it yourself. They just brought him in about two hours ago, and there was no way of getting hold of you."

"Where are they now?"

348

"Icing that monster of a black eye that Heller gave the Regis guy and having a celebratory beer, I think down at the Century Club." I turned and started for the basement as he called after me. "They left a report on your desk, but do you want me to call them?"

"No." I continued down the steps to find on the table the weapon in question, an HK416, a wicked black-metal assault rifle with a broomstick foregrip and a stubby, hooded scope.

It looked like it could do the job, whatever the job was.

"That you, Sheriff?"

The voice had called from the row of cells in the back, and I moved that way, opening the security door and moving down the hall to the second cell.

Jordan Heller was reclined on the bunk, an arm over his face. "It's not mine."

I grabbed a folding chair from the wall and opened it, having a seat. "What was it doing stuffed under your camper?"

"Hell if I know."

"You don't seem overly concerned."

"I'm not. It's not mine, and anybody who says it is will have a hard time proving it. I've never seen it; I haven't touched it . . . Nothing."

"You're sure?"

"I am." He removed the arm and rolled my way as Dog ambled in and joined me. "Aren't you supposed to have a warrant or something if you start searching a place?"

"Unless you've got consent, search incident to arrest, plain view, exigent circumstance, or hot pursuit — do you know what all of those mean?"

"No."

"How about you just tell me what happened, and I'll tell you if they had a right to do what they did."

"You'll be straight with me?"

"Have I been up to now?"

He slipped his legs off the cot and sat up, carefully rubbing his face with his hands. "Yeah, but there are these bars between us . . ."

"I can't do anything about that until I hear what happened."

He yawned. "Did you ask them?"

"I could, or there's a report on my desk upstairs, but I'd rather hear it from you first."

He stood and came over to the bars and kneeled down to pet Dog, who licked at his hands where I could see he'd sustained some damage, the knuckles on his right hand being bloodied. "They showed up this afternoon, and I was just sitting in my chair the way I always do on my day off, and they started asking me questions. They got pushy with the questions, and I got pushy back . . ."

"Describe *pushy.*"

He looked up, and I could see the damage to his face where he'd been beaten. "Oh, the one in the suit jacket, he started asking me about my service, and I didn't like the way he was asking or the direction the questions were going, so I told 'em to leave."

"What happened?"

"They didn't."

"And?"

"I punched the guy in the suit jacket." He regarded the damage to his knuckles. "It was a hell of a lick."

"He put up much of a fight?"

"Yeah, he got back up and landed a few before that deputy of yours got the cuffs on me."

"And that's when they did the search and found the rifle?"

"Yeah, the guy in the suit jacket spotted the rifle sticking out from the undercarriage of my trailer by the steps and showed the deputy, which is bullshit because there's no way I'm going to leave a seven-thousand-dollar rifle hanging under my trailer for cris'sake. Did you look at that thing? It's an actuated model with an ATN ThOR night vision scope . . . You actually think I'd leave something like that out there where the mice could chew on it?" He chuckled. "If it was mine, I'd sell it and buy a decent truck . . ."

"Well, just for future information, if you assault a police officer you'll likely be put under arrest and that gives them the right to search the immediate vicinity — that's SIA, or search incident to arrest."

"Is the guy in the suit jacket a cop?"

"Nope." I stood, folded the chair, and leaned it back against the wall. "And that's why I'm going to get you out of here."

He called after me as I walked back down the hall and through the security door to retrieve the keys. "You don't think that rifle is mine?"

"No, I don't." I approached again, unlocking the door, and swinging it wide as Dog backed out of the way. "C'mon, let's get you doctored up."

I sat in one of our guest chairs with Dog at my feet as Barrett Long expertly administered to the scratches and bruises on Heller's face, smiling as Heller winced whenever he applied the anti-infection ointment, and bandaged him. It had taken more time to wrap his knuckles, as it turned out.

He raised his hand and flexed the fingers, impressed with Barrett's work.

"You do a good job."

"I've had a lot of practice."

There was some noise from the front door and the stairwell as I stretched my legs out over Dog, crossed them, and waited.

"What is he doing out of the cell?"

Barrett stared at Saizarbitoria and Mike Regis as the two of them made the landing, finally nodding toward me.

"I let him out."

Stepping in a little farther, they both looked at me, and I could see Regis's eye, which had taken, by all accounts, a hell of a lick. He gestured toward Heller. "Do you know we found the weapon that shot Jules Beldon on him?"

"I know you found a weapon under dubious circumstance."

Saizarbitoria stepped toward me. "Boss . . ."

I lifted a finger. "You better think about it before you say another word." I looked at Regis. "You — out of my county and gone, do you understand?"

He stared at me through one and a half eyes. "Look, Sheriff, I don't know what this

353

is all about but —"

"Gone . . . By tomorrow."

He glanced at Santiago and then back to me. "Did you hear what we said about that rifle?"

"Did you hear what I just said?"

He made a sound of indignation, looking back at Heller, who stared at him impassively. "Look, I can call up Tom Rondelle and —"

"Call him — I offered to toss him through a window just yesterday."

Regis shook his head and started to speak again but then thought about it, turned, and extended a hand to Saizarbitoria. "Good working with you, Deputy. When you get ready to make your move up here and stand for sheriff just let us know and we'll be happy to help pitch in."

I watched Regis walk past Sancho and go down the steps before he turned at the door to look back up at me. "I think you're going to regret this, Sheriff."

I sat there, glaring at him. "The only thing I'm going to regret is not throwing you through a window too."

He stared at me a moment more and then shook his head and slipped through the door without looking back.

I sat there for a moment more, just to cool

my temper, and then faced my deputy. "You arrested him for striking Regis?"

His dark eyes flashed. "Yes."

"He's not a cop. Did he identify himself as one?"

"No."

Heller joined the conversation. "He just acted like one."

Saizarbitoria glanced at him and started to say something but then held his tongue before turning back to me. "You saw the HK on the table downstairs?"

"I did."

"It's the same caliber as the one that shot Jules Beldon. How do you explain that?"

"I don't have to. I'm not disputing that; I'm not even disputing that it's the weapon that may have done the deed." I raised my finger again, this time pointing it at Heller. "What I *am* disputing is whether it belongs to that man there." I leaned back in the chair I'd been occupying since they'd come in. "Have a seat."

"I'll stand."

I petted Dog, who I knew was upset by my tone of voice, and then slowly brought my eyes up to Sancho. "I've become privy to some facts about your buddy there that just don't sit right."

He stared back at me for a moment. "Just

355

doing my job, Boss."

"No." I glanced toward the stairs, where Regis had disappeared. "I think you're doing his."

His eyes dropped, and he stuffed his hands into the pockets of his jeans and stood there a moment more before turning and walking down those same stairs and out the door.

"Wow, that was intense."

I turned to Barrett and then to Heller. "C'mon, I'll give you a ride home."

The bandaged young man stood and nodded. "Can I have the rifle since it's supposed to be mine?"

"No."

"I was kind of worried if I was in jail on Monday that I'd lose my job."

I drove along Route 14/16, taking the right turn toward Absalom and following the Powder River. "You'd get fired for missing a day?"

"Yeah, the manager's looking for a reason to cut me loose, as near as I can tell."

"How come?"

He shrugged and then reached into the back to pet Dog. "I told him I was going to punch his lights out."

I shook my head. "Is that your major form

of communication?"

"Pretty much, these days." He turned back and stared into the darkness of the rolling hills, a few lights in a few houses dotting the landscape. "How did you handle it when you got back?"

"For me it was incremental." I drove thinking about those years that didn't seem so very long ago. "As punishment, the provost marshal shipped me out to this rock in the middle of the Pacific Ocean — Johnston Atoll. Ever heard of it?"

"Nope."

"Neither had I. There's about fifty square miles of lava rock and sand there and a couple of landing strips that were built during World War II."

"The Japanese never tried to take it?"

"As I recall, the Japanese subs hit the refrigeration unit, so I guess they had to go without ice cream for a week."

"Doesn't sound much like punishment."

"Later they launched nuclear weapons from the island, some of which failed and left residual radiation. It was also used for chemical weapon storage."

"Nerve gas and shit?"

I nodded, lifting my hand to look for the scars that were now only barely visible. "Agent Orange, sarin, VX, and even mustard gas . . ."

"And that's where you decompressed after Vietnam?"

"Yep, and then I got discharged and took a job on the North Slope up in Alaska."

"How was that?"

"I almost got eaten by a bear in a ghost ship." I slowed my truck, pulled through the gate that led to his place, and parked alongside the camper.

"My lawn chair is sounding better and better."

I nodded as he climbed out. "I think you should get a different job."

"Yeah, I'm thinking that too." He closed the door and spoke through the open window. "You hiring?"

"I may have to, as of tomorrow." I took in the desolate landscape. "I also don't think that sitting out here and dwelling is such a great idea."

"Is that what I'm doing, dwelling?"

"Yep."

He smiled and reached in to pet Dog one last time. "Is that what you did on that island and up in Alaska, dwell?"

"Yep."

Pulling his arm out, he rested it on the sill, turning to look at his portion of God's little acre. "You wanna know something,

Sheriff?" He pushed off my truck and stepped away. "I think you're still doing some dwelling yourself."

I smiled, pulling the truck into reverse and starting to back out.

"Can I ask you one last question?"

I stopped the truck. "Sure."

"How do you know I didn't shoot that guy?"

"A feeling. When you've been doing this as long as I have you get to a point where you begin questioning your instincts, which is a mistake, because they're the reason you've been able to do this kind of thing for very long."

"Ever been wrong?"

"Yep, but I also happened to look under your camper when I was out here the first time, and that rifle wasn't under there then." Backing up, I swung around and started north but took the time to look back and could see him seating himself in the camp chair, his face lit by the lighting of a cigarette.

On the drive out, I'd noticed the lights were still on at the Red Pony and thought I might stop in there and have a beer before returning to my little cabin, but then I knew it was likely that I'd just annoy Henry by bringing up Vic.

So, she was gone.

It wasn't something I could easily wrap my head around.

As I debated stopping back at the bar, I saw a set of headlights in my rearview mirror approaching fast. Slowing, I steered into a pullout that doubled as a gate entrance and sat there.

Ignoring my driving lights, the SUV blew past, so I flipped on my siren and emergency lights, then, pulling back onto the road, I hit the gas. I was pretty sure it was the same vehicle I'd seen the night Jules Beldon had been shot and had driven into the Red Pony.

It was a long straightaway, and I was having trouble gaining on whoever it was, watching the taillights grow smaller. I floored my truck and was impressed with the acceleration of the old beast that Jim, the county mechanic, had patched back together after my adventures in Montana. He'd said he'd rechipped the big engine, but I really hadn't had any reason to see what that meant until now as all ten cylinders came online.

I was doing a good hundred and twenty when the taillights went around a corner, and I lost the Lincoln in the distance. When I went through the same turn, I couldn't see it at all.

Slowing, I looked to the right, where I could see headlights tracing the hillside on the road that led to my ancestral homestead on Buffalo Creek. Turning the wheel as I got there, I accelerated in the straight, getting a little airborne, and even caught sight of the taillights as I came over a hill.

Whoever it was, they weren't going as fast on the gravel, and I started gaining ground, as I was sure the softer suspension of the SUV wasn't taking to the rolling landscape as well as my truck and was likely bottoming out.

I also knew this road like the back of my proverbial hand, having driven it since I'd been fifteen, but whoever was piloting the SUV was pretty good and appeared to be determined to get away.

We'd just reached the ridge that looked out over the river with a drop off on the other side when I saw the SUV again, this time sliding sideways before dipping over the berm and eventually rolling, the headlights now aimed at the sky.

Sliding to a stop where the vehicle had flipped, I jumped out and closed the door behind me quickly so that Dog wouldn't follow. I could see the vehicle lying on its roof in a cloud of dust and dirt, the motor still running and the tires still turning as I scrambled down the hillside.

I didn't expect the thing to explode like they always did in the movies, but whoever was inside was bound to be in need of some medical attention.

Slipping to the side, I finally braced a hand against the Lincoln and stooped down to look in the window, where I saw, hanging from the seat belts, an unconscious Ruth One Heart.

I reached an arm under her and I saw something of interest but then focused on the job at hand. Unclicking the buckle and pulling her out, I dragged the two of us from the Lincoln and propped her up after we got a safe distance away. I smelled alcohol on her breath as I gently patted her face a few times until I finally saw her eyelids flutter. She stared up at me. "You?"

"Who were you expecting?"

She tried to push my hand away but then gave up and relaxed against my arm. "I thought you were an HP or something."

"You're not supposed to run from them either." I pulled her up some more as the engine on the SUV finally sputtered and quit. "What were you doing?"

"Having a drink in Absalom." Her head

lolled against my chest. "A few drinks, actually."

"I just drove by there and didn't see your car."

She looked around. "What, you're following me?"

"No, I was dropping off a suspect out at his place on the Powder River and drove by, twice."

"What, you guys make deliveries now?" She tried to sit up but fell back again. "Suspected of what?"

"Shooting Jules Beldon."

"Oh, you're still working on that?"

"Yep." I tried to gauge if I could carry her back up the hillside before dropping her and falling back down myself. "Do you think you can stand?"

"Yes." With my help, she was able to bring herself to a semi-upright position but still swayed a bit as she bent over.

"Really, we're in no hurry, and I think you just survived a barrel roll without the benefit of your plane."

She belched loudly. "I think I might throw up."

"I know I would."

She laughed, and I could tell that after a few moments she was feeling better, because she looked at what had been a sleek, shiny vehicle — now, a little worse for wear. "Well, shit . . ."

"New?"

"Worse, it's a rental."

I reached a hand out and took her shoulder as she stood upright. "I think you've bought it."

"I think you're right." She slumped a bit with the first step, but I was able to hold her.

"Take it easy and don't talk — conserve your breath till we get to the top."

Half-carrying her, I was able to get back to the berm where she'd gone over before we both slumped onto the ground, leaning against each other listening to Dog, barking in the cab of my truck. "Now, wouldn't this have been a lot easier if you'd just pulled over?"

"I thought I wasn't supposed to talk."

"That was before; you can talk now."

"I don't want to talk about it, and trust me, you don't want to hear it."

"Try me."

She pushed off and sat there gesturing down at the wreckage. "Now, there's a metaphor for my entire life."

"I thought your life was going pretty well?"

She laughed and threw an arm over my shoulder. "Fooled you."

"Well, how 'bout we load you up and talk about it while we get you into the hospital for a quick going over."

Her head turned, and she stared at the wreck. "I'm fine."

"Maybe you are and maybe you're not — let's have you looked at."

"No."

I turned my face to her. "Ruth . . ."

"No, I'm fine. Other than calling my insurance and the car rental place, I'm fine."

"You're going to need at least one wrecker to fetch that rental."

She sighed, and then her voice became soft. "Well, now that you mention it, I do need one other thing."

"What's that?"

She turned and smothered my lips with a kiss.

I tried to pull away, but, with her arm around my shoulders, she held me fast, even going so far as to climb onto my lap and allow her weight to push me backward, where my hat fell off. Then she slipped the arm from around my shoulders and took my face in her strong hands, holding me there.

There was a frenzy in her movements, and I'm pretty sure things would've gotten out of hand fast if I hadn't brought my own hands up and taken hers.

Her face drew away as she sat there strad- dling me, her hair forming a curtain over our faces, only inches apart. "I have had a crush on you my entire life, and I don't care what you say, that was a truly superb kiss."

"I think you did all the work."

"I'm willing to do some more."

"I can't."

Her eyes stayed locked on mine for a mo- ment, then she slipped to the side, partially dismounting me, and sat there. "That other somebody?"

"I'm afraid so."

"I thought that was an on-again, off-again thing?" She climbed the rest of the way from me and straightened her hair and blouse. "I was hoping this was the off-again portion."

I sat up. "To be honest, I'm not sure what it is."

She nodded her head but wouldn't look at me. "I was brokenhearted when you got married . . . I always thought that someday, somehow, we'd end up together, you know?" She laughed again. "And here we are sitting on a hillside looking at my wrecked rental after I've made an ass out of myself."

"You didn't make an ass out of yourself. My life is just . . . complicated."

She laughed, but it was flat and emotion- less. "Is life ever not?"

I reached a hand out to her in an attempt to make things normal. "Good question."

She stood. "I'm going home."

"What?"

"It's only a couple of miles, and I need time to think."

I also stood and then moved toward her. "I'm not letting you walk off down the road in the dark after rolling your vehicle."

She glanced at me, and I could see the grin on her handsome face. "If you'd kissed me back you might've had a say in it but seeing as how you didn't, I'm a free agent." She started off.

"Ruth, please."

She called back over her shoulder and reached down to pat the semiautomatic still at her hip. "Don't feel bad for me, Walt, feel bad for whatever runs into me out there in the dark."

I took a few steps after her and then stopped — what was I going to do, cuff her?

Standing there for a long while, I thought about what had just transpired and tried to sort through it all, but something was niggling, something that wouldn't let go.

I walked back to my truck and pulled open the door only to be confronted by a hundred and fifty pounds of insulted canine. "C'mon, let me in."

He stared at me, standing in the seat, unmoving.

"C'mon, I want to go home."

He still didn't move.

"I didn't want you running down there and getting crushed or burned or something, okay?"

I finally began pushing my way in and he had no choice but to move. I had him by a hundred pounds, and even though he had fangs, I had opposable thumbs.

Firing my truck up, I switched on the headlights and could see Ruth about a hundred yards down the road. I suppressed the urge to take off after her and spun the wheel, turning back and heading for the paved road.

After a few miles, I sat at the turnout, chatting with the dispatcher over in Campbell County, figuring it was closer and that they could send a wrecker out from there. After assuring her of the exact location, I hung up the mic and stared out the windshield and thought about what had just happened.

Whirling the wheel, I hit the gas and spun around, spraying gravel onto the road as I jetted back from the direction I'd come. Blasting through the straightaways, I drifted through the curves with Dog looking at me from the passenger seat as if I'd lost my mind.

Finally parking at the exact same spot where I'd stopped before, I threw open the door and jumped from the driver's seat with Dog right behind me. Scrambling down the hillside, I slid to a stop at a rock outcropping even though Dog kept going down toward the overturned Lincoln.

Halting at the driver's-side window, the beast looked back up at me for verification.

I nodded and started off again, trying to catch my breath. I finally reached the vehicle and leaned against it, looking down at him. "You knew something was wrong, even if I didn't know exactly what it was, huh?"

He wagged, and I reached down to ruffle the fur between his ears, but then he did something strange and backed away from my hand.

"What?"

He barked, although I realized he wasn't looking at me but rather back up the hill toward my unit at least fifty yards away. I'd left my headlights on and I thought I could see something moving in the beam. My keys were still in the ignition, but I didn't think anybody, whoever they were, would be stupid enough to steal my truck. "Hello?"

369

Dog continued barking, and I took a step up the hill. "Hello?"

There was no sound in return, just the clicking of my emergency lights.

"Hey?"

Still nothing.

Dog took a few steps in that direction, but I took hold of his collar. "No, that's okay, I know who it is."

I raised my other hand to put it by my mouth in hopes of amplifying the volume of my voice. "I know you're up there!"

I waited for a moment more and when there was still no response, I jiggled Dog's collar to get his attention. "Stay. Do you hear me? Stay."

He sat, but his eyes still darted up the hill.

Crouching down, I reached past the seat where I'd fished Ruth from the Lincoln and felt along the side of the black leather seat, between it and the leather console, when I could finally feel what it was I'd thought I'd seen.

Wrapping my fingers around a black plastic triangle, I wedged the object loose and pulled it out past the seat, drawing it with me as I turned and stood, thinking about Jules Beldon as I held in my hands another Heckler and Koch model HK416 5.56x45mm NATO.

13

It was after midnight, and I probably should've gone home, but I didn't, instead finding myself slowly driving along Buffalo Creek, following it toward where the old Pennsylvania truss-style bridge spanned the Powder River between Wyoming and Montana and far larger things.

The moon was full, and the river looked like a thick stripe of mercury reflecting the light as I made the turn and drove across the bridge, stopping when I saw someone standing on one of the girders some twenty feet above, about halfway across.

Killing the engine, I climbed out of the truck, letting Dog out with me. I glanced around and then trailed over to the walkway and shouted up to her. "Hey?"

She didn't answer but spread her arms out.

"Ruth?"

She still ignored me.

371

"You're kind of worrying me here . . . What are you doing?"

Her voice was, and sounded, very far away. "Flying."

Dog and I stood there looking up at her, and I couldn't help but smile. "Like in the laundry cart?"

I thought I could hear a smile in her voice. "Exactly."

Leaning against the railing with Dog, I looked straight at her as I listened to the water flowing below. "Do you really think you should be up there, considering your condition?"

She flexed her fingers, rustling them like primary wing feathers. "What's my condition?"

"Um . . . Slightly inebriated?"

"No worries, I've puked off the bridge twice now."

"Maybe you should come down?"

"I don't want to."

"How come?"

"I don't like it down there — too confusing. I just want to keep flying."

I nodded, petting Dog. "Everybody's got to land sometime."

Her arms slowly sank until she was just standing there, leaning into the slight breeze that smelled of the sluggish water. "Pity, isn't it?"

I glanced around. "Nice night."

She slowly crouched, still looking out at the reflective stripe between states, and then sat on the girder. "To jump?"

"Human life is a valuable commodity . . ."

"Doesn't feel like it right now."

I leaned the small of my back against the railing and looked up at her as Dog sniffed the silver I beams and then joined me. "Besides, I think the river's only about four inches deep right here."

"Far enough to break my neck?"

"Probably." I kept my gaze on her.

"Got anything you want to tell me?"

"Like, I'm an idiot?" She leaned forward and looked down at us. "Sorry about what happened back there."

"That's okay, we all have our moments, and I might've been giving out mixed signals. Can I give you a ride home?"

Her eyes went back to the sluggish water. "I'm good."

"I'd really like to give you a ride home."

She smiled. "What? You're worried about me?"

"A little." I massaged my neck. "Hey, I'm starting to get a crick. Do you mind coming down?"

She placed her hands on the I beam and

slumped. "I'm fine, honest — I just need a little time to lick my wounds and recover my pride, and you're the one person that can't help me with that."

"I just want to give you a ride."

She laughed, pulling her hair away from her face and then turning her head west, where the moonlight caught her profile to perfection. "You're just not going to let me walk away from this, are you?"

"No. I'm sorry, but I can't."

She pulled her leather jacket around her a little tighter, the mouton collar still framing her face from far above. "I wanted to be a fighter pilot."

"Why didn't you?"

"Allergies."

"You're kidding."

"Nope. During a preflight at Wright-Patterson I was in a pressure chamber, this big tube they put you in to pump the air out and simulate high altitude. On the second simulation I was coming down from fifty thousand feet when I thought my sinuses were going to explode all over the plexiglass. I fought it for a while with Afrin and then steroids, but nasal steroids didn't exist at the time, so I got an asthma inhaler and rigged up a baby bottle nipple, cut the tip off and used it to get the stuff into my sinuses. It eventually caught up with me when they found traces of the steroids in my drug screening and grounded me."

"I'm sorry."

She nodded. "No problems getting in the marines?"

"No, they weren't being very selective at the time." I moved to the side to get a better look up at her. "Hey, you're making me a little nervous . . . Would you mind coming down?"

Her face went back to the river, and her voice took on a different tone. "You ever think the world would be a better place without you, old friend?"

I took a deep breath and stood there a moment before answering, trying to give my words the gravitas I hoped they would carry. "No, old friend. I don't."

A moment passed before she spoke again. "I do, sometimes."

I started looking back and forth in an attempt to find a route to her. "Okay, I really need you to climb down here or I'm going to have to come up there, and I really don't want to have to do that because I'm much more likely to fall off than you are."

"My life's a mess."

"Don't say that."

She barked a laugh. "Why the hell not?"

"Well, go ahead and say it, but you should know that's the way it is with all of us."

She looked down at me again but said nothing.

"When you're born it's a mess, and it does nothing but get messier. You get married, you have kids, it's nothing but a great big glorious mess . . ."

"I wouldn't know about those two."

"Then you avoided a couple of them, congratulations." I scrubbed my face with a hand. "The point being that you can get through life relatively unscathed and clean as a pin, but what's the point? The scars and stains are what make us who we are, or at least who we eventually become."

"I think it's different for men."

"It might be, but we're all in this boat together."

She swung around, lifting a leg, straddling the girder, still looking down at me. "That's where you're wrong — I'm pretty much on my own, more and more every day."

"I'm here." I reached down and pulled at the beast's ear. "And so is Dog."

She laughed again and then called down. "So, you are, but you're not all here, huh?"

"It's complicated, this relationship I think I was in, and things might be even more complicated now that it's over."

"Now you're coming around to my way of thinking." She studied me, and even from the distance I could sense a little pity. "You want to see the old homestead?"

"I want to see you home, safe."

She sat there for a while longer and then smiled. "Safe." I watched as she leveraged herself up and stood on the girder like a tightrope walker, then turned, grabbed another beam, and lowered herself onto another, then walked a bit more, and worked her way down another before arriving at ground level and striding back toward us in a pretty dexterous display. "I like the sound of that."

Dog nosed up to her, and she kneeled down to caress his bucket head. "Safe, it is."

She stood, walked around the front of my truck, and then spoke to me again through the open passenger-side window. "I'll take you up on the ride."

She pulled the door open and climbed in — Dog jumped to the back, and I walked over and climbed behind the wheel. We drove in silence, and I gave her that in hopes that she'd open up, but she only sat there looking out the windshield at her homeland, or what used to be.

We rounded a curve on the northern side

of the river and headed west. I slowed, looking at the open fields that were bisected by
a single two-track, and for the first time, she
spoke. "Turn here."

I did as she indicated and then pulled up
to a rounded drive that ended in two garage
doors with a cantilevered and very modern-
looking house, which was lodged into the
rock hillside overlooking the river to the
northwest. All windows and angles, I was
pretty sure a house like this would cost a
couple of million, at least. "I don't remember this house."

"I swore I'd never live in the one where
Ella died." She pulled the handle and
climbed out. "C'mon, I'll fix us something
to eat."

"Is your stomach up to that?"

"I think so. If not, I'll just fix something
for you — I owe you that much, after saving
me."

There was a regular door beside the
garage and a spiral staircase that led to the
living quarters above. She didn't notice that
I'd scooped up the HK416 from behind the
seat and brought it into the extravagant
house with me. She stepped across the
marble flooring and turned with her arms
spread wide, continuing into the open area
kitchen, set apart from the living room by

an island with a built-in range and overhead grill.

I surreptitiously propped the rifle against the railing and continued toward a mammoth refrigerator that could've held half a cow but from which she pulled breakfast ingredients. "Nice place."

"Yeah, I might've overdone it."

I sat on a stool as Dog sniffed around the room. "Government work must've been good."

"I had some friends in finance who turned me on to a couple of investments in a few tech firms." She cracked some eggs into a stainless-steel bowl, added some milk, and whisked the makings as she flipped on a burner and then quickly sliced up some mushrooms and an onion and tossed them into a skillet with butter. "Blew it all on this house."

"And that nifty airplane?"

"Yeah, that too." She reached behind her, pulled a couple of mugs from the cabinet, and set them next to a complicated coffee maker exactly like the one Mike Regis had bought for our office before I'd banished him. She hit a button, and the machine went to work like a square, plastic barista. "That, and a few other toys . . . I figured I wasn't going to have kids, so I might as well blow it all on me, right?" She spilled the eggs into the skillet and moved them around with a spatula. "Now I just wander around the place trying to remember why I came into a room."

I sat on the stool opposite her, placing my hat on the island as Dog settled in at my boots. "It can get lonely."

She scraped some eggs off into our plates and poured cups of coffee before picking up a fork and poising a bite at her lips. "Do you?"

"My job doesn't allow for that much." I shook my head, sipped my coffee, and picked up my own fork. "Sometimes I wish it did."

"How long has Martha been gone?"

I took a bite and chewed. "Almost nine years now."

"Does it seem like long?"

"Every day."

"I think Ed and I were divorced about that same length of time ago."

"Ed — that was his name?"

"Ed Bishop, he was the one who taught me the trick with the nose steroids. He was a flight surgeon."

I ate some eggs and then asked, "What happened?"

"We just grew apart, and when I decided

to move back here, that was the last straw." She glanced around, sat on a stool, and ate a few bites. "I suppose I could sell it, but I'd never get what I've put into it."

"I may end up selling my grandfather's place."

Her eyes came back to mine. "Really?"

"Yep, I'm afraid it's going to take too much work and time to get it into shape. Cady doesn't want it, and I'm pretty sure it would be a full-time job for me."

"So?"

I nudged my jacket back, revealing the hardware. "In case you haven't noticed, I have another line of work."

"Aren't you thinking of retiring?"

"I always am."

"And wasn't there mention of a certain someone else out there on the bridge?"

"There was, but she appears to have fled the coop."

Ruth made a face. "Really?"

I sipped my coffee. "Yep."

"What happened?"

"I asked her to marry me."

"And she ran off?"

"Yep." I shrugged. "Not exactly the response I was looking for, but there it is."

"Did you know her long?"

"About four and a half years now."

"That's weird." She sipped her own coffee and studied me. "Must've been something else."

"Somebody?"

"Not necessarily." She finished her eggs and clattered the fork on her plate in finality. "How long has she been gone?"

"The better part of a week."

"Less than a week?"

"Well, yep . . ."

"That's nothing — maybe she's getting herself together." She stared at me, finally shaking her head. "It's a big step, you know."

"Right."

She scooped my plate from under me, taking the fork from my hand and chucking it on top of hers before depositing breakfast in the sink. "Get out of here."

"What?"

"Get out of here. Go home and get some sleep and figure your life out."

Not particularly knowing what else to do, I stood and picked up my hat. "Are . . . Are you sure you're going to be all right?"

She picked up two coffee cups and placed them in the sink too and then started off toward the greater part of the house, leaving me standing there. "Yeah, I'm fine . . ." She stopped about halfway across the living room to turn to me. "You're the one who needs to get his shit together."

I didn't say anything more but listened as she walked down a hall muttering to herself. "Men . . ."

I turned to Dog, who looked as confused as me. "I guess we should go."

Walking back toward the stairwell, I grabbed the assault rifle from behind the railing and headed out with Dog in tow. "Boy howdy."

Henry leaned against the bar and stared at the menacing looking rifle that lay between us. "What, you are putting together a collection of these things?"

"Seems like it, doesn't it?"

His eyes met mine. "So, why did you bring it in here?"

I reached down to pet Dog, whose head rested on my knee — something he did only when he knew I was upset. "I'm kind of at a loss as to whom to trust."

He studied the rifle. "She was drunk?"

"I thought so, but now I'm thinking she just used that and the pass at me as a diversion."

"Yes, I cannot see any sober woman making a pass at you." He picked up the HK416 and balanced it expertly in his hands, finally bringing it up and sighting it over my shoulder with a frightening ease. "Why would she have this particular gun?"

"It's popular, and she did work with the ATF Rapid Response Teams and was Air Force Intelligence . . ."

He lowered the weapon. "This does not seem like Ruth One Heart."

"I know, but maybe we don't know who Ruthless became."

"Why would she shoot Jules?"

"Somehow, she's involved in all this." I shook my head. "Why else would she come popping back into my life?"

"For the same reason you have not been to your grandfather's homestead for thirty years? It is possible that it is coincidence." He placed the rifle back on the surface of the bar, leaned on the edge, folded his arms, and gripped his chin. "You say she came back when you went down the hill and retrieved this?"

"Someone was there, and I'd have a hard time believing it was anybody else."

"But how could she have gotten to the bridge that quickly after you saw her?"

"Good point."

"Did she seem guilty?"

"She seemed upset."

He reached back and picked up his usual seltzer water with the lime twist as I sipped my beer, both of us studying the rifle. "Go talk to her again."

"I intend to. The question is, do I go ahead and send this thing down to DCI with the other one?"

"No, the question is whether or not her friendship is worth risking if you do. It would seem to me that even in possession of this weapon, she should have no concerns about you having DCI look at this rifle if she was not the one who shot Jules."

"That makes sense."

"Thank you."

"You're sure you Indians aren't just banding together against me?"

He released his chin and refolded his arms, the muscles bulging. "Need I point out to you that you had in custody a white person with this exact rifle yesterday and just let him go?"

"I haven't arrested Ruth either."

"So you are oh for two." He looked at the clock on the wall, pointed toward the door, and then back at me. "Go home."

I took another sip of my beer. "I have to say, the hospitality around this place has gone to hell." I rattled the can, emphasizing my point. "I've still got half a beer left."

He sighed. "I am assuming that things did not go well down in Cheyenne?"

I thought about it. "Well, I found out about a lot of things . . ."

"Such as?"

"It's possible my grandfather didn't kill Bill Sutherland because of this SWF."

"And what is the SWF?"

"The Sovereign Wealth Fund, a precursor to the PWMTF, and a possible ghost fund that's floating around out there, somewhere."

"And that is good, yes?"

I shrugged. "But that he probably killed both Carr and Grafton for murdering Sutherland."

"Well, that is not so good."

"Lucian says they needed killing."

He grunted. "In my experience, he has said that about a great number of individuals."

"Yep, he has."

"So, now the question becomes, who knows about this . . . What did you call it?"

"SWF, Sovereign Wealth Fund."

"This SWF, who controls it, and how far will they go to keep it hidden?"

"Enough to kill Jules Beldon and my friend Nina Yadav." I took the last sip of my beer and reached down to pet Dog. "And I'm the one who put Jules on the job of trying to find the body of Sutherland and pointed Nina in the direction of what happened back in '48."

"Perhaps they thought they could scare you." He cocked his head, smiling. "In which case you have an extraordinary advantage."

"And what's that?"

"They must be monumentally stupid." He took my can, crushing it and tossing it in the trash behind him. "Go home."

Instead, I found myself wheeling the truck back out to my grandfather's place, where I turned down the main road and circled the fountain before parking and then lowered the windows and switched off the ignition.

I sat there thinking about what had just happened and wondered if I'd done the right thing or that I'd just been played.

Dog grumbled, so I let him out and then shut the door behind us, walking over to the broken fountain and sitting down, as he sniffed the surrounding area in the moonlight.

Looking over at the broken Indian maiden, I couldn't help but think that my life was kind of coming apart at the seams and that pieces of me were falling off. "What do you say, ol' girl? You're the only female I seem to be able to keep around . . ."

My eyes drifted toward the barn where I saw something strange, something gleaming in the ambient rays of the moon.

I stood and walked that way, crossing the turnaround, and making it to the corner, where I could see the front wheel of what looked like a motorcycle. It was some kind of space-age off-road BMW that I'd never seen before. Walking toward the back I saw the plates were a strange red and white with a numerical code I didn't recognize.

There was a helmet and goggles hanging from the handlebars, but nothing else.

I turned and looked back at the main house where Dog stood just off the porch, at attention and staring intently at the front door.

I walked in that direction and could now see prints from some heavy boots that had walked around the place a bit and then had possibly gone up the steps and onto that same porch.

Reaching down, I took ahold of Dog's collar, stepped onto the stone, and pushed the door open, which creaked wide, ever so slowly.

There were no lights on in the house because I hadn't paid the Powder River Energy co-op, but there seemed to be some noise coming from the study, which sounded like someone rustling paper and moving things around.

Walking carefully, I got to the door and could see a thick-looking individual sitting at the partner's desk with a fire going and a few candles lit, making his dinner from a black rubber dry bag while studying the chessboard. I hung onto Dog's collar and slowly stepped into the opening.

He sat there with a can and a can opener in his hands, unmoving. "There is knight missing."

I studied him. "Since my childhood — we never knew what happened to it."

"It was replaced by metal child?"

"Yep, they call it a Kewpie doll."

"Kewpie doll, this I have never heard of."

"From a comic series in the early part of the last century."

"Kewpie." He smiled, revealing a gold incisor. "I am sorry — I thought place was abandoned." His voice was rough, like he'd spent his life shouting and his vocal cords had finally given out. His accent was eastern European, but the edges were softened by time in America.

"Well, it is, kind of." I looked down at Dog. "Sit."

He did as I commanded but kept his attention on the tough, whose hair stood up at odd angles. He had a silver Dizzy Gillespie cookie duster under his lower lip, and I judged him to be in his forties.

"Do you mind if I ask who you are?" He sat the can and opener on the desk and started to stand, but Dog growled, and he froze, for which I didn't blame him. "You can stay seated, Dog here is kind of territorial until he gets to know you."

He nodded and then reseated himself, going so far as to extend a hand that carried a number of tattoos. "Maxim Sidorov."

I gestured toward the beast. "I better not let him go, just yet. Are you lost?"

"No, at least I do not think so — even though GPS appears to have given out. I was following main road and saw sign for Powder River and decide I want to see."

"Not much to see, is there?"

"No." He glanced down at his repast. "Would you like food? I also have red wine —"

"No thanks." Dog sat, so I released him and then pulled off my jacket and hung it on the back of the chair and also sat. His eyes focused first on my star and then the holster, mags, and cuffs at my belt.

He smiled. "You are police officer?"

"Sheriff."

"Ah . . . Then I am in trouble."

I shook my head, sliding a hand down and unsnapping the safety strap on my Colt. "No, I own the place, and you're welcome to stay here tonight." I motioned toward the trunk of his body and a bulge under his leather jacket. "Is that a weapon?"

He didn't move. "I was told that I should carry gun while traveling in open country."

"You want to take it out and place it on the table where I can see it?"

"Da." He did as I asked, and I leaned forward in order to examine the strange weapon. "Poloz 9mm, newest Russian design."

"And where are you traveling from?"

He continued smiling, and I noticed the gold tooth again. "Cathedral Heights, Washington, DC."

"Russian?"

"Yes, very good." He gestured toward the tin. "Tushonka pâté?"

"No thanks."

"Is very good."

"I'm sure it is, so don't let me stop you." I leaned back in my chair, keeping a hand near my sidearm. "So, Mr. Sidorov, what brings you to Wyoming?"

He picked up the opener and wrestled with the can. "I have always had interest American West, from watching all Westerns

I think. I finally have free time . . . ."

"And a new motorcycle?"

"You see it?" Getting the can open, he placed it on the table and began unwrapping the paper from a block of crackers. "It is magnificent machine."

"And what is it you do for a living?"

Taking a butter knife that he must've borrowed from one of the drawers from the table, he began spreading the pâté on some crackers before reaching one out to me. "Please, I insist."

Taking it, I continued staring at him.

"Retired, but used to be security analyst for politics, mostly computer systems."

"Ever work with drones?"

He took a bite of his cracker, chewing as the smile faded. "Drones?"

"You know, the flying things that take pictures and video?"

"No, that sound more tactical and technical than things I deal with."

"Are those diplomatic plates on your motorcycle?"

"Yes. I do contract work for embassy, which has privileges." He pointed at the chessboard between us. "This your game?"

"It is the board on which my grandfather taught me to play." I adjusted the Kewpie doll piece. "This actually might be a game he and I were playing."

He continued studying the board. "You are white?"

"I was."

He grunted and then smiled. "You are in grave danger. I can see why it is you stopped."

"Yep."

He continued to study the wooden squares on the weathered board. "They are very good, or you are very bad."

"Probably a combination of the two. You play?"

"It is birthright in my country, yes." He carefully spun the board on the lazy Susan. "Would you like to finish game?"

I thought about how long I wanted this song and dance to go on but decided there was no harm in getting to know my new opponent. "Are you sure you wouldn't prefer white or to start a new match?"

He studied the board. "I would simply play game out, but since this is first time we face each other, perhaps is best to start new?"

"Agreed." I spun the board again, and we both began to reset our pieces. "In which case I insist you take white and the first move."

He set his pieces and quickly opened with

the Smith-Morra Gambit. I accepted the sacrificed pawn. "Mr. Sidorov, I'm going to ask you a question, and I want you to think about it for a good long time before you answer me, okay?"

He sat there, staring at me and taking another bite and chewing as we traded pawns.

"Do you know a fellow by the name of Mike Regis?"

He continued to stare at me before taking another bite of his cracker and sustained the longest pause I'd ever borne witness to in an ongoing conversation. "I am under suspicion of something, Sheriff?"

I took a bite of my own cracker and chewed, but not quite as long as him. "You answer my question, and then I'll answer yours."

He studied me, but then I watched as his eyes flicked to the Poloz for only an instant and then returned to the bishop I had moved forward. "You're not going to convince me that you're here by accident."

He made himself another cracker and moved his queen. "No, a friend invite me here; he said fishing terrific."

"Fishing?"

"Yes."

"Fishing for what?"

He bit and chewed. "Trout, I think."

"Well, I believe you're fishing, but not for trout." I gave him my most becoming smile in return. "You were the one in the alley behind my daughter's house in Cheyenne."

He tried to swallow but choked with a laugh, finally recovering with a hand to his chest and staring at me. "I admit was warned about you."

"Warned by whom?'

He stopped laughing and shook his head as he advanced a bishop and, after I moved a pawn, another one. "They say that I should not underestimate you."

"They?"

"The powers who be, Sheriff. You see, when individual is brought in to attend to situation when they become more a problem than powers who can contend, I am sent for."

After a few more moves I was finding it difficult to discover a suitable posting point for my queen. "So, you fix for the fixer."

"That sound so clandestine. It is really not anything so covert . . . You were in military, Sheriff?"

"I was, a long time ago."

"As was I — Spetsnaz special forces. You?"

"Just a marine."

"But perhaps you still recall chain of culpability?"

I took a deep breath and released it, realizing I was in more than one trap. "In what sense?"

"Accountability, responsibility, answerability, liability, or, as I refer in your language, blameworthiness. There is great deal of misconception in the world as to role of those who take drastic action — murderers, hired guns, hit men, assassins . . . What is one thing these people have in common?"

"A complete lack of morality?"

He shook his head and moved another pawn, prolonging the game. "They are disposable. Hollywood like to portray killers as confident professionals, but who need competence when all need do is pull trigger? Much cheaper hire someone down on luck or with opportunity to advance themselves in organization — people who do anything to better situation."

"And you're that kind of man?"

"I am just one in long line of men." He gestured with the one hand and smiled. "Long time ago, my type gave up on evading your type, so instead of risking knights and bishops we move with pawns and sometimes yours — much more cost-effective." He glanced at the board and then at me. "Check."

I stared at the board, attempting to see some way out, acknowledging only a repetitious delay that would momentarily put off the inevitable. Keeping one hand on my sidearm, I reached out and toppled my king in resignation. "This sounds like a threat."

"Oh, no. More of warning." His other hand slowly lifted, and he carefully sat another, identical Poloz 9mm on the table, his hand still on it. "In my business, Sheriff, an individual always carries two. I will not make mistake of underestimating you, because I do not like to think of myself as disposable. I gotten to point in existence where life has certain value to me and that something of revelation. I am sure man like you places value on life, whether family, property, wealth . . . Any number things."

"You're asking me to turn my head."

He gave out a long sigh, but then the smile returned. "You seem like good man, Sheriff, and that is why I am here. Let me to tell you something — you are in very above your pay grade on this. These powers who be, they are not to send just one guy like myself against you, they are to send whole army, and they will make it look like it your fault."

"And you came here to tell me all this?"

"I come here to give options; it seem like only decent thing to do."

"Thanks."

"Do not mention." He carefully aimed the 9mm at the wall and returned it under the table where it disappeared like a vapor. "Now, you can arrest, but in pursue of title 22, chapter 6 United States code — I assure you I be out in twenty-four hours, and there nothing you or anybody else be able to do about."

"You're sure of that?"

"Unfortunately for you, yes." He stood and began wrapping up his meal and putting it away in his dry bag. "The more time I spend in your country, and that is almost as long as I spend in mine, the more I come to conclusion is not much difference — or whatever difference was become less and less every day." He held up a metal water bottle. "You are sure you not share wine with me?"

"Under the circumstances, I don't think it would be appropriate."

He nodded. "I retrieve other weapon or that also inappropriate?"

"Drop the clip."

He did as I said, placing both in the dry bag, then, making an exaggerated movement, brought out the other 9mm, dropping the clip and then the weapon in the dry bag with its brethren and then zipping it. "I be going."

"You're sure you don't want to spend the night?"

He slipped the strap of the bag onto his shoulder and came around the corner of the desk as Dog watched him like a T-bone. He extended his hand, and I stood and shook it as he looked up at me, at the scar over my eye and the missing piece of ear. "I am afraid, under circumstance, it also be inappropriate."

Dog and I followed him into the entry hall and then out onto the porch where he stepped down and swaggered toward his high-tech motorcycle in the heavy knee-high boots as I caught him with my words. "Hey, you can tell the powers who be that I'm not likely to resign as quickly as I did on the chessboard a few minutes ago."

He slowly spun, the smile still on his face. "That was message I was to convey, yes." He started to turn again but then stopped. "So, you never play against Sicilian Defense, Smith-Morra Gambit ending Siberian Trap?"

"I have. I just know it by another name."

"And what that?"

"My grandfather used to call it the Longmire Defense."

"Truly." He nodded in contemplation. "It

last used in tournament play, Rohit-Szabo in Spain 2001, and before that, '90 and '87."

"My grandfather used it against me when I was thirteen."

Calculating my age, he stared at me. "He truly ruthless, this your grandfather."

"You could say that, yep."

He started to go but then stopped again. "Sheriff, before, when I say you are in very above your pay grade on all this?"

"Yep."

He began backing away. "I should have say, you are in very, very, very above your pay grade on this." Chuckling, he turned, and, after a moment, Dog and I watched him motor away, the single headlight climbing the hills and disappearing into the darkness.

I snapped the safety strap on the holster of my .45 and petted Dog's head. "I guess I need to very, very, very up my pay grade."

400

14

Dog and I slept in the jail cell but were awakened by the creaking of springs in the opposite bunk as the early morning sun crept through the high, barred window.

I rolled over and pried off my hat to find Santiago Saizarbitoria sipping a cup of coffee. "Morning."

Sitting up, I rubbed my face and noticed it was my mug he was holding. "You didn't bring me a cup of coffee?"

He gestured with the mug. "I'm lucky I could figure out one, but you're welcome to it."

I appropriated it and studied him as I took a sip. "What's up?"

He held his hand out to me, and I noticed his badge was there. "I'm resigning."

"Really?"

"Yeah."

"Why?"

He leaned back, his spine resting on the

concrete wall with a thump. "I've just got a feeling that you and I have reached a parting of the ways and I shouldn't be here anymore."

"All because of this Mike Regis character."

"More than that."

I took another sip. "I'm listening."

"Look, Boss . . . I know Vic is your heir apparent, and I'm not sure if I want to hang around here under another administration. I'm thinking it might be better for me to move on."

"What about the Basque mafia that wants you to stand?"

He shook his head. "That's still a year away . . ."

"But that's where you're headed?"

"I haven't even thought about it."

"Sorry to bring this up, but what would you do in the meantime?" He stared at me for a moment and then placed his badge on his knee in avoidance of my eyes. "Why do I think this all has to do with Mike Regis?"

"He did offer me a job opportunity."

"As?"

"A consultant."

"And you don't find the timing in all this a little odd?"

"What do you mean?"

"I don't want you to take this the wrong

way, but you're a deputy in a rural county with four years' experience and along comes this corporate fixer and he offers you a high-paying position?"

"I didn't say it was high paying."

"Then what's the attraction?"

"Like I said, opportunity." He sighed and looked back up. "I'm tired of herding loose cows with my cruiser, Boss."

I nodded, resting the mug on my knee. "You're a young man, and I can understand that, but you're putting a lot of yourself in one basket, and as near as I can tell there are some rotten eggs in there."

"Look, I know you don't like Mike —"

"No, I don't, and I met another of his associates last night, a Maxim Sidorov, and I don't like him either." I thought about it. "Actually, I like him better than Regis. At least when he comes at you it's straight ahead."

"You don't think you might be a little off kilter by this whole involvement of your grandfather?"

"No, I don't. I'm thinking that my reasons for stirring up this hornet's nest might not be completely valid, but they're not the reason I'm going to see it through. The man who was killed, Bill Sutherland, proposed the Sovereign Wealth Fund back in '41 that may have been co-opted and implemented without his knowledge, and it's been siphoning money from the state for the better part of a century — theft on a monumental scale, and it needs to be stopped."

"And you're sure these are the guys who are doing it?"

"If not, they're the ones who are protecting the ones who are."

"You're sure of that?"

"Yep."

"How?"

"This Sidorov character pretty much told me in plain terms."

"Well, maybe he's involved but Mike's not."

I leaned forward, filling the space between us. "Will you listen to yourself for a minute? Mike Regis is the so-called problem solver for Tom Rondelle and this Sidorov is the muscle. Now, they've already tried to kill two people I know in an attempt to shut this investigation down, and I don't know who else they've got on their side, but I'm starting to worry about you."

He stared at me for a long while before retrieving the badge from his knee and holding it out to me. "I don't want to work here anymore if that's how you feel."

"You don't think your allegiances are a

little suspect lately?"

"No, but you do, and if you don't trust me anymore, then I'm out of here."

I stuck my hand out. "If you change your mind, you know where I am."

He stood. "No, I don't — half the time nobody knows where you are."

I took a breath and let that one pass. "You're sure you don't want two weeks to think about it?"

"No, I'm done thinking."

"Okay then, I'll miss you, Sancho." I watched him walk out of the cell and down the hall as I dropped the star in my pocket. I petted Dog's head. "C'mon, I bet you need breakfast — or are you quitting on me too?"

Ruby was waiting at her desk when we came up the stairs. "And then there were none?"

"Pretty much."

She motioned toward a package on her desk. "Woody shipped the other rifle back up, the one that didn't shoot Jules Beldon. He says he forgot to give it to you when you were down there."

"Roger that."

"He also sent up four bricks of ammunition that he said he has no use for."

I nodded and walked over, picking up the

405

package and the boxes of ammo. "You want to call up Double Tough down in Powder Junction and tell him he's being transferred for now?"

"Sure."

"How close is Barrett to heading to the academy in Douglas?"

"Another four months."

I leaned against the counter, cradling the rifle in my arm as she petted Dog and then made her way over to the kitchen area to pull out a bag of dog food and a stainless-steel bowl, filling it with kibble. "Know anybody who's looking for a job?"

She lowered the bowl to the floor. "Not right off."

"You want to be a road deputy?"

"I might be beyond that kind of thing, Walter."

"Any word from Vic?"

"No." She shook her head and looked at me with melancholic eyes. "I'm not sup-posed to be saying anything, but would it make you feel better if I were to tell you that I know for a fact that she's fine?"

"You spoke with her?"

"I didn't, but someone else did. That's all I can say."

"And why is that?"

"Because this person asked me not to say

any more."

I studied her. "Okay."

"And I have some more news."

"I'm listening."

"Trisha Knox, the young woman who was setting up camp in the local motels?"

"Yep."

"She's dead."

"How?"

"Strangled."

I thought about the woman who thought she was tough — the problem with being tough being there's always somebody tougher. "Where?"

"Absalom. She evidently checked in to the motel connected to that bar out there last night, and when they went to clean the room this morning, they found her."

I thought about the AR, a bar so named because the B had fallen off and blown away, along with the couple of dilapidated motel rooms a stone's throw from Cody Richard's trailer out on the Powder River. "Who's got it?"

"Campbell County."

"Sandy Sandburg?"

"None other, along with two cashiers and a bag boy."

"Can you get him on the phone?"

"Maybe, if there's service out there." She

walked over to her desk and immediately began working her magic on the computer and the ancient conference phone as I continued into my office, Dog having abandoned me for the quiet under Ruby's desk.

Sitting in my chair, I propped the rifle up and set the bricks on my desk. I looked at my Rolodex and twirled it, somewhat surprised when Vic's name came up. I stared at the card that had her home, cell, and even the numbers of her assorted family members back in Philadelphia. I thought about making a few calls to see if I could track her down through her family, but it didn't seem right. If she needed time, then I was going to give it to her, and if she was gone, she was gone.

Hell, everyone was gone these days.

The little red light on my phone began blinking as Ruby called out. "Sandy Sandburg, line one!"

I picked up the receiver. "What've you got?"

He chuckled and then continued in his used car salesman tone. "Hi, Walt. How are you?"

I cleared my throat. "Sorry, I'm kind of in a hurry."

"Well, Trisha Knox isn't."

"What happened?"

408

"Checked in last night with some guy waiting in a car outside, no ID on the vehicle or that individual, go figure. Preliminary from the cashier says she was raped and strangled. What's your connection?"

I adjusted the phone in my ear. "She'd set up camp in two of the local motels where she got beat up pretty bad. We got her squared away at Durant Memorial but then she took French leave a few days ago and I lost track of her. She supposedly had a client . . ."

"Anything on him?"

"About as much as you've got, supposedly he had a, and I quote, 'bitchin' car.' "

I listened as he scribbled in a notepad. "Bitchin' car, got it — that should narrow the search."

"When they get through with the whole room, let me know if they find anything?"

"Will do."

I hung up the phone and sat there, looking at the wall, then picked up the phone and dialed Durant Memorial, a number I'd memorized decades ago.

After a moment, a voice came on the line. "Durant Memorial Hospital."

"Hey, is Doctor Dave there?"

"And who can I say is calling?"

"Sheriff Walt Longmire."

"Yes, sir. Hold on just a minute."

I listened as she placed me on hold and waited until a familiar voice came on. "Doctor Nickerson, can I help you?"

"Dave, it's Walt. I was calling in to check on Jules Beldon?"

"I was just getting ready to call you about Lazarus."

"You're kidding."

"Nope, I'm in his room right now and he's having some chicken soup and a Diet Coke as we speak."

"I'm on my way over." I hung the phone up and hustled out front with the HK and ammo and slapped my leg to retrieve Dog. "Jules Beldon has risen from the grave."

"My goodness." Ruby came around with Dog and stared at me. "What are you going to do, Walter?"

Dog and I started down the steps toward the front door. "Go talk to him."

She stood at the top and looked down at us. "No, I mean about everything else?"

"I'm not so sure there's anything I can do." I shrugged. "Maybe put an ad in the paper?"

"Not funny."

I surveyed the photos of the men on the wall, a combined hundred years of sheriffing. "I'm thinking there were times when they had to work alone too."

"Are there things you're not telling me?"

I thought about it, lodging the rifle under my arm and balancing the ammunition boxes in my other hand. "I'm not aware that I've told you anything."

"What's going on with this MNLOP thing?"

"It may have a connected fund that some people are trying to hide."

"And is your grandfather involved?"

I started to turn and go. "I'm not sure, but I think he killed the two guys who had probably killed Bill Sutherland."

"Oh, good."

I turned back to look at her. "Oh, good?"

"Well, we all knew he was a killer, I'm just relieved that he wasn't a thief."

Shaking my head, I sighed. "You know, Rube, this is a strange business we're in."

"How's lunch?"

I sat in the guest chair watching the high-plains desert rat sip his soup. "Marvelous, my compliments to the chef."

I glanced back at David, who leaned against the door with his arms folded, evidently amazed that the old man had taken a licking and had continued ticking. "How do you feel?"

He dropped the spoon in the soup and reached up, brushing his fingers over the bandages that adorned his scalp. "My head hurts and my chest hurts, but I've had worse."

"When?"

"Pusan Perimeter in Korea, fer one."

I nodded. "Any idea who shot you?"

Beldon scratched at the bandages until Nickerson came over and pulled his hand away. He gave the doc a look but then recommenced spooning soup into his mouth. "First shot came from behind and got me in the chest, I guess. I knew I'd been hit and that if I didn't get to the Jeepster that I'd just bleed out there on the ground. So, I leaped through that sagebrush like a jackrabbit and worked my way toward the car."

"Did you see anybody?"

"It was sunset, and the sun was to the west and they were backlit, so it was hard to see anything. I made it to the car and was climbing in when I got clipped in the side of my head. I'm not sure, but I'm thinking I might've blacked out, at least for a minute or two. I do know I woke up because I could see someone walking through the sage with a rifle, one of those fancy new ones."

"HK416?"

"Hell if I know, all I do know is that they saw me moving and started shooting again, so I hit the switch on the Jeepster and went bouncing along on that two-track, finally making it out onto the main road where I headed north." He spooned in some more soup, finally taking a break to sip his Diet Coke. "Where did they find me?"

"I found you after you ran your car into Henry Standing Bear's Bar."

"He mad at me?"

"I don't think so."

"How's Wilma?"

Nickerson asked, "Who's Wilma?"

"My car, the Jeepster."

"Um . . . Salvageable."

He went back at the soup. "Oh, good — don't know what I'd do without Wilma."

"Jules, if there's anything you can remember about the person who shot you, I'd appreciate it, anything at all. Male, female? Big, small? Did they say anything?"

"No, they was just shootin'." He stopped for a moment, caught in thought. "There was something, but it probably ain't nothing . . ."

"What?"

"When they got close, after I woke back up, they were cussing the rifle 'cause it must've jammed or something."

"What did they say?"

"Hell if I know, it wasn't English."

"What was it?"

"Damned if I know . . ."

"Did it sound European, eastern European — maybe Russian?"

"Don't know, I never heard Russian."

Nickerson stepped forward and after a moment of tapping into his phone, he held it out and played a video of two men talking in strong Russian dialects. "Like this?"

Beldon listened for only an instant, and then his eyes lit up as he pointed at Nickerson's phone. "That, it was like that."

When I exited Durant Memorial, there was a one-man welcoming committee leaning against the railing on the steps and smoking a cigarette. "I heard you were hiring?"

I walked down the steps and stood in front of Jordan Heller. "Could be. What happened with the tire shop?"

"I punched the manager."

"Is that supposed to be part of your résumé?"

"Not really, but it's the truth." He smiled the crooked smile. "C'mon, your dispatcher says you need help."

"I do, but it has to be trained and sworn help, which means six weeks down in Douglas at the Law Enforcement Academy."

He stubbed out the cigarette and dropped the butt in his shirt pocket. "From what I hear, you need help now."

I started off toward my truck. "And where did you hear that?"

"Your dispatcher."

"Well, I do."

"Then hire me."

"You're not listening —"

"I am." He reached out a hand and caught my shoulder. "Look, that ass who tried to frame me with that HK, Mike Regis, who, by the way, came back by my place again last night."

I turned to him. "I'm listening."

"He was still nursing that black eye I gave him, but he offered me a job."

"And what was that?"

"Wanted to know if I'd kill someone."

"He said that?"

"In as many words, yeah."

"Who does he want you to kill, Jordan?"

"He didn't say — was just generally feeling me out on the subject."

"If you were to take a guess, who would it be?"

"You."

I stared at him. "Me."

415

"He didn't say as much, but he meant you."

"And what did you say to him?"

"I told him I wasn't in that line of work and that he needed to get himself another boy." He walked past me looking out at the cottonwoods and then turning back. "He said that if I didn't want the job that was fine, but that if I told anybody about this, he could make my life a lot harder than it is, and I told him to do his worst." The crooked smile again. "You check that rifle they say they found under my camper to see if I might've killed that gravedigger?"

"I did, and you're clear."

"What're you going to do with it?"

I smiled and shook my head. "You're really tied up with that rifle, huh?"

"You don't get accused of murder every day . . ."

"If no one claims it in the next twelve months, which I doubt anybody will, it'll be destroyed or sent down to Douglas for training at the academy if they want it or to Cheyenne to be used by DCI in their weapons cache for testing."

"No auction?"

"No."

He nodded and then stared at me. "I could be a lot of help to you with that weapon."

I waited a moment and then stated plainly, "You need to stay out of this."

"I believe I'm already in it."

I glanced around at the empty street. "Look, there's nothing I can do."

"Deputize me."

"You've seen too many movies; it doesn't work like that anymore — it's a question of civil liability and reasonable conduct and I don't think what's going to happen here can be confused as any kind of reasonable conduct."

"They're gonna kill you."

I looked down at the ground. "Maybe."

"No maybe to it, they're out there looking for somebody to do the job, and if they can't find anybody to do it, they'll do it themselves." He moved over to where I stood. "Now, I don't know what you've done or what you're digging into, but they intend to stop you with extreme prejudice."

I looked up at him from under the brim of my hat. "It's been tried."

"This ain't *High Noon* — I'm offering my help, Sheriff."

"Why?"

"I think you're a good guy, and you treated me fairly when I'm not sure I would've."

417

"That doesn't make this your fight."

"Yes, it does — or at least they did."

I started for my truck. "Go home."

"I haven't got one." I climbed in my truck as he called out after me. "Or a job either."

I sat there, giving Dog a pet. "Did you fill out an application back at the office?"

"No, I wanted to talk to you first."

"Go fill out an application."

He started to walk past my truck toward the parking lot but then stopped. "I don't think you're going to be around much longer, so who do I give it to?"

I started my truck and pulled out, mumbling to myself. "Good question."

I thought about going back to the office but instead decided to head out toward Absalom, rather than call Sandy Sandburg, and see for myself what had happened to Trisha Knox.

On the drive out, Dog kept glancing over at me. "What?"

He said nothing, so I kept driving. "You think there's another way I could've done all this? Well, I agree." I liked talking with Dog because we rarely disagreed, even when we disagreed.

Driving past my house, I thought maybe I should check in and make sure coyotes

418

hadn't decided to take up residence, but the thought of facing the lonely place was more than I could bear. As I drove by the Red Pony, I looked for Rezdawg, but Henry appeared to have gone home — besides, I seemed to be boring him these days. Driving on, I passed the cutoff to the family place but put the kibosh on that too, simply because it would only lead me back over to Ruth's place and a confrontation over one of the rifles I had in my truck.

I could pull over and sell weapons by the side of the road, but that seemed a little imprudent.

By the time I took the cutoff from the main road and crossed the bridge, I could see the cop convention at the AR was still going strong. Parking at the far end of the bar, I got out and walked over to where the Campbell County Sheriff was talking with some of the DCI crew. "Look, I've got dinner reservations, and I can't hang around here for another two hours."

"Dinner reservations with whom?"

Smiling, he turned to look at me. "My wife, if it's any of your business." I don't think I'd ever seen him not smiling. "What are you doing out here?"

"Checking on business — anything new to report?"

He nodded toward the row of motel rooms, and I figured anything I was going to get was going to be from the DCI cashier or bag boys and so started off in that direction. "Hey Walt, are you going to be around here for a while?"

I shouted back at him. "I can be."

His voice and predictable words faded away. "Well, there goes your new primary investigator . . ."

When I got to the walkway in front of the rooms, I could see two men talking and another dusting the desk for prints. "You guys moving in?"

I recognized the taller man as he stuck out a hand. "The legendary Walt Longmire."

"Investigator Price." I shook the hand. "Nobody else wanted the job?"

He looked past me at Sandy. "Yeah, Sandburg's been trying to get out of here for an hour."

"No liaison officer from the department?"

"He's on vacation, so I got the call, but I'm afraid Sandy's forgotten how to work."

I smiled. "He used to work?"

"So they tell me."

I looked past him and into the tiny room, a room I remembered as the one I'd stayed in during one of my very rare undercover investigations a few years ago. "What've we got?"

"Jeff Simmons, how are you, Sheriff?" The other individual, a shorter man with a few too many pounds and a walrus-like mustache, stuck out a hand. "We already processed the body and are just about done in here." We shook and he turned to the tech who had just gotten up from the floor. "Right, Eric?"

"Oh, sure. Minutes away."

I watched as he collected fibers from under the bed, and I could see where the sheets had been removed and bagged. "Anything?"

He turned, pivoting on the floor. "As near as I can tell, nothing. I have never seen a crime scene wiped this clean in my entire career. It's almost as if she strangled herself and then fell down on the floor."

"She fight?"

"Did she ever, but speaking from a preliminary viewpoint, there's nothing. I mean usually there's tissue or blood or something, but not this guy. Whoever he was, it's like he killed her and then evaporated."

"Prints?"

"Nothing." He looked past me to the DCI investigator. "Look, in all honesty, I'm not going to get this done in two hours —"

I interrupted. "You don't have to; I think I just got handed the primary on this one."

"You're right." Sandy hung an arm on my shoulder. "Did you know her?"

"Oh, she tried to camp out in a couple of motels over in Durant after her car broke down."

"She a pro?"

"Yep, I think so. I took her out to dinner and tried to get her squared away, but . . ." Something loomed in my memory, something I was trying to recall, but I knew better than to force it and so I just let it hang there in my mind like an itch.

Sandy moved his arm off. "Hard to figure how she got out here, but I guess if you're going to jump off, the first thing you do is go to the end of the world."

The tech, Eric, interrupted. "I don't think it was her choice."

Sandy patted me on the back, momentarily breaking my concentration. "Well, you got the best man for the job right here, so I'm going to beat feet." He glanced at Price. "Keep me up to date?"

"Will do."

Watching the Campbell County Sheriff waltz off toward his crew-cab dually, I moved away from the doorway, sat on a rickety lawn chair, and stared out at the

Powder River in a reasonable impression of Jordan Heller.

"You okay, Sheriff?"

"Yep, I'm fine." I listened as they worked in there, trying to remember what it was that had snagged in my stream of consciousness.

"Hey, Sheriff?"

I looked across the parking lot to where another member of the DCI crew was standing by my truck. "Yep?"

"Want me to let your dog out? He seems kind of antsy in here."

"Sure." I watched as he cracked the door. The big beast leaped out, galloped across the parking lot, and came down the walkway. He glanced in the room but then planted himself in front of me, once again placing his head on my knee. "You worried about me?"

We both sat there for a moment more, and then his hundred-and-fifty-pound body slid to the wooden planks, and he sighed.

I thought about the things I had to do next, including sending the newly acquired HK416 down to Cheyenne to get it tested and then start doing two things I wasn't particularly good at doing: making phone calls and asking for help. It was becoming obvious to me that I wasn't going to be able to do all of this myself, and if I wasn't aware of it before, then I certainly was after my conversations with both Jordan Heller and Maxim Sidorov.

As this thought crossed my mind I watched as a familiar green International Scout came down the main drag slowly and then pulled up and stopped right in front of us, just off the edge of the planked walkway. "Fancy meeting you here." Jordan glanced around at the collective manpower. "What's going on?"

"A woman was killed."

He switched off the engine of the Scout. "Anybody I know?"

"Trisha Knox out of Minnesota?"

"Nope, don't know her. You say she was killed?"

"I did."

"Right here?"

"Right here."

He got out of the International and came around, sitting on the edge of the porch and reaching over to pet Dog's head, which Dog allowed without protest — at least that was a vote in his favor. "I dropped off my application. I like your dispatcher, she's real nice."

"I'll tell her you said so."

"You have a picture of her?"

I thought about it. "Of Ruby?"

"No, the woman who was killed."

"I don't, but I'm sure we will."

"She involved in this mess you're dealing with?"

"I don't think so, but you never know." The nagging thought returned to my mind and once again I couldn't shake it.

"Something wrong?"

"No, just trying to remember something."

Price, the lead investigator, exited the motel room and glanced over at me. "Sheriff, I gotta go take a piss, so you mind just keeping an eye on things while I run over to the bar?"

"The AR, sure . . . You can't go here, I know that from the last time I stayed in this room, the toilet was busted, and I doubt it's ever been fixed."

"Actually, it has." Eric came out of the room with a collection of sealed evidence bags and headed for a van we euphemistically referred to as the Deathmobile. "There's a brand-new toilet back there in the bathroom."

"Toilet . . ." Of their own volition, my boots dragged under me and my legs straightened. I stood as the three men and a dog watched me, and then I turned and entered the room. Walking back to the bathroom, I pushed open the door and looked at what had been a used commode, but a great improvement over the one that had been here when I was here last.

The others followed as I walked over to the toilet and carefully lifted the lid off the tank, noticing that it had been broken before but had been glued back together.

Slipping a hand into the murky water, I felt around on the left side where there was more room, finally wrapping my fingers around something and then pulling it from the water and holding it over the tank where it could drain.

A relatively new cell phone in a turquoise-and-rhinestone waterproof case.

15

"The battery is dead."

I looked over DCI Investigator Price's shoulder at the device, one which I knew absolutely nothing about yet but still offered an opinion. "Can we charge it?"

"Unfortunately, it's an older Samsung, maybe pre-2009 when the companies got together to use a universal design for their chargers." He continued punching hidden buttons and then finally gave up, turning toward his partner. "Hey, Jeff, do we still have all her stuff in the van? She's bound to have had a charger somewhere."

Simmons looked at the van, the picture of dubious. "It's all in there and tagged, but —"

Without waiting for a full answer, Price shouted at the tech out by the back of the vehicle. "Hey, do you remember bagging a phone charger?"

The younger man, Eric, turned to look at

us. "You're kidding, right?"

Price held up the phone. "We found this, and it's dead."

Jordan Heller, leaning against his International, pulled a battered and scraped up phone from his pocket and held it out. "Is it like this?"

Price nodded. "Holy crap, exactly — you got a charger in your vehicle?"

The young man shook his head. "No, but I've got one at my trailer."

"Where's that?"

I answered. "About a mile down the road."

The investigator turned to me. "You want one of us to go with him?"

"No, I'll do it," I said as I took the phone from Price. I gestured toward Heller's International. "Yours or mine?"

"Mine's closer."

"You mind Dog?"

He glanced back at the overloaded Scout. "No offense, but I don't think there's room."

"I'll put him in my truck." I called to the beast. "C'mon." He followed I let him jump in the driver's seat where he turned to me as I closed the door. "Sorry."

I'd taken only two steps when the monster cut loose with a harrowing howl that rattled the windows of my truck. I turned to look at him as he stared at me through the glass, trying to rearrange his lips after the audible display. Then he jostled against the door in an attempt to get me to come back and open it. "No."

Shaking my head, I walked back, wondering what had come over him.

I stopped at the International and turned to Price and Simmons, holding up the phone. "You guys already dusted this thing for prints, right?"

Price smiled. "You trying to tell us how to do our job, Sheriff?"

"I don't even know how to turn it on." I pulled the handle and attempted to climb into the Scout but had to wait until Heller had snatched enough detritus and thrown it in the back to make room for me.

"What are you smiling at?"

"Oh, this just reminds me of somebody."

He hit the starter. "It's a mess; I'm living out of the thing a lot."

Pulling out, we headed south. "Why?"

He shrugged. "I get depressed at the camper."

I smiled again.

"What?"

"I'm in no position to judge in that I haven't been home in more than a week."

He drove, glancing at me. "Where the hell

429

do you sleep?"

I studied the storm clouds building to the west, hoping they'd head this way. "In the jail."

"You're kidding."

"Nope, I have for years. Mostly since my wife died."

"I'm sorry."

"No, it's okay." I thought about it. "It really is." And it was, at least more than it used to be.

Wheeling across the cattle guard, I waited as he pulled up to the trailer in his usual spot, the one where I'd seen him parked the first night I'd met him. I pulled the handle, climbed out, and followed as he made his way toward the trailer. "The charger is beside my bed."

"Do you want me to wait out here?"

He glanced west at the dark cloud bank that was piling up. "Nah, come on in out of the wind — you can be my first houseguest."

He held the door open, and I followed. "Close quarters."

"Yeah, sorry about that." He held out a hand. "You've got the phone?"

"I do." Pulling it from my jacket pocket, I handed it to him as he sat on the bed. Fishing a cable from near the wall, he plugged the thing in before slipping past me to open the small refrigerator door and producing two bottled iced teas. "Here, from my experience with these chargers it takes about five minutes for the phone to show any signs of life."

I took the tea and sat on one of the bench seats beside the sink. "This really is a nice camper."

"Thanks." He unscrewed the top of his tea. "A going-away present from my parents, as in don't let the door hit you in the ass on your way out."

I frowned. "That didn't seem like what your uncle was intimating the other day."

He laughed. "Well, there's what my parents say to him, and what he says to me." He lifted the tea. "Here's to parents."

I unscrewed the plastic top and touched the neck of my bottle to his. "Cheers."

He watched me swallow and then asked, "What was your relationship like with yours?"

"My parents?"

"Yeah."

"Pretty great, actually — it was my grandfather that I never got along with."

"What'd he do?"

"Rancher and a bank president."

"No, I mean what did he do to you?"

I took another sip of my tea. "Taught me

431

how to play chess."

"Well, I can see why you'd hate him for introducing that kind of misery into your life."

"Actually, those were the few moments when I didn't hate him." I glanced at the young man. "You don't play?"

"No, I just never had the patience for it — it seemed like torture the few times I tried." He looked at me again. "So, what *did* he do?"

"My grandfather?" I thought about it. "I guess he didn't approve of me or anything I did."

He leaned back on the bed, propped himself against the wall, and sipped his tea as the first raindrops began hitting the metal roof of the camper like buckshot. "And you think you're the first person that's ever happened to?"

"He was pretty active in his displeasure." I shrugged. "It was when I was young."

"Probably thought he was doing you a favor."

"Probably."

"Ever think he was trying to toughen you up?"

"It occurred to me." I took another sip of my tea and put it by the sink, then leaned back in my seat and looked out the front window toward the river as the sheets of rain continued to cross the high country like a bedspread. "How's the phone doing?"

He sipped his own bottle and glimpsed the screen. "Nothing yet."

I yawned. "The sun is going down, and that storm is really coming in."

He nodded. "Yeah, when it gets over there to the mountains it really disappears."

"So, you do turn your chair out there sometimes?"

He spread his hands in supplication. "A whole new world."

I yawned again.

"You sleepy?"

"I guess so . . ." I listened to the rain on the roof. "I haven't slept much lately, and I guess the sound is getting to me."

He glanced at the phone again. "It still isn't charged — it must've really been dead. Go ahead and close your eyes — I'll wake you up when it comes on."

"No, I've got too much to do."

He shook his head. "You can't do anything or go anywhere until this stupid thing charges, so you might as well catch a few winks."

I had to admit that it sounded inviting, but I just couldn't do it. Instead, I sat up and massaged my head. "No, I'm good . . ."

My hat fell to the floor, and I reached down, having trouble picking it up. "Wow, I am tired."

"So, where are we on the gravedigger case?"

"Jules Beldon?"

"Yep, that guy."

I sat my hat on the table and propped my head up with a fist. "He's awake."

"You're kidding."

"No, he's the one I was visiting at the hospital when you found me."

"He say anything?"

I stretched my jaw, trying to clear my head. "About what?"

"About who shot him?"

"He said he heard voices." I reached for my tea that I'd put on the edge of the sink.

"What kinds of voices?"

"Another language." I reached for the plastic bottle but my fingers slipped, and it fell to the floor between us. "Oh, no . . ." Jordan pulled himself from the bed, and I watched as he took a roll of paper towels from beside the sink. "Sorry . . ."

"Oh, that's okay, you drank most of it, and that's something hardly anybody does."

I struggled, trying to find his face as he stood in front of me. "What?"

"Ketamine, GHB, Rohypnol . . . I can't

remember which one it was, but I put enough in that bottle of tea to drop a rhino — you're gonna sleep, whether you like it or not." Swallowing, I tried to stand, but he put a hand on my shoulder, forcing me back down. "Do yourself a favor, Sheriff, and just stay seated. If you stand, you're going to fall like a poleaxed steer and that's not going to do either of us any good."

"You . . ."

"Yeah, me." He moved toward the door and opened it, the cool air rushing in but doing little good in reviving me. "The trick is how am I gonna get you into my truck? I guess I can just drive it over here and park right by the door."

Reaching to my back, I tried to retrieve my .45 from the pancake holster but then felt another set of hands there as they took my weapon and pushed me back. "No, let's not have any of that. There are some really important people who want to have a little chat with you, and we don't need you shooting up the place."

I felt the hands push me back as I fell on the bench seat, staring at the ceiling as it continued to rain.

Jordan came into view, holding the phone out for me to see the still-dead screen. "The charger doesn't work on this phone, which isn't mine, by the way. She had two phones; do you believe that? Anyway, if we did get this one charged, it would just show you a bunch of shit that you don't want to see — trust me." His face came in closer. "You still with us?"

"Gotta . . . Gotta get up."

He shook his head and examined my Colt, dropping the magazine, and then reinserting it. "It's embarrassing to see you like this; just relax, and it'll all be over with soon, I promise."

"Gotta . . ."

"No, just sit there and go to sleep."

And I did.

I slowly became aware that I was staring at my lap, but it was confusing because it was the same room that I'd been playing chess in with my grandfather. I felt as if I was surfacing through something heavier than water, heavier than thought.

Thinking I might see my grandfather's boots, I glanced around the floor, but there was nothing there and the carpet seemed older.

Strings of saliva strung down from my chin as I closed my lips and felt the dryness there, coughing and then swallowing what little moisture was left in my mouth.

"Hey, he's coming around."

I tried to raise my head, but the muscles in my neck wouldn't cooperate.

"Yeah, he's making noise."

Moving my arms wouldn't work either. I could feel a dull ache in both of them as I tried to bring them around, but they remained fastened behind me. Turning to one side, I was finally able to leverage the trunk of my body and could see that I was, indeed, in my grandfather's study. The chessboard was in front of me, and I could hear and smell the fire that was burning in the fireplace behind me along with some candles scattered around the room as I looked out the windows at the darkness.

A hand caught my chin and tipped my face up as someone looked down at me. "Damn, I didn't think you were ever going to drop off."

I shook my face, attempting to clear my head, but all that did was confuse me even more.

"I didn't think you'd wake up this soon either."

I could see the legs of somebody else standing beside him as my head dropped.

"C'mon now, wake up."

I tried again to raise my head, but it was like it was a boulder and I was downhill.

The hand grabbed my chin again, pulling my face up. "And don't say something stupid, like, 'Where am I?' or 'Who are you?' "

I cleared my throat. "Jordan Heller."

"None other." He studied my eyes as I tried to find his. "How do you feel?"

"Drugged."

"Good. You might as well stay that way for what we've got in store for you."

"And what's that?"

Another voice answered. "Oblivion."

I tilted my head in Heller's hand so I could see the second person, Mike Regis. I attempted to wipe the saliva from the corner of my mouth but didn't quite make it. "You just keep showing up like a bad penny, huh?"

"Sheriff, you're a problem that just won't go away, aren't you?"

I cleared my throat and swallowed, attempting to work up some spit so that I could speak again. "I do my best."

He pulled up a chair, dragging it around the partner's desk and having a seat, and I noticed both of them were wearing tactical BDU outfits in matching black. "Every one of us has given you an out, and you just wouldn't take it."

"How many of you are there?"

"A crowd, trust me. Not to worry though, you're a command performance so the gang will all be here. You must've made quite an impression on Max, in that he wanted to get you over to our way of thinking, but I told him that just wasn't going to work out."

"Sidorov . . ." I could feel my head starting to clear. "And Rondelle?"

"He will be. Hell, they all will be — I made it a requirement. I mean we've done some shady shit trying to keep this covered up over the years but nothing like killing a sheriff."

"So, that's the plan?"

"For what it's worth, yeah. I called what they refer to as an executive meeting, which means that all parties will be present at your demise — making sure that everybody keeps their mouths shut for good."

I took a deep breath, clearing my head. "Kill me, huh?"

"Well, you're going to just disappear, if that's what you're asking."

"And you don't think there will be questions?" I regarded Heller, standing there in his tactical gear and ball cap. "Especially for you, since you're the last person to see me alive?"

"Hey, nobody was in Absalom when we came back through, and I even drove your truck up here. We'll do something that makes it look like a suicide, and then they'll just never find the body — I tell you, this Powder River Country is great for that."

"Where's my dog?"

He laughed. "The dog? At a time like this you're worried about your dog?"

I stretched my arms against the handcuffs, the wood of the chair making alarming sounds. "Where's my dog?"

"Easy there, Sheriff, easy . . . I don't know. He wasn't in the truck when I got back there — somebody probably stole him or he got out and ran off. Anyway, what do you care, you're about to die."

"I can be hard to kill."

"Not half-drugged and handcuffed to a chair you're not."

Regis pulled his own chair in a little closer. "You don't have any idea the dollars you're dealing with here, do you?"

"Millions?"

"Billions. The initial Sovereign Wealth Fund never has been monkeyed around with by the state legislators with tax revenues set aside like the PWMTF, no severance tax, diverted savings tax, or citizen dividends like Rondelle is being forced to do. The SWF has just sat there soaking up money since the middle of the last century."

"How did you keep it hidden?"

"I don't know the details like Rondelle, but it basically came down to the state thinking the federal government was in charge of it and the federal government thinking it belonged to the state. Everybody was making money, so nobody asked any questions until you came along and started poking your nose in where it didn't belong."

"So, this was Harold Grafton and Bob Carr's baby, and when Sutherland came home from the war . . ."

"Yeah, from what I'm to understand they had to get rid of Big Bill. It's a shame, because I don't think they had any idea what this thing was going to grow into."

"Who killed them?"

He stood and shrugged. "I don't know, probably your grandfather, who appears to have been a much more reasonable man than you."

"Carol Wiltse knows what's going on."

"Who?"

"The state treasurer."

"Oh, her . . . Well, she's probably going to be taking a long trip to nowhere too."

Another voice sounded from behind them. "You're telling him too much."

Regis looked over his shoulder. "What does it matter, he's going to be feeding the coyotes in no time."

Past them I could now see Ruth One Heart seated on the arm of the tufted leather sofa. "Oh, no . . ."

She looked away, but then her eyes came back to mine. "Sorry."

"You too?"

"Money is money, Walt, and we're talking about a lot of it."

"So much of it that we can take all we want and never scratch the surface." Regis lowered his face, looking into my eyes. "The head honchos are going to be here in any minute, so if you want to have a change of heart and come over to the winning side, you need to do it some kind of quick."

I gasped a small laugh. "What makes you think you could ever trust me?"

"I don't."

"Then why the offer?"

"I just wanted to hear you turn it down."

I nodded. "Who killed the woman, Trisha Knox?"

"The hooker?" He made a face. "At a time like this, you really want to know about the hooker?"

"I don't like loose ends."

"I did it — I killed her."

"Why?"

"Really, the dog, the whore?" He shook

442

his head and laughed. "It was an extracurricular activity, a penchant I picked up out there in the real world, Sheriff. Not all lives matter, and some are just plain disposable." He stopped speaking as a set of headlights cast across the windows from outside. "Which you're about to find out."

Heller walked in that direction, pulling the curtains and cranking open the window for a better look. "They're here."

Regis looked back at me. "To be honest, I wasn't so sure they'd show up, I mean, Tom isn't too keen on getting his hands dirty but I told him that if we were going to do this that we were all going to do it just to make sure we didn't have any backpedaling. Skin in the game — if you know what I mean."

"You're never going to get away with this."

He stood. "Sheriff, we've been getting away with it for a long time."

Heller started toward the opening leading to the entryway, rapping his knuckles on the exterior wall. "It's too bad; we could burn this place with him in it, but the damn thing is made of stone."

Regis began following Heller but then turned and looked at Ruth. "I've got a feeling this is going to take some coaxing." He glanced at me. "You've got him?"

She folded her arms. "Where is he gonna go?"

I watched as the two men headed out into the entryway, but I could still hear them discussing something out there.

"Any last requests?"

I turned to look at her. "I can't believe you're a party to this."

"Well, Walt, some of our lives don't turn out the way we plan."

"I don't think that response covers the particular situation here."

She shrugged. "I fell in with a bad crowd, what can I say? I just got offered a better deal."

"Paying off your house?"

"Among other things."

"Is there anybody else I should know who is involved with this?"

She stood and walked toward me. "What, are you still investigating? They're going to kill you. You get that, right?"

"Are you?"

"Am I what?"

"Are you going to kill me?"

She continued toward the bookshelves and then stopped. "So, you still remember the Count of Monte Cristo?"

"Now is an odd time to ask, but yes I do."

"What do you suppose is the message in

444

that story?"

"Vengeance?"

She turned and looked at me. "It's more than that, and you know it."

I took another deep breath with the realization that there weren't that many left. "I'd say it's a tale of providence, of patience and hope, determination and faith."

She shook her head, looking at me sadly. "I think it shows how laws serve the men who society holds responsible for enforcing them and that those laws are as faulty as those men."

"Do you think that's why my grandfather killed Grafton and Carr?"

She turned her head to Lloyd Longmire's portrait. "I think he killed them because they killed his friend, and it was made easier because they were doing bad things."

"And what are you doing here?"

"What I have to." She turned to look at me. "Not all of us have the luxuries in life that you've had, Walt."

I rattled the handcuffs. "The luxury of being murdered, chained to a chair?"

She came over, crouching down and looking at my face. "I didn't want this."

"Then don't do it."

She looked toward the entryway, where the voices faded as the front door opened

445

and new voices joined in outside on the large wraparound porch, before turning her face back to me and sweeping away a wave of dark hair, a wide grin on her face. "Had you going, didn't I?"

"What?"

"White boys, you're so dumb." She moved to the side and then I felt her fiddling with the handcuffs that held me. "Peerless, but my key is so worn down I'm not sure if it'll work."

"You're still working for the Justice Department?"

"Yeah, and more importantly . . ." Her head swung around, the electrifying gray eyes and the effervescent grin in full display as I felt her fussing with the cuffs on my hands. "I saved your dog."

16

I glanced around the room as the voices and laughter sounded from out on the porch. "Are you armed?"

"Always, but it's not enough."

"Give me the key you've got, and I'll see if I can get it to work."

"They're going to kill you."

"Well, we'll have to see if we can stop them, huh?"

She pressed the key in the palm of my hand and then walked away, standing near the opening, next to the wall where she'd been before.

There were more voices from outside, and I listened to the front door open just as I fitted the key into the cuffs. Luckily the shank went in and the bit length fit, it was just going to be a battle trying to get the thing to turn without the key wards actually fitting. That and the fact that I was trying to do it behind my back.

"Hello, Sheriff."

I looked up to see Tom Rondelle standing in the doorway with Sidorov and Regis as Heller walked past Ruth and moved toward the fire where he pulled out an iron and adjusted the logs. His line of sight put him where he could see my hands, so I cupped one hand over the key and remained motionless.

"Want to throw me out a window now?"

"More than ever."

He laughed, walked over to the chair Regis had occupied, swept his long coat aside, and sat. "Nice place."

"Thanks."

"Comfortable?"

"Not particularly."

"Well, I'll try not to take up too much of your time." He flicked a piece of imaginary lint from the black wool of his topcoat. "I'm here to try to save your life."

"Are you, now?"

"Look, there's no reason this situation has to go where it's headed right now — nobody has to be hurt."

"Tell that to Jules Beldon and Nina Yadav."

He nodded, looking at Sidorov. "Yes, well some of my associates have behaved a little overzealously."

"Overzealously, is that what you'd call it?"

He spread his hands. "Fortunately, no one was killed."

"Trisha Knox."

He stared at me, blankly. "I'm sorry?"

Regis interrupted. "Nothing, nothing to do with anything."

I nodded toward the man to his left. "Your problem solver murdered a woman in a motel about fifteen miles from here."

Rondelle sighed deeply and turned to look at Regis, who shoved his hands in his SWAT outfit and looked away. "Not the first time, but be that as it may, I'm here to make you an offer."

"Not interested."

"Really, Sheriff? Really?" He leaned in, looking at the chess pieces on the board beside him. "I'm talking about some real money here. What if I were to offer you —"

"Don't waste your breath."

"I don't think you understand the kind of money we're talking about."

"I don't think I care."

He looked disappointed. "You do realize what's going to happen — you're just going to disappear. There will be no body, no weapon, no DNA . . . I mean nothing."

"Oh, there will be something, there always is, especially when my friends come for you, trust me." I glanced back at Heller. "If I were you, young man, I'd be concerned about being the lowest on the totem pole in this room. These guys are going to throw somebody to the wolves, and I'm betting it's going to be you. I don't know what they've paid you, but it probably isn't much."

He walked from behind me, pretending to look at the books on the shelves. "Shut up."

"You were the last one to be seen with me, the last one in possession of crucial evidence in a murder case, and they already planted the weapon that shot Jules Beldon on you."

"I said shut up."

"They're going to need to burn somebody, and boy, from where I'm sitting, you're flammable."

"I could say the same thing about you."

I started working on the cuffs again. "How long have you known these guys, a couple of weeks?"

"What of it?"

"You don't think they sought you out for a reason? With your background and temper, you're the perfect fall guy."

He looked at Rondelle and then at Regis and Sidorov. "I know too much."

I felt a little tension on the lever mechanism of the cuff on my left wrist. "The hell you say — they aren't going to let you live." I did a little glancing around myself. "Who's got my gun, because that's the one you should be looking out for."

Heller immediately stared at Regis.

"Makes sense in that he's got the most to lose; he killed a woman. Did you give him that cell phone? Because if you did, then you're dead. They're going to kill me and make it look like you did it, and then they're going to kill you and make it look like I did it or they're going to make it look like you killed that woman — either way, you're dead."

"Shut up."

"Are you armed? Because I'd be worried if I was the only one in this room without a gun."

He glanced at the others.

"This is a chess game, Heller — and you're playing checkers."

The click of the rachet in the cuffs was loud enough for all of us to hear, and I figured I'd done enough to get them riled with the most potent weapon I had, the truth. Lurching forward, I swung the chair at Regis and Sidorov as Ruth yanked out her 9mm, firing a few rounds toward the windows.

Rondelle scrambled backward as I bolted for the door, assisted by One Heart, and we both ran for the front as the others tried to get their bearings.

Ruth swung open the door and I ran for it, figuring the first thing I needed to do was get my hands on a weapon, but there was someone in a ball cap rushing toward us from the black Suburban near the fountain. "Shit."

She quickly slammed the door as I hooked her arm and headed toward the kitchen. "C'mon."

I could hear noises as the others were shouting as we pushed through the swinging door and then carefully eased it closed behind us. I whispered to her. "We either have to get some backup or get more weapons. Do you have any idea where my truck is parked?"

She raised up, looking through the porthole in the door and then lowered back down to look at me. "I would imagine out front."

"There's one of those HK416s out there and about four bricks of ammunition, along with the Weatherby."

"Well, that would do the trick."

"If they're still in my truck." I began moving toward the cupboard that led to the cellar.

"Where are you going?"

"We aren't going to be able to get to my truck from the front, and I'm betting they'll search the entire house. Fortunately, they don't know it as well as we do."

She followed as I opened the slatted doors and ushered her in, closing them behind us as we heard footsteps approaching. Pushing on the false-front cabinet, I stepped on the pedal at the floor and eased the door open as she moved forward with her phone, shining the light down the cobwebbed stairs. "You first."

"Thanks a lot." She continued, and I followed, closing the door behind us just as I heard the kitchen door open. "Aren't there lights down here?"

"There are, but somebody didn't pay the electric bill."

Each large wooden step was cupped at the center from the century of use in hauling the laundry, ice, coal, and firewood from the outbuildings. There wasn't much light from Ruth's phone, but it was enough to get us down to the larger area at the bottom where the buttress for the handcart sat to keep the thing from rolling into the stairs.

We started moving forward, walking between the narrow-gauge rails.

"I don't remember this being uphill."

"That's because you never had to push the cart."

She laughed softly. "You're right."

"It was built this way because when it was rolled under the house it was generally full and when it was pushed back it was usually empty." We kept going, and I figured we had a few minutes to talk. "So, where's Dog?"

"My place. I figured something was up when the guy at the AR called me, so I drove over and got him."

"So, when were you going to tell me you were working undercover for the feds?"

She started off again. "I needed to get Rondelle in the thick of things. Financial crimes are kind of hard to track, but the attempted murder of a sheriff, that's pretty concrete."

"I thought that's how you guys got Capone?"

"No, I think syphilis eventually did that."

I trailed along after her. "So, you were using me for bait."

She stopped and turned to look at me, the apology on her face. "In all honesty, Walt, I didn't think it would get this far. I didn't think they were this desperate, but I guess with the amount of money we're talking about . . ."

"How did you guys find out about the Sovereign Wealth Fund?"

"Carol Wiltse and Linda Roripaugh, the CEO of the PWMTF; once we got looking the whole thing fell into our laps pretty easily."

"So, this all started with me finding my grandfather's rifle."

"I guess it did."

Using the mismatched key, I got the other cuff off my wrist and then stuck the entirety in my back pocket. "I wonder what Grafton and Carr would've done if my grandfather hadn't killed them?"

She turned and continued down the tunnel, careful to step on the ties that supported the rails. "You don't know that he did it, Walt."

"Yep, I kind of do . . ." We were almost to the outbuildings when I heard something behind us. Touching Ruth's arm, I stopped her and whispered. "Just a minute." At the far end from where we'd come, I could hear noises. "Did you hear that?"

"No."

"Well, I did. Turn off the phone light but keep going." Allowing her to go ahead, I waited a moment and then saw the general illumination of phone lights, similar to the one that Ruth had been using, shining down the steps at the far end.

Hustling on, I caught up with her even in the darkness and whispered . . . "There's somebody back there, and they're coming this way.

"I can't go very fast when I can't see."

"I know, but if you turn on that light, they're likely to throw a few shots this way just to see if they can hit us." She stopped, and I ran into her. "Sorry, what is it?"

"The coal cart, the steps should be right on the other side."

As the words left her lips, the string of lights I'd mentioned before glowed to life and illuminated the entire tunnel.

"Damn, they must've gotten the generator working. Get up the steps, quickly."

She did as I said but then paused just before throwing back the trap door on the floor above. "What are you going to do?"

I moved behind the heavy cart, still loaded with coal. "Something creative."

She disappeared upward, and I crouched behind the cart and looked down the length of the tunnel as somebody moved down the steps. He was wearing a ball cap, and I was pretty sure it was the guy who had come at us from the Suburban out front, possibly the driver.

I saw a logging chain that lay across the rail, chocking the large metal wheels of the cart.

I took one last look at the individual at the far end who was moving my way and leading with a handgun, so I reached down and yanked on the chain. Nothing happened, and I yanked again, figuring the thing must've been rusted to the rails. Peeking over the cart, I could see the driver was almost halfway through the tunnel and must've heard the noise from the chain.

Wrapping my hand around the thing, I gave one great heave and watched it break loose at the same time a shot ricocheted against a support timber off the wall beside me. I ducked down with my back against the still-unmoving conveyance.

There was another shot and another ricochet as the round bounced off the metal bracings on the side of the cart and into the ceiling, breaking one of the naked bulbs like a firework.

Putting my back into the cart, I lodged my boots against the buttress on this end and pushed like a blind mule. There was a brief shift and then nothing.

Bracing my boots once more, I hit the thing like the lineman of yore that I used to be and felt it give way and slowly begin rolling.

There had once been enough of a walkway on one side to make your way through the tunnel without stepping on the tracks, allowing you to pass if someone, namely Ella, my grandfather's housekeeper, was rolling the thing, but collapsing dirt had filled in that area.

As near as I could tell, the driver had nowhere to go but back the way he'd come, which he did at a panicked pace.

As I stood there watching my cover roll toward him, he quickly realized what was happening. Throwing one more quick round my way, which whizzed by me and hit the wooden steps, with splinters going everywhere, he turned and began to sprint.

I don't know for sure, but if he'd just started sooner and not taken time to throw that shot at me, he might've made it, but maybe not. Considering the cart itself and the full load of coal it carried, the thing probably weighed something close to a thousand rolling pounds, which explained the rate of speed it was rapidly attaining.

Forgetting about me, the guy was now in full retreat, fleeing for all he was worth when the toe of his tactical boot must've caught one of the ties. He'd had the misfortune of tripping close to the buttress at the far end, and I watched as he crumpled into the timbers there, trying to half-scramble, half-crawl away before the cart crashed into it.

He didn't make it, and the high-pitched scream broke off suddenly and terminally as the half-ton of cart and coal slammed into him and the timbers with a force enough to shake the entire tunnel.

I climbed the steps to find Ruth holding her cell phone up in an attempt to find a signal. "It won't work here."

"I figured I'd try. Was there somebody?"

"Was . . ." I glanced around the outbuilding at the coal bin, the laundry tables, and the old tin-lined ice vault for a weapon, any kind of weapon. "Do they just have handguns?"

She moved toward the window and wiped some of the dust away to get a better view. "Who knows."

Reaching up, I took an oversize icepick from one of the rafters. "We've got to get to my truck."

"That's going to be difficult, because I'm thinking that's where they're gathering right now."

"Rondelle isn't going to have the stomach for this and will try to get out of here, especially now that I killed his driver."

She peered over my shoulder toward the hatch in the floor. "He's dead?"

"I'm pretty sure."

"Why didn't you get his gun?"

"It's buried under about a thousand pounds of coal."

She glanced at me. "Regis and Heller will stay."

"What about Sidorov?"

"He's something of a wild card."

"He might try to get out of here with Rondelle." I moved toward the door and stood there looking the length of the cattle barn to the right of the main house and the icehouse where there was the sound of a motor running — a generator, had to be. How in the heck had that thing stayed operable? Unless it was Tom Groneberg who had kept it in service.

Good ol' Tom.

Glancing back at the barn, I revoiced my plan. "If I go through the stalls, I can get pretty close to the front where all the vehicles are parked, including my truck."

"You?"

"We need backup." I turned to look at her. "You've got to take that phone and go find service. I think you can get through if you go up there at the family cemetery on the northeast ridge."

"And leave you down here with them — are you nuts?"

"I know this place better than anybody, with the possible exception of you."

"Walt . . ."

"We need help."

She tried to hand me her sidearm. "Here."

"No, you keep it." I held up the icepick. "I'll take a page from the Henry Standing Bear handbook."

She attempted to shove the 9mm into my hands. "Walt, how old are you?"

"Old enough to know better." I started moving toward the door. "I'm not letting you go out there without a weapon. Period." Cracking the door open, I looked outside at the luckily overcast sky. "Now, I'm going to go across to the barn and then work my way to the left while you head behind the outbuilding toward the icehouse where there's a dipping vat, a channel you ran cattle through."

"I remember."

"It's about six feet deep, and after you get through it, you'll be near a corral by the river. If you stay near the river, you can get over the bank and work your way east and then climb up the back side of the ridge with nobody seeing you. Now, once you get close to the main gate, you should be able to get service. Call in everyone — my department, the Campbell County Sheriff, Highway Patrol, everyone."

"Walt —"

"I have to stop them." I motioned for her to move. "Go!"

She shook her head, but I stepped out and held the door for her as she went and turned right, following the route I'd given her. I stood there until she disappeared behind the icehouse where she could get to the river and be out of harm's way.

As I turned, I could hear voices out front but to the left near the fountain, which was probably where they were. I couldn't see my truck but assumed it must've been to the right, near the standing stall where I'd first seen Sidorov's motorcycle.

I held the icepick in my right fist, for whatever good that was going to do, and crept across the opening toward the main entrance of the barn at the center. Constructed of the eighteen-inch-thick stone, it was divided into two parts, one side for cattle and the other for horses, with loft space above.

A door hung partially open, the thick-planked floors still holding up against the wear and tear of more than a century. The interior walls were also made of stone, the corners rounded, so as to not scrape the sides of the big draft horses that did so much of the work in that era.

Standing in the breezeway, I could see to the end of the building, stalls lining both sides. Walking in that direction, I wondered what they might've done with my sidearm but figured I'd find out soon enough.

I thought I might've seen something at the far end of the barn, near the loafing shed overhang where the far doors opened up. Moving to the side, I stood there completely still, shadowed by the grain and hay chutes that led up to the loft.

Somebody was there — I'm not sure how I knew, but I knew.

It was possible they knew I was here too.

The only thing to do was to stand still, like a blood trail waiting to happen.

I wanted to get going to see if I could retrieve a weapon, but I also knew that my adversaries were out there.

Movement.

It was also possible I was being bluffed by a raccoon or an owl, but I stayed put.

Movement.

This time I could see the outline of an individual doing the exact same thing I was, standing back against the stall divider and glancing around. It was about then that I saw the night vision goggles, just bare traces of the phosphor image intensification screen behind the optics.

Leaning back, I covered myself, unless the damn goggles could see through a wooden stall divider, and ducked, then peered through a crack between the heavy wood slats and could see the shooter checking the stalls with a short rifle that looked to be the HK from my truck. He went about it in a purely professional sweep and hold.

There was no one else with him, but he was moving this way and in a few moments he'd be on me — and I had an icepick.

Standing back up, my shoulder hit something, and I felt at it, realizing it was a light switch in a conduit box with a cable leading up into the loft.

What were the chances that the generator was also connected to the service line leading to the barn? What were the chances that the switch actually worked? What were the chances that the light bulbs were intact and operable?

It's not like I had a lot of options, me and my icepick.

I stuffed my sole weapon into my belt, then pulled the gloves from the pockets of my jacket, put them on, and flattened my chest against the divider, standing there and waiting with one hand on the light switch and the other ready to divert the barrel of the assault rifle when the shooter came around.

I could hear his footsteps barely scuffing the wide planks as he worked his way toward me, pausing at each stall.

The noises stopped at the double stall next to me, and I knew the moment was about to happen and just hoped I didn't deflect the barrel of the assault rifle down and bury about thirty rounds from a STANAG detachable magazine into my leg.

The barrel of the HK came first, and I palmed it, pushing it down but hanging on to it with my best death grip as I flipped on the lights. They didn't flicker the way they had in the tunnel but blew on, full bore — one of them right above us.

The HK went off, but the shooter fell backward screaming as the electronically enhanced, image intensifying phosphor blasted into his optic nerves like twin solar flares.

I tried to yank the rifle away from him, but it was attached with some kind of harness, so I had to settle for driving him farther backward and across the breezeway, bouncing him off one of the timbers and smashing his back into the heavy wood of the manger in the stall on the other side, then hitting his head on the feed dump with a resounding crack.

He slumped to the ground, and I listened as the air left his body. Reaching down, I disconnected the harness, picked up the rifle, and noticed that the barrel was now bent about three inches from the muzzle, just past the fire break.

"Well, hell . . ."

I walked back across the breezeway and flipped off the light. There was more shouting from outside.

I figured my cover was blown, so I moved back over and checked to see who the shooter was, pulling the ball cap and night vision goggles off to reveal the face of Heller. "You should've stayed out there on the Powder River, my friend."

Checking his pulse to see if he was still alive, I removed the cuffs from my pocket and attached him to the stall divider and then checked for a sidearm but found nothing. I thought about taking the night vision goggles, but my unfamiliarity with the damn things might lead me to do something stupid, like shooting myself.

Standing, I took the useless rifle with me, figuring I could use it as a club or a bluff. I worked back to the midway point in order to look across at the outbuilding and the main house and then to the far end of the barn where I could see an individual running across into the end of it.

With nowhere else to go, I pushed open one of the doors and stepped out. There still weren't any lights on in the main house windows, but I wasn't sure if the generator in the icehouse was connected there at all.

Leading with the bent rifle, I moved across the fifty yards quickly and got to the kitchen side where I glanced in the window but could see nothing. Ducking down, I went past the window and got to the corner of the porch. I could see the Suburban still idling out near the fountain, where, amazingly enough, there was water spraying up from the maiden's broken pot. Obviously, the generator was connected to the pumps that brought water from the river to the fountain.

There were two men talking next to the idling vehicle, and I could tell from their outlines that one was Rondelle, which left at least two unaccounted for — Regis and Sidorov, the two I had to worry about the most, both of them being high-level specialized combat vets.

But I had a rifle with a bent barrel and an icepick.

I retreated, circled around to the back door of the kitchen, and entered through there. The pantry door hung open and so did the trick cabinet that led to the tunnel, but nobody was there. Maybe they'd already checked on their friend, or maybe they'd left him down there to rot.

Moving through the kitchen, I raised the HK in a battle-ready position just in case I ran into anybody and could possibly bluff my way out. I glanced through the porthole window in the kitchen door and could see the fire was dying in the study — that didn't necessarily mean there was anybody in there, but I probably needed to know. I still needed a weapon, and the only place I was certain where there was one was in my truck. It was possible that the one in my hands was the one from my truck, but I'd be damned if I knew.

Maybe this wasn't the weapon from my truck.

Maybe there were more weapons in my truck.

Maybe my truck wasn't locked.

Maybe I would get lucky and be able to shoot around corners with the bent barrel of the assault rifle in my hands. I sighed, slowly pushed the swinging door open, and stepped quietly out onto the wooden floor of the entryway where I concentrated on the windows and the balcony above.

I could still hear voices outside and figured that was the direction I was going to have to go in, but first I needed to make sure nobody was coming up behind me with an operable weapon.

Moving to the left, I could see into the larger portion of the room that somebody was seated in the chair opposite the one I'd occupied. I leaned into the opening and could see it was Ruth, handcuffed to the chair the same way I'd been.

"You do not think we let her get away, do you?"

I turned to see Sidorov leaning on the bookshelves on the right, the dark gleam of my own Colt .45 apparent in the minimal light.

I also noticed it wasn't pointed at me.

"Is that my sidearm?"

"Is, da." He pushed off from the wall. "I do not wish shoot her, but also not wish shot by NATO round in HK — it would, for Russian, be bad form." He glanced past me as he moved toward Ruth.

"Are you all right?"

She nodded, sighing. "Yes, I just feel stupid."

I looked back at Sidorov, who was momentarily distracted, and casually flipped the switch on the left of the rifle I held to full auto. "I don't suppose you'd like to play another round of chess for her?"

"I wish I have time, Sheriff, but am afraid associates like finish business and move on."

"I'm surprised Rondelle hasn't already left."

Sidorov laughed. "Businessman. He anxious, yes." He moved to the left, circling around Ruth. "You kill driver downstairs?"

I tracked the muzzle of the HK along with him. "If he's dead, I did it."

"And you have rifle, so you kill other man?"

"Heller? No, I just knocked the shit out of him — I try not to kill people if I don't have to."

"Ah."

"Am I going to have to kill you?"

He shrugged. "If you fire, so will I and woman dies."

"No way to get you to come over to our side, is there?"

"I do not think you have amount of flexible capital they have."

"Probably not." I raised the barrel of the

470

HK in the air, keeping the muzzle in the shadows. "Okay, here you go." I laid the thing down on the chess table with the butt toward him, which spilled the pieces to the floor.

He stared at me, somewhat unsure.

Then I moved around Ruth and pulled her cuff key from my pocket in order to release her from what I assumed were her own cuffs.

Sidorov quickly reached out and took the HK, just as I knew he would. "What you are doing?"

Getting her loose, I pulled her up to a standing position and then began backing away from him. "We're leaving."

"No, cannot allow."

I pushed Ruth behind me and continued moving back, making sure there was a good twelve feet or so between us. "Well, then, you're going to have to shoot."

I watched as he lifted the barrel of the HK toward us, I'm sure being of the thought that it would be more intimidating than my Colt .45 that he tossed onto the chessboard the way I had. "Do not do this thing, Sheriff."

"You do what you need to do."

To his credit, he aimed down at one of my legs and then pulled the trigger. Just as I'd anticipated, the first round lodged in the barrel and the subsequent rounds hit it and exploded the rifle in his hands.

It was a quick blast, because he must've gotten his finger off the trigger as fast as he could, but the result was the same. I've seen a few sidearms misfire and explode on the range and even a few back in my military training, but this was far worse than anything I'd ever seen. The top rail of the barrel splintered backward and into his face. He dropped the thing, but it simply bounced on the floor as he fell backward clutching his eyes.

I grabbed my Colt and leaped forward, quickly checking to make sure that it was loaded, cocked, and ready to fire — which it was. I turned to Ruth. "Check him for weapons and see if he can be saved."

She moved toward the moaning man lying on the floor, who was still covering his face with his hands. "What are you going to do?"

"Stop them." I started toward the front door with a half-hearted smile. "If I can."

"I was able to get a text off before they caught me, but I'm not sure if it went through."

"Let's hope it did." Going through the opening and into the entryway, I stopped at the front door in order to set up along the wall to the left, away from the front door that swung open in that direction.

There were some noises from outside but then nothing.

I glanced over at the front windows where there was more light, so if anybody were to show themselves I'd easily see them first.

It was a long wait, but I heard some scuffling noises on the porch and finally saw the knob begin to turn and the door slowly open, a semiautomatic leading the way.

"Freeze."

They didn't, kicking the door toward me and shooting wildly, so I fired.

Two shots splintered the heavy slab, leaving two dime-size holes on this side. I heard something hit the ground on the other and then once again waited. There was no return fire, so I moved forward, kneeled down, and pulled the door open with two fingers.

Rondelle lay on the stone surface of the porch, copious amounts of blood pooling out from his head and upper chest. A 9mm was at his side as his body twitched once, then twice, and then was still.

The idling Suburban remained parked near the fountain and by my truck near the barn. Standing, I swung the door back slowly and looked both ways before stepping out onto the porch.

By my count, there was still one of them out there, somewhere.

Stooping, I placed a few fingers at Rondelle's throat, but there was nothing.

I stood and looked out into the night, mostly around the still-running SUV, but couldn't see anyone.

I'd just started to take a step when I heard and saw the shot and then felt it barely strike me on the side of my head as it passed.

Falling backward over Rondelle, I landed in his blood but still brought my Colt up and aimed at the side of the building where the sound and muzzle flash had come from. I lay there with my arm outstretched, ready to fire. "I guess you finally got Rondelle to put some skin in the game."

"I did." Regis's hollow laugh echoed from around the block wall at the corner of the porch. "Everybody else dead?"

"I've been working on it."

"More money for me." There was a pause. "Did I get you?"

Palming the side of my head, I pulled back a bloody hand and felt an oncoming headache where the bullet had grazed my skull. "Come see."

"I think not." The laugh again. "So,

Sheriff, this is where we talk — man to man."

"Is that what we do?"

"Look, I'm not a bad guy . . . There's no reason for us to shoot each other out here in the wilderness. We're talking about seventeen billion dollars. Did you hear me? Seventeen billion with a B. Hell, move away and go buy yourself another county."

Pushing off the ground, I sat up, keeping my .45 trained on the corner where his shot had come from and where his voice carried. "I like it here."

"You're not being very flexible in this negotiation."

Scooting my legs forward, I sat on Rondelle's dead body, only slightly disconcerted as the air exhausted from his kidney-colored lips. "Your boss is dead. How are you going to get the money?"

"Oh, Sheriff, you really need to get with the times. It's all electronic these days, a few clicks on the computer and a quick check of the Basel AML Index to see who has the safest rating this week and then the money goes to the Cayman Islands, Haiti, Laos, China, Yemen, or some other goddamned place where the Financial Action Task Force, the World Bank, or Transparency International can't get a toehold." His voice sounded a little closer now. "C'mon, Sheriff, it's found money."

"Stolen money."

"From who?"

"The people of Wyoming."

"Oh, for God's sake, the people of Wyoming, including your sanctified attorney general, Joe Meyer, or that high-and-mighty state treasurer, Carol Wiltse?"

"Carr and Grafton killed her great-uncle to cover that money up."

"Yeah, and your grandfather killed them for doing it . . . Look, Sheriff, let's just stop the killing here, okay?"

"Is that what you told Trisha Knox before you strangled her?"

Silence.

"Look, I'm going to make it easy for you, okay?" There was a sound and suddenly a 9mm semiautomatic Glock 19 landed in the grass off the front steps. "There, now can we talk?"

I eased up off the dead man and slowly stood. "I thought we were."

"Face-to-face, I just want to get the hell out of here, Sheriff. I'm going to walk out to that Suburban and just get in and drive away and out of your life."

Angling to the side, I pressed myself up against the stone wall and leaned forward just a bit. "Can't allow it."

Another shot rang out and another 9mm slug dug into the stone right above my face, sending splinters of sandstone into my forehead as I ducked but then watched as Regis stepped around the corner with another weapon raised. "Never walk the walls, Sheriff, it's where you make noise and where the bullets live."

I began to get my .45 back up, but that small measure of distance meant I was going to come in second — no place in a gunfight.

There was the blast of gunfire again, but I held aim on Regis as he turned to look behind himself. At that point he pivoted back to stare at me and dropped the second Glock from his loose hand. Then he stood there for a few seconds and walked away, a little unsteadily, toward the idling vehicle near the fountain.

He'd taken about five steps when he swayed like a strong wind had hit him. He steadied himself and then paused again before raising a fist as if he were at a rock concert. Then his knees buckled and he fell into a crouch where he silently genuflected, almost as if in prayer, and then fell over into the dirt.

I stepped forward to the edge of the porch

and stared at him as I picked shards of sandstone out of my forehead, finally turning to see Ruth hanging out from the study window with Sidorov's smoking Poloz 9mm in her hands.

I holstered my Colt. "Thanks, Auntie."

EPILOGUE

"How long have you known?"

The medical tech continued pulling the rock shards out of the side of my face because I had refused to go to Durant Memorial Hospital. I sat there on the tailgate of my deputy's truck. "In his security box, among his financial papers, were the receipts from when he'd paid for you to go to Wellesley."

She leaned against the SUV of one of the DCI guys out of Gillette. "That's it, that's all it took?"

"Well, I couldn't help but wonder why he'd paid for your entire college education, but no, I still remember the way he looked at you when we were kids. Before he died, my father hinted at it, but never told me the whole story." I took a breath before asking the next question. "Did you know that Lloyd and Ella were a thing?"

She smiled in the harsh glow of the emergency lights from the investigative team who were working across the square in the main house. "A thing . . ."

"What would you call it?"

"I think they were in love."

I paused as the tech dabbed at the holes in my face and waited for him to get out of the way. "I didn't mean . . ."

She shrugged. "It was a different time."

"She was thirty years younger than he was."

"Those Longmire men, they have their wiles."

"He took advantage of her."

Her eyes came up, defiant. "No, he didn't." She pushed off the SUV and walked a little ways away, finally turning and looking at me sideways. "The dynamic of these conversations has changed in that I'm Lloyd's daughter, okay?"

"There's no excuse —"

"Stop it, just stop it." She took a step toward me. "You found receipts, but I have the letters that ended with the same phrase every time — Never let go."

I stared at her as the med-tech excused himself to get some bandages, but he likely just wanted to get out of the line of fire.

She watched him go and then turned back to me again. "He was widowed and begged

her to marry him for years, begged her —
but she was still married, and it was a different time. She didn't want to hurt her husband or the rest of my family. I know you didn't like him, Walt, but he was a good man."

"Bill Sutherland —"

"He didn't kill him, and you know it; they probably took that rifle in hopes of incriminating Lloyd and hid it. If he killed Grafton and Carr, then they deserved it." She glanced past the fountain toward the ranch house. "The same fate Regis and Rondelle deserved — some rats can't be retrained."

I nodded, glancing back at the hubbub of cashiers and bag boys. "What about the kid, Heller?"

"He's stupid, and sometimes there's a price for that too."

I stared at her. "You know, I'm seeing more and more of him in you every minute."

She actually laughed. "I hope so."

"So, what are we going to do, you and me?"

She came over and sat on the tailgate as well. "Go on living our lives . . . As extended family." She took my hand, turning it over and studying it for what, I wasn't sure. "I knew it was wrong when I kissed you, even though it felt so good." She laughed again.

I waited a moment and then repeated myself. "What are we going to do?"

"Walk away, Walt. Just walk away."

"You have his toughness."

"No, you're the tough one." This time she didn't laugh. "And you're going to have to do it, because if you don't, I know I can't." She slipped off the tailgate but still held my hand. "I've got another two years before retirement back in DC and who knows if I'll keep my parents' place or not."

"I thought it was your place?"

"It was, but I don't know if I want you as a neighbor."

"I'm that bad, huh?"

She stared at me with those spooky gray irises for what seemed like a very long time before pulling her hand away. "Go home, Walt."

"You also have his eyes."

She didn't turn back this time. "And so do you."

I started to get up, but the med-tech was back, along with the DCI investigator, Louis Price. "How do you feel, Sheriff?"

"Better than most of the folks around here." I tried to look past him, but Ruth seemed to have disappeared into the darkness, just as I knew she would.

He laughed, nodding as he handed me my

hat. "One wild night is all I can say."

"Heller?"

"On his way to a holding cell in Gillette, unless you want him?"

"I do not." The tech finished patching up my face and then snapped his kit closed and walked away without another word, evidently having heard enough of mine. "Sidorov?"

"The Russian . . . he's going to lose the one eye, but he'll make it." He stuffed his hands in his pockets and jingled his change. "He'll turn state's evidence — he's just the type."

"Do I have anything to worry about?"

"Legally, no. With the recordings we got from One Heart, the state treasurer's office would've sent those sonsabitches to prison for the rest of their unnatural lives."

"Recordings?"

"The ATF agent, Ruth, she recorded the whole thing with Rondelle and Regis on her phone — no need for wires anymore."

"Well . . ." I sighed. "They were judged by a higher court."

"Feeling sorry for yourself?" He studied me, but when I didn't answer he continued. "I wouldn't, they were gonna to kill you, Sheriff, sure as anything."

I slipped off the tailgate and stood, stretching and yawning even though it hurt my face. "And yet, here I am."

"The legendary Walt Longmire."

"I'm not feeling very legendary right now, Investigator."

"Don't worry, it'll come back to you." He patted my arm. "In answer to your question, no you're not in any trouble with the law, but both Regis and Rondelle were powerful men with a lot of connections in the state."

"Is that a warning?"

"Just some friendly advice."

"Thanks." I placed my hat on my head. "Where's my dog?"

He nodded past the fountain amid the gathering herd of official vehicles. "One of your deputies showed up and corralled him from One Heart's place."

"Do you need anything more from me?"

"Nope, we'll do the follow-up in a few days, if that's okay with you — you look like you haven't slept in a week."

"Non-drug induced, I haven't."

"Go home and get some sleep, Sheriff."

He patted me on the back as he walked off and I circled around my truck where I found Saizarbitoria petting Dog's head which was sticking out of the driver's-side window. "Hey, Boss."

"Howdy."

"How are you doing?"

I stretched my jaw, feeling the bandages that were holding my face together. "I'm okay."

"Look, I . . ."

Fishing into my shirt pocket, I took out his badge and handed it to him. "Here."

"I don't think I can take that." He stared at the star in my hand. "I don't think I deserve it anymore."

Both of us stood there in the uncomfortable silence until I pushed it toward him again. "Fortunately, that's not your choice for another year."

He continued to stare at the badge. "Yeah, I need to talk to you about that."

"What?"

"I'm not going to stand."

"For sheriff?"

"Yes, sir."

"That's a shame, you'd make a good one."

"I used to think so, but now I'm not so sure."

We stood there, silent for a moment, before I finally reached over and stuffed the star into the pocket of his uniform shirt. "A little uncertainty is a good thing in this line of work." I patted his shoulder. "Now, get out of my way, I'm going home and going to bed for the next two days."

He stepped aside. "You sure you trust me to hold down the fort?"

Opening the door, I pushed Dog back as he licked my face and then turned and sat, attaching my seat belt and hitting the starter. "I gave you back your star, didn't I?"

It was a long drive to my house, the house I hadn't been back to in more than a week, so long in fact that I actually pulled into the parking lot of the Red Pony in hopes that Henry might be there with a pot of coffee to help me make it the rest of the way.

It was still very early and the sun was just showing glimmers of rising over the foothills of the Bighorn Mountains, the tips up near fourteen thousand feet showing the violet and purplish hues of the high-altitude sunshine as I climbed out of the truck and trudged to the door, only to find it locked.

Taped to the glass was half a sheet of paper torn from a spiral-ring notebook. A message in cursive looped across the page: GO HOME.

What was it with him and wanting me to go home, anyway?

I flattered myself by thinking that the message was exclusive to me until I came to the conclusion that indeed it was and perhaps not so flattering at that. Turning, I trudged back to the truck and climbed in, finally directing it for home.

Driving up the short ranch road from the county road, I slowed to a stop in front of my tiny cabin and almost fell over on the steering wheel, right there. Staring at the little log starter-kit through my half-lowered lids, I thought about the great manse I'd just left and of the man I'd thought I'd known so well but, as it turns out, hadn't.

Dog jumped out first as I slid from the seat and just stood there, unable to move forward. I like to pride myself on my ability to keep going no matter what, and I couldn't help but think that I was hitting the gas, but the tank was truly and deeply empty.

Taking another deep breath, I pushed off and trudged toward the front door with my face down, my neck muscles refusing to hold my head up.

I made it to the porch when I tripped. Hitting the wide planks, I slid into the front door and lay there crumpled against the wood, my hat knocked to one side of my head, thinking this might not be such a bad place to take a nap. Dog's claws skittered across the porch, and I felt his nose sniffing my head under the brim. "Go away, I'm busy dying."

He ignored me.

"Git." I listened as he sat, waiting for me to open the door.

It was likely that Grafton and Carr took my father's rifle and killed Sutherland, but would my grandfather have hidden it or did they? What good would it have done for them to hide it, other than to get rid of any forensic traces of how the deed had been done? Why would Lloyd have hidden it? Everyone in the town had seen him win the Weatherby rifle that had killed Sutherland — or was Lloyd Longmire the kind of man you just didn't ask those types of questions?

In the final analysis, I don't think my grandfather had anything to gain by the death of the state accountant, but he was, by all accounts, a vengeful man who wouldn't have thought twice about killing two men he knew to be killers and thieves.

Would I pursue that? Probably not, preferring to file it under just desserts.

Perhaps, like Lucian Connally had said, it was sometimes better to let sleeping dogs lie.

Sleep.

I had an aunt or a half-aunt or great-half-aunt, or would it be second cousin once removed or a first cousin twice removed? It didn't matter, it was comforting to think that our little family had grown by one.

Sleep.

It was always like this whenever I lay my head down to rest, a million and three things would suddenly come to mind, spinning around like the Rolodex on my desk that Vic always made fun of.

Vic.

I wondered what it was I'd done wrong.

I just hoped wherever she was she was safe and happy. Maybe I'd take a trip to Philadelphia to see if I could find her. That thought also comforted me, and I could feel my eyes starting to close.

Sleep.

It was funny, but as I lay there drifting off, I started remembering lost moments with my grandfather, just glimpses of the man, and he was smiling. I couldn't hear the words, but as I looked up at him from a child's perspective, I watched him laugh and remembered things I'd most certainly forgotten. One remembrance in particular when I reached out and grabbed ahold of his finger.

He pulled, and try as I might, I couldn't hold on.

He extended the finger again and I clutched it in my tiny hands as he pulled once more, but this time he allowed me to hold him fast in a world of imperfect grandfathers, fathers, and sons.

For once, I remember the gray eyes softening as he stared down at me and his voice was soft and reassuring. "Never let go."

It was about then that the door swung wide, so I figured that Dog must've leaned against it and, with his bulk, pushed it open.

Then I felt hands take ahold of my head and turn it, knocking my hat away.

Tarnished gold eyes looked down at me, framed in brunette hair pulled back in a kerchief, which made her look like an entrancing housekeeper. "Where the fuck have you been? I moved all my stuff in here, and I've been cleaning this place for a week."

I started to speak, but she interrupted, turning my head, and studying me with a horrified inspection. "What happened to your face?"

Never let go.

ABOUT THE AUTHOR

Craig Johnson is the *New York Times* bestselling author of the Longmire mysteries, the basis for the hit Netflix original series *Longmire.* He is the recipient of the Western Writers of America Spur Award for fiction and the Mountain & Plains Independent Booksellers Association's Reading the West Book Award for fiction. His novella *Spirit of Steamboat* was the first One Book Wyoming selection. He lives in Ucross, Wyoming, population 26.

The employees of Thorndike Press hope you have enjoyed this Large Print book. All our Thorndike Large Print titles are designed for easy reading, and all our books are made to last. Other Thorndike Press Large Print books are available at your library, through selected bookstores, or directly from us.

For information about titles, please call:
  (800) 223-1244

or visit our website at:
  gale.com/thorndike